FROSTBOUND THRONE

SONG OF NIGHT
SONG OF WINTER
SONG OF HEAVEN AND ICE

MAY SAGE

Frostbound Throne
Court of Sin Book One to Three
The complete trilogy
May Sage © 2019

Edited by Hot Tree Editing and Theresa Schultz
Map by Francesca Baerald
Cover art by Jeremy Chong
Typography by Rebecca Frank
Interior Design by The Illustrated Author Design Services

COURT OF SIN

PART ONE

SONG OF NIGHT

PROLOGUE

This was how she died. She knew it, felt it to her bones. There was no other way, not here. Saving herself would mean condemning every breathing soul in the city of night. As little as she liked most of them, and however much they hated her in return, she couldn't bring herself to destroy so many just to save herself.

She should give in now. Drop her bow, accept her fate. Yet she shot one arrow after the next, desperately holding on to life.

Devi took down enemy after enemy, her mind processing each kill with a cold, analytic indifference. They were relevant because she knew there had been fifty-one arrows in her quiver. Each fae she killed represented one arrow lost. There was every chance she'd run out of weapons before she reached the gates.

She was at the very center of the city, in the large Square of Dawn, famous for the obelisk erected at the end of the last war. The closest exit was a mile east, and there were three dozen enemies around her right now and more coming at every passing moment. It was a credit to her skill with a bow that none of them had managed to get close to her yet.

A horse whinnied to her left, and Devi's head turned sharply. She expected enemy knights. She'd managed until now because she'd only had to deal with foot soldiers; fae knights were another matter altogether.

When they came into the square from the south avenue, there were only two riders. She stiffened in alarm, until her eyes took in the colors of their habits and then their faces.

Devi had no issue recognizing the two males, although she'd never seen either dressed in anything other than their fine court attire. Now they wore plain reinforced gear under dark unseelie coats.

Neither of them looked any less intimidating for it.

"Vale."

The name fell from her lips in a tone she had never used to say it. With relief. Barely conscious of her decision, she adjusted her position to aim at the enemies following Vale and his second, rather than foolishly carrying on attempting to clear a path out of this nightmare. Vale was more important. If he lived through the night, there would be hope for the Isle.

Her shot hit the mark, killing a fae right behind the prince. As the enemy tumbled, Vale turned to see where the arrow had come from, his eyes landing on her.

He was on the other side of the square, but her vision could distinguish him quite clearly. For the first time since they'd met, he wasn't amused. His trademark smirk had disappeared. That shouldn't have come as a surprise given the circumstances, but his expression wasn't what Devi might have expected. Vale wasn't confused, shocked, or scared, unlike her. The dark prince seemed downright pissed right now. His violet eyes, so like his mother's, watched her with pure fury.

Devi's heart hit her stomach. Was this her fault? Had the attacks started because of her? It wasn't impossible at all, given her history.

Then, to her astonishment, Valerius Blackthorn, the dark prince, lord of the court of sin, lifted his hands, pulling on the reins to turn his horse away from the road leading to the eastern gate. Away from safety. Instead of heading out, he rode at full speed toward her. *Her*. The half-breed who was "nothing," according to him.

Devi regained her senses just as he reached her, in time to take his hand and hop behind him on his black mount.

"Fucking idiot!" he yelled before leaning forward and whispering sweet spells at the horse, who obeyed his master's urging, rushing through the streets of the city of night.

ONE
THINNER THAN WATER

Valerius Blackthorn wasn't one to cower before any ordeal, and yet he stopped before two winged giants of stone. They stood tall either side of a shimmery metallic doors of the throne hall, holding a vast basin filled with the purest of waters on their shoulders. Gazing upon the statues and their burden, he recalled the legends. They said the guardians of the doors were just the hilt of a cup the gods used to drink from in the dark days. Looking at the twenty foot high giants with their extended wings, and the seven foot wide dish they bore, Vale was glad the gods were dead.

Vale took one step, then looked right and left, checking his surroundings. Never had he so wished for an interruption. A rider with news from the borders, a messenger bearing an invitation, an acquaintance he simply had to greet—he would have taken any excuse that might have called him away.

No one came to his aid. The cavernous halls of Wolven Fort were cold and empty.

Cold, they'd always been. Empty was new. He knew why no one, neither lord, clerk, nor kitchen maid roamed the corridor. Everyone who was anyone now waited for him behind the imposing doors.

"Go on," said his companion. "Standing about isn't going to make this any easier."

Vale sighed, and flicked his wrist, holding his hand up in the direction of the heavy doors. They were made of pure gold and might weigh a hundred stone. He could have knocked, or announced his presence. Most would have, as all magic had a price, depleting some of their energy. A common fae might have been in need of a nap after making such a heavy object move, but Vale was no weakling. Pushing the doors cost him very little.

The doors slid open and Vale entered the throne hall. At first glance, he found the court of night unchanged. The noise of the rabble overwhelmed all his senses, but if he was uncomfortable, displeased, and wary, he did not let it show. The court saw nothing but power, and powerful lords did not display signs of weakness.

He took one step, and every male and female present ceremoniously bowed before him. All except for one fae: the queen, his esteemed mother. His eyes cut through the crowd and focused on Shea Blackthorn, who stood next to her masterfully carved iron throne, holding her arms outstretched in a deceptively welcoming stance.

She wore a dress of shadow and sin, made for slaying fae, in every possible sense of the term. The two long slits on either side of her hips were practical: she could, and would, leap into action if she needed to protect her court and her throne.

The throne was a statement. At all times, she subtly touched it, leaning against it or letting her bare arm rest on it, wordlessly reminding the crowd of one fact: she was more. More than any of them, more than any fae in the Isle. Mighty as they were, iron burned all fae, except her.

And him.

"Valerius Blackthorn. We have missed you, son."

He stifled a grin in response.

Fae folk couldn't lie, but they certainly were well-versed in the art of twisting the truth. When she said *we*, she spoke on behalf of the court; she, however, was another matter. No doubt, she would have preferred if he'd stayed away.

The foolish curse that plagued their kind also prevented him from responding that he'd missed any of them. Instead, he replied with a half-truth of his own—"You know I can't stay away for long"—while morphing his expression into a charming smile that didn't reach his eyes.

The platitudes might have carried on for a while, but in that moment he felt a presence. Among the entire assembly, he clearly distinguished her essence, her aura, her power.

How peculiar.

He stopped for an instant, and tilted his head, just enough to catch a glimpse of the female who so demanded his attention from the corner of his eye.

The female was still looking down, head bowed in a sign of deference.

She was a stranger, an icy high fae he'd never met in his long years; not at court or anywhere else. He would have remembered. She held her back very straight, and kept her shoulders back like a good little well-bred lady. She emanated a familiar mixture of power, entitlement, and indifference, wearing it like a scent. Vale was used to that. It disgusted him enough to render him immune to sensual lips and fine eyes. Usually.

Not this time. He found that he was not, after all, quite indifferent to beauty. His gaze hungrily took in the curve of her elegant neck, and the tight blue fabric of her formal dress. She had hair of night, so dark it almost seemed blue. Her skin was sun-kissed, so unlike the complexions of the rest of the court of night. Her bare golden throat was whispering, beckoning him.

He knew better than to listen to its call. The female was nothing more than an appealing trap. But still he looked, because it wasn't her appearance that had called his attention.

She felt different. One thing mattered to the high fae of this court and all others: power. The entire unseelie court reeked of it. There were, in this very room, over a thousand ancients who could with very little effort set fire to seas and stones if they felt like it. The queen's wrath could shake the ground from one end of the Isle to the next. And yet amidst all this, Vale noticed her soul.

She didn't belong here. Not really. The stranger's attitude may have resembled that of the rest of the females of the court, but when he paid attention, Vale saw a clear lake, mountains, and forests in her mind. He saw a child lying back in the snow and laughing as she watched the stars. The other fae in the hall were aroused by gold, silk, flesh or control. Sometimes, all four. In her, he saw innocence, and another kind of beauty.

Vale froze when he realized he'd reached out, caressing the edge of her mind to see its nature, its true color. It had been centuries since he lost control of his aptitudes in that manner. He didn't ever invade the mind of anyone without meaning to these days. And yet he'd done just that with this female.

The beauty wasn't a woman of the court. She was wilderness. Wilderness in a pale blue silk dress that hugged every one of her delightful curves; wilderness that could effortlessly and elegantly maintain a curtsy for an extended period of time. Wilderness tamed by his mother.

Shame.

It took some effort, as his interest was seldom piqued, but Vale managed to pull his attention away from the enticing female. No one had identified the object of his focus , although all eyes were on him. His intrusive inspection hadn't lasted more than a second. He carried on walking toward the platform where the throne had been raised thousands of years hence, when the forests and mountains surrounding the unseelie realm had been young and kinder.

Once he'd reached the three steps elevating his mother above the rest, Vale dropped to one knee and dipped his head. The rest of the attendees finally rose as one.

The dark prince of the court of night, lord of the court of sin, who'd stayed away for sixteen years, was finally home.

Party time, they thought, no doubt. They expected a spectacle. He was to torture, threaten, fuck, and drink his way through the upcoming solstice. By the time he was gone, everyone would recall what a wastrel he was. This was his role, and he'd play it well.

There were various reasons why he had to stick to that script. The first one was obvious to anyone who knew the game of king, queens and heirs. Shea Blackthorn had ruled for over a thousand years now. It was expected that monarchs should relinquish their power to their heir after a time. Their race may be immortal, but the elders' understanding of the world became obsolete after a while. How could old souls rule over a nation they were fundamentally unable to understand?

Many times in the history of the Isle, the people had demanded that a previous ruler pass down the throne to their heir. The Seelie and Unseelie Courts were alike in that respect: both governments included a Senate who advised the Throne and discussed the laws their monarchs proposed. Ultimately, the monarch had the last say, but the Senate had the right to demand the abdication of an unfitting leader. Considering the way Vale acted, no one would think of suggesting it in their case.

Vale had no desire and no intention to rule over the entire unseelie realm any time soon. Carvenstone, his domain, the land running along the northern borders of the realm, was his home and the only place he cared to oversee.

The second reason was the fact that now, thanks to his unpredictable persona, absolutely no one wished to visit him in his court. He was known to be mercurial and cruel; why would anyone seek out the likes of him?

And the last reason why Vale wouldn't disappoint the audience, who were secretly delighted to watch him disrupt the course of their mundane lives, so long as his attention wasn't directed on them, was because drinking, threatening, fucking, and torturing those who displeased him was the only way he could stand spending time in this accursed place. The court of night? A better description would be the court of hypocritical, elitist swine. He seldom returned—only when it was entirely unavoidable.

Shea waved her hand, and he rose along with Kallan, Vale's loyal second, who'd stopped a step behind him.

"You should have sent a messenger ahead," she stated with a slight frown that meant she was absolutely livid.

Her expressions rarely changed at all and every minimal twitch of her eye had meaning.

Vale shrugged indifferently. "I had no intention of traveling south, just three days ago, or I certainly would have sent word. But Kallan and I did let those spies of yours see us ride south. Surely they warned you, Mother, or you wouldn't have had time to gather such a welcome."

The queen sighed. Without a word, she turned on her heels, heading out of the throne hall. She snapped her fingers, summoning him. The formalities were apparently already over with. Good. After one hand gesture of his own, ordering Kallan to remain behind, Vale followed her like an obedient hound.

They took the corridor to her left, leading to one of her studies. Vale entered the familiar octagonal room, stiffening as he pulled the door behind him. He expected to be informed of his dozens of failures and told to grow up. The tiresome business was unavoidable.

The instant they were alone, two soft and seemingly frail arms wrapped around his shoulders. The embrace was short-lived, fleeting, yet shocked him to the core, as any display of affection from Shea Blackthorn did.

Vale was glad when it stopped.

"All right." He had a perfect explanation. "The world is ending."

His mother chuckled, offering him a thin smile for half a beat.

"Basically. Thank fuck you're here." Her verbiage was far from formal while away from her subjects. The curse didn't alarm Vale, but he didn't fail to note the fact that no reprisal crossed her lips. "I didn't think you'd come. You seriously need to get better at answering messages, Vale."

She'd sent him three letters over the last month. They had been opened, but not by him. Valerius got Kallan to run through correspondences like those. What were subordinates for, if not dealing with the things he didn't want to think of?

Kallan had told him his mother wanted to see him on some pressing matter, so he'd planned to make the journey at some point within the next year or so.

What had occurred three days ago, close to dawn, had changed things though.

"I truly didn't intend to visit the court this winter," he assured her. "That said, a seelie contingent has passed through my land. A hundred strong, including their actual fucking king."

Among other things, Vale had inherited his mother's love of four-letter words. There may have been an endless array of suitable terms in his vocabulary, accumulated over the course of seven centuries, but more often than not, "fuck" happened to be exactly what he wanted to say.

"And you figured I should be warned before they get there. I thank you, Valerius. When will they arrive?"

"Two days—three, tops. Kallan and I used the fastest paths and changed horses seven times to get here directly.

They have carriages and civilians. They'll need to take the main roads, and travel slowly."

He was familiar with the queen's expression. She was calculating, scheming, plotting. As was her way. Vale only wished she shared her findings.

"This warning is incredibly valuable. Pick whatever reward you desire."

He didn't attempt a reply, too taken by what he saw now that he was paying attention. Shea truly seemed wary.

She stood at five foot four, the shortest high fae Vale had ever seen, and yet more imposing than any of them. Shea Blackthorn looked youthful and as beautiful as the most delicate of roses, thorns and all. Usually, the queen was ready to fight against a whole army before breakfast. Right now, it looked as though she'd already killed them all and was waiting on a second assault.

"What is it, Mother?" he asked.

Tell me. You may trust me.

The plea went unpronounced, and yet it was answered.

Shea moved to her desk and started to shuffle through documents. She laid out a dozen handwritten reports before standing behind her chair.

She never sat if it could be helped.

After a lengthy pause, the queen replied.

"War is coming. See for yourself."

TWO
DARK AND CHARMING

Some fair folks were lucky. Their minds simply conjured nightmares of imaginary monsters in the darkness, but upon waking, their dreams were all over. They fled in the moonlight.

Devi's subconscious was a bitch. No clawed, furry beast chasing her, no ghost under the bed for her. Oh no; instead, her haunting dreams played on her memory.

Her throat tightened painfully as she fought against one intense desire. One need: to breathe. She just wanted to breathe. But if she succumbed to temptation, water would invade her airway and flood her lungs in no time. The conscious part of her brain acknowledged that, but her body, her instincts, just wanted her to take one breath....

Her feet kicked, never hitting anything. Her vision started to blur, but she still saw the three silhouettes. One of them was holding her head underwater, the other one pushed her shoulders down, and the last remained a few feet back. Their words, the sounds they made, had been undistinguishable when the scene had occurred thirteen years ago, but now, in her dreams, she heard them clearly. They were laughing.

Devi remembered the moment she'd snapped. The moment when she'd realized she had to do something or they'd claim her life. The moment she decided to stop being weak prey, she turned into something else altogether. A rush of power had violently jumped out of her skin.

This was always the moment she woke up.

Her four poster bed, and the rest of her large, elegant room carved white in stone and furnished in dark wood, was a cold mess. She'd broken the glass of her window again. Once, it had been ornate, but after the first time she'd destroyed it, it had been replaced with plain glass. Devi sighed. No wonder that the servants of Wolven Fort hated her. They had to replace something in her apartment every other day.

Knowing there was no point in attempting to get back to sleep now, she dragged her feet to the hole in the wall, carelessly walking on the shards of glass. None broke her skin.

It was before dusk; the streets wouldn't come to life for another two hours or so. It wasn't without cause that Asra had been named the city of night.

Devi winced as the sun blinded her sensitive eyes. She'd woken way too early again. Using her hand as a visor, she stayed to watch the sunset, enjoying the warmth of the sun on her skin. She seemed dark compared to the unseelie fae, but in fact, she'd never been paler. Her mother had raised her to live during the day and sleep at night as a child.

In the last few years, she'd missed the sun sometimes. Not of late. She'd woken up early enough to see it for a while now. The nightmares—the memories—had started a year ago, although it had been three years since she'd finished her time in the toxic royal unseelie academy, and over a decade since that fateful day at the riverbank. Her body and mind were restless, bidding her to stay on her guard, reminding her of a darker time.

Her plight was over. It had been a long time since she'd had reason to fear for her safety. There were plenty of decent folk around her now. She'd even managed to make some friends, most of whom didn't have a drop of high fae blood. Common fae were far more understanding.

Devi had a particular friendship with the two fae who'd started their protector internship at the same time as she, Jiya and Rook. They were all suffering the same torture under the tutelage of Drake Night, the formidable and sadistic master in charge of their training. As they were the first batch of apprentices he'd personally trained, no one else could quite understand their misery.

Her days consisted of six hours of agony with Rook, Jiya, and Drake, lunch, two hours of further training wherever she was sent, a free period where she was expected to perfect whatever Drake had endeavored to teach her, dinner, then sometimes, two hours down in the secret rooms carved in the belly of the castle under the dungeons. A restless sleep, rinse, repeat. This was her simple life. In her little cocoon, she'd let herself forget what it was to have to remain cautious, expect the worst, and watch her back. Her dreams served as a daily reminder, showing her what occurred when she wasn't vigilant.

She'd wondered whether she was simply paranoid, but just when she was convinced that her imagination was driving her mad, a rumor had reached her.

The previous night, Devi had heard that the seelie king was coming to Asra. She sincerely wished that it was nothing more than stupid whispers without cause, but her mind wouldn't be at rest until she knew for sure.

After the sun went down, Devi moved from her window and hopped in the bath her servants had poured, moaning in delight. She knew better than to take such pleasures for granted.

"Perfect temperature, thank you."

She persisted in speaking to the staff, who persisted in ignoring her. They hadn't talked to her for thirteen years, and she didn't expect them to start now, but it wasn't going to discourage her.

The lesser fae employed at the palace never uttered a word to any resident or guest, except the queen herself. Devi knew they could talk; she heard them babble amongst themselves quite frequently. It was just one of many oddities of the court of night. Sometimes she wondered if it was the same throughout the rest of the continent. Then she remembered she'd never know. She wasn't welcome in the Seelie Court, wasn't likely to return to the elven realm, and she would never be invited to Corantius. No one was. The unseelie realm was her home, for better or worse.

By the time she managed to convince herself to get out of her bath, she was running late—again. Devi rushed to get dressed and headed down the castle's main staircase, jumping four steps in each leap.

Punctuality had never been her forte, so she'd done that almost every day since she'd arrived. It was the first time that she missed a step, and it was entirely his fault.

Wincing, Devi got back to her feet and lifted her eyes toward the dick who had caused her fall.

Her jaw fell open. *Fuck.*

She'd been there the previous evening when he'd arrived at court. Devi had curtsied and kept her eyes on the ground like everyone else, but not before stealing a glance at the elusive prince she'd never met before. Rook had told her that his last visit to the court had been sixteen years ago, and she'd only arrived three years after that.

Her first glance surprised her. The two fae entering the throne hall were both striking, yet they couldn't have been more different.

The first one had been gorgeous. Long blond hair, bright eyes, flawless skin, a ready smile, perfect bone structure, and his lean stature was elegant. High fae were a handsome bunch in general, but the fair-haired male had been at another level.

The male standing right beside the stunning stranger was… magnetic. Charismatic. His shoulders were a little broader, and he stood a good half head taller than his companion. His eyes were ice, his presence edgy, threatening, commanding. There was something in the way he moved that said hunter. Wild beast. It had been hard to turn her eyes away from him, because frankly her every instinct told her to keep the predator in her sights. His features were distinctive: his jaw too square, his cheekbones angular, his nose so very straight. He might have been quite beautiful had he not seemed so menacing. As things stood, Devi decided he wasn't handsome at all. Just dangerous.

The blond was everyone's idea of a striking prince, yet Devi instantly knew that Valerius Blackthorn was the beast. He had his mother's violet eyes, her commanding presence, and something more. Something alarming.

After the prince had officially been welcomed by the queen, Devi had hurried the heck out of the hall, returning to her apartments. Her heart had been beating a little too fast, a little too hard. She was glad Valerius never stayed at court for long, and while he was present, there was no reason why they'd interact at all. She was a twenty-eight-year-old nobody—very young and inexperienced by fae standards. She asked questions that made older folks smile condescendingly. "Aren't you cute, asking about this thing I figured out three centuries ago," they always seemed to say. Younglings rarely mixed with elder fae.

It occurred to her that the prince's apartments, like hers, were in the residential wing of the queen's castle. Devi quickly dismissed that concern; it was a fucking big wing, after all. But she was also the queen's ward, an adopted daughter of sorts. Maybe she *would* have to meet him someday. Shea might wish to introduce them.

Devi was no coward, but she was painfully aware of the fact that she had to avoid stressful situations when she could—not for her own well-being as much as that of the people around her. If she lost control of her powers, who knew how many people she'd hurt this time?

And now here they were face-to-face. Or face to knee, because she was on her ass.

Everyone else, she felt or heard before they were anywhere near her, but Valerius Blackthorn had literally appeared out of thin air, in perfect silence.

Surprised to find him right in front of her, she'd lost her balance and ungracefully tumbled down the stairs, twisting her ankle in the process. She had enough coordination to avoid falling face-first, but it still hurt.

Valerius briefly smiled, like her plunge entertained him. She stared openmouthed. She hadn't expected much contrition, but an apology wouldn't have gone amiss.

"Don't worry," the prince told her, eyes shining with laughter. "Not the first time a female has thrown herself at my feet."

Was he seriously flirting with her right now? She had no words for this male. None. She shouldn't have been that surprised, actually. After all, the prince was known for fucking anything with tits and tormenting those who didn't fall in the former category.

Still, no one had ever mistaken Devi for a fuck toy before, particularly not when she wore supple, reinforced leather gear from neck to toes.

"You must admit it was pretty entertaining," he stated, noticing her astonishment.

"I hurt my damn foot, you fucking idiot!" she retorted before recalling who she was speaking to.

Being Shea's ward didn't change the fact that she was supposed to be deferential toward the prince and heir of the realm. Someday, when Shea wouldn't be here to protect her, he'd be king. She'd be at his mercy then. What if he recalled that, on their first meeting, she'd called him an idiot—a fucking one, no less?

Valerius didn't seem upset at all; if anything, he seemed a little more amused.

"My, what a dirty mouth you have on you. I wonder what else it can do."

Fuck deference. She held her hand up, the middle finger extended in a universal gesture: fuck you very much.

Standing, Devi tested her ankle. Not broken. She could apply a little weight on it. Good, she'd be able to hobble away to the infirmary easily enough.

Once his royal pain in the neck was at a distance, she felt some relief, realizing that the prince hadn't made her feel anxious at all, actually. Today, she could still see the wildness she'd read in his eyes, and the way he moved didn't conceal his inherent brutality, but somehow she didn't find any of it threatening up close. He'd seemed a threat to everything around him the previous night, a volatile creature likely to explode at the slightest provocation. Who could blame him? She certainly remained on her guard when the court was assembled around her. She now faced another person altogether.

Devi was smiling to herself, glad she didn't have to be concerned about him after all. Then his voice resounded in the empty hall.

"Where are you going?"

Valerius had a nice voice, all things considered. Deep. Raspy. Did he smoke a pipe? She tried to picture it but failed.

"Where do you think? The infirmary, dumbass," she grumbled in response, annoyed at herself for liking anything about him at all.

Devi limped away without gracing him with so much as a glare in his direction.

So she had a temper. She blamed her mother for it. While Loxy Rivers hadn't gifted Devi her luscious, deep red curls, she'd been so good as to bestow upon Devi every other characteristic usually attributed to redheads.

She realized that trait was definitely not working to her advantage right now. She should at least attempt to play nice with the future king.

Suddenly, without so much as a warning, Devi was swept off her feet. Frozen in confusion, she stared at Valerius as he carried her down the hall like it was the most natural thing in the world.

Just for the record, it really, really wasn't.

She wasn't used to having strangers invade her personal space. Most people stayed away, having heard the rumors about what had occurred that day in the river. The members of the court knew what she was capable of. Besides, she was a master in the art of sending an unambiguous "stay away" vibe.

Devi was shocked into silence for at least a dozen steps before she started kicking her feet and yelling. "What the fuck are you doing? Go away! Let me walk, dammit."

"Walk?" Valerius questioned mockingly. "You were wobbling, at best."

"Which is my prerogative."

"Falling for me and now being swept off your feet.... This is turning into quite an experience for you. No doubt, you'll speak of it to your grandchildren. 'Little dears, let me tell you of the night whence I met a charming lord....'"

"Can you fuck off and die?"

"Oh, shush. I'm a goddamn prince. Carrying damsels in distress is literally in the job description."

"Give me your sword. It looks pointy. I need to poke your eyeballs and see if it makes you shut up."

"I'll shut up if you let me carry you."

She considered this dilemma and decided that losing her dignity for ten minutes was totally worth it, as long as he kept his mouth closed.

As promised, Valerius remained silent, and she stayed still the rest of the way. It wasn't long before she discovered it wasn't the best idea after all. When he wasn't talking, it gave her leave to notice certain things that weren't entirely unpleasant about the cocky, arrogant, infuriating, self-important jackass. His smell, for one. He smelled nice. He also had large, strong hands. And he was pretty warm too. His heartbeat was steady, like he carried full-grown females up and down stairs every day without breaking a sweat. He probably did. All in all, she had to admit that being carried by him was, in fact, rather pleasant. If asked, she'd deny it fervently.

As they passed the threshold of the infirmary, she was still deep in her clinical observations, noticing that, unlike the previous evening, there was now a little bit of scruff around his face.

Realizing they had arrived, Devi wiggled to try to get down, making him sigh.

"And here I thought you were actually capable of remaining reasonable. Beck!"

Thus summoned, Beck Stormhale, the healer-in-chief, appeared, coming out of his office. His eyes widened at finding Devi wincing in discomfort in Valerius's arms.

"Oh dear. Whatever happened?"

"I was on my way to work when this buffoon decided to cut me off. I fell and hurt my ankle."

"You mean," the healer translated, "you were rushing down the stairs because you were late, again, and you finally got what was coming to you."

Would sticking her tongue out be childish? Probably. She did so anyway.

"Room to the left."

"I'm just fine. I simply need—"

"No, Devi, you're a patient. I'll tell you what you need. You're not doing a thing until I come examine you. Go now. I'll let headquarters know you'll be late." There was no arguing with his tone.

Valerius took her to the room Beck had pointed to and gently laid her down on the cot.

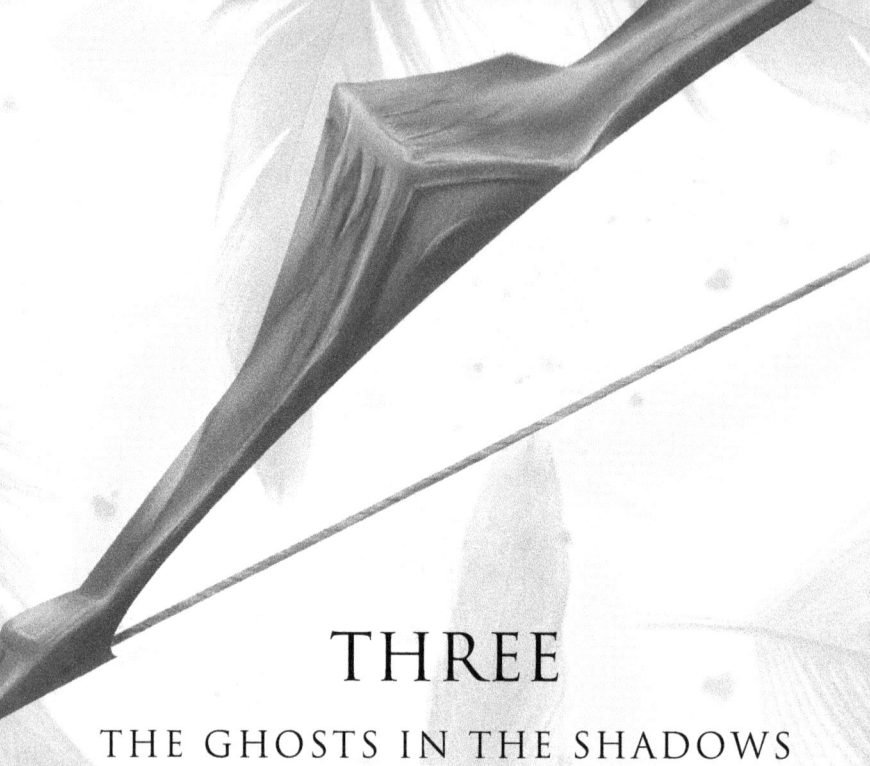

THREE
THE GHOSTS IN THE SHADOWS

Just like the queen, the prince was mostly expressionless. Devi could often boast of understanding the slight variation in Shea's face: an almost imperceptible twitch of an eyebrow, a blink that came out of place, the movements of her mouth.

After years of studying the mother, she found that reading the prince wasn't impossible. She could tell he was amused, although he'd only smiled once. She could tell he was also intrigued and suspicious of her. Clever male.

He broke the silence with a short statement. "You know the healer."

Small talk. Not very interesting small talk, at that. Devi guessed that he was either bored or he'd figured out that she was attempting to make sense of him. He wished to put a stop to her observations.

Very well. She certainly could do without his unnerving eyes burning holes in her soul.

"I work here occasionally," she replied. Valerius lifted a brow, just a fraction. "Well, I intern here," she amended. Devi pointed to her own chest, explaining, "Protector in training here. Healing is one of the skills we have to hone in order to get the job."

Protectors were the most esteemed jacks-of-all-trades of the realm. Mostly, they specialized in defense—or attack, when necessary—but their status was three steps above that of a guard or soldier because they also doubled as strategists, diplomats, and healers. Whatever the realm required of them.

It would be another decade before she'd become a full-blown protector, but she was almost done with her healing course.

They didn't need to learn as much as actual healers though. Devi knew her way around most simple spells, could create salves and potions, but her hand wasn't as steady as it could be. She wouldn't feel confident leading a major surgery, for instance. Had Beck given her leave to do so, she would have taken care of her own ankle without any issue. She just needed some of his supplies.

"And here I thought you were just a pretty little doll in my mother's collection. Didn't expect you to be a useful one."

He'd somehow found a way to demean absolutely everyone in one breath. So, the members of the court were dolls, were they? Of course he'd see them that way. Dick.

Devi wasn't on great terms with most high fae, but even she saw their uses. There were thirteen members of the queen's council, fifty-three senators, a hundred and seven lords, three judges, thirty lawyers, nine generals, and one commander at court. Factoring in a staff of two to thirteen members, a minimum of two guards per person, and about two family members, this represented a thousand folks of high rank. Adding the senate brought those numbers to seven thousand three hundred and eleven fae at court, a third of which were of great importance.

Not to His Highness, apparently. Why was she putting up with him again?

"Thanks for bringing me—against my wishes. You can go now."

Valerius sat on the seat next to the bed, extended his feet to rest them on her mattress, and folded his arms behind his head, making his intention to stay obvious. She suspected it was just because she'd told him to go.

"You're a dick."

"I do happen to possess one of those, but mighty as it may be, I can't say I'd use the term to describe the entirety of my person."

"If I swore my firstborn child to you in a binding oath, would you leave me alone?"

Fae had a thing for oaths.

"No. No one else is awake right now, you're mildly interesting, and I'm bored. I'm staying."

She grumbled and sighed—fruitlessly, one might add. The prince ignored it, determined to keep her company.

"So, Devi—Beck called you Devi, right?" She made no reply. "Why did you decide to become a protector of the realm?"

"I like the uniform."

The prince smiled. A real smile, not the fleeting ghost of a grin disappearing within an instant. Devi understood why he seldom used this particular weapon. It was a thing of wonder, rendering him more glorious than his handsome blond friend, and just as frightening.

Thankfully, it didn't last. Valerius shifted on his seat, leaning forward to close the distance between them.

Devi treated him like the predator she knew him to be, glaring right back at him, not attempting a sudden movement.

The prince tilted his head. "You know that if I were in a different mood, you'd be screaming in agony right now while I tormented your mind for your insubordination."

He said it in a matter-of-fact, conversational manner, as though he'd been speaking about the weather.

Devi wondered if his posturing ever worked. She gasped dramatically. "You'd hurt an innocent, defenseless female?" She batted her eyelashes for good measure.

There was no doubt that Valerius was dangerous, but he wasn't one to threaten. If he'd intended to harm her, he would simply have done so. Right now, he was just taunting her, testing her reaction.

"Don't bother using the female card with me again. I'm the son of Shea Blackthorn. I've long ago learned that what's between your legs has absolutely nothing to do with your strength."

Screw him for saying something she approved of. Devi was entirely resolved to dislike him, and imagining him as a sexist pig would have helped.

"I may just be a protector in training, but they don't let us in unless we can kick ass, Blackthorn. You'd *try* to hurt me. I'd try right back. You really don't want to find out who'd win."

She meant every word, but the dick seemed even more amused. He smirked. Fucking smirked. And damn him, but it was just as disturbingly beautiful as his smiles. He truly rubbed her the wrong way, getting under her skin with little effort. She was itching to lash out, but doing her very best to contain herself when Beck finally came, interrupting their stare off.

Devi redirected her glare toward the healer.

"I could have sorted my ankle with a charm," she told him.

"Indeed, but if I had let you do that, I wouldn't have had the chance to get you to do your psychophysical exam."

Oh, that. He had asked her to pop by to do it… twice? Maybe three times over the course of the last couple of months. Devi had glanced at the deadline and resolved to book the day before it was due. If memory served, she had seventeen days left.

But now he'd cornered her.

Shit.

She pointed to Valerius. "He can't be here for that. Make him get out."

"And he wouldn't have been here if you'd scheduled ahead of time at your convenience. Your Highness, feel free to stay. Devi never learns if there's no repercussion."

"Hey, I'm not a five-year-old," she protested, although one could argue that she was presently acting like one. "Plus, these exams are private, you know."

"Technically," the prince said, visibly loving every second of this, "these exams are demanded by the head of the protectors' order to ensure that our trainees are physically and mentally able to do this job. Newsflash, that's me."

Her jaw hit the floor. How come she'd never heard of this? To her knowledge, Drake Night was the current master of the order, hence why he was in charge of the training.

Valerius winked at her obvious astonishment. "Drake may have been elected master recently, but as prince *and* protector of the realm, I outrank him. He just sits on the council because I'm generally absent from court. Poor substitute, I'm sure you'll agree."

"Healer Beck, I think His Highness's protuberant ego is more concerning than any of my conditions. Surely you'll wish to see to it first."

Ignoring her, the tall, bulky healer smiled as he placed his hands on either side of her head, ever so softly. Beck was always gentle for such a giant. At first, an acute pain made her brain and ears buzz, but she dropped her mental shields and let him in.

Beck wasn't one to use kid gloves. He went right for the good stuff, replaying her nightmare. Drowning. Always drowning.

After reading everything he wished to know about her, he moved his hand, sighing.

"You should have come to me for sleeping droughts, young lady."

"I intended to. It's just…."

"That you don't wish to speak of it."

Biting her lip, Devi glanced toward Valerius.

"Get out of here, Vale." Beck's tone allowed no protest.

"What? We're just getting to the good stuff."

The healer's hand lifted and a golden flame appeared in his palm, to Devi's astonishment. Was he really threatening Valerius? She awarded Beck a hundred badass points for that. The prince sighed and backtracked.

"All right. Sounds like I'll just have to read the report." He winked playfully on his way out, like the dick he was.

Beck's hand, now void of offensive magic, waved and the door closed behind the prince.

"Vale," she repeated. "You're on a nickname basis with his mighty pain in the ass."

Beck chuckled. "We go way back. I'd like to say that his demeanor improves over time, but Valerius loves nothing more than getting under people's skin. And evasion won't work. I have every reason to believe you'll be an excellent protector, as long as you can deal with this."

Devi immediately parroted, "I can deal with this."

The healer nodded once. "All right, I'll bite. Tell me about it. Not the dream. Tell me what happened then."

Devi had seen this coming. Physicals could be improved; the protectors' exams were about the trainees' abilities to fare under duress. She'd known he would want to touch sensitive subjects, hence the reason why she'd delayed the ordeal to the last possible moment. But she was ready. She'd prepared herself.

"When I arrived at the Royal Academy, I was the new girl, intruding into circles of friends established a decade before. Generations before, actually. It's a high fae school, and every other student was a legacy. And I am the exact opposite of that."

"How so?"

He knew how so. He wanted her to say it.

"I'm a hybrid." How she hated that word. "No one liked that. Some disliked it more than others. I tried to stay out of their way, but they had no intention of staying out of mine. One day, we were out on a hunt. They cornered me at a river and tried to drown me."

She'd said all of that while staring at the ceiling, reciting a simple story like it hadn't been her own, as though it was nothing more than a dream. Now, knowing her future depended on it, her eyes cut to Beck as she said, "And I killed them. I killed them all."

At age fifteen, Devi had little control over her powers. It had just burst out of her, freezing everything. Everyone.

She still recalled standing in front of the teachers after getting away.

"What happened, Ms. Rivers?"

But although Katena Warlow asked, she already blamed her; Devi could see it in her eyes. "I... I...."

She ended up in the headmaster's office, being told that she was expelled.

Then Shea Blackthorn had stormed in and informed her staff that, actually, Devi wasn't, nor would she ever be, expelled from her academy. "I am queen, and this is my wish. If you desire that your other pupils survive the next ten years, I suggest you keep them in line."

The queen's intervention served to endear Devi to exactly no one. She'd killed three high fae of the court and gotten away with it. They'd hated her; after that, they also feared her.

She ran through these events, but Beck wanted more than a report; she saw it in his eyes.

Devi offered, "I don't regret it. They might have removed the screws from my chairs, painted my lockers and hidden my gym clothes, but no one's threatened my life since. If it's kill or be killed, I'd do the same again. I believe that's why I chose this career."

"No doubt." The healer watched her very carefully for a beat before breaking into a kind smile. "I can see you playing me, Devira Star Rivers. You're good, very good. And no wonder, since you learned from the best.

But I see you're only giving me what you think will get you out of trouble."

Oh. Well, shit.

"You're used to your elders underestimating you, aren't you?"

She had to laugh. "Not all of them."

Beck chuckled. "The queen is the exception to most rules. Unfortunately for you, so am I. Tell me what's wrong."

Devi sighed in defeat. "Okay. What's wrong is two kids were holding me down, but I don't know what the third kid was doing at all. He could have been encouraging them, or telling them to stop. I'll never know. When I was about to drown, my power just lashed out and they all died, him included. I wasn't in control. What I said stands. I don't feel guilty. I don't regret it. If I hadn't defended myself, I wouldn't be here today. But I also don't particularly want to speak of it."

The healer considered it and finally concluded, "That's fair, and I'm proud of you. You came a long way in a very short decade, Devi. Consider my stamp of approval sealed on your folder. Now, I still want to speak about those dreams. They're highly unusual for various reasons. Firstly, because they're a new development, occurring long after you've dealt with the issue. Secondly, because they trigger something that makes you use your power unconsciously, hence the broken window tonight."

"I've thought of it." She nodded. "It's like... I don't know, it feels like a warning. I know I'm no seer, but the queen says those with magic should be mindful of our dreams regardless. Maybe there's something coming."

Beck thought it out. "Not a bad theory."

But he was obviously thinking about something else. "What's your take on this?"

"I have multiple ideas, none of which quite make sense. But staying on your guard is a fabulous idea regardless."

The healer went to the cabinet against the wall and opened a drawer. He pulled a circular charm out of it and threw it at her. Devi caught it in midair and pressed it to her ankle before pushing energy through it. Within seconds, she could move her foot without any residual pain.

"Thanks," said she, hand extended to return his charm.

Beck shook his head. "Keep it. I had new ones made, so we have some surplus. Now get out of here. I told Drake you'd be back in training within a couple of hours."

"Thank you, sir." She leaped off the cot and rushed toward the door, stopping at the threshold. Dare she ask?

"Sir? Valerius Blackthorn…." She tilted her head. "Should I be worried?"

"You mean, if you've piqued his interest?" Beck chuckled. "Be very worried. He's quite irresistible, and he never takes females seriously."

Devi lifted a brow and crossed her arms over her chest defiantly. She hadn't asked for dating advice, dammit. Valerius was known to be quite cruel to some; she was simply wondering if she should expect him to actually harm her, should the mood strike him.

"I'm not one to fall for pretty faces or for a title, sir."

"And that would be helpful if Vale was, in fact, just a pretty face or a title."

Devi dismissed that comment as she left the infirmary, running to the protectors' headquarters.

Once she made it to the master's training room, she was greeted by a long baton flying right at her at full speed. Devi dropped to her knees, barely avoiding it, and caught the second one Drake Night threw at her.

Fuck. She should have worn gloves.

"Fifty-four minutes late, Devira."

Each of the tall high fae's steps were menacing. She knew better than to give justifications. Drake came at her with everything he had, each blow powerful and fast. She managed to avoid the first hit, stop the next two, and attempt an attack herself. The moment she advanced, he used her momentary imbalance to put his baton between her legs and pull it, flipping her over.

Dammit. That was twice today.

Drake knelt beside her and whispered, "Fucking you doesn't mean I'm going to make allowances for you, understood?"

Devi's eyes widened at the insult. She moved to wrap her legs around his muscular torso and used the position to flip him onto the ground.

"Once. I fucked you *once*," she reminded him. "While being entirely too intoxicated, one might add. And I've *never* asked for any fucking allowances. I'll stay an extra hour, just like everyone else."

Drake's eyes flashed with something she recalled a little too accurately.

There was no rule against a master and an apprentice ending up in bed; unseelie fae had very few rules at all when it came to sexuality. If it felt great, it was probably allowed, or even encouraged. The issue was that Drake Night just so happened to be Shea Blackthorn's consort.

Even if Devi had felt so inclined, she would have passed on a second rodeo with the protector-in-chief. The queen frequently shared him, as their relationship was very open. Still, the thought of bedding Shea's partner made her sick to her stomach—when she was sober, in any case.

Devi ignored the heated glance, wishing he'd stop sending her signals, and slowly got to her feet.

"Where am I to train today, sir?" she asked as formally as she could.

Drake stared at her for a good second. Then he stood up and replied, "Rook and Jiya are patrolling with the guard. Join them. I want you to take a post in the street after midnight."

She nodded once, clicked her heels together, and straightened her spine before turning toward the door. She'd almost crossed the threshold when the master added, "Also, Rivers? Do yourself a favor and stay away from Valerius."

Devi blamed Beck and his big mouth. Damn him. The healer did say he'd warn Drake, but he hadn't needed to give him a damn play-by-play. She was wondering how to politely tell her superior that he should mind his damn business when Drake added, "He'd eat you alive and spit you back out."

What in the ever-loving hell is he on about? Boiling at his out-of-place remark, Devi took a leaf out of the prince's book. She turned and smirked at Drake; now she knew nothing was quite as infuriating as a mocking grin.

"I'll have you know, most females do enjoy being eaten, sir." Then, still mimicking the prince, she winked. "Take notes."

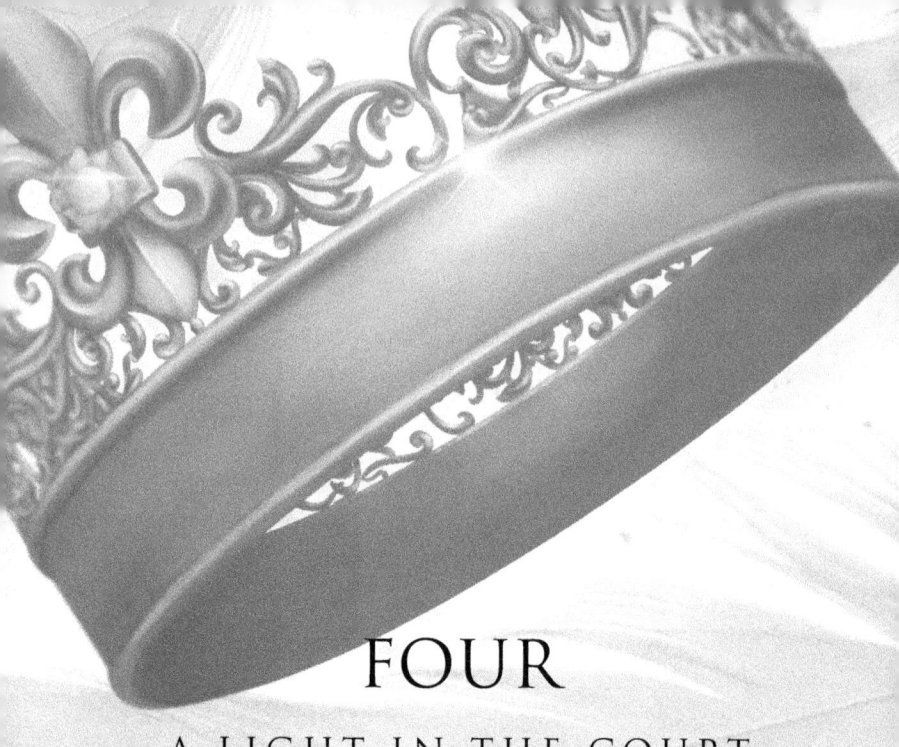

FOUR
A LIGHT IN THE COURT

The winter solstice had once been about mages, sorcerers, and barefoot priestesses performing rituals in the moonlight. Nowadays it was that and so much more. The entire court celebrated. There was music in the street, magicians and artists established along the main road, and the queen herself attended the festivities, meeting her people. There were games, of course: games of speed, games of agility, games of intelligence, and games of pure, brutal force. It was a beautiful chaos.

Vale held his own revels in Carvenstone, but he had to admit he'd missed the grand festival of the city of night.

"Elar Dorrel. You know I mostly come back home for your pastries," he told the short lesser fae who had curved antlers coming out of his skull.

The baker had set up a stand outside of his shop, and the smell was so enticing it made Vale feel dizzy, faint. He *needed* cake, now.

Vale couldn't recall how many times as a child, the old male had given him an extra portion of cake in secret and winked. Food had been rationed back then, during the War of the Realms. The last war the Isle had known.

Elar wasn't known to the new generation; his name was nowhere mentioned in history books. He was just a lesser fae who could take a bit of milk and flour and turn it into a cake suitable for a king, somehow. He was also the civilian who'd rounded up dozens of people and walked right to the front lines to bring fresh food to the armies.

Vale hated the system. Elar was a hero and should be celebrated as such.

"Your Grace." The male inclined his head cautiously, minding the direction of his long horns.

"None of this nonsense, just feed me. Are those creamers?"

Chuckling, Elar shook his head. "Don't you touch any of those, young prince. Nor you, Captain," he said, addressing Kallan. "I have some freshly baked goods resting at the back. An assortment, sirs?"

"Always," Vale vowed solemnly.

That was one oath he was willing to keep until the end of time.

The baker winked and rushed inside his store, coming back with two bags that emanated an impossibly delectable scent. Vale could have fainted.

"Can we kidnap you?" Kallan begged after inhaling the first beignet in two mouthfuls. "By the gods, I swear these get better every time."

The man snorted. "Me, in the court of sin? I think not. You'll have to come back if you want more Dorrel goods."

Vale sighed dramatically, all the while wishing he could talk. He'd tell the old man just why he should pack up and move to Carvenstone as soon as possible.

They spent the next two minutes arguing about paying. Defeated, Vale and Kallan had to retreat with the contents of their purses intact.

They reached the mile-long Square of Dawn, the largest open space in the entire city. It was situated right in the middle of Asra, where every main road intersected. The square was seldom quiet, but the week leading up to the solstice, it was a mess. One glance and Vale spotted everyone of importance—his mother, most high fae, the bulk of the guards, soldiers, and protectors on duty, along with a swarm of common and lesser fae.

And, of course, there was also that damn female.
Devi.

What was it with the girl? There were thousands of people in the square, but again his eyes were drawn to her.

It was entirely natural that he should notice the nobility. Lords were surrounded by dozens of subordinates wearing their colors and holding their houses' sigils. Devi had no such entourage, making her stand out. There was no reason at all why he should have noticed her in the thick crowd.

Like every guard posted in the square, she was still adorned in the plain brown leather he'd seen her in right after sunset the previous night. She stood a few steps away from the activities, surveying from a distance, like a good little protector. She was obviously on guard duty for the night; the job description was to be entirely invisible, blend in, not attract attention. She did her job very well, so Vale had no rational reason why he saw her at all.

The square had been divided in four sections. Northeast, they'd set up a track, and northwest, an archery contest. Southeast, there was a sanded circle around which the bulk of the crowd had assembled to watch contenders spar.

Devi stood in the shadow of the building erected around the last corner, where a more civilized kind of battle was taking place: chess. It was one of Vale's favorite games, which admittedly had grown tiresome now since he rarely lost.

Purposefully avoiding the area the female surveyed, Vale headed over to the sparring ring, where the queen had settled herself.

Someone had carried her portable throne, the one she used in battle.

Unlike the iron statement in the throne room, this one was a handsome throne, with pure white stone engraved with precision and art. If one cared to pay attention, the little figures sculpted on its back told a story, one of war, of monsters, and of the thirteen families who had triumphed over both. The tale of the formation of the four realms.

Their continent, the Isle, was old. It had borne many names, and its borders had changed shapes a thousand times before their realms had been built. The sixteen million square miles had been hundreds of nations once. Now there were but four, and all were at peace. Their one enemy lay behind the walls erected in the ocean surrounding their land.

When he thought of the throne and its bloody history, Vale's respect for the female to whom it belonged was undeniable. But as soon as he looked into her violet eyes, some of that deference disappeared, replaced by something darker. More dangerous. A doubt had been sown in his mind long ago. The knowledge that while Shea was one of the many reasons why there was peace, she also was the last person who should be trusted to keep it.

She plotted, always ten steps ahead of everyone else. Her goal, no one knew, not even Vale. If she desired order and harmony, all would be well in the end. If she wanted power, war, and chaos, there were few who could stop her. She was perhaps the most dangerous person in the realm, though that was arguable. Some might say it was Vale's father, or his half-brother.

Others would name him. Time would tell if they were mistaken.

"Greetings, Mother," he said, as Kallan bowed reverentially.

Shea didn't so much as grant them a glance, simply waving a vague hello. She kept her eyes fixed on the fight, entirely engrossed.

"Who did you bet on?"

"Brooke," she replied, leaning forward when the lean female stepped back after a hard kick in the stomach.

Count on Shea to put her money on the underdog. Brooke was fighting Lance, a male who looked like he ate metal poles for breakfast. He was built of pure muscle, and what was worse, he knew how to make use of them.

"You know, if you want to give your money away, you could just chuck it out the window."

"Hush, mini me. Just watch and learn."

He resolved to remain until the end of the fight, in the hopes of seeing his mother lose for once.

Brooke took a lot of hits, until Lance basically considered the fight won; he got cocky, turning his back on her. One kick to the chin, a rotating one to the head when he was kneeling forward, and she had him at her level. She punched him in the face, hard, breaking his nose. Lance was powerful, but slower than she. Finding his footing and counterattacking was entirely impossible while the female kept coming at him.

Five minutes later, Vale was sighing, reminded of one of the many reasons why his mother was annoying. She was never wrong. After a while, Lance was just protecting his face behind his knuckles. He ended up tapping out.

Dammit.

"Let me guess." Vale pointed to the victor. "You're training that female."

Shea laughed. "No, Brooke came to me already lethal. She's Loralei's little sister."

Ah, that explained a lot. Loralei Night, the queen's first advisor, came from a long line of badass people. The Nights also had another value: they were known to mostly give birth to daughters. That fact was one of the many reasons why Shea had taken Drake Night, Loralei's twin, as her principal consort.

"Remind me to put my money on her next time."

"This, my son, is why you occasionally lose," Shea replied, finally turning to him. "Brooke isn't a sure thing. No one is. It simply depends on who she's facing."

"I don't know. Some would argue that statement, given the fact that *you* are yet undefeated. Betting on you is the very definition of a sure thing."

"Flattery will get you everywhere," said the queen, rolling her eyes. Then her good humor disappeared. "My spies, as you call them, tell me the seelie will be here by dawn. They'll be shown to their quarters, and we'll welcome them at nine tomorrow night. Can I count on you to stand by my side?"

Vale nodded without hesitation. Despite what happened behind closed doors, showing a united front in front of the strangers made sense.

"Also, is that Dorrel patisserie I smell?"

Vale curved his fist around his bag and glared.

"No. Just no. His shop is right outside of your castle. I have to ride thirty-nine hours nonstop to get here. I'm *not sharing.*"

Kallan's will was weaker. He handed the queen a cake, and Shea devoured it in no time.

"This man's baking skills are an art." She moaned in delight. "Now, let us talk. You're aware of my having a ward these days."

"I've heard of it," he acquiesced.

There was nothing extraordinary about the queen sponsoring an orphan; she did it every other century. It was a clever move meant to increase her popularity, nothing more. Vale hadn't bothered to make further inquiry into the current ward. He didn't doubt that it was someone useful to the queen—the heir to a fortune or to a strategical stretch of land.

"She has a certain history with the Seelie Court. For that reason, she'll join us when we greet them. I'll keep an eye on her when I can. If I have to step out, can you ensure her safety for me?"

Vale pondered upon the point, frowning. Not only because his mother never asked a favor of him. Not only because it seemed so unlikely that the seelie would attempt anything against a ward of Shea Blackthorn.

Because at the back of his mind, a little voice was telling him there was more to this query.

"This ward of yours," he started, tense, eyes narrowed, "who is it?"

The queen's response came as no surprise. "She goes by Devi. Devira Star Rivers. You may not have met her yet. When you do, you'll understand. She's a power to be reckoned with. And the seelie will either want her in their hands or out of the way."

Vale laughed. He should have known there had been an angle. "How predictable you are, Mother dearest."

Every half century or so, the queen attempted to catch his attention with an appealing little thing who could bear him heirs—daughters, specifically. He'd always been a great disappointment, as he was her only son, when the queen's powers could only be transmitted to daughters. Shea Blackthorn had tried to match him twelve times. In this instance, she'd definitely found a fetching prize mare, he had to give her that.

"How so?" the queen asked innocently.

"You're thinking of my liking this ward of yours well enough to give you that granddaughter you so wish for."

Shea chuckled, turning her violet eyes on her son. "I can assure you, in no uncertain terms, that I had not once thought of you possibly pairing up with Devi. She's not your type."

Valerius had to snort. Not his type? No female he'd encountered had ever been more his type. Still, Shea had said each word with a purposeful clarity. He frowned, trying to guess her game. There was always a game.

"Had. You're thinking of it now."

Shea shrugged. "I can't deny that I wish you'd direct your attention to a worthy lady. Devi certainly qualifies."

He sighed. "I'm never going to settle on a female unsuitable for me. Give me leave to find someone who fits me."

Why was it so hard for her to grasp that concept? She'd certainly taken her time to pick a consort she desired.

"And in the meantime, you fuck every tramp in the realm. Are you attempting to father a bastard with lesser blood? Our court would destroy such a child."

"Don't be obtuse, Mother. If a tramp is indeed unworthy of my royal seed, I fuck her ass."

Shea tried very hard, but in the end, she couldn't help laughing.

As she often did, she turned to Kallan for support. "He listens to you. Tell him seven hundred and thirty-eight is a fine age to settle."

Kallan winced. "I would, but he might call me a hypocrite, given the fact that I am the same age and quite as single. Besides, you may have noticed that His Grace only listens to me when my opinion exactly matches his own."

The queen smiled, reaching out to touch Kal's cheek. "I missed you and your smart tongue."

She didn't need to talk on behalf of the court this time, because she truly had missed Kallan—the son she wished she had. Valerius had stopped wishing he and his mother could share this kind of affection a long, long time ago. They were too similar in many respects, all the while being too different where it mattered.

Leaving them to their little chat, he walked away, unnoticed.

Vale's aimless steps led him toward the chess competition. He told himself it was quite natural, given that it was his game of choice. It had absolutely nothing to do with the dark-haired beauty with hazel eyes who stood quite straight next to the justice building.

But now that he was close, failing to greet her would have been rude.

Valerius realized he was attempting to fool himself, and failing at it. He was quite simply heading toward the chit because he wanted to.

He approached her, relishing in the way she sighed.

"I've had a long night," she warned him, her tone making it clear that trying her patience wouldn't be without consequences.

Vale had a hard time preventing himself from smiling. She was almost threatening him again. How adorable.

"No doubt. You look a fright. Quite a disgrace, really. Is that dribble on your face?"

Her eyes narrowed suspiciously, but she believed him enough to pull the sword attached to her belt out of its sheath and checked her reflection on its surface.

Finding it unmarred, she told him, "I hate you."

It wasn't often that anyone could boast of driving a stranger to hatred in the space of two nights. It might have been flattering, if it had been true. The words had crossed her lips freely, perhaps because she was convinced of their veracity, but he knew better. He had more experience with emotions. He saw much in her eyes: frustration, anger, resentment, confusion. Vale could see how a youngling might mistake the cocktail of alarming feelings as hatred, but she was so wrong. Hatred was cold. Iron and ice. Devi Star Rivers's eyes were filled with fire when they set on him.

Admittedly, that was just as dangerous.

"Have you ever fucked anyone you hate, Devi Rivers?" he taunted her.

Pushing her was becoming addictive. She'd snap eventually—hopefully before he left the court of night.

The female shook her head in disbelief. "I can't make sense of you."

"I'll take that as a no. Your loss. There's nothing quite like passionate sex. And you're too young to have known love, so hatred would do."

"Let me guess, you're volunteering as my test subject for the trial? How generous of you." She rolled her eyes. "Go away. I'm working."

"You're standing uselessly. No one is going to attack at the busiest time of the night, five sunsets before the solstice, when the guard has been doubled."

"No? When would you attack Asra?" she asked him.

Valerius gave the question some consideration. "You're trying to get it out of me because the question is likely going to come up on your next test, aren't you?"

"Damn straight. If you're going to stalk me, you might as well be useful."

She was fucking adorable. If his mother truly wasn't thinking of her as a potential Mrs. Valerius Blackthorn, the queen was stupid. And given the fact that the queen was the very opposite of stupid, he had to conclude that she'd somehow lied to him.

Rolling Shea's words in his mind until he'd made sense of her meaning, he laughed when he got it. "I had not once thought of you possibly pairing up with Devira," she'd said. *Not once*. So she'd thought of it more than once, then.

An idea suddenly came to Vale. What if she hadn't *simply* thought of it? What if she'd taken steps to ensure that Vale was quite captivated by the little trap dressed in leather?

Vale had seen spells of obsession cast before they were banished, and the queen wasn't above making use of trickery.

Interesting.

His silence had lasted long enough for Devi to take notice of it, so he indulged her, giving thought to her question.

"I'd attack right before dusk. Place my troops nearby and get a small group to kill the guards posted around the city first. Once the gates are unmanned, I'd send my armies in and take the city while the court sleeps. The elders may be politicians, or landlords now, but seven hundred years ago, there was war. Most of us can take care of ourselves. I'd ensure I hold most of the territory before they can defend it, giving them little choice but to flee or perish."

Devi nodded. "Smart. Underhanded, but smart. But Shea would know when her city is at a disadvantage. She'd post additional troops during the day, would she not?"

"Indeed. But the guards are night creatures. Regardless of their number, they would be tired, quite ready to be relieved. You asked of our most vulnerable time. It is the late afternoon."

She seemed upset to hear it; he could practically see the wheels of her mind turning as she attempted to come up with a solution, a way to reinforce their defenses.

Vale didn't interrupt her thoughts to let her know that dozens of strategists with far more experience than she were working on the matter. First, because he knew better—many a time, a fresh young mind had found answers no one had thought of. But mostly because he took the occasion to study the female closely.

He liked her mouth. Plump. Kissable. Her skin was tanned, sun-kissed. Unusual for an unseelie.

Her eyes were fascinating. Dark blue at the rim of her irises, then gray, green, gold and yellow. When the light caught them, they seemed entirely green, only to change to a vibrant blue the next instant. Looking deep into them, he found stars. An entire unknown constellation he could spend a lifetime studying. He'd never seen a fae with eyes quite so mystic. The word hazel didn't cut it at all. Her eyes were life.

It was then, while frustratingly trying to make sense of her, that he realized the very first fundamental thing about Devira Star Rivers. He wasn't certain what clued him in—perhaps her presence, her aura—but she wasn't unseelie at all.

"Mother says you're called Rivers."

She dropped her eyes. Vale found that he didn't like that. He put his hand under her chin and tilted it until she was looking at him again.

"Answer me."

"Was there a question?"

Good point, smartass.

"You're a Rivers. As in a jewel of the Seelie Court, descended right from one of the thirteen families who shaped this world. One of the last to bear the name, I'd wager. And yet you're here."

She rolled her eyes. "I was born north, quite close to Carvenstone, actually. Between the border of the elven realm and your own domain. On unseelie land. At age fifteen, I was called to court and raised here *by your mother.*" Devi slapped his hand away. "I'm a citizen of the unseelie realm."

She was right, by the definition people went by these days. Being born and raised on unseelie ground made her an unseelie fae.

And yet she wasn't. Not where it mattered, not in her heart and mind, from the little he'd seen from her.

High fae were malicious and selfish at the core. Since the old days, they'd wielded magic, but their gifts didn't come without a price. It took a toll on their body and mind. Some spells could render them unconscious for days. They could even kill them. As their powers often came from natural elements, they also suffered with nature. Earth mages hurt when forests were razed, air mages became sick in polluted areas, and so on.

Their trials had made them cruel. They'd started demanding payments for use of their powers—payments which were always meant to cripple those they "helped" so they might feel some of their plight.

They'd divided into two realms a long time ago. The seelie fae went east and swore an oath to hold themselves to a better ideal. They swore to act for the greater good and deny their nature if they must. They had rules, and used oaths like they were going out of style. Those who failed to follow the ton paid for it in blood, or in curses.

The unseelie fae, in their great wisdom, took one look at the long charter of nonsensical regulations and said "fuck that shit." They chose to do as they pleased. Their laws were few, and seen as guidelines.

The female before Vale's eyes was a seelie fae, whatever she may say.

If her eyes could have burned a hole in his, they would have. She hadn't truly meant it when she'd professed to hate him a few minutes ago. Now she almost did.

Vale was itching to find out why this was such a sensitive subject. Hundreds if not thousands of fae with seelie blood lived in their city, and there were also a few unseelie who'd migrated east.

He wanted to know, and he could find out. He could look in her mind, crack her mental defenses open like an egg. Blast through it.

Instead, he found himself wishing that she'd speak to him. His tone was demanding, but still, he asked, rather than extracting the information he wanted from her pretty head. "Tell me. Tell me why you're ashamed of this."

Devi rolled her eyes.

"Go away. I'm *working*."

"Tell me and I'll leave you alone."

That did get her attention.

"Forever?" she asked, so visibly hopeful he laughed.

She wouldn't have liked if he'd truly left her. Not now. Not before taking her wildly against every available surface they could find. Their chemistry was volatile, combustible. She might find it confusing and frustrating now, but she'd work it out eventually. Especially if he kept pushing her.

It wasn't the first time he'd encountered a fae who was compatible with him. In his seven centuries, there had been three males and nine females with whom he'd shared an intense chemistry. Vale recalled his first. He'd been older than Devi—twice her age, at least. And yet he'd felt bothered, annoyed at himself, and at the object of his lust. Out of control. Once or twice, he might have wondered if he'd hated her.

I know what you're going through, little fae. And I know how this ends.

As the words came to him, he wondered if they were quite true, because for all his years, he'd never felt such an acute attraction. The intensity was entirely new, and he knew better than to trust it. The fact that Shea had the female under her thumb for years couldn't be forgotten. There was a very good chance that there was magic involved.

"Forever is a long time," he stated, not about to let her induce him in a vow he didn't intend to keep. "For the rest of the day."

"Why do you care?" she grumbled, her frustration evident.

"I can't say I *care*," he carefully lied. "But I told you before. I'm bored. You're a new development in this court, and therefore, it makes you entertaining. Satisfy my curiosity, and I'll probably leave you alone in due time."

This also felt like a lie.

She nodded, guessing she wouldn't get a better offer from him.

"I'm not ashamed. I'm *careful*. My mother and I were banned from the Seelie Court."

"Why?" he pressed.

"Because my mother ran away."

"Why?"

"Because she received a proposal she wasn't able to refuse, and she was not inclined to accept."

"Am I going to have to pry each word out of you? *Why?*"

"Because," she said with a defeated sigh, "the proposal came from Kravin Farel. The seelie king."

Oh. Well, that explained it. No wonder Shea wanted her watched around the seelie. They had a long memory, and too much arrogance for their own good. That a female could have jilted their king wouldn't have sat well with the seelie, and Devi was a living reminder of their shame.

"Hey, is that a bag from old Dorrel?" she asked, noticing the paper bag he carried in his left fist.

Valerius groaned. "What is it with females wanting my pastries? I don't share," he stated, quite resolved.

Devi softened her eyes, staring right at Vale for a long moment. Then she pouted.

He didn't know how or why, but all of a sudden his arms were rising, holding the bag open right in front of her.

He let her pick two pastries before walking away, grumbling.

Sorcery. It had to be sorcery.

FIVE
THE DAWN OF NIGHT

Vale had made no promise to keep an eye on Devi, as his mother wished, yet he knew he would. Now that he knew the chit could be in real danger, he was left with no other choice.

He hid it well, but he felt like trapped prey, circled by wolves. Helpless. He'd played right into Shea's hand, he was sure of it. His mother had set her trap, and he'd run right into it, like a bug taken in a spider web.

Devi Star Rivers. A very appealing spider web. Chemistry aside, the female was fun. A lot of fun. How long had it been since anyone had treated him that way? Like someone normal. Someone she could insult, brush off, and belittle.

And yes, he realized that these weren't characteristics one should value quite so much, but it did beat the horde of spineless drones that fell at his feet. Although, she'd technically done that. Vale found himself smiling again at the memory. She'd seemed so shocked and lost, like it was the first time she'd ever lost her balance. And it might have been.

After leaving the girl in the square, Vale headed back to the castle, needing to clear his mind. Kal joined him on the way, and they walked in companionable silence.

"Tell me we're not staying long," were the first words out of Kallan's mouth as soon as they walked back in his apartment.

They were settled as far as possible from his mother's place, atop the west tower, whereas the queen lived on the first floor. He'd chosen his rooms at court long ago, to ensure he never, ever heard his mother fuck. That strategy had failed half a dozen times over his long existence—six occasions forever branded in his mind.

"Why, Kal, not enjoying my mother's attention, the fine ambrosia, the scantily dressed women throwing themselves at you, and the—" Vale stopped his list when his companion threw a knife his way.

Vale laughed as he caught it between two fingers and started playing with it, twirling it around his hand. Truth was, he knew how uncomfortable Kal was with the queen's attention. He had no reason to be; it wasn't his fault that Shea preferred him to Valerius, and Vale wasn't about to begrudge his friend, who'd never known any other parental attention. They were now all quite old enough to accept these facts. Just not mature enough to stop teasing each other.

"You know you're supposed to be my second, right?" Vale reminded Kal. "Pretty sure attempting to kill me isn't part of the job description."

"It is when you drag me to court. Shea wanted me to talk about my life and aspirations, dammit. You *owe* me."

Vale sighed. The male had a point. "I'm sorry. It's been sixteen years though. Even if the damn seelie hadn't seen fit to screw with us, I would have had to show my face within the next two seasons. You know what would have happened if I hadn't come. And Shea would have had reasons to think something may be amiss had you not accompanied me."

Kallan would have had to be reasonable if he had said anything at all, so he remained silent and brooding. If it was possible, his friend hated the court more than Vale. But there was a price to pay for their freedom.

If Vale never showed his face, his mother would pack her court up and head over to see him. The queen considered it a duty to ensure that her heir was well from time to time. She'd done it once, four hundred years ago. Hiding what he was up to in Carvenstone had taken a lot of fucking effort.

People had called his domain the court of sin long before he was ever born, because the duke who owned it had settled his mistress there. They imagined the deepest depravity every day and night, and he needed them to carry on believing exactly that.

When the queen had come to him in 3179, he had to evacuate entire villages, empty most of the city, and create what she expected to see in less than six hours. His people still recalled that ordeal. Never again. Now he was playing by the rules, like the dutiful son he wasn't, and ensuring mummy dearest wasn't paying him any mind.

"I know. Still sucks. We're only staying a few days, right?"

Vale made a noncommittal sound that somewhat resembled a yes. That was the plan in theory, but in practice....

Kallan sighed. "Now what?"

"Nothing. I want to get back as soon as possible. The seelie delegation will likely be gone right after the solstice, and we'll go after they've returned to their land."

"Don't bullshit me, I know all your tricks. What's making you evade a direct answer?" Then comprehension hit, and Kal just laughed. "The girl. The one who wore a blue dress. I saw you stop in front of her. She got under your skin three nights ago."

One of the problems with hanging out with someone he'd known since childhood was that he couldn't get away with lies.

"No," he lied. A technicality allowed him to do that. The girl in the blue dress hadn't gotten under his skin three nights ago; she'd done that the following dusk, dressed in a plain brown leather tunic and breeches that did wonderful things for her long legs. And she'd retained his attention because of the words that came out when she opened her sensual mouth.

"I know you too well. You want to find out what's up the girl's skirts. Can't say I blame you. I don't think I've seen anyone half as exquisite since we went to Corantius. And man, what I'd do to her ass—"

Vale didn't even think. The next second, the knife was sailing back through the air at Kal, aiming for between his eyes. It was only seven hundred years of rigorous training that allowed his friend to evade it in time.

Fuck.

A silence stretched between them. Just as Vale opened his mouth to apologize, Kal started to laugh. Hard.

"Damn. This is going to be fucking epic."

"Disastrous," Vale corrected. "Disastrous is the word you're looking for."

Kallan simply laughed harder. Then he managed to stop long enough to say, "You remember your girl in 2867? The one you kept for seven years before your mother found out."

Teria. She'd been good fun, but Vale had had no intention to make their little affair a permanent thing, hence why they'd parted ways once Shea had started pressing the issue.

"Of course I'd remember one of my former partners. Do you have a point?"

"As a matter of fact, yes, I do. How many times did you let me play with pretty Teria's shapely ass, Valerius?"

Right now, Vale wished he had another knife at hand. As there was no weapon in the vicinity, he settled for glaring.

He'd had no issue sharing Teria. Sharing was quite the norm for his kind, in any case—definitely before forming a permanent union, and sometimes after. Statistically, there were about three males for every high fae female born. No wonder that their race had a natural inclination for pansexual and polyamorous relationships.

Vale was monogamist in his affections. Caring about more than one person at a time was quite unnatural. And besides, it sounded like too much effort. That said, sexually? He was just as open to mixing things up as any other high fae. Who was he to deny his partner an extra pair of balls if he or she felt greedy? Sex was simple.

Vale demanded a heart, mind, and soul focused on him, but when it came to flesh, he was the opposite of possessive. Watching his lovers writhe in pleasure as multiple hands, tongues, and cocks worked them over was one of his baser predilections.

So he couldn't decide what had happened to him right then. He should have been hard at the thought of Kal fucking Devi. Instead, the mental picture rendered him absolutely furious.

There was magic involved; he had no other explanation.

He wasn't quite as put out as he should have been about that development. Vale joined in, chuckling at his own expense along with Kal, all the while feeling a little anxious.

"I have no idea where that came from, mate. Seriously. I'm sorry. I'm telling you, my mother probably slipped a spell in my drink or—"

"Or found a girl who hits every single one of your boxes and dressed her to your taste before dangling her in front of you like a carrot. Shea is no fool, and whether or not she keeps you at a distance, she knows you better than anyone." Kal gave it a thought for a second before adding, "Except me, perhaps."

Vale wrinkled his nose in distaste. No, that wasn't it. He hadn't attacked his closest companion because he'd met a pretty girl. There was more to it, and he'd find out before he left. Not staying on top of his mother's games was dangerous.

The Blackthorns passed their immense powers down from daughter to daughter; therefore, no one had been surprised that Vale had ended up inheriting his father's gifts. He was redoubtable, fearsome. The name they called him, "the dark prince," had been earned by many deeds fair folks still whispered of when they told stories meant to terrify one another around bonfires.

Yet for all that, Vale was of little use to the queen. She wanted a Blackthorn with Blackthorn magic: elemental powers.

He was her firstborn, made the very first time she'd attempted to conceive a child. But she'd failed to birth another babe for over seven hundred years, hence her insatiable thirst for grandbabies.

Vale had quite honestly believed that, given the severity of the current climate, she would set her plans aside. Then he'd talked to Devi, a youngling who didn't shiver when she looked into his eyes.

Come to think of it, it made sense. If war was truly coming, the Blackthorns needed fresh blood in case ill befell their house. They were two now—the mother and the son. For the first time, Valerius genuinely put aside his own distaste at the notion of finding a female to bear his heir for practical reasons and admitted how pressing the matter was.

Be that as it may, he wouldn't let his mother trick him into obedience.

"There's more to this. Shea is cunning. I think there could be a spell brewing."

Kallan nodded before summarizing, "So, basically you're staying because of your many mommy issues and because you want to bang a new girl."

Fair assessment, but he corrected it nonetheless. "I'm not touching the female until I know for sure what makes her get under my skin. If Shea played with magic to bind her to me, fucking her is likely to make things exponentially worse. I've seen obsession spells at work before. I won't be able to stop thinking about her. Leaving court before sorting it out would only make things worse. I need to break whatever hex my mother started."

While saying all this, Vale frowned.

He had studied the art of spells, like any gifted high fae who'd ever attended the Royal Academy. Although he had no skills in the making or breaking of hexes, he recalled enough of his schooling to know that any such spell needed a part of him: a hair, a drop of blood—hell, some saliva. He'd been away for over a decade, and he'd come practically unannounced. How could Shea have created a spell that needed weeks of preparation in such short notice? And how could she have done it at all? The queen had earth-based elemental magic. They had a handful of mages in the Unseelie Court, but none were of a high caliber. To create a spell of that sort, the queen would have needed the services of someone infinitely more powerful and versed in the dark arts. A sorcerer. There were only three of them left in the realm, and none resided in Asra.

His theory didn't add up, but he clung to it. It still made more sense than the alternative. Because if he wasn't hexed by his damn mother, then he was simply enchanted by Devi for no reason at all. That was a frightening thought—for him and for her.

Vale was known for playing with his favorite toys until they broke. Tough as she may think she was, Devi was infinitely too young and innocent for the likes of him.

"Enough of the girl. We're here because the seelie king is heading for the court of night, and that spells trouble. I'm going to have to mingle. Meanwhile, you can watch what's happening in the shadows. Shea believes war is coming, and I'm not entirely certain she's wrong."

Shea had showed him thirteen documents to support her theory. Any one of those would have seemed innocent enough on its own, but all together, they painted an alarming picture.

The lord of Duneran wrote to inform Shea that the seelie were fortifying their borders, erecting walls of the magic and mortar variety. The spies on the coast reported merchants risking the perilous travel along the line of the Isle's Wall, the potent energy barrier that separated their world from the monsters roaming the seas, all in order to bring cargo to the court of sunlight. The spy wrote that he would endeavor to discover what exactly was loaded on those boats. No other missive bore his distinctive handwriting. Then there was talk of seelie friends in the court leaving the unseelie realm. Reports told of food provisions being amassed throughout the entire seelie realm and being brought to their court. Seelie lords posted outside their borders were being ordered back. And so on.

The court of sunlight and the court of night had been on opposite sides of every single war. If the seelie were preparing, Shea was right to be wary.

Twelve of these reports were various shades of disquieting, but Valerius could have brushed them off, concluding that the seelie had probably heard the winter would be biting this year. They were known to dislike the cold.

The thirteenth was incontestably daunting. There was no way to dismiss it.

It said that the elves had sent more troops to their borders. If Vale knew one thing for certain about elves, it was that they never did a thing without cause.

SIX
SWORDS AND SNOW

Devi swung her sword with all her physical, and some of her mental, strength, yelling a battle cry as she charged. Her opponent sighed and waved her hand. Devi's body flew backward, hitting the wall with a resounding *thud*.

Fuck. She painfully got to her feet and cracked her neck.

Devi didn't take it personally; it wasn't a testament of her skills. This was just the sort of thing that happened when one faced the unseelie queen.

"What did you do wrong?" Shea asked.

"I said yes when you suggested sparring," she shot back immediately, making the queen roll her eyes.

But Shea also wanted to smile, Devi knew it. She'd managed to extort a grin from the grave, somber queen before they were done tonight.

Their little tête-à-tête was always a lesson, but Shea liked to switch things around. Sometimes she told Devi about the history of long-forgotten ages that weren't taught in any class or recorded in any books, and other times, the queen had tried, and mostly failed, to help Devi control her powers.

It was rare that Shea offered to fight these days. Devi couldn't deny that the change of pace had sounded like a reprieve at first. An hour into it, there were bruises on all her limbs, and she hadn't so much as entered Shea's space.

Shea had trained her for over a decade, but now Devi realized that she'd always held herself back in the past. Tonight she wasn't pulling punches.

"You didn't scan me. Mages prepare their attack. Checking what your opponent's aura says before launching is Fighting 101. If you'd checked…."

"But no one *can* check your mind." Devi frowned, confused.

Shea was known to have the strongest mental shields. It was said that the overking himself, the all-powerful ruler of their entire Isle, couldn't get past the queen's walls, although he was the single most powerful psychic in the realm.

"Fortunately for you, my mind isn't what you're fighting right now. I'm using earth magic, so you're fighting gravity and stones. Know your enemy, know their power, and learn to anticipate where it's going to come from. You have a unique advantage, Devi. You know every elemental magic. How it feels. How it behaves. Identify it, and then use your knowledge."

Still frowning, Devi nodded once, showing her willingness to try rather than a conviction that she'd manage to hold her own against the unseelie queen.

"All right, ready," she said, bracing herself.

The queen finally managed a smile for the first time that night. "Aren't you always. Now concentrate."

Devi opened her mind and tentatively felt the energy around her. Finding too many conflicting voices, auras, and magic coming from all around them, in every room surrounding the queen's apartments, she closed her eyes, trying to shut out everything and everyone except Shea.

The flare of power hit her mind a millisecond before it moved into motion, intending to push her again. It came from behind her this time. Devi felt it rise like a wave—a very specific wave with a set trajectory not even Shea Blackthorn could change on a whim.

Devi leaped out of the way, and Shea immediately sent another hit from a different direction. Devi ducked and rolled on the practice mat, getting to a crouch, ready to move in whatever direction she needed to next.

"This isn't a dance, Dev. We said sparring, not jumping around like a monkey."

Oh, yes. Recalling she had a sword at her belt and was meant to make use of it, Devi unsheathed it and redirected her attention to the queen. The moment she did, another wave hit, directly coming from the ceiling this time. She tried to move but was firmly thrust on her back.

"Dammit."

Shea laughed softly and crossed the distance separating them, offering her a hand. Devi accepted the assistance to get back on her feet.

"You did well."

It was now Devi's turn to roll her eyes. Her bruises said otherwise.

Truth be told, Devi wasn't at her best on one-on-one. Her strength was magic. She understood why Drake and Shea made her train like this, but at the back of her mind, she wondered if there was any point. If she couldn't kill her enemies from a distance, she was probably screwed.

"I haven't spent that much time on my ass since I learned snowboarding," she replied.

Shea tilted her head, her interest piqued like it always was when Devi shared a little piece of information about her life before the court.

The queen never asked anything, but when Devi talked, she listened.

"That's basically strapping a board on your feet, and—"

"I saw elves snowboard in the war," Shea replied. "It made them deadly in the mountains. Deadlier than they generally were, which is saying a lot. They came down at high speed, too fast to target. And yet they could still shoot an arrow right between their enemy's eyes."

There was no bitterness in Shea's words, although the elves may not have been on her side.

She was speaking of the last war. Every nation had fought for themselves at first. Then there had been alliances, betrayals, and more alliances. Finally, it had ended when Orin got every king and queen on their knee, forcing their submission and their allegiance. He was crowned overking of the realm, and all swore to obey him.

To most, this was history. Shea had lived through the entire thousand-year conflict, as the youngest daughter of a warlord first, and then as the leader the unseelie had rallied behind when there was no hope, no strength, and no one to believe in.

It blew Devi's mind that the rather short, seemingly young female in front of her was also a legendary commander, famous for a war that had ended almost seven centuries ago.

At the same time, she'd seen Shea's glare. It made strong fae shiver and weaklings piss themselves. The legend made total sense to one who'd witnessed the queen's anger.

"I get they've used their snowboards as a military strategy, but nowadays they do it for fun," Devi said, feeling a little awkward. "I mean, as I said, you spend day one on your ass a lot, and that doesn't change much for a month or so, but suddenly you know what you're doing, and the speed, the freedom, the adrenaline rush…."

She closed her mouth because words failed her, as they always did when she spoke of her year in the elven realm of Wyhmur.

"Sounds like something I would have liked to try in another life," Shea said before glancing toward the window. "It's late. We should call it a night. Before we part ways, however, I want to talk about the seelie delegation."

Devi swallowed her saliva with difficulty.

"It's not the first year there's been a delegation at the solstice," Devi said, because that's what she'd told herself again and again on repeat since she'd heard of the seelie's arrival from the rumor mill.

Rook and Jiya had spoken of nothing else tonight.

"Indeed, there have been a few seelie here every year since your arrival," Shea confirmed. "Just like I send diplomats to attend their celebration at the court of sunlight. But usually that delegation doesn't include their king."

Devi's eyes widened, and her heart stopped.

Shit. She hadn't wanted to believe it. Now that the queen had confirmed it, her mind raced, and finally she said the one thing that made sense.

"I can head home," she offered. "Make myself scarce until it's all over."

Shea tsked. "Don't be silly. He knows you're here. If I hide you, he'll believe we're scared that he might wish you ill."

Devi chuckled. "That may be because he's put a price on my head. Just my head. It doesn't really have to be attached to my shoulders."

"In his kingdom," Shea retorted. "You're a welcome guest in my house, and a lady of my realm. He'll have to respect that here."

Yeah, right. She could see that happening.

Not. That just wasn't how proud nobles functioned.

"Besides, I'm not talking of King Kraven. His Grace has passed the reins of the kingdom to his son, Devin. He was enthroned not a fortnight ago."

Oh, that changed things. Possibly.

Her mother had been betrothed to Kraven, and Devi was the living reminder that she'd rejected him. Actually, that was a mild term. Her mother had run away, leaving the seelie realm, and had gone to Shea for asylum. Loxy Rivers was disowned by her family and banned from the seelie realm under penalty of death. At her birth, Devi was awarded the same sentence.

Hopefully Devin didn't feel quite as strongly about the matter.

"Right. What's our play?"

"You'll stand by my side when we're greeting him. I'll present you. Our play depends on his reaction."

She bit her lip but nodded, because there was only one response to anything Shea Blackthorn dictated.

"As you wish."

The queen gestured her forward, and knowing what it meant, Devi came closer before bending down. She was over a head taller while standing up. Now that they were at the same level, Shea pressed her lips on Devi's forehead, holding on to her head for an instant.

The queen wasn't known to be warm, or expressive. Nice was one term that had never been used to describe her. Nonetheless, when she kissed her that way—each time they parted ways in private—it felt like home. It felt like love.

"Now go, child. Sleep well, for the days ahead may be strenuous to your young heart."

Devi chuckled. "The way you and Vale go on about my poor little inexperienced self, you'd think I was a babe in diapers."

She understood it, as the queen was over a thousand years old, and the prince close to it. But she was twenty-eight. It had been three years since she'd come of age. Some lesser fae had a lifespan of just half a century; she would have been considered an adult among them.

"Vale, is it?" Shea asked.

Her tone had changed. *Shit. Am I in trouble?* They'd always been rather informal together, but perhaps she was expected to call Shea's son by the title due his rank.

When she looked to Shea's face, she found no annoyance. There was a small degree of teasing however.

Devi groaned. "Why is absolutely everyone assuming that I fancy the guy? He's not my type."

"Child, you forget: I know you can lie."

Shit.

"He's annoying, haughty, extremely egocentric and—"

"Save it. I'd give consent to a union, if I were asked. Just bear that in mind."

Devi had been quite exhausted a few instants ago, but left the training room irritated and too furious to hope for sleep.

Instead, after a short cold bath, she got dressed and headed to the library.

The royal residential wing of the castle was large and mostly empty. Rather, it had been empty most days before. Her apartments were on the second floor, the last guest suite at the very end of the corridor. The safest spot in the wing, according to Shea; if intruders were invading the palace, they had to enter through the main building before they reached it. "It gives you plenty of time to flee," she had said.

Devi had always hated the thought of fleeing anything, but she gracefully took the apartment she was given.

She had to walk through the elegant halls and down to the ground floor before stopping at the round door leading to the library.

During the earlier hours of the night, it was generally occupied—scholars often requested to study some of the priceless volumes in the queen's private collection—but it was close to dawn. At this hour, no stranger was welcome in the queen's home.

Behind the door, the room was dark and silent, but she knew Valerius had taken refuge there. She felt him; his presence was too distinctive to mistake it.

Devi stood still before the door. She had truly wished to spend time in the library, perhaps her favorite room outside of her apartment, but the last thing she needed was more of Valerius Blackthorn.

She looked down self-consciously. She was wearing a long white chemise and a comfortable bathrobe. Flushing, she turned her heels and rushed through the empty halls until she was safe behind her door again.

Come to think of it, fleeing wasn't such a bad idea at times.

On the other side of the red circular door, holding a book of spells, hexes, and countermeasures he'd ceased reading thirty-seven seconds ago, Vale found himself smiling. Devi was rushing upstairs, running away from him. It took all his strength to remain in his seat rather than chase his prey.

SEVEN

LADY OF THE COURT

Valerius didn't often make use of his abilities. Knowing exactly what people thought made life incredibly dull. Besides, he'd come to see it as an invasion, a weapon one only used against enemies.

As dozens of seelie poured into the court of night, he didn't hesitate, willfully breaching the minds of every single one of them and seeing what lay underneath.

He had good reasons to be suspicious. For one, only a third of the party he'd seen pass through his lands had made it to the court, mostly nobles and private guards. They'd left their soldiers somewhere along the way. Valerius could conjecture a million motives, and none of them were remotely friendly.

He was completely unapologetic about figuring out where they'd conveniently stowed their missing soldiers, as well as the intentions behind the king's presence. It made no sense whatsoever, especially with no warning.

The problem was the seelie had been ready for him. Among the thirty-four high fae who entered the throne hall with every flourish characteristic of their kind, wearing tons of gold, complicated hairdos, and too much perfume, thirty had their minds completely bared. None of them had done anything even remotely interesting in their entire existence, long as it may have been.

The last four were another story. The king, his two guards, and his advisor were completely blocked; he couldn't even get a peep out of their minds. No shields were that strong, not even his mother's. This wasn't their power. They were using some sort of artifacts to keep him out.

Vale swore under his breath. He couldn't do a thing. Or rather, he *wouldn't* do a thing, because pushing against the barriers was akin to raping his way through their minds. It wouldn't go unnoticed. They'd scream in excruciating pain. And doing that to the king of the realm of sunlight would have been a clear act of war.

Valerius swore under his breath. He was stuck, unable to act. He was standing next to his mother, and they were flanked by her head of staff and first advisor. Then there was Devi, to whom he wasn't paying attention. Openly, in any case. With the eyes of the entire court on him, it wouldn't do to leave right now, but something had to be done.

An alternative came to mind, and his eyes searched through the crowd until he found Kallan in the second row of fae standing before them. He held Kallan's eyes for a beat until his second understood what he needed. It was almost physically painful for him, Vale could tell, but Kallan dropped his mental shield, allowing Vale to get in.

"*They're up to something. Only the king and his three closest subordinates know what,*" Vale informed him.

"*What do you need?*"

"*Get one of the guards they posted outside the city.*"

Kallan made his way out of the hall entirely unnoticed, as the eyes of the court were on the uninvited guests.

Finally the seelie reached the queen and her party.

The king was a handsome high fae who hadn't yet seen his first century, Vale could tell. Devin's aura held no weight. One look and he categorized the boy as a puppet in someone else's game. Probably his father's. His subjects knelt before Shea in deference. Devin inclined his head, as was the way of sovereigns.

Shea was doing her thing—giving him her trademark stare that made grown men squirm and avert their eyes.

At long last, she returned the greeting.

"Devin of the house of Farel." Her voice was cold. "An unexpected honor."

In short, she meant "Why didn't you fucking ask me permission before stepping in my fucking kingdom, fucking prick?" The little king seemed to get that. Vale saw him swallow and glance toward his advisor. After a beat, the male regrouped.

"Your Majesty," he replied pleasantly, with all outward signs of respect, "I was enthroned not a fortnight ago, and my first thought went to your court. For centuries now, our great nations have been on friendly terms because of the pleasant rapport between yourself and my father. When we received your invitation to attend the winter solstice, my advisors and I saw it as an opportunity to rekindle this relationship now that my reign has started."

So, the boy isn't entirely brainless. Good for him.

Truth was, said invitation was nothing more than a formality; some seelie went to the Unseelie Court for the winter solstice, and some unseelie went to the Seelie Court for the summer solstice. Devin knew he'd messed up, but he was turning it into the innocent gesture of friendship of an inexperienced new ruler. Well played. Vale would even have believed it, if Devin hadn't gone to great lengths in order to keep his mind so carefully closed off. There was more to this.

"We're glad to have you," Shea assured him before introducing her escorts. "You may not recall my son, Valerius. The last time you met, you were—"

"Ten years of age and very impressed to be standing in front of the legend known as the dark prince," Devin said with a chuckle.

Strangely, the laughter reached his eyes. He advanced to shake Vale's hand, all the while saying, "You did not disappoint. I asked you if you could truly torture people just with your mind, and you made my music teacher scream in agony for a brief instant."

"Did I?" Vale replied with an indifferent shrug. "Well, that definitely sounds like something I'd do. In my defense, I'm generally drunk during any visit to the court of sunlight. You guys can definitely brew ale."

In truth, he recalled the incident just fine. The musician had some inappropriate thoughts toward most of the boys he taught. Vale had made quite certain that he never acted on his sick inclination. One acute dose of pain served along with one compulsion. If he ever thought of harming a child, he'd feel that pain again.

This was exactly the sort of thing Vale never would admit to, lest he be mistaken for an honorable person.

"No hard feelings," Devin said. "I never liked Sir Trunchin much."

Vale reluctantly, and cautiously, decided that he didn't have any clear alarm bell ringing against the little king. He reserved judgment, but his first impression was that of a male intending to do his best for his nation. Vale could be reading him wrong, or Devin could be led astray. Young and out of his depth, the king probably heavily relied on his advisors.

"Solerus Dane, my head of staff. Loralei Night, my first advisor. Drake Night, my consort. And Devira Rivers, my ward," Shea introduced.

As they were presented, Devin shook hands with a polite, "How do you do," as was the way. Everything was quite uneventful, at least until the king arrived in front of Devi Rivers.

Valerius saw the young male freeze. Then Devin's eyes widened.

Vale knew that look.

"Rivers. Of course." The king shook his mind out of the funk. "I knew your mother. You look almost exactly like her, but for the hair and eyes."

Vale wasn't the only one watching closely; the entire court of night and every seelie guest were fixed on them.

"Loxy said she liked my name. I see she made good use of it," Devin added.

The young king seemed at a loss for words then, and Devi appeared uncomfortable as fuck. It was painful to watch the confident female who'd told Vale to fuck off seem so lost right then.

Instinctively, without any conscious volition, Vale moved, finding himself standing right behind her.

Fuck.

As an afterthought, he reminded himself that his mother had asked that he protect her when he could. He was doing nothing more than his duty. This would have been logical reasoning, had he considered it *before* he found himself hovering over the girl protectively. Devi lifted her gaze to Vale, and as their eyes held, she breathed out, regaining some of her composure.

His mind eased. This wasn't about his mother at all. He'd seen a female in need of help, and he'd responded. There was nothing more to it.

"Sorry, yes," she said, finding her voice. "My mother once told me she named me after a boy. I found the thought quite upsetting as a child."

Devin laughed good-humoredly, extending his hand. Devi looked at it like it was a venomous snake. Almost imperceptibly, she stepped backward until she was close to Vale, nearly leaning on him. Vale wasn't sure she was even conscious of the movement. Everything she did seemed to scream "save me."

So he did just that.

As Devi hesitantly raised her hand to shake the king's, Vale circled her waist with his arm, silently, but clearly, making one statement.

Mine.

Vale could almost feel his mother smile. *Dammit.*

Could he plead insanity? But if he was truthful, he knew exactly what he was doing. His mother had said the seelie would want to recruit or eliminate the female, and for what it was worth, neither option was acceptable to Vale.

Devi was a lady of the unseelie realm, a jewel adorning the crown he would inherit someday.

No one was poaching her. No one.

EIGHT

A TASTE OF MADNESS

In any other circumstances, she would have yelled at Vale to keep his hands to himself, and kicked him in the nuts for good measure. Right now, the uninvited arm around her waist felt like a lifeline, an anchor keeping her firmly on the ground.

What was the seelie king playing at? Speaking of her mother fondly and laughing over the name they shared. This was not how she'd pictured this encounter going. A glare, maybe veiled threats, would have been more appropriate given the fact that there was a price on her head ordered by his father. But of course, Shea had been right; he wasn't going to try anything here, in public and right in front of the unseelie queen, who'd introduced Devi as her ward.

The king stressed her out. A crown did little to impress her, and she didn't doubt that, should any other man try to harm her in any way, she could have taken care of herself. The issue was that using her powers against him, or kicking his ass, *wasn't* an option. Starting a war by age thirty wasn't something she wished to add to her list of accomplishments.

Devin Farel's green eyes went from Valerius to her, and something flashed, disappearing too quickly for Devi to identify it, but she could guess. He'd planned insults and intimidation, or worse, if—or when—he caught her alone. Now that the dark prince, who he obviously feared, had pretended to make a claim on her, he couldn't do anything.

Devi covered Valerius's hand with hers, playing along. Vale was wearing black leather gloves, but somehow the touch felt warm.

The king's eyes softened, and he spoke with the appearance of pleasantness. "I understand she died when you were young. I'd known her from the very day I was born until the day she left sixty years later. If you wish to speak of her during my stay, it would be my pleasure."

Devi stiffened. Right, like she was going to voluntarily spend time around him.

"I do apologize for spoiling the fun," Vale said. Nothing about his stance seemed apologetic at all. "But Devi and I are going to be swamped until the solstice, aren't we, darling?"

It was another lifeline thrown her way by the most unlikely savior of all. Devi clung to it, wondering if it would cost her her soul. Surely he'd demand payment for his kindness, one way or another.

"Yes, so much to do."

Hopefully no one would ask her exactly what she had to do, because outside of work and catching up on some sleep, there was nothing on her agenda.

"My offer stands if your schedule opens up," the seelie high fae assured Devi before finally turning his back on them, returning to his company.

Devi's chest rose and fell more freely now that he was at an acceptable distance.

"Thank you," she whispered softly.

Vale's answer was swift and final. "Later."

She got it. They'd started a game, and they had to continue to play by its rules. But she wasn't one to do as she was told. She could very well play the part of the besotted arm candy while saying what she wanted to say.

Devi twisted her neck to look up toward him with a smile. "And here I thought you were kidding, but you do take your duty to rescue damsels quite seriously, don't you?"

"Or perhaps I simply thought to save the poor, unsuspecting fellow from your filthy mouth. It wouldn't do to let you embarrass the court."

She glared, and Vale pinched the bridge of her nose fondly.

"Be good. Let us not make a spectacle of ourselves."

Too late for that. The welcome ceremony was carrying on. King Devin introduced his subjects while Shea shared words of welcome and offered wine, but the attention of everyone in the room was entirely focused on them.

Realizing that, Devi wondered how much of a bad idea this whole charade was. It certainly had helped to push the son of a man who hated her very existence at arm's length, but that only helped her for a week;

pretending to be with Valerius Blackthorn might have consequences until the end of her life.

She brushed the thought aside. If the seelie were allowed anywhere near her, the end of her life might come a lot sooner than expected.

The introductions finally came to a cheerful conclusion when the queen announced, "Let us drink and dance."

"Great fucking idea," Devi replied under her breath.

"Drinks first," Valerius opted as he herded her toward the closest bar, his arm still around her waist.

The crowd parted to let him pass, and Devi realized that the little game came with good perks.

"I'll have a nectar," the prince said to the common fae minding the bar, then removed his gloves and loosened the top button of his white linen shirt. Devi was surprised when he turned to her. "Your poison of choice?"

"You know," she said, "you actually strike me as the kind of guy who orders for your dates without asking."

The prince rolled his eyes, telling the bartender, "Make that two."

She only had herself to blame for that.

She would have liked to appear badass, but truth was, Devi couldn't hold nectar. No one her age could, except her friend Rook, perhaps. She'd seen him drink some without making a complete fool of himself.

She was far from a lightweight. Her mother had served her watered-down wine in her youth, familiarizing her with alcohol. It was a custom among the nobles so their children could toast with important guests without passing out. Drinking spirits all night long was no problem for Devi, but nectar was basically the equivalent of a cocktail made with equal parts rum, whiskey, vodka, and gin, then sprinkled with a touch of aphrodisiac on top. What was worse, it tasted refreshing, light and fruity, like incredibly delectable water flavored with a hint of fruit or flower.

Older fae had had the time to build an immunity to it. But the first time Devi had tried it, she was halfway down her first glass when suddenly she'd found herself topless and riding Drake Night's dick like the world was ending on the morrow. Trying to recall the events leading to that unfortunate occurrence, she'd actually remembered quite clearly that she had accosted him in the most brazen of fashions.

It had been five years ago. Since, she'd taken sips here and there to get used to it, but there was no possible way she could handle a full glass.

Devi clicked the bottom of her glass with Valerius's and sipped it carefully. The prince downed the contents of his in one go before gesturing for a second one.

"Show-off."

Valerius bit back a smile.

"And the lady will have wine, now that she's learned that her sharp tongue can easily get her in trouble," he added with a knowing wink. "Let's not let that go to waste."

He lifted his hand, intending to take her drink. She let it go, but for the briefest instant, their fingers touched. A jolt of energy struck her with an astonishing force, and a gasp escaped her lips. Devi looked up to him in confusion, wondering if he'd used some sort of magic, only to find Valerius watching her with just as much puzzlement.

She chuckled. "Static."

"Right. Of course. Static," he repeated before downing her drink. "Ah, and here's our bartender."

"Are you seriously going to finish three nectars in as many minutes?"

No answer was necessary. The bartender handed her the wine and Valerius his third drink. The prince promptly downed it like it was water.

"I'm not carrying you to bed."

"That truly breaks my heart. Keep them coming," he told the bartender.

"No," she objected firmly. "If you're to stay with me, I'll not have you act like a fool tonight. Bring him wine."

The poor bartender's eyes went from his prince to Devi. She made things simple for him, removing a gold coin from her purse and handing it out. It was always an open bar at the throne hall, but gold spoke everywhere.

"Did you seriously just tell me what I could drink, and bribe the fucking bartender too?"

She shrugged.

"You realize I have more money than you, and that I could, regardless, *order* him to serve me."

"You'll keep your money and your egocentrism to yourself for another half hour or so. Then I'll excuse myself, and you'll be quite free to drink yourself stupid and act as you please," she informed him.

"And now I understand why you're still single."

"I'm twenty-eight," she replied, rolling her eyes. It was rare that a common or high fae her age would commit at all; most didn't form a bond before they'd seen their first century, at least. "And I have plenty of offers, thank you very much."

"Of course you do. I simply doubt they come from anyone who's heard you speak more than two sentences in a row."

"You really are a dick."

"And you are a prickly shrew."

She wasn't sure how or why, but Valerius was now standing quite close to her, so close there wasn't more than an inch between her chest and his. Valerius towered over her frame, although she was tall. He'd inclined his head toward her so she might hear his insult over the brouhaha of the two courts.

They were, in fact, close enough to kiss.

She had no clue why that thought crossed her mind, but she banished it as quickly as it had come. She blamed the whole thing on the sip of nectar. Kissing *him?* She should have thought, *Close enough to knee him right where it hurts.* That was more likely.

"Well, be that as it may, we have to pretend to get along for the rest of the evening, so try to keep your more dickish instincts in check. In return, I'll attempt to do something about the prickliness. Deal?"

"Why, are you offering a pleasant evening with you, my lady? How could I possibly refuse? Come. Let us mingle."

The Unseelie Court was an odd mixture of formality and chaos. One minute they were all curtsying to the seelie delegation, and the next, everyone danced, laughed, drank, and fucked in dark corners.

Devi itched to leave as soon as the chaos started, wanting to return to her apartments and catch up on some sleep or some reading. Hell, she would even have headed to work, given a choice, but Drake and all her superiors were in this hall, making it clear that she wouldn't find anything to do if she stopped by the protector headquarters.

She wasn't against celebrations per se, but there was quite a crowd today. As well as Valerius Blackthorn, who was known for unbelievable dramatic escapades, they now had the highest members of the Seelie Court and their flamboyant escorts in attendance. No one wanted to miss the chance to shake hands and rub elbows.

That sort of things held no appeal for her, and she had personal reasons to want to stay far, far away from the seelie. However, Valerius wasn't cooperative.

"Don't you look at the exit yet, dearest. Your absence will be noted and indeed seen as an insult at best. Cowardice at worst."

She wished she could disagree. "It's a circus, and everyone is staring at me, thanks to you," Devi said with a sigh.

Valerius chuckle. "No, I assure you, I'm quite innocent in the matter. They're staring at you thanks to that fucking dress you're wearing."

Devi narrowed her eyes. She liked her formal dresses, and her occupation didn't provide her enough occasions to make use of them. Tonight she wore a backless, dark green silk halter neck that fell to the ground and embraced all her curves along the way. She'd paired it with black bracelets around her left bicep and her right forearm, black shoes, and dark makeup. Her hair, usually tied in a knot and out of the way, was braided and thrown over her right shoulder.

Black and green were the colors of the court of night. Her dismissal of lighter tones, such as blues and silvers, which were the seelie's colors, was entirely purposeful.

"Your disapproval is noted and disregarded."

"And again, you misunderstand me entirely. I can't quite decide whether it's willfulness, modesty, or coquetries. I was paying you a compliment, Devira Star Rivers."

"If those are the kind of compliments you pay, no wonder you're still single."

She'd really tried to stay civil, but she couldn't help it. He'd practically begged her to poke at him.

"I have plenty of offers, thank you very much." He echoed her previous reply with a wink.

"No doubt. You do come with a pretty set of jewelry. Almost makes up for the rest. Not quite though."

"All right, now I have to shut that pretty mouth."

She had a reply at the ready, but he stole her voice, as well as her capacity to move or think, when his lips quite suddenly descended on hers, swallowing her gasp. He covered them softly at first, and then, finding them unresponsive, he coaxed them to life by pressing his lips harder on hers.

She had no explanation as to why she stepped closer, entirely closing the distance between them, or why she wrapped her arms around his neck and threaded her fingers through his luscious brown hair. Valerius's large hand circled her waist and pulled her against him as his tongue licked at her bottom lip. Devi was lost, at the brink of insanity, pushed to a point where she had cause to believe that she might just die from this. And yet one resounding thought came to mind. *More.* She needed more.

Valerius obliged. As he held her against his hard frame, his lips moved from her mouth. He kissed her collarbone, quite softly, and then trailed his lips along her neck until he'd reached her earlobe. He teased it with the tip of his tongue before nipping at it cruelly.

One of her hands moved to his torso, fighting with the top button of his shirt, needing the damn material off him, but the prince took a step back.

The sudden sense of loss was overwhelming one second, and the next, she was livid. Absolutely livid. What the *hell* was he thinking, the womanizing piece of trash! Working her up like that, and in public! She had an honorable reputation, dammit. He was reducing her to nothing more than a fucking court slut.

Devi didn't question why his touch had awakened her that way. With seven hundred years of whoring himself, it was no wonder he was skilled with his damn maddening lips.

"What the fuck was—"

"Shush. There are hundreds of eyes on us. We couldn't very well have sold our little farce without sealing it with a kiss, could we? Now come. I see they've set out a buffet."

NINE
WILD BLOOD

Devi liked food, apparently. Or at least she liked sweets. Ignoring the little pies and sandwiches, she went straight for the cupcakes, picking out one with blue icing. She took her time savoring the sugary frosting before devouring the cake in three bites. Then she reached for a chocolate melt.

"All right," she said after she'd eaten her first bite of dessert, "maybe you had a point. A public display of affection might have been in order. I'd appreciate a warning in the future though."

"Duly noted," he replied, amused.

She seemed far less angry once she'd had some food, he observed, storing the information in his mind. A minute ago, she'd been ready to ax off his head, and now she'd calmed down, recognizing that his excuse for kissing her had been valid. Fae were tactile and affectionate. There was no way anyone would have believed that they could spend a whole evening together without so much as exchanging a touch. It was a clever reason; however, it had come as an afterthought, just like his excuse for rushing to her aid in the first place. He'd simply kissed her because he'd looked at her lips and all of a sudden, he desired to taste them. He might have been able to help himself, with reasoning and logic, but he hadn't wanted to.

Now Devi seemed to have accepted the necessity of. Perhaps he should take to carrying sweets and pop one in her mouth when she was growling at him.

Vale smiled at the idea. He could kiss her to his heart's content and feed her when she was displeased with him.

"So, what now?"

"Now, Devi Star Rivers," he replied, saying every part of her name slowly, savoring it, "we're perhaps an hour away from the end of the party. The crowd will start to thin out, and we'll be able to make our way out without causing offense. Let us kill some time. Tell me about you."

If he didn't find a way to distract himself, he'd be right where he had been ten minutes ago—deep into madness as he lost himself to her softness.

A fucking kiss. It had just been a fucking kiss. He hadn't so much as groped the damn female. Valerius had fucked countless faceless females and not felt a tenth of what that simple, fleeting touch had awakened. It was a hunger he doubted would ever be sated. He'd had a taste and now he wanted more, craving it so much it scared him.

He could see just how much she wanted him to take her right there, in the middle of the throne hall. He'd felt her respond to him and smelled her response, her arousal. It was a delicious temptation he so wished to unwrap.

His theory that his sudden and violent infatuation was born of magic fresh in his mind, he had to keep his distance.

"Not much to say, really," she finally answered.

"Coming from the daughter of a seelie princess once betrothed to the king of the realm of sunlight, I sincerely doubt that. There is a story. Come on. Give me something. I can tell you don't belong at court. Where were you raised?"

Something dark flashed in her eyes as the female held his gaze. He'd obviously touched another sensitive subject.

"Sorry if my manners aren't to your liking, sir," she stated, her tone making it clear she wasn't sorry at all.

Yet he liked her voice. Steady, a little raspy, deeper than expected. He liked the tone she took with him. It was a far cry from the usual high-pitched flirtiness he was used to within these walls.

"I've heard something of your mother, and yet nothing at all about your father," Vale prompted, and he immediately knew he'd hit the nail right on the head.

Her entire body tensed; he would have felt it even if his hand wasn't resting on the small of her back.

"I'm technically an adult female. What does it matter who my parents are?"

"It matters because you're uncomfortable when anyone speaks of it. I want to know why." His inquiry was met with silence, unsurprisingly. "I could just fetch the answer from your pretty skull. I might even enjoy invading the intimacy of your mind."

"Then do it and leave me be," Devi challenged.

Poor dear. No one had warned her about poking a dormant beast.

Vale wrapped his hand around the back of her neck and tilted her head until her hazel eyes met his. Then his upper lip curved as he bit the lower one in anticipation.

"You've quite literally asked for it, sweet thing," was the last thing he said before entering her very soul.

Devi Star Rivers's life had been simple once. Her mother was pretty, gentle, idle, and quite happy to let her daughter roam the countryside by herself. At the time, it hadn't struck her as odd. Later, Devi realized that no creature of these parts would have dared lay a hand on her.

They owned a picturesque manor tucked between a forest and a beautiful clear blue lake. It was the sort of home that seemed to have been built in another age. In the winter, it was incredibly cold, so servants lit fires in every single room. In the summer, every room was a sauna, and Devi used the slightest excuse to take a dip in the lake. There was talk of selkies, nickers, nymphs, and other creatures who'd gladly pull an unsuspecting soul all the way to the bottom of the lake. When Nanny hysterically warned them, Loxy Rivers simply laughed it off.

"Aren't there any water sprites, then, Mama?" Devi had asked.

"Of course there are," the elegant high fae replied, bending down to look her daughter right in the eyes. "But they'd never harm you, little princess."

It would be a while before she understood any of that.

Devi had many friends, ranging from the dogs to passing strangers and mysterious spirits who never spoke and never quite showed themselves as they lingered in the shadows.

"I know you're over there, by the way," she'd sometimes say. "I can feel you, you know. Mama says to trust my magic, and my magic tells me there's someone watching me."

Sometimes she swore she could hear a soft laugh in the wind. It mattered not; the shadow was a friend.

All in all, it had been an enchanting childhood, and like every enchanting childhood, it came to a sudden, unexpected end. Her world crashed the day Loxy Rivers—the best mother on Ertia, according to Devi—died suddenly.

She was just fourteen and became quite lost, unsure of where she belonged.

Looking up from the boat with her mother's remains burning in the middle of the lake, she saw him for the first time—a very tall grown-up male, quite handsome, and dressed in a way that seemed odd to her eyes. It was not the dress of a soldier, a noble, or a servant. It was made of dark earth-toned, durable cloth embroidered and finely shaped, but cut in a peculiar way.

He had the pointed ears, stature, and air of a high fae, but also something else underneath. Wilder. Stronger.

It was the shadow, and he had her eyes.

Vale pulled away, letting go of her mind before breaking it. When he returned to the throne hall, Devi's eyes were wide, horrified. She was breathing hard, and a few beads of sweat had gathered on her pretty forehead. She'd strained to resist him.

How sweet of her.

"What the fuck was that?"

He shrugged.

"Seriously. I know psychics. I went to school with a few. They can sometimes tell what you're thinking right then, with a lot of effort, after breaking down shields. My shields are always up. You just waltzed past them, and you fetched exactly what you were after. How is that possible?"

Her interest seemed entirely academic; she was so curious she'd forgotten to be put out. Endearing. But he wouldn't let her distract him, not now.

"I'll tell you when you satisfy my curiosity. I asked first. That shadow of yours was an elf. Your father."

It wasn't really a question—he knew it. He'd recognized the male's dress, although at the time, it had seemed foreign to her younger eyes. The shadow had worn the dress of a noble from the elven realm. That explained everything. She was a half-blood. A rare thing, indeed. He hadn't noticed earlier because elves somewhat resembled high fae.

Lesser fae were often short and stocky, sometimes so small they never grew to stand past his knees. Common fae could stand up to his shoulders, perhaps. Sometimes they were blessed with wings or pointed ears; more often than not, they weren't. They distinguished themselves by having plain features.

High fae and elves were tall, generally muscular, and prone to beauty. Both races had pointy ears. Elves didn't have wings, and therein lay the one outward difference. Inwardly, it was another matter altogether.

Vale had met plenty of elves he liked well enough, though he doubted that any of them would think so well of him. Their race was strange, brutal sometimes and inclined toward violence. Confronted by ten strangers invading his space, an elf shot ten arrows before asking any questions. Yet they could be so wise.

Her nature explained the fascinating hazel eyes he found himself trying to read too often, as well as the feelings he'd extracted from her mind the first time he'd seen her.

No doubt living at court was difficult for her. Trees, water, snow—her blood would constantly be called by the wild, but it wasn't simply that. Elves weren't liked, and half-bloods were rarely accepted. The blessing of the unseelie queen wouldn't have protected her from the cruelty of court. There were nasty whispers trailing her steps when his mother's back was turned, no doubt.

"A little elfling," he whispered as a thousand other questions came to mind. Did she have wings? What gift might she have inherited with such an exotic parentage? All he said was "I should have guessed. That explains your wild soul."

Devi narrowed her eyes defensively, shoving his hand away and taking a step back.

Come to think of it, his words could have been taken as an insult; not just the friendly teasing that had so quickly become their normal, but a nasty affront on her nature. And because she'd no doubt heard millions of slights before, she took it that way.

The disgust and disappointment in her eyes was quite real now. It hit him like a slap in the face.

He should be glad of it. Let her believe he was a snobby, ignorant bigot. Let her believe he thought himself above her because of her blood. Let her believe he was the despicable, useless, spoiled brat this court thought him to be. Every single member of the court needed to carry on thinking exactly that. This was for the best.

"Come on, elfling. If we can't talk with any degree of civility, let us dance instead."

"I don't think so," she replied before turning her back on him and walking away.

Vale watched her for five steps, stunned at first, as he didn't think anyone had ever left him so unceremoniously, and then because the view of her bare back was quite enticing. Regaining his senses, he wished he could dart after her. He wished he could afford for Devira Star Rivers to know him. Know that when he said wild, he meant pure and beautiful, certainly not flawed.

He understood the confusion. Rare were the high fae who shared his beliefs.

Valerius didn't give a damn about castes, about blood, about inheritance. His home was a haven where all lived as equals.

In the court of night and the rest of the unseelie realm, lesser fae could only work baser professions. Vale had thrown that law in a bonfire; there were lawyers and captains of the guard amongst their race in his court.

He kept it secret for many reasons, the main one being that his rules were technically outlawed. He would have braved the legalese if necessary, but the principal reason why talking of Carvenstone freely wasn't an option was that, for centuries, his lands had sheltered creatures from each corner of the Isle, those who were hunted, mistrusted elsewhere. Those who'd never had a place to call their home.

There were rogue dragons, dire wolves, sphinxes, centaurs, chimaera, unicorns, griffins, and manticores that called his land their home. All of them were hunted for sport, killed for fun or for gain. If word traveled, they'd never be safe.

There were also elves. Elves who'd wished to leave their realm, and who would not have been welcome anywhere else in the Isle.

Protecting them was his duty and his burden. He'd lied and made himself look like a fool for centuries in order to preserve Carvenstone. No one at court could know—that was the one rule.

She wasn't worth risking the lives of thousands. She *wasn't*, he insisted, repeating his conviction to himself. Thankfully, before he could talk himself into reaching for the female and setting records straight, something caught his eye at one of the side entrances.

Kallan.

Vale allowed himself one last look toward Devi, who'd joined a short, redheaded common fae female in an alcove. The girl looked particularly uninteresting, but he memorized her nonetheless. One of Devi's friends, no doubt.

It cost him to walk away from her right then, but there were pressing matters to attend to.

Later, he told himself.

He turned on his heel and went to Kallan, following him away from the hall and up toward the residential wing. Once they'd reached the tower Valerius had claimed, instead of heading up toward his apartment, they followed the steep corridor leading down to Vale's dungeons.

It had been a long time since he'd made use of them, other than that one instance two hundred years hence when he'd tied up a pretty young female with heavy breasts.

"You've succeeded, then?"

He'd never doubted that Kallan would complete his mission. His friend was a master in the art of moving quietly, without being seen.

"Obviously. Delivery of one common foot soldier, as instructed. Hard nut to crack though, that one."

Kal pushed the heavy door of a windowless cell open, revealing a high fae.

Shiny armor, polished shoes, not an imperfection on his handsome face. A noble from a lower family, Vale guessed. But a noble who was careful not to show his colors. Like Vale so often did, he wore black from head to toe. That was unusual for a seelie; they were a proud lot, using every occasion to flaunt their heritage if they had cause to boast.

It was obvious that Kallan had started the interrogations, because the high fae's left hand was nailed to the wall and thick dark blood dripped down along his shining armor.

"I see my second has already shown you the sort of hospitality the unseelie realm shows to uninvited guests," Valerius said pleasantly.

The high fae laughed. "Nothing you do is going to make me talk, bastard."

This made Vale pause, then smile, showing all of his teeth. "And yet in those few words, you've already told me plenty, guest. There's only one kind of fae in the Isle who'd think to call me a bastard."

Something like regret flashed in the male's eyes.

"You're not a seelie at all," Vale deduced. "You come from Corantius. Strange, is it not, that a high fae of the court of crystal would ride alongside the seelie king, and with an entire battalion."

"I'm not saying—"

"Anything, I know, I know," Valerius completed, his tone entirely disinterested and more than a little condescending. "That's what you have to say to pretend that you have balls. At first, in any case. You'll soon change that tune." There was pure hatred in the eyes of the Corantian. Vale smirked. "You know me to be a bastard, and I'd wager you know exactly whose blood runs in my veins too?"

Vale's parentage was no secret, but fae had a way of letting time bury truths.

When he was born, Shea had been in a very public relationship with his father, so all had known whose son he was. Then they'd parted ways at the end of their hundred years binding contract. Vale's father had returned to his land, and Shea to hers. They'd both taken new consorts, and their short fling had become nothing more than a blip in history. They hadn't wedded or exchanged vows; no archivist thought to take notice. If historians were to record every relationship greater faes entertained in the course of their long lives, archives would resemble gossip columns.

The overking's subjects found the fact that their leader had fathered a child from an unseelie fae shameful. Shea said she'd rather not talk of her past lovers. With the elders induced into silence, within a generation, no one knew that Valerius Blackthorn was the son of Orin, the king of Corantius and overking of the four realms.

The waste of air in his dungeon was a fae of the court of crystal, no doubt about it. To the rest of the Isle, Valerius was the dark prince, heir to the unseelie. Only the Corantians thought of him as a disgrace. What the hell was this fae doing here? It made no sense, but there was no doubt in Valerius's mind that he would find out.

"You're too weak to make me talk," the noble said spitefully, attempting to hide his anxiety.

Valerius simply laughed out loud. Devi amused him because she believed herself capable of inflicting a degree of pain upon him, but her mistake was born of ignorance. This fae knew Vale's power. His denial was nothing short of comical.

"Oh well. I guess we'll find out, won't we? Kal, is this floor still soundproof?"

"Yep."

"Great. Let us begin."

Mere moments ago, when he'd entered Devi's mind, Vale had done so carefully, coaxing his way in, ensuring that he broke nothing on the way. It had felt like a caress, and still she'd pushed against it, exhausting herself. The moment it might have gotten painful for her, he'd stopped, pulling away.

What occurred now was very different. For one, it wasn't Vale in charge of his mind. It was the dark prince. The inner beast he usually kept on a leash by preventing himself from using too much of his power. Now he let go of all control. The room darkened around him; his aura, typically quiet and purple, to those who could see these things, became a mist of night and thunder. His eyes shone in the shadow.

The prince was free, and he liked it. He smiled, flashing canines as he lifted his hand and violently crashed against the Corantian's mind, punching his way in. The prisoner's body was lifted upward; if it hadn't been for the chains and the nail keeping his hand in place, he would have been plastered on the ceiling.

The noble was strong, Vale had to give him that. But still, he immediately started to scream, and then he pissed himself while begging and cursing him all at once. The prince was delighted. He unrelentingly pummeled against the walls shielding the fae's mind, his lips curling a little higher yet. The enemy's distress had a sweet scent; the powerful feelings fed the prince, enthused him.

Vale barely recognized himself when he let go of his restraint. He turned into a creature with simple needs. Air, water, food—they were nothing. The only thing he desired, the one thing he sought, was power.

Recalling that there was a purpose to his torture took some time. Oh yes, he'd meant to check into the fae's mind once he'd destroyed his mind and subdued his soul.

The fae's mind had been altered by someone who knew how to prevent a psychic from looking too deep into relevant information, but Vale still caught flashes, jumbled visions.

A female. A child. A bed. A throne. *The* throne.

Vale had only visited the court of crystal once, at his father's invitation, over six centuries before, yet he perfectly recalled that imposing throne, inscribed with incredibly fine words in a foreign tongue. He wasn't sure why, but he'd known that the delicate, translucent crystal throne was no simple seat. It held a strange power. A power the dark prince found himself greatly desiring now.

Vale never thought of the throne one way or another before that day. It was his father's, and it would go to his brother when the overking passed.

Vale understood that. The dark prince didn't care.

Enough was enough. He'd let the dark prince take over for too long already. Vale slowly, clearly enunciated the spells he used to control his powers in his mind, and reluctantly the dark prince retracted.

Vale released his hold, and the noble immediately passed out, spent.

A sudden and overwhelming fatigue took Vale's limbs and mind. It had been a long time since he'd let himself embrace the darker part of himself. He supposed that, like any muscle, his shields became rusty when he didn't flex them. Reining himself in had taken some effort. He needed rest. Food. Water.

But his needs would have to wait. The fact that they'd found a Corantian within their walls needed to be reported to the queen immediately.

"Let me know when he wakes up?"

"You got it," Kal replied. He hesitated before asking, "Are you okay?"

Kal knew what it cost Vale to use his power that way. Torturing the mind of an enemy, all the while feeling everything his victim endured, was a curse. It didn't bother the dark prince at all while he did it, but Vale was left with consequences. Each time he did so, part of his soul suffered for it.

Vale was painfully aware of Kal's concern: his second wondered if someday, Vale might lose his apathy and become the beast he used.

And if he was honest, Vale didn't believe the concern was unfounded.

Carvenstone was his anchor to the world, the one thing that allowed him to hang on. He was determined to protect it—even from himself, if necessary.

Vale sighed. "It needs to be done." This was no reply, and Kallan knew it. "I'll be at my mother's if he wakes within the hour. Then I'll try to catch some rest. Get Beck and that damn poser, Drake, to guard him in turn. Only those two. I wouldn't trust anyone else."

TEN
A NEW KING

Jiya was being quite impossible. Devi had headed to her friend in a quest to get away from Valerius, but the damn female just wouldn't stop talking about him.

"Seriously, how could you keep the fact that you're boning Dark and Handsome from me?"

Devi sighed, repeating herself. "New development. He arrived two nights ago. I've barely seen you since."

She wished she could simply tell the truth, but it wasn't advisable in a roomful of creatures who all had an acute sense of hearing. It would have to wait.

The crowd was still thick and paying attention to her. Valerius might have had a point about the dress. His words kept her planted where she stood; if she left early, some might believe that she was too cowardly to remain when her protector had left. A retreat might have been wise, but her pride prevented it. She wouldn't leave quite yet.

"I heard elders whisper around me. They said that while Valerius is known to fuck his way around the court, he's *never* singled out any female before tonight."

Devi shrugged wordlessly, glancing toward the exit Valerius had taken, annoyed at him, and at herself too. What if he'd gone off without a word of apology? She shouldn't give it a thought after his insult. But she did. Damn her, she found herself looking at that door far too often.

"Go on, give me something. Anything."

"Tomorrow," Devi promised, sipping on her second glass of wine. "There are too many ears for my liking now."

At least that much was true.

Jiya sighed, defeated, then started to talk, but something she saw behind Devi's shoulder made her gasp and stare, eyes widened.

Devi turned, half expecting to find Vale. If only.

She was seriously considering the nefarious consequences of having too much pride; she should have gone back to her apartment, dammit.

King Devin stood behind her, hand extended, smiling pleasantly.

He was very handsome, and so exquisitely exotic. His skin was golden, darker than Devi's, and his hair was black as night. Keen green eyes lightened his features, making him appear young and mischievous.

"Devira. I'd be enchanted if you were to grant me this dance."

She practically grimaced, staring at his hand like it might bite.

"I'm sorry, I do find myself quite worn out."

He dropped his right hand to his side while his left one scratched his head awkwardly. "I see." He hesitated before adding, "You're not quite comfortable in my presence."

"As comfortable as I can be with any stranger, sir," she lied easily, offering him her best smile.

"Right. Of course. In any case, I offered a dance because I wish to speak to you privately regarding a matter of some sensitivity."

The king glanced to Jiya purposefully.

"Perhaps we ought to make an appointment for a later date if the matter is confidential. Anywhere in this hall, a dozen ears will catch it, at the very least."

"Right." The king paused. "But at a later date, I am correct when I say that we'd talk in the presence of Valerius Blackthorn?"

"Probably."

The prospect was obviously not appealing to Devin. "I do not wish to make this an official matter between our two realms. I am simply rectifying a matter that should never have occurred." The king put his hand in the pocket at the side of his embroidered silver and blue coat, pulling out a small piece of paper adorned with his seal.

"This is one of the twelve copies ratified and filed, restoring you as a member of the house of lords, and revoking my father's orders against your person. I came to express vows of friendship to the queen and her court. They do extend to you."

Devi broke the seal, opened the folded piece of paper and read the short order. She was to be called Lady Rivers. Her lands in the banks were restored. She was no enemy of the Seelie Court. Just like that.

She chuckled. "That's…." Finding the right word took an instant. "Nice. I guess. Not having a bounty on my head is certainly pleasant. But I'll never step foot in the Seelie Court. I'll never join a realm where females are expected to wed the lords who put a claim on them. I have no interest in that foreign land that bears my name. It has done well enough for the last century without my meddling in its affairs."

The king was startled, but not outwardly displeased. His features relaxed.

"Good. This piece of paper won't change the ways of the members of my court. You'd find little welcome in my realm. Nevertheless, know that I bear no ill will toward you. Not all of us seelie are quite as backward as you may have cause to believe."

He seemed very sincere, and hadn't twisted his words in a way that might have allowed him to hide a lie.

"Glad to hear it."

"How about that dance now?" he asked cockily, an open and teasing smile on his lips.

She laughed good-heartedly. "Thanks, but I'm really tired. I'll be retiring in a minute."

The king's mouth was very expressive, she noted. It dropped and pouted in a way that struck her as handsome and adorable all at once.

"Shame. The music is quite engaging, and I have a mind to join the dance. I know no one but the members of my party."

His eyes had returned to Jiya at least twice. At first, Devi thought he was simply checking whether she was eavesdropping—and Jiya most definitely was. But finally she understood. Feeling foolish, she exclaimed, "Oh!"

Devi took Jiya's hand and pulled her forward. "May I introduce my closest acquaintance, Jiya Duniel."

Jiya wasn't used to nobility. As an apprentice protector, she was admitted as part of court, but that didn't change the fact that she was a common fae. She was mostly ignored by all who didn't need to deal with her.

Devi winced, knowing she would later pay for putting her on the spot like that. Jiya had little magic, but she was twice the fighter Devi was when it came to games of fists and kicks. She was also fast; potentially fast enough to hold her own against Shea.

The ruthless warrior waved awkwardly, bent her knees and said, "Hi."

Devin smiled politely, extending his hand again. "Hi back. May I request this dance, Lady Duniel."

"There's no lady here, but sure, I guess. Thanks."

And they were off, leaving Devi amused and grateful. Left to her own company, and with the eyes of the room focused on the seelie king, she could finally slip away unnoticed.

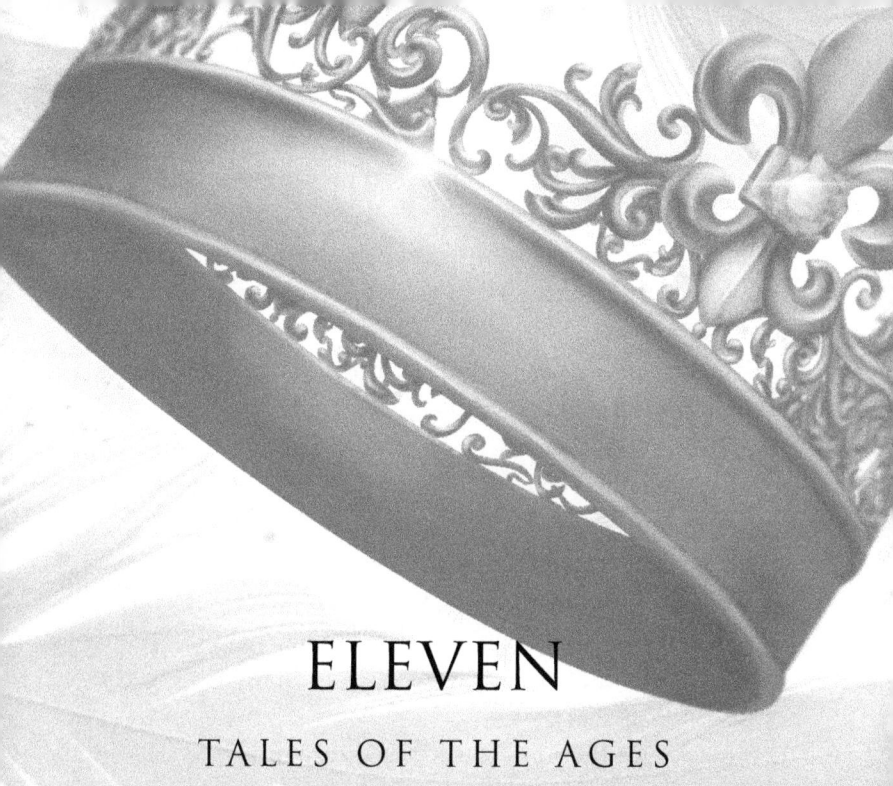

ELEVEN
TALES OF THE AGES

The elegant corridor leading up to his mother's chambers on the ground floor of the residential wing was large enough that six men as broad as him could walk side by side. Along the wall, sculptures of great warriors, beautiful maidens, and a naked Adonis had been planted, and in between each priceless piece of art, there was a guard who surveyed him darkly, threateningly, as if daring him to look the wrong way.

Vale wasn't surprised to see Drake Night come out of the room just as he reached its curved double doors, but he still threw up a little in his mouth.

The issue wasn't that his mother was having sex, exactly—although, had she been good enough to abstain, it would have certainly helped his nausea. It was that she'd chosen to do it with a male who'd grown up along with Vale and Kal. They'd never been friends—they were too competitive for that—but they'd had each other's back in battle. Drake had bled to take a hit intended for Vale, and vice versa.

"No need for the grimace," said the protector. "I was here in my official capacity."

"Aren't you always?"

Drake rolled his eyes. "Go on in. She's waiting for you."

Of course she was, although Vale had decided to visit her not even ten minutes ago.

"Kal will wish to have words with you," he told Drake, leaving it at that, as there were far too many ears in the wide-open space.

Drake nodded and took his leave, and Vale passed the doors leading to the queen's chambers.

It hadn't changed, at least not in the last seven hundred years. Behind the large heavy doors, there was an impersonal hall that befitted Shea's rank. A circle of polished white columns supported her bed at the very center of the room. The bed was large enough for a dozen people, and Vale was quite certain that his mother had tested whether a dozen people would indeed fit at one point or another.

The ominous piece of furniture gave him the creeps. Young and beautiful she may seem, but Shea was his mother, and he hated everything that reminded him of the fact that she also happened to be a grown-ass woman very fond of the pleasures of the flesh.

The queen was seated in her study, fully dressed, and Vale couldn't discern the distinct scent of sex around the room. Thank all heavens, Drake hadn't deceived him.

"You're no seer, and yet you often know things well before they occur. How does that work exactly, Mother?"

"A lady has her secrets," she replied. "And a little bird has whispered in my ears long ago, telling me that I would reveal some of them to you tonight."

Vale lifted a brow.

"Tell me of the prisoner down in your little playroom."

Count on her to know of his dungeon. "He's not saying much yet, but I've learned a few things regardless."

He explained his findings. Shea remained expressionless while he spoke, but Vale saw no surprise in her eyes.

"And you knew everything I just said," he stated as a conclusion.

She sighed, patting the seat next to hers.

Vale did as he was bid, all the while trying to recall whether he'd ever been invited to sit in his mother's bedroom. Probably not. As an adult, he'd never remained within those walls long enough to have any reason to take a seat.

As a child…. He allowed himself a smile, imagining the awe he might have felt, had the great and magnificent beauty he called queen asked him to sit in her presence, back in those days before he'd known that he was her son.

"You've always been a curious boy. What do you know of ancient history, Vale?"

He frowned. "Are we to discuss my education? Perhaps you could quiz me on dates. I quite like this game." Shea set her stare on him until he had to point out, "That glare isn't working on me, Mother. It's basically like looking in a mirror."

"If you're able to keep your tongue in your mouth for a moment, I'll tell you what you need to know."

Vale closed his mouth and forced himself to keep it that way as the queen began her tale.

"I'm not talking about your lifetime, or mine for that matter. Have you ever looked into the times before the age of gold, and before the age of kings?"

"I can't say I have," he admitted.

He had enough things to worry about in the present. Getting lost in old volumes about the golden days of the past wasn't his style.

"Shame. Well, I'll have to run through it quickly. This world was quite different back then. More populous, for one. There was a lot more infrastructure, technology. And war. Everywhere around Ertia, there was war."

The queen pulled out a map that showed the Isle, the waters around it, and its walls, separating it from the horrors behind them. The bulk of the map was covered by dark patches of lands and sea. But the long parchment also showed other light stretches of land, some larger than the Isle, all fitted with the same golden walls around it.

"There's more safe land in the world?" he guessed, frowning.

It had been his understanding that the Isle was the last safe harbor of their kind.

"Indeed. There were once five continents, and three remain unaffected. But there's no time to run through all of this now. I wish to tell you of a bygone era, five thousand years ago. Back then, the world was inhabited by a race of mortals, with short life-spans and a high reproduction rate."

"Common fae, then," Vale translated.

Shea shook her head. "No, not quite. These beings called themselves humans. There are some left in the lands of dragons, on the other side of the Dead Waters.

Humans had a love for the arts and enough intelligence to build marvelous things, but what they truly excelled at was destroying one another. Among other weapons, they created a virus meant to incapacitate their enemy, but it was more volatile than they'd imagined. That was their doom. Over 97 percent of their population was infected with it. Some survived it, in a manner of speaking. Their bodies would remain alive, and yet their minds were truly gone, leaving nothing but a beastly hunger for any flesh they could find. It was a thing of horror. All would have been lost to this fate, if help hadn't come to them."

"Help?" Vale prompted, now quite attentive.

These were some interesting facts he'd never heard before, but part of him grew impatient. He had pressing concerns, and he had no idea how the lesson was supposed to be helpful to him now.

"Yes. Unbeknown to the bulk of their population, the human evolution had been overseen, and often tweaked, by a higher power—creatures who came from another world far in the skies."

Now he laughed, actually laughed out loud for a long while. Then, seeing his mother's expression, he added, "You're kidding."

"Are you truly egocentric enough to believe that in all of the stars you can see, just with your naked eyes, there could be no other planet with life?"

"Yes," he replied without hesitation.

"And yet these creatures came from the skies. To the humans, those beautiful, immortal creatures were nothing short of gods. Over the next years, they battled those we call orcs, those turned humans, until almost none of those foul beasts were left in the Isle. The gods were mighty, but few. A few dozen of them could not hope to defeat billions of vermin and keep the remaining humans unaffected by the virus, so they erected energy walls to keep us safe from what lies beyond. Two continents, and most of the seas, are still swarming with these evil creatures. They've depleted their resources by now, eating every living thing around them. Without the mind to farm or gather the food they need, they're desperate to get to us. Eat our animals, and our flesh, if they can."

Vale now perfectly understood why children were simply told that an enemy lived beyond the wall. The detailed version would have given any youngling nightmares for years.

Vale had seen orcs. Occasionally, a few made it through the walls and they needed to be put down. Never had he considered that they could possibly have been anything close to fae.

He expressed his doubt. "You say they're all behind the wall, and yet I certainly have killed my fair share of orcs."

The queen nodded. "They're constantly attempting to cross the walls. Sometimes a few pass through. Battling ten, or even a hundred of them is one thing. Fighting against billions would be quite another. The walls prevent an outbreak."

Vale nodded carefully, attempting to accept this revised version of the history of their kind.

"All right. That's… a strangely fascinating tale. But the fact remains: I fail to see the point of hearing it tonight."

"Impatient," the queen chastised him, clicking her tongue.

He was, which had something to do with the fact that he'd depleted his energy less than an hour ago. He needed food, rest, maybe a fuck too. Not a lesson.

Still, if Shea believed he had to hear it, he had to hear it. "Sorry, go on."

"Some of the gods remained here on the Isle. They built a stronghold in the cold of the north. You know it. You've seen it." As Vale remained silent, she explained, "The city of crystal."

His mouth opened and closed again, as he found no protest. The white city with its shining high walls had seemed foreign to him. He didn't recognize the materials, hadn't understood the devices and the transports people used. Everything was strange about it—both ancient and too advanced.

He'd always thought of it as a place from another world. Alien.

His mother was still recounting her tale. "For a time, they lived there quietly, but it isn't in their nature to stay idle. The human population had considerably decreased. Where there used to be billions, there were only thousands. The air had become toxic, changing the very core of the human constitution. Physically, they changed, but that wasn't the problem. Their previously rapid reproduction rate slowed down considerably. Many young died before they came of age. It was easy to see that the race might soon become extinct. So the gods fixed it."

"Fixed it?" Vale was confused.

"Tweaked a thing or two on a cellular level. Modified a few genes. Made the mortals longer-lived so they had the time to reproduce again. They didn't stop there. Some were made prettier, a little more like them. Eventually some could even bind energy and matter, just like them. Others were blessed with wings. Some experiments didn't go as well, of course...."

Despite his exhaustion, and the slight headache he suffered from, Vale had finally connected the dots.

"You're talking of the castes. Lesser fae, common fae, high fae."

Shea nodded. "Imagine a teacher grading a paper. A lesser fae is an experiment gone wrong. A common fae is deemed acceptable. High fae are successful test subjects. Elves were the last creatures they made, once they'd perfected the process."

Vale couldn't believe what he was hearing. "You're saying we were nothing more than lab rats to aliens who played at being gods?" The notion was enraging.

"No, Valerius. I'm saying our people were nothing more than lab rats. You and I are descendants of the gods."

Spotting a full glass on the queen's desk, he asked, "Is that alcohol?"

"Water."

He sighed. "All right. Explain."

"There were only a few gods in all of Ertia. Fifty, perhaps fewer. No more than a handful chose to live in the Isle. Most of them paired with high fae at some point during their long existence, giving birth to half-bloods. Scions, we're called. Those children were exponentially more powerful than the fae who'd been genetically modified to have those powers, needless to say. The Blackthorns are one of the first of those lines. There's perhaps a sixteenth of divine blood in my veins, but it makes me who I am."

One of the most powerful fae in the Isle.

Vale would have loved to find something illogical in what his mother was saying, but all of it made too much sense. He sincerely wished she'd told him all that when his cerebral capacity was at its optimal level; right now, he just hoped he'd taken in all of it to reanalyze it later.

"So, if there's a sixteenth of their blood in your veins, that makes me a watered-down version of that?"

But even as the words crossed his lips, he knew how wrong they were. No. If Shea was indeed some sort of demigod, then his father, the overking of the Isle, was just the same.

Or worse.

"Are you telling me my father is one of those gods you speak of?"

Shea inclined her head in concurrence. "Indeed. And most of those who now live in his realm are either gods or their direct descendants. The rest of the Isle call them fae and they laugh at it. They're right to. Don't get me wrong, Vale, I can hold my own against anyone in this realm. I can defeat any seelie. I may even bring down some elves. But they're another matter. The weakest scion is worth ten high fae in battle. As for your father…." She hesitated. "He didn't wish to get involved in the War of the Realms. Corantius stayed out of it. It was his belief that they'd interfered with our fate enough. That the gods ought to leave mortals to their affairs. The moment he changed his mind, demanding peace, everyone bowed, because his kind could have killed us all with absolutely no effort."

Vale's mind went to the fae in the dungeon. Or the demigod. Had Shea said scion? Whatever he was. Kal had told him he'd grabbed a simple foot soldier, and yet Vale had had some trouble reading past his defenses. He'd needed to push hard.

His mother's words changed everything he knew, and yet explained so much.

Still.

"I don't get it," he said finally. "I mean, I understand everything you said. I'll admit that it makes sense, strangely. I just don't get why there's a scion amongst the seelie guard. It feels… underhanded. If they could just kill us all, why the sneakiness? It makes no sense."

"I didn't say I had all the answers. I simply wish you to understand what you'll have to face."

Silence stretched as he considered everything.

Finally, he concluded, "This doesn't come from the overking. If Father had wished for war, he'd come at us directly. And by the sound of it, we'd be utterly screwed."

Shea smiled. "Indeed. Thankfully for all of us, your father believes in peace."

"But not everyone among his people is the same. Someone from the realm—someone high in the hierarchy—is pulling strings."

"That is also my belief. Now, son, I have given you much to think about for a night. And you do look quite exhausted. Go and rest."

"I will if you tell me there's a plan in place so we come out of it alive."

The queen chuckled. "You should know me better by now. There's always a plan."

He got up and moved to leave, but at the doors, he hesitated.

"Tell me, Mother, where does Devi Rivers stand in your machinations?"

The queen held his gaze. "Well, I never. You do like the girl," she said, laughing.

"Let us not pretend that it wasn't your doing."

"It wasn't," Shea replied unequivocally. "And to answer your question, son, Devira is at the very center of it. Just like you."

He didn't like that. Not one bit.

"You'd put a youth who hasn't seen her first century in the way of harm?"

If one thing could be said of his mother, it was that she didn't hide who she was.

"I'd throw a thousand youths in the way of harm to protect the realm. I am queen, Valerius. One day, you'll understand what that means."

Hopefully he never would.

TWELVE
A RED AND GOLD STORM

The dream had changed. She was still drowning, but then the sun flashed above water, so bright she had to close her eyes. When she opened them again, the three children had disappeared. In their stead, there was a figure—a male, she would have guessed. His face was unclear, but he had dark hair, and he smiled, extending his hand to her.

Devi wanted to take it more than anything, let him pull her to the surface, but her wrists were bound at her back.

She woke up sweating, her breathing erratic. Her room was intact this time, window and all.

Devi frowned. This dream had little to do with her memory. If anything, it seemed like a clearer warning.

She knew three men with dark hair like the shadows in her dream. Three men who smiled and fancied themselves her champion of sort. Rook—and every god knew there was no cause to be wary of him—Drake Night, and Valerius Blackthorn. What did the dream warn her of exactly? Relying on one of them, or not putting her trust in them? She shook her head, chasing away the nonsensical visions. A part of her wondered if she should reach out to Beck and ask him what he thought, but the healer might make a fuss about it.

She could ask Shea. But the queen had bigger problems with Devin Farel and his posse strolling through her city like they owned it.

There was someone else who crossed her mind, but she immediately dismissed the very notion. Valerius would just find a way to make fun of her and wouldn't be of any help whatsoever.

She bathed, got dressed, and made her way down to headquarters.

At this time on any ordinary day, the castle would have just started to wake, but there was a full house of active servants rushing through the corridor. Where one guard would usually be posted, there were two. Everyone was visibly on their guard.

She arrived at headquarters and found the master's office closed. Rook was resting against the door.

He was an odd one, a common fae as tall as any high fae, and with very long pointed ears—a lot longer than most high fae, like a handsome knight of old carved in ancient sculptures.

Rook was lean, seemingly frail—seemingly being the key word. Devi had seen him effortlessly carry loads that she would have struggled to move two feet. His features were delicate, almost effeminate. Above all, Rook distinguished himself by using his wings.

Every high fae Devi knew had wings, which they kept firmly hidden under their skin. Showing them was something akin to showing boobs in public. Common fae rarely were bestowed wings at all.

Rook's looked like a bat's, dark and velvety. Devi was certain they were soft, although she hadn't touched them, of course. Grabbing his dick might have been less personal. He kept them out at all times and flew whenever he could. There wasn't any regulation against it, but it certainly earned him his fair share of disapproving glances.

Devi's bet? People were envious of his freedom. There was no noble name for him to disgrace and no patriarch who'd threaten to disown him, so he did as he pleased.

Devi was certainly jealous, but it was for another reason.

She had wings, all right. Wings that hurt like she was being split in two when she forced them out. Wings so heavy she couldn't lift them to fly at all.

Flying was a skill parents taught their children, along with swimming and swinging a sword. After one try, Loxy had cried along with her little girl and promised she wouldn't make her go through that ordeal again. She'd been six at the time, but Devi recalled it well enough to keep her own wings where they belonged—tucked inside her skin. She truly envied Rook, who was so very comfortable with his.

Rook had cut slits into his uniform so his wings could come out at any time. For once, they weren't on display.

"Who are you and what have you done with my best friend," he growled darkly, eyes narrowed. "Devi

Star Rivers has never, ever been early to anything in her entire life."

"Har, har," she replied, rolling her eyes. "Couldn't sleep."

He shrugged. "You never sleep. You generally just hang out in your room until the last possible second. Not that I blame you. It's like the size of my entire place. Plus the neighbor's. And you have people wiping your butt too."

Devi's life was an unending source of entertainment to him. Sometimes she was a little ashamed of having so much when others worked very hard for little flats atop a fishmonger's shop. Rook purposefully kept his uniform in his locker here at the palace so it didn't smell of fish like the rest of his stuff.

Then she remembered why she had no reason to be ashamed at all, and she kept her head high.

Devi owned the land where she was born, Farj. There were thirty-seven thousand fae of all castes who lived there, and every day she served them by residing in the court of night.

As a landlady and member of the court, she had a seat in the House of Lords; she could give her opinion on things such as tax reforms. For ten years, she'd let a delegate speak for her, but when she'd turned twenty-five, she'd sat alongside him at every meeting to learn how she could be of service. She was one of the only voices who spoke for the good of the people, rather than out of self-interest.

With her work came a generous income. Shea also had given her an allowance. On top of that, she earned a fair living as an apprentice protector. Devi only kept her protector salary. The rest went to helping orphans around the city, and perhaps building a dam where it was needed, or redoing the roof of a farmer's house in her land. She did her best with the nice set of cards fate had dealt her. Having her own place would actually cut into the budget she spent on helping others, given the fact that living at the castle cost her nothing.

So she shrugged off the comment. Yes, she had servants, and never in her life had she thought of having to dust her own curtains. But Rook had never rebuilt a mill after a nasty storm, or taken in the three dozen children she fed and clothed in the little shelter that bore her mother's name.

"Jiya isn't in yet?"

"She's off today. You've got tomorrow. They've changed our rotation so we can all be on duty this weekend."

Devi groaned. The last thing she wanted to do was work over the solstice, but she got it. Everyone was on alert because of the seelie's presence.

She could use a night off anyway.

"Jiya sent me an owl last night," Rook said carefully, giving her a meaningful look. "If half of it is true, I missed quite an interesting gathering."

Devi sighed. Rook used to have a crush on her, and she really, really fucking wished she could return the attention, because he was awesome. But her taste tended to lean toward assholes, so that was a hopeless cause.

She'd said no to a date three years ago. The awkwardness had lasted a few weeks, but now all was well. Except when he alluded to her dating life, of course.

Not that she was dating Valerius Blackthorn, but still.

"It certainly was interesting," was all the reply she gave.

Thankfully, Drake Night walked inside the headquarters, interrupting the course of that particular discussion. Or so she thought.

The master looked worn out and ill-tempered; no doubt he'd stayed awake most of the day. He looked at her, slowly taking her in from the tips of her toes to the top of her head before saying, "Well, didn't we have fun last night?"

Could someone kill me now?

"I don't know what I've done to make anyone think that my personal life should be discussed at work," she replied. "But if you're done gossiping, I'd love to know my assignment for the day."

Drake glared. Devi half expected to hear another warning about Valerius, but he simply waved toward the doors. "You're both to assist the guard for the rest of week. We need all eyes in the streets right now. Should anything, and I do mean *anything*, seem out of the ordinary, I want to be notified directly."

They saluted and walked out, hiding their smiles. It wouldn't do to let the tyrant know that they enjoyed working with the guards. It was easy, and yet entertaining; plus, it actually meant that they got to see some of the festivities.

On their way to the main guard post, near the Square of Dawn, Rook dug some more.

"Do you really think you can get away with the evasive crap, by the way?"

"Watch me."

"Devi, you and Jiya made me run a play-by-play of my night with Lily and Tristan, and it wasn't *that* interesting. This is *major* gossip. Spill."

She groaned.

"Come on...."

"There's nothing to say, okay?" The walls had ears in the court of night, and she didn't want people to whisper that it had all been a ruse by the time the guests woke in a few hours. So she did what she had to do. She lied.

Actually lied.

Devi only rarely made use of that simple and yet extremely useful gift. Fae couldn't lie, and thus they often considered spoken words to be the absolute truth. No one had ever stopped to think that as a half-elf, Devi could say whatever the fuck she wanted.

She skirted the truth, knowing lies were more believable that way.

"We met when he arrived a couple of nights ago. I'd never interacted with him before."

"Really?" Rook pushed doubtfully. "Carvenstone is close to Farj. The talks say you were old acquaintances, and that you'd frequently met up north."

"Ew." She grimaced. "I left Farj at fourteen."

"But you've visited."

She nodded, once. "Yes, to oversee projects, meet with contractors, and partake in official ceremonies. I just met Vale. He's the reason I was so late to work the other night, actually. We randomly bumped into each other and, well, bumping a little more into each other seemed like a great idea at the time."

She shrugged. Sex was simple to unseelie. Until someone was bound, mated, or promised, they were fair game. Devi knew most fae were bisexual and likely to jump on each other simply because they had nothing else to do.

She wished she was a little more like that, in a way. It took a copious amount of wine—or a glass of nectar—

for her to feel like casual sex was a good idea. Probably the seelie in her. Seelie were monogamous and often heterosexual. That caused plenty of problems, given the fact that there weren't as many high fae females as males. For three males, only one female was born, according to their recent census. No wonder the seelie seemed so grave and severe—they were sexually repressed.

They could have easily sorted that issue, had they simply been willing to pair up with a common or lesser fae. There were as many males as females among them for some reason. But while pairing below their class wasn't encouraged in the unseelie realm, it was entirely forbidden to the seelie folks.

Stupid.

"So that's it? You just had sex?" Rook frowned. "Jiya made it sound like you were basically tying the knot."

Devi snorted. "Hardly. The fae king was making me feel uncomfortable, and you know how it is. No one walks away from the king in the seelie realm. Here, I could probably have told him to fuck off, but then…."

"Potential diplomatic incident that may or may not end up in a bloody war," Rook guessed.

"Yes, that. So Valerius stepped in. Having him claim me as his in public like that was one way to make sure Devin backed off. I mean, if the seelie king was bothering the plaything of the unseelie prince…."

"Potential diplomatic incident that may or may not end up in a bloody war," her friend repeated.

"Basically."

They were in the middle of the square now, close to the large edifice that served as the guards' headquarters.

"Poor you. So many sexy alpha males fighting for your attention."

She rolled her eyes, laughing reluctantly.

"Hardly. Devin was more into Jiya, if anything. There are family matters that made the idea of talking to him quite awkward, that's—"

She'd been about to say, "that's all," but suddenly, and without a single warning, a violent blast pushed her twenty feet back until her back hit the obelisk at the center of the square. Her ears buzzed. Everything hurt. Smoke and dust burned her eyes when she tried to open them.

But finally, she saw it.

There was nothing but ruins in front of her eyes. The guard tower had been blown to pieces.

"I'd attack right before dusk. Place my troops nearby and get a small group to kill the guards posted around the city first."

"Devi!"

She heard it like a whisper, although the word had been shouted, no doubt. Devi grabbed the healing charm on the pouch tied to her belt and sorted out her ears first, then her leg, which was bruised or broken in two places.

"*Vide*," she said, hands on her temples, and her vision cleared.

There was nothing but a mess of dust, fire, and ash, but now her eyes caught heat signatures where they couldn't see farther than a few steps away.

Catching Rook's silhouette high above the cloud, she yelled, "To the queen! Now! Warn the queen."

The fae remained there for half a second before batting his large wings, heading toward the castle.

Her enhanced vision saw a volley of arrows aimed at Rook, coming from every side. She gasped. Had she sent her friend to his death?

Lesson one: when in danger, don't fly.

She recalled that from her very first day as a protector. At the time, she'd shrugged off the advice, because she never flew anyway. But it made sense. Fae always had bows and arrows. It was smart to kill your enemy from a distance, given the fact that their race was strong, fast, and lethal. Hand-to-hand combat was messy. With so many archers among their kind, flying was one way of making oneself a damn easy target.

But Rook had signed up for this. He was a protector, just like her.

She removed her own bow from her back and got it at the ready, prepared to shoot the first thing that came at her.

"Once the gates are unmanned, I'd send my armies in and take the city while the court sleeps."

At a distance, her eyes caught various explosions around the city. East, north, south. Not west. The enemy hadn't taken the western flank, probably because the only way to reach it was through the elven realm, and no fae was stupid enough to venture there armed.

"Devira."

She almost knelt before registering that the voice had come to her in her mind. The queen wasn't actually there.

"They attacked," Devi mentally sent back.

"I know. Never mind any of that. I need you to get out of here."

She froze. Out of here? No, she had to fight. Push them back. Make sure whatever enemy dared to attack them was destroyed.

"It's an order, Devi. Go now. Go to your father's. Take the portal of Daryn. I need you to live."

The words were downright terrifying, and Shea made it worse by stopping the connection the moment she'd said them.

Devi had her orders now though. She could work with that.

She started to run west when a sharp cry made her turn the other way.

There was a girl, little more than a child, screaming as she tried to run, and behind her, a legion of men in red and gold.

Red and gold. The colors of the overking. The male who ruled over all high fae. The male who'd forced every king to bow before his will and ordered them all to be at peace. The male to whom they owed seven hundred years of peace.

It made no sense.

Without even thinking about it, Devi released the first of the fifty-one arrows she had in her quiver, and the enemy fell. The child had half a second before the rest of the legion caught up, and she managed to use it, climbing up the first house and getting to its roof. The soldiers ignored her; she was of no consequence.

Instead of following the harmless girl, the legion descended upon Devi.

THIRTEEN
IN FLIGHT

Strange that Devi should be his first thought as the world ended, and yet not strange at all, if he was right and he was under a spell.

His sleep was always light and restless, and he woke up with a start, sensing a presence that didn't belong in his rooms. His unease didn't decrease when he opened his eyes to see his mother at his door. It was the first time that the queen came in person to his tower; usually she sent a messenger. But he'd already begun to comprehend that this night wouldn't be ordinary.

The queen wore tight black protector gear under her green coat. He knew this outfit. In fact, she'd worn nothing else for his first twenty years.

This was how she went to war.

"Mother."

"You need your sword, bow, and a full quiver. Dress as warm as you can and go, now." The queen moved to his wardrobe, pulling out leather shirts and coats as she spoke. "This will do."

She'd settled on a skin coat lined with fur, something he'd only worn up north in the dead of winter.

"What is—"

"No time for questions."

He opened his mouth, but suddenly the very floor vibrated as a thundering sound made them both snap their heads toward his window. High in his tower, Vale had a full view of the entire city. Usually at this time of day, the streets were asleep, quiet and peaceful.

Now the city was burning. A building around the square went first—the guard post, he guessed. Then three of their four main gates exploded.

"Devi."

The name was nothing more than a whisper kissing his lips, but Shea heard it.

"I've ordered her to get out and head to Wyhmur through the portal of Daryn. That's also your destination. You must get to safety. The realms depend on it, do you understand?" Shea had never talked that urgently, pleadingly.

He had so many fucking questions, but his body had acted on autopilot, packing his essentials. Daryn, then Wyhmur, with Devi. He got it.

"Kallan...," he said aloud, his mind racing.

"He's getting your horses. Don't think of anyone else. Just go."

There was an urgency to her words, and a certain vulnerability too. This was Shea Blackthorn worried—

something he'd never thought he'd see in his life. And she worried about *him*.

"What of the kingdom? What of my home, Carvenstone? And—"

"I want you to listen to me very carefully. Your home will be burned to ashes within the hour. The city of night will fall. The world as you know it ends tonight. Safety, peace—forget it. They died with your father."

His heart skipped a beat. The overking was dead? The god she spoke of not even twelve hours ago? It made no sense. Who could have killed someone like him? But even as he asked, Vale could guess. It took one monster to destroy another. One of his peers had done this. Someone in the realm of crystal. Someone in a position of power.

"Aurelius," Vale guessed.

His elder brother, first son of Orin. No one else would have the authority to command his armies this way.

"I don't know," was Shea's answer. "Much is yet clouded to me. All I know is that war is coming to us from enemies I cannot hope to defeat. I need one thing from you now. You must live."

"Where are you going? I'll be of more use to you in command of a—"

Shea moved toward the door. "I'm going to join my armies, and *you* are going to the Elvendale, in Wyhmur. There, you will ask Elden, the elven king, for his aid. Without it, we're all lost."

Everything in Vale wanted to protest against that order. He was no coward. His place was next to his queen and mother in battle, if that was where she was headed.

But the queen said the one thing that made any protest impossible.

"This may be how the Isle falls, unless we can unite the realms. To that end, you're one of my best weapons. Stay alive."

Valerius bowed his head, holding his hand over his heart in a sign of compliance. Again, the queen turned to walk away.

"Do not think that I send you always to safety, son. Every god, every assassin, every hunter, every spy against us will be after you. This fight ends with your death or your coronation."

That made no sense. None whatsoever. But Vale had his orders, and he recalled enough of war to know that questioning them further would only result in delaying the inevitable.

The city of night was to fall. The court of sin was too far to think of saving it. His people would either manage to get to safety or they would perish.

If they did, Valerius Blackthorn would be prince of nothing more than ashes and ruins.

Kallan had the mounts ready, and they were soon on their way, holding nothing more than the essentials. They could hunt and find more water along the way.

"The eastern gate hasn't burned down yet. If we want to keep the horses, we'll have to take it."

This was problematic because it meant taking the long avenue all the way toward the square, where no doubt they'd have to face plenty of enemies. His mother's warning about the strength of the weakest among them fresh in thought, he wanted to put as much distance between them as possible for now.

The scions had entered the other gates and would no doubt be slowed down by the guards and protectors along the way. He and Kallan had a fair chance if they took small and direct roads. But they'd still need to cross the Square of Dawn, or what was left of it.

Vale led the way, his sword in his fist, holding the reins with his other hand.

The enemy crossed their path two blocks away from the square, but they were on foot. Outnumbered a hundred to one, Vale decided to make a dash for it. He yelled to Kal, "Don't slow down to take them out. We need to go." His mother's words were vivid in his mind; he was part of a bigger plan, presumably a way to win this war in the end. He had to get out of there.

Another thought made him rush forward at high speed rather than slow down and kill as many of those vermin as he could, as part of him wished he could do.

Shea had said that Devi had her orders to go the same way. No doubt she'd also head east, as it was the last remaining gate. He shouldn't even have spared a thought to the young half-blood he'd met not a week ago now, as the city was under siege. Yet the thought of getting her to safety was paramount to his every move.

The foot soldiers were getting closer, somehow catching up, although they had no horses. *Fuck.*

Vale looked over his shoulder. The closest ones had almost reached him when an arrow shot straight, hitting the soldier right in the eye. The scion fell, and two of his peers tumbled with him.

Vale's eyes followed the direction of the shot, and he froze in horror.

Devi. She stood alone in the square, with a bow and arrow. *What the fuck is she still doing here? Mother told her to get out over twenty minutes ago! She should be at the gate, or near it.*

He didn't even have to think it through. Vale turned his horse and headed to her. She took his hand and jumped on the back of his horse.

While he'd diverted his course, Kallan had halted and was shooting as many enemies as he could.

They had golden helmets covering their skulls, mouths, and noses, and their armor had few weaknesses. Other than a small slit around their eyes, there were softer points under the arms, at the groin, and knees, but that was it. Kallan managed to take down a dozen in half a minute. Now the rest were upon them.

Vale blamed Devi for this entirely.

"Fucking idiot!" he yelled. No doubt she'd remained out of some misplaced sense of obligation, risking her life. He lowered his voice and whispered calming chants to his horse, compelling it to go forward. Now that his mount didn't need attention, he turned to Kal and outstretched his hand, pushing as much energy as he could muster toward the soldiers approaching his friend.

They all froze in place for a few precious minutes, allowing Kallan to catch up.

"What was that all about?" Kal screamed over the racket. "Are we to also stop for tea?"

"Shut it. This isn't over. They know they haven't blown the east gate."

They were close enough to see plenty of red and gold soldiers posted before the gates, butchering their way through the civilians who'd gone that way in hopes of finding a path to safety.

Shit.

"Valerius," Devi called from his back, "can you feel if there are any of our guys on the gate?"

"What?" he shot back.

"Can you?"

Using his energy for so pointless a task seemed wasteful, but it wasn't strenuous, so he scanned the towering gate and the brick wall surrounding it.

"No, just theirs. They've killed all our guards."

He'd only just said that when he felt a pressure on his shoulder for one short moment. Looking up, confused, he swore out loud.

What the *fuck* was she thinking? She'd used him as a stepping stone and launched *herself* at the goddamned gate.

Halfway up, when gravity would have seen her fall, bright golden feathers exploded out of her back, shredding her uniform. She extended the longest, largest pair of wings he'd ever seen on any fae, him included.

Devi didn't beat them, but a sudden, unnatural wind pushed them up, leading her to the very top of the gate.

She landed on it, ignoring the hundreds of arrows shooting her way. Some hit their mark, others didn't.

With a scream, Devi Star Rivers punched the marble gate, sending a resounding jolt of energy that hit Vale harder than a punch in the teeth, although he was at a distance.

The stone crumbled to pieces, destroying the gate as well as the wall around it for half a mile on each side. The soldiers on and around the wall didn't have a chance. They fell, along with some unseelie fae. The remaining unseelie took advantage of the new overture and ran outside the city.

"She's a power to be reckoned with," the queen had said. Only now was Vale beginning to comprehend what she'd meant.

Devi was an elemental mage, that was obvious. He'd clearly identified air magic; she'd made use of it to get on the gate. Then things got complicated. He couldn't tell whether her blast had been earth, fire, or water magic. His senses had picked up characteristics from all three. Which was downright impossible.

He'd never heard of one person who could master more than one element at all, and yet she'd at the very least used two.

It made no sense. Individuals could pick up more skills along the way, like his mother had, but elemental magic was tied to the bloodline, implemented in a person's very genes, like the color of their eyes or their height.

And yet he was certain he'd observed at least air and earth.

"Okay, so all things considered, I guess I get why you had to stop to get that one," Kal said. "Fucking amazing rack."

Oh, that. Devi was still topless. She herded the people toward the new entrance, encouraging them to go faster.

Vale held up his middle finger to Kal, trotting to the ruins of the gate until he'd caught up with the female.

She was wincing, obviously in pain and exhausted, but none of that, or the fact that every male obviously eyed her firm boobs, stopped her from trying to help.

"Come on up, little elf," he said, holding his arm outstretched.

She hesitated.

"You should go, and fast. No one here is a target. You are. I'll stay with them and take them somewhere safe."

"Safety, peace—forget it."

"You, without a shirt, against a whole army when they rain down on these plains?"

She set her jaw stubbornly, intending a no doubt well-prepared argument he had no intention to listen to.

"This wasn't a question, Devira. My mother made it clear that she wanted you to go somewhere, did she not? Would you defy the will of your queen?"

He saw her resolve falter and didn't let her think of it any longer, extending his hand and pulling her up when she took it. This time, he made her mount the horse in front of him, where he could hold her.

"There's a shirt in the bag at my side," he told her. "And if you look, there'll be some dried meat. Eat. Get some rest. Good job, protector."

Vale would have fought his way out and dashed to the Graywoods of Wyhmur, get to Daryn as he was instructed. Whoever made it out of the city tonight would do it because of her.

"Don't think of anyone else."

Those were the queen's orders, and for a while, he'd tried to let them direct his course.

Then he'd seen Devi in the square, shooting at those who came at *him*, rather than protecting herself. He'd seen her trying her best to help this little group of irrelevant fae who were, for all intents and purposes, already dead. They wouldn't survive the next assault. They wouldn't survive the winter outside of the city.

But still, Devi was trying, because such was her duty.

And if a half-breed, half-naked youngling could think of them, Valerius, protector of the realm, heir to the throne, would not forsake them.

"Kal, ride ahead of the townsfolk. I'll take the back."

Both Kallan and Devi turned to stare at him, eyes wide.

"The army is concerned with taking the city for now. I doubt we'll be followed within the next hour or so. We're leading this group to Elham before going on our way."

This would eat into the precious hours they had to put as much distance between them and their enemies, but it would also give him a chance to think and prepare himself for what was coming next.

War.

FOURTEEN
HEIR OF DARKNESS

Court of Crystal, One year ago.

"Who would you choose between us?" Lyn's drunken sister demanded to know, pouting and playing with her hair.

The rich nobles Arya usually targeted always picked her, of course. Arya spent whatever she earned on fineries and had her hair braided by professionals before she went out to the Cauldron each weekend. Lyn tagged along, as she had nothing else to do, but she had no intention of spreading her legs for the first male with a heavy purse. Even those as handsome as the stranger Arya had set her eye on tonight held no appeal to her.

The stranger was somehow familiar, although she couldn't tell why. He had long blond hair and was taller than most. His eyes were a pure crystal blue, and his features couldn't have been more perfect had they been carved by the gods of art.

He tilted his head and smiled.

"I'll take you both. You," he said, staring right at Arya, "to fuck mindlessly." Then he moved slowly, like some kind of predator. Lyn took a small step back. As his legs were much longer than hers, he was still standing right before he. "And your shy little friend here, I'd worship."

She froze. His voice… she didn't know why, but she couldn't resist it. Breathing hard, she let him touch the side of her face and tilt her head. The stranger lowered his head to her ear and whispered, "I'll have you sit on my mouth and cry my name as your friend rides me. What say you, beautiful? No doubt a virgin hasn't had better offers."

It came to her suddenly why she knew this face. She'd seen it before from far away, and then he'd been wearing formal red and gold armor, but there was no mistaking this male.

This god.

Somehow, Lyn remembered she had a spine.

"Am I supposed to suddenly wish to let your mouth anywhere near my pussy while you fuck my sister because there's a crown, no doubt too small for your fat head, attached to your name, sir?" Aurelius, the elder prince, heir to the realm, smiled cruelly. She didn't let it intimidate her. "Perhaps I would have considered your proposal had you offered your friend as a fourth companion to our little party." She raised a brow, purposefully observing the man who stood behind them. His guard, or perhaps his companion.

The other male hid his smile.

She'd known it was going to get to the royal, arrogant as he was, and she'd been right. He took another step forward, this time invading her personal space, his intense gaze locked on her.

She took a step too, refusing to back down, standing so close she could feel his breath. Lyn didn't quite reach his head, but it was close enough. She knew each word was going to leave a hot breath on her sensitive skin. "I would have had you watch while I used my mouth on him," she whispered.

She knew the rules of this game. She had simply never played her cards before.

Leaving the prince utterly stunned, Lyn winked and walked away.

It wasn't a fortnight before her parents received a summons in her name. She was called to the palace, where she'd join the harem of the overking's son.

Lyn would have refused, had anyone given her a choice, but she was twenty-four and, as such, a charge of her parents. Her inclination didn't matter. Not for another year.

Her parents liked the amount of gold that the prince was offering, and the fact that they'd have their daughter in the palace to boast about, so her fate was sealed.

She had to go and become the dick's little plaything.

Lyn's first weeks at the palace were painful. Aurelius stretched out the torture by leaving her to her own company for days, making things worse. She was given a flock of ladies who bathed her, plucked eyebrows, and cut her hair into shape before dressing her up like a doll.

She was to walk around the castle at certain hours, and always in the company of her ladies—four mindless, self-important females who made her nonviolent self want to pull their hair out. During the day, she was expected to listen to lessons in etiquette, teaching her how she was supposed to address a prince, a duke, a simple lord, and how to eat with the various cutlery set for formal meals.

Every night, before dismissing themselves, her ladies would dress her up again, in a very different sort of getup this time. Silk or lace. Some dresses, shorter than some of her shirts and open at the middle, scarcely hid anything. Why they bothered making her wear anything at all, she didn't know.

Every night she lay in bed, unable to sleep for more than a few minutes at a time. On the eighth night, finally, what she'd dreaded occurred. She caught the noise as the doorknob was turned and pushed. Lyn sat up and tried to breathe.

Aurelius entered her room.

He was as handsome as she recalled, and he smiled in the exact same way as when she'd pushed him at the Cauldron in her little village.

The prince took a step toward the desk she'd never touched, tucked in one corner of her room. As he advanced, two other figures followed. One male—the guard who'd accompanied him when they'd first met—and one female.

The female was exquisite, the single most beautiful thing Lyn had ever beheld. She had silver hair and eyes made of night. Her every move was gracious, elegant.

It wasn't the first time she'd seen her either, but at a distance, she'd never realized just how perfect Kelina Stormhale truly was.

The daughter of the advisor to the king, and Aurelius's fiancée, from what Lyn knew.

What sick games were these three into?

She wasn't a crier, but she fucking wanted to cry right then. She wouldn't give them the satisfaction though.

"You know, I was actually not going to do this," Aurelius said conversationally. "You were just a mousy little thing I'd seen while slumming with commoners for my entertainment. But my friend here"—he gestured to the second male in the room—"ended up taking a strand of your hair that night."

She frowned, trying to understand what was going on.

"It's crazy what a strand of hair can tell you, you know? To those who have access to the right technology, in any case. It contains all your DNA. Enough information to see a lot of things about you, Lyn Reyland."

Aurelius removed his coat and left it on the desk.

"I'm not going to beat around the bush. I'm not going to lie to you either. I'm no rapist. I won't take you against your wishes."

She breathed out in relief, somehow believing him.

"But I will take you nonetheless, because you will let me once I'm done talking."

She snorted in disbelief. What a fucking entitled prick.

"I'd wager you know of the origin of my house, as does any Corantian. We're not of this world. My father came five thousand years ago, and it took him four thousand years to find a female with whom he could have a child."

She nodded cautiously.

"I'm born of a common fae who just so happened to have compatible genetics. And just like my father, I will not have a child unless I find the right partner. I have reasons to believe that you may have the right genetics, Lyn."

Oh. Somehow, this was reassuring to her. That he'd sought her out for practical reasons, rather than out of cruelty or revenge, was a relief. She still wasn't going to fucking ask him to her bed.

"Here's the deal, sweet thing. You've been fed various concoctions that ensure you're quite fertile tonight. Let me take you, and if our coupling is unfruitful, you get to go home. You can keep the hundred thousand marks, and you'll be free. Refuse me, and you'll stay until I see fit to release you."

Oh, the dick was good. One night. He was asking for just one night, not the whole year she'd dreaded.

Lyn looked away. She wasn't for sale, dammit.

While thinking through his offer, she noted that he'd failed to cover a third option. "And what if I am with child?"

Aurelius tilted his head. "Well, you'd remain here until he or she is born, of course. The rest? That's entirely up to you, little Lyn. Would you leave a child to be raised away from its mother?"

She bit her lip. If she was with child, she'd be trapped here, for months.

Or forever.

But what she recalled of her reproductive studies was in her favor. Hell, Aryn was fucking her way through downtown and not being very careful about it, yet she'd never had so much as a false alarm. Fae couples were known to try for years, if not centuries, before they managed to give birth to a child.

It would be just one night….

She bit her lip. It could be worse, really. The prince was charming, and no doubt he knew what he was doing.

She nodded, not managing to get a word out of her mouth.

"Well then."

Lyn just had time to register that he hadn't requested the others leave the room.

"Turn around, come to the edge of the bed, lift your skirts, raise your hips."

She did as she was told. Promptly and without warning, he was behind her, pushing his incredibly stiff member deep inside her, hard. Aurelius moved his hips back and forth, faster, deeper, and unexpectedly, Lyn found that she didn't dislike it at all. Something inside her boiled and screamed for more, and just when it was about to be sated, just when she could feel the edge, Aurelius thrust deeper, faster, making her scream in pleasure.

He came with her as her walls tightened around him, emptying himself.

Lyn remained still, motionless and stunned, attempting to understand everything that had occurred. Decide how she was feeling about it. Understand why she wanted more.

He paid her no mind, speaking to the woman who'd entered with him.

"Will it hold?" he asked with indifference.

Lyn could tell he expected a no. This was the tone of someone who was used to getting the same answer over and over.

Kelina Stormhale stared at Lyn with something strange in her eyes. Something akin to hatred.

"I can't believe it. A goddamn common fae! But yes. Yes, she'll be pregnant."

Oh.

Fuck.

At first Lyn was in denial. How could they have known for sure that soon? But there was a very simple answer: Kelina was a seer.

When the morning sickness started, she had no doubt, and no hope.

Lyn gave birth to a perfect little boy she named Alyx. The moment her nurse put him in her arms, her boy was hers, and she knew she'd remain in the castle amongst vipers, liars, and monsters who'd scheme to either control or eliminate her little boy. She'd protect him with everything she was.

Aurelius had kept his promise. He'd only asked for one night. As their child grew inside her, he came to her rooms often. Read there sometimes, observing her in silence.

Four times, he invited her to ceremonies where she was at his side. He presented her to his father, calling her "my Lyn."

Orin, the overking himself, said, "Welcome to the family, my dear."

She'd known it would stop the moment the child was out of her though. They'd try to take him away from her. Eclipse her.

One of the nurses went to get Aurelius after the child had been handed to her. She was crying when the prince entered her room that day.

Aurelius walked slowly, reverently, and knelt at her side before kissing their son's head. Then he got to his feet and looked at her.

Wordlessly, and just as slowly, the prince bent to drop his lips on her forehead.

"You won't take him from me."

She managed to make a statement, rather than asking a question, finding her strength.

Aurelius laughed. "No one is taking our son from his parents, little Lyn. No one."

Lifting her eyes, she saw him and knew he meant every word. She also saw something else. In the background, close to the door, Kelina and the guard whose name she still didn't know were watching her like she was a worm they couldn't wait to squash under their talons.

This was two nights before the winter solstice. The following day, black flags were raised around the city of crystal, indicating that the overking had died. At dusk, their armies were descending upon the city of night.

FIFTEEN
THE QUEEN'S ARROW

The enemies had come in the day, while the sun was still shining and while the high fae of the Unseelie Court slept. They'd taken the gates two hours ago, pouring into the streets of the city of night, killing all who crossed their path and encountering little resistance.

Devi didn't understand.

Their land was at peace—had been for hundreds of years. Just a day ago, seelie and unseelie had all been drinking and dancing together, celebrating the upcoming solstice as one.

She just couldn't comprehend what could possibly have compelled the army of gold-clad soldiers to attack them now. They came from Corantius, if one was to believe their colors, and the soldiers of Corantius answered to Orin Dreigo, their overking, the person who had demanded peace in the first place.

Her utter ignorance and helplessness wasn't helping matters. From the moment the guard post had blown before her eyes, she'd been fighting her own instincts, keeping them in check. Everywhere there had been screams, blood, and chaos. Although she would have loved to pretend otherwise, her response to that hadn't changed in ten years.

Attacking. Lashing out. Destroying everything around her.

Even now, as Valerius's horse carried them away from the city, her hands trembled under her struggle. She closed her eyes and forced a calming breath. Useless. She'd never felt as volatile. Or dangerous. Not after her dream, not even from under the water all those years ago.

Devi had released some of her energy at the gates, but she'd purposefully kept the most lethal part of her from coming out. If she'd let herself make use of it, she wouldn't simply have destroyed the pile of stones she stood on. None of the people walking ahead of them right now would have been spared. Valerius and his pretty friend would be dead, along with anyone in a mile radius.

She was a fucking mess.

What now? These people were bound for Elham, and no doubt the prince had a plan after that. What was her next move?

She knew her orders. She'd been asked to go to her father. To a place she recalled on the rare occasions where she found herself dreaming. A city high on a snowy mountain, surrounded by ice sculptures and built of polished black stones. A castle more splendid than that of the unseelie queen, older than anything she'd ever laid eyes on. A realm of power and beauty, where she may not be welcome.

There was nowhere else to go, however. The thought of her destination did nothing to ease the torrents blowing in her mind.

She was holding on to the front of the saddle. Feeling a strange tingle at the ends of her fingertips, she glanced down and gasped. The leather under her palms had turned a blueish white. She let go of it, resting her hand on her own legs, where it would do no harm.

A second later, Valerius was wrapping his right arm around her torso.

Bad idea. Very bad idea, for all kinds of reasons. For one, she might lose it and kill him without meaning to.

"Can you please let go of me?"

He sighed. "Now's not the time to argue, Dev." Dev, he said. No one called her that, save for his mother. She found herself not protesting. "We might be going slow, but if I see anything gold coming out of the gates, I'll have to gallop without any warning. Plus, the horse might spook if we're attacked. You're too tired to hold on, so I'm securing you."

His tone had changed, she noted. This wasn't the person she'd met five days ago. This wasn't the idle spoiled brat who infuriated everyone he crossed paths with just to pass time. There was no humor in his voice; he wasn't teasing her. If anything, he sounded grave. Burdened. Devi found that she didn't like it.

"Count on you to find any excuse to feel up a gal," she challenged. She didn't have to turn to know he smiled, if only a little.

"If you think that's feeling you up, you seriously need some action, little elf."

That was more like it. She found herself smiling too, and to her astonishment, Devi realized that some of her own anxiety had evaporated. Her hands weren't shaking. She wasn't quite back to normal, but she didn't feel like a bomb ready to detonate at the first provocation. Each breath she took calmed her further. She looked down at the hand pressed against her stomach and frowned.

He'd helped. Somehow, he'd achieved what she, and his mother, had attempted for over a decade: getting her under control when she was ready to blow.

"Are you using your brain mojo on me?" she asked, confused.

He chuckled low. "What makes you think so? You and I both know I'm not beyond making use of my powers for my amusement, but I'm actually conserving my resources. I may have to use it later."

"Oh."

Then how the fuck was he soothing her deadly edges? She decided against mentioning it, knowing it would simply invite a bunch of questions she had no intention of answering right now.

"You really should rest. I don't need to probe your mind to feel that you're all over the place, in pain, and depleted."

Well, that showed how much he knew. Out of his three observations, only one was accurate. All over the place? That, she couldn't deny. But she felt no pain, and the very core of her problem right now was that she was very, very far from depleted.

The incident at the river hadn't been the first time her power had lashed out that way, just the most notable. The first time around, no fae had died.

Devi recalled the days when she played around the family manor so innocently, plucking flowers in the spring, making angels in the snow during the winter, and talking to her shadow friend. The creature who watched her from the Graywoods at least once a week. By age ten, she was brave enough to actually venture to the dark, misty woods and seek it out, her favorite bow on her back.

"I'll catch you today!" she'd say, running after it as fast as her bare feet could carry her and laughing at their games.

She knew the shadow played with her. Sometimes it almost let her get close enough, and then, when she was but a few yards away, it took to the trees, moving at an impossible speed. She'd never catch it, but little Devi didn't intend to stop trying.

Her mother had been right when she'd told her no one would harm her on their land; no living creature had every tried. This was perhaps why it took ten years for her power to come to her.

It happened because of a stupid little root she hadn't seen. Her feet hooked inside it, and the next instant, she fell face-first with a cry. Devi felt it then. Something came out of her along with her voice, something that resonated deep inside her.

Her head hit the ground, hard. Harder than it should have; it wasn't the first time she fell on a bed of grass, but it was the first time that it felt like a solid wall. Opening her eyes, she blinked in confusion, for it was summer and yet the ground was ice.

She looked around, fearful and confused, only to find nothing but white as far as her eyes could see.

"Shadow?"

She felt it—it had come back, and it was close.

"I'm scared."

That day, the shadow had a voice—a voice deeper than her sword master's and softer than the wind. "There's nothing to be afraid of," it had said, and she'd believed it.

"Go home, little princess." He'd called her that, just like her mother did. "We'll play again someday."

And then it disappeared, leaving her alone in her midsummer winter.

Devi turned and retraced her steps, heading back to the manor. In her path, she found all sort of creatures: rabbits and foxes, those forest dwellers who ran from her heavy steps, knowing to fear her bow. They didn't run that day. They stood there like ice sculptures, entirely frozen and—she could tell—dead.

She'd killed everything.

"There's nothing to be afraid of," the shadow had said. That day, she learned that the shadow lied. There was something to be very afraid of, and it was a girl called Devi Star Rivers.

She told everything to her mother, and found that Loxy was also a liar, because she echoed the shadow's words. "Don't be afraid of your own power. It's quite normal, and I'll show you how to control it." Loxy Rivers held her arms high up toward the ceiling, and before Devi's wide eyes, her mother created the most beautiful thing out of nothing: a delicate sculpture of ice. She'd made a fae with large, extended wings.

"Someday, you'll be able to mold water and ice as you please, just like me. And you know, a hundred years ago, when I was just your age, it burst out of me too. Now I'm a danger to no one." Then Loxy tapped the tip of Devi's nose with her index finger. "Unless they want to hurt my little girl, that is."

Devi sighed in relief, glad to know that she'd be okay, someday. Loxy kissed the side of her head and moved to her desk, pulling out some writing paper, ink, wax, and her seal. "Go get some rest now. You must be very tired. And we have a lot to do tomorrow."

The very next day, Loxy started her training.

"How did you learn to walk, sweet?" she asked, and Devi frowned.

"I don't remember, I was too little."

Loxy chuckled. "Very true, that. Well, your little wiggly bottom started to crawl first, and then you had to learn to stand up on your own. Only after that did you take your first step. And you fell on your face."

Devi had pouted. "Doesn't sound like fun."

"Indeed. It was a long, tiresome process, because you had to learn to use new muscles without quite understanding how it worked. But by mimicking, and then strengthening them, you got there in good time. I'm not going to tell you that this is the same. It's worse. It will take years. Decades, perhaps. And when you've lived a hundred years, you'll find that you're learning a little more about it. But you walk just fine now." Loxy winked. "You'll figure it out."

Step one—wiggling her butt, as Loxy had eloquently put it—was finding the damn muscle in the first place. It had come to her out of nowhere, but consciously managing to make it come back wasn't as easy as it seemed. Loxy got her to jog around the house, or dance, or even read a book. Then without warning, she'd poke at her, surprising her. It took weeks, but they were out in the gardens and Devi tumbled, kicking a bucket of water, and magic finally came to her. She'd stopped the bucket in midair, still full, and instinctively she'd managed to hold it in place.

"Look, Mama!"

And Loxy had looked, but contrarily to what Devi had expected, she didn't seem happy at all. She seemed frightened.

Loxy did a lot more writing after that, sending plenty of letters.

"Who are you writing to, Mama?"

"Friends. It's nothing to worry about, little princess."

She definitely knew by then: those words really were a lie.

Masters came to observe her, and within months they'd all come to the same conclusion.

"I don't know what to say. It shouldn't be possible, and yet here we are. Your child displays an aptitude for controlling every element. She's learning at an unprecedented rate. I wouldn't be surprised if she surpassed you by the time she's of age, my lady."

Loxy sighed. "Well, she will be pleased. You may report to the queen. Let her know that her little experiment has paid off."

"I'm sorry," said the master, and Loxy laughed.

"What for? I knew what I signed up for. And I'm glad that my daughter may have a purpose."

When the master left, Loxy said, "You know, eavesdropping is quite unladylike." Devi opened the door her ear had been plastered against, unapologetic.

"Although, I can't blame you. I'd be curious too if people talked of me behind closed doors. Come, Devira."

She'd walked to her mother, asking, "What did you mean? What purpose am I supposed to have?"

"Sit. Let me explain."

So, she'd sat and listened.

"If we were to put a fae, an elf, a mage, and a dragon in a cage, who would win?"

"The dragon," she'd replied immediately.

"Probably. But what if the elf, mage, and the fae worked together against the dragon?"

She'd had to ponder it. "Then they'd probably win, I think."

"Indeed. They'd at least have a fair chance." Devi was very young then, but Loxy didn't hesitate to tell her, "We're in a cage. This island of ours is circled by walls, and what lies beyond is too formidable to face. We've nowhere to go, and there are creatures living among us who are much, much more powerful than dragons. Some among them believe that because we're weaker, we ought to be nothing but slaves to do with as they please. Our peace will last another thousand years perhaps, but my friend, the unseelie queen, has spent a long time working on a way to make us stronger, to give us a fighting chance when the time comes."

"How would we fight something worse than dragons?" At ten, she couldn't imagine a creature more formidable than a great fire-breathing beast.

Loxy's reply remained branded in her mind, even now. "We'd make dragons of our own, little princess. I come from a very old family, and my great-great-great-grandma, your ancestor, was one of those creatures."

"The things who want us to be slaves?"

"That's right. You may call them scions. In my veins, there's an old power that I gave you. And in the veins of your father, there's another power, something just as strong. But before you were born, the queen had a strange idea. What if she was to also bless you with her strength? And with another strength too. We had hope that it might make you a lot stronger than any of us. And we were right. You will be."

Devi took everything in and decided that she quite liked the idea of being stronger than even a queen someday.

"So, my purpose is fighting bad guys?"

Loxy laughed. "Not quite. I doubt there will be anyone to fight at all for hundreds, if not thousands of years. Your purpose is to have strong children, who'll have children of their own. Now that we know it works, the queen will arrange for other children to be blessed just like you, and when the dark times come, our kind will have thousands of warriors strong enough to defend us against the scions."

Devi pouted, for the thought of having children wasn't as appealing as that of defending her mother with her sword, her bow, and her magic.

Eighteen years had passed, and the dark days Loxy had believed would come to another generation were upon them now. It looked like she was getting her wish after all.

She'd been bred to be a weapon of the unseelie queen, in defense of their entire kind, and that was exactly what she intended to do.

SIXTEEN
TWO DEADLY ROADS

Their little company advanced in silence and at a declining pace. The two dozen fae had been fast at first, eager to put the burning city behind them, but as time passed, cold, tiredness, and thirst prevailed. No one had left entirely prepared, not even Vale, although he'd had a little more time than the rest of them. The dried meat he'd offered Devi was the last of the provisions he'd packed before leaving Carvenstone. What he had, he shared, not taking a single sip from his own water bottle.

This part of the realm was known for its beauty; the eastern road was seldom used, as it led nowhere of note. There were a few villages here and there, planted every other hundred miles to ensure those traveling that way may find food, water, and shelter.

The road led south to the seas, and east to the forest of Graywoods, which marked the borders of the elven realm.

Neither destination was safe at the best of times. Tonight, they had plenty of reasons to be tense.

Valerius could feel Devi struggle to remain upright, forcing herself to stay conscious.

"You should sleep," he told her.

She snorted. "Yes, I ought to take a nap. Never mind the fact that our city has fallen, our realm is at war, and there are probably soldiers after us right now."

He smiled because she'd retained her sharp tongue, despite everything. He wondered how long it would last.

"We are indeed at war, Devira. And wars are won by well-rested, well-fed soldiers. Sleep when you can."

She attempted to relax, he could tell. Then she gave up.

"Will it help if I order you to get some rest, as your direct superior?"

"I can't. Not on horseback."

Vale chuckled. After a month of this, she'd be able to. As long as she was still alive. The thought was sobering and forced him to look to the future.

They could already see the borders of Elham on the horizon. It was but a small irrelevant town that may not get completely razed by the enemies, with luck. It wasn't strategically placed, and the hundred or so peasants, merchants, and clerks who inhabited it posed no threat. But there were so many reasons why it might fall nonetheless: because it was the first village out of Asra, because the army just happened to pass it by, because they were bored, because they wanted to stretch their muscles.

Elham might fall. He was going to leave the flock of commoners who now traveled with him there regardless. They considerably slowed him down; he had no other choice.

Valerius's mother had told him to head to Wyhmur, and to Wyhmur he intended to go. But not alone with Kal.

Devi had wanted to remain behind with the commoners. She might express the same wish again, but Vale was bringing her with him if he had to knock her out and drag her unconscious. Who knew what she'd do when left to her own devices? Attempt to take on an entire army, no doubt. No, she was to go with him. He just had to convince her that it was a good idea.

"After Elham, what was your plan, little elf? Do you intend to follow your orders?"

"Little elf," she repeated, "is going to the elven realm as she was told. They need warning, and I need resources if I am to join the queen."

Vale wasn't surprised that she wished to join his mother. Not surprised, but still somehow annoyed.

"How convenient. It also happens to be where I'm headed."

Devi turned sharply to watch him, her expression confused. "You? To Wyhmur? Elves and fae don't mix."

"And yet here you are," he said, quite amused. "Surely they must mix occasionally."

She rolled her eyes and faced forward again.

"Tell me of your parents. How they met. It must be quite the story. A seelie princess and her woodland elf."

"Oh, I think not. You demand I tell you everything about me, and yet you give me nothing in exchange."

Bartering. He wholeheartedly approved.

"And what would you ask of me, little elf?"

"That you stop calling me that, for one."

He could, but getting under her skin was a pleasure he wasn't inclined to deny himself. "Request denied. Find something else."

She sighed. "Well, I suppose you want me to sleep. You could tell me about you. It ought to be sufficiently boring."

He gave it some thought. "I'm the sole heir to the crumbling unseelie throne. Pretty certain most of my life has been bared to the entire world."

The parts he talked of, in any case. Something told him he could trust Devi with the secrets of Carvenstone, but now, more than ever, they had company. He would not speak of it with so many ears around.

"Everyone has secrets. Tell me something that's not common knowledge."

He gave it some thought.

"All right. This is no secret, but I wouldn't call it common knowledge either. I was born in battle, during a time of war. It was two decades before we were at peace again. Both of my parents were invested in my safety, I'm sure, but my father already had an heir. My mother took the matter more seriously. She kept me hidden in plain sight as a servant boy. Pretended that my 'master' was her son. She doted on him openly. Many a time, that child was attacked. When peace came, and I was presented as Valerius Blackthorn, her son and heir, all were surprised. None as much as me."

"You didn't know? Not at all?"

Vale smiled. "The child, Kallan, was told, of course. I wasn't. And I could never have guessed. My mother didn't spare me a glance in nineteen years. Yet I recall once, after an attack on Kallan, when I'd gotten hurt attempting to defend him, she came to me and bound the wound herself. I didn't question why. Later, I knew. My mother might just care a little." He shrugged. "In her own way."

There was silence for a few minutes. She finally broke it to say, "How fucking messed up is that? No wonder you're a head case."

He laughed. She certainly never disappointed.

"I mean, now you totally should be over it, but I get why it would have fucked with you as a child. And yet I understand Shea. I might have done the same in her place, to ensure my boy was safe."

Vale found himself thinking of a boy standing next to Devi. A boy with violet eyes.

He smiled. When had he seriously thought of having a child? The spells of the queen were fucking with his mind again, no doubt.

He recalled that his mother had clearly professed to having nothing to do with his infatuation, but trusting anything the queen said was foolishness.

"Yes, Shea does use everyone around her as pawns on a chessboard, but she does so with the best of intentions."

"Indeed." Devi laughed. "You know, I once told her I was willing to be used, so long as I got to be a knight rather than a pawn. She told me I could even be the queen if I wished." Before he managed a reply, she said, "Ah, look. We're almost there."

They'd reached the border of the town, and a few alarmed folks met them, walking right up to Kallan with water, food, and plenty of questions about the smoke coming from the city in the horizon.

"*Prodire*," Vale said, charming the word as it escaped his lips. The horse picked up his pace until they reached Kallan. "We don't have time for this," Vale told his second.

"And no answer to give them in any case. We need to change the horses, or at least make these ones drink if the horse masters are out, and we're out of here. Agreed?"

"No argument here." Then, looking at Devi, Kal made use of his best charming smile. "I don't think we've met. Kallan. Second to His Highness."

"My, I've heard of you. Just now, in fact."

"Have you? Funny that. I might have brought you up a time or twenty over the last few days, and yet I haven't heard a word about you. Not even a name."

"It's Devi." She was smiling freely, charmingly, and she hadn't given Kallan so much as an insult.

Vale dismounted and held his hand up to help Devi get down.

The wind blew a little harder, making him notice that the temperature had gone down considerably. He thought of undoing his coat and giving it to Devi, but dismissed the temporary fix. She'd need something warmer if she was to reach Wyhmur without freezing to death first.

"Come. Let us see if we can get you a warm coat."

"I'm fine."

He lifted a brow. "You're wearing a cotton shirt. It'll snow before morning, and we may not find a roof to sleep under."

She shrugged, repeating, "I'm fine."

And now that he paid attention, he saw she truly was. She wasn't shivering, and her skin hadn't reddened at all. The temperature bordered on freezing; she should be entirely blue and begging for warmth.

"Devi?"

"Hmm?"

"Pardon my asking, and you may find it rather odd… but what the heck are you?"

It might seem rather rude, but the question was valid nonetheless.

She chuckled humorlessly. "Let me know if you figure it out. All I know is that I'm not normal. I'm just pretending to be. Or I was, I guess. But we're not in the city now. We're out here by ourselves, in danger and in a hurry, so I'm not going to make us waste precious time pretending I need a bloody coat. Let's get horses."

"You don't feel the cold at all."

She just shrugged. "No, I do. It's simply that it can't harm me."

The towns along the path of Duran existed to supply travelers with what they needed. They had provisions, food, and horses, and they also happened to have coats. He bought her one.

Devi rolled her eyes. "I said—"

"That you didn't *need* it. But this isn't cutting into our timeline, because we do need to stop for supplies. Besides, we'll pass another five towns before reaching the forest. How many eyes would fail to notice a female rider in nothing but a shirt as the snow falls? Can you be sure that none of these eyes belong to someone who'd give our direction away for a purse full of coin, or under torture?"

She shut her mouth and followed him to the horse master's domain at the eastern edge of the village.

Thain Fairfolk was the man to talk to when it came to horses, and his children ran a shop that provided travelers with whatever gear they needed, as well as other random things they might sell to the villagers.

"We have ten minutes," Vale said, gesturing to his left where the ladies' clothes hung.

Thain came to greet him directly, and with Kallan, they talked in low voices about their requirements.

"We need three horses, the fastest you have."

"We've seen the smoke, and we got them all ready in case the queen requests our services," the horse master announced proudly.

That would help.

As they carried on discussing the matter, Vale watched Devi from the corner of his eye. She looked through the racks of coats and pulled one out within a minute.

She tried it on; it was a dark coat lined with fur. Its hood fell down to her eyes when she pulled it up to try it in front of a mirror.

Catching his own reflection, as well as Kallan's, Vale frowned. He preferred understated tones, but everything about his dark habit still screamed unseelie; there were slashes of green through the black fabric.

Once they'd agreed on a deal for the horses, the master left to get their mounts prepared, and Vale asked Thain's son to show him to the males' coats. None were displayed in the front of the store.

The merchant shook his head. "We ran out, sir. We have brown capes though. Nothing fancy, and it won't help with the cold, but I reckon you could wear them over your coats."

"It's perfect, thank you."

Vale moved to pay the man, but Kallan stopped him. "A moment. Just one of the capes, please. And some hair dye too."

Valerius stared at his second, his first and perhaps only true friend. He needn't ask what Kal had in mind. They knew each other too well by now.

He grabbed him by the arm and pulled him to the front of the shop, out of hearing range.

"No."

"*Yes.* It will gain you some time. Besides, I need to return to Carvenstone and see the damage there. You know this."

"I will not have you do this. Not again."

Devi joined them, interjecting, "What am I missing?"

Vale didn't attempt a reply, too busy staring Kallan down.

"I'll play the decoy, so you and Vale may slip by unnoticed. I'll ride north along the border of the Graywoods until I've reached Carvenstone. There, I'll be safe. It won't pull everyone off your trail, but this should at least divide anyone who'd follow us."

"You're *not* doing this," Vale insisted.

"Of course I am. Don't get worried on my behalf, it's insulting. I'll be just fine. I know these roads, and they don't. They'll never catch up with me."

"These aren't wayward orcs from the walls. These aren't seelie foes. These aren't even *elves*, Kallan. We're facing something entirely new."

Kal shrugged. "I've seen them fall. I've seen them bleed. They're as killable as anything else. Sure, they're fast, but we have a head start. And if you're right and they truly are beyond our skills, we're all dead anyway. Let me do this."

Valerius couldn't bring himself to reply for a moment, not when he knew he had to say yes.

"You will go as soon as the horses are brought to us. Take the most direct road, and stay alive."

They exchanged coats to make the deception more believable, as Vale's was imbued with his scent. Kal retreated to the back of the merchant's shop to apply the hair dye, with the help of a shop assistant.

Too many eyes had seen the exchange, but still, it may work.

For the sake of his first companion, Valerius hoped it wouldn't.

SEVENTEEN

RIDE OF THE DYRMOUNTS

His wings extended behind him, the traitor surveyed the burning city from the top of the castle wall. To his right, he watched a gold-winged fae destroy the gates. Devira. What a perfect little goddess she'd turned out to be. He was glad she'd made it, and he hoped she lived through the next year.

To his left, he saw the cowardly queen of the unseelie flee, no doubt planning to join her armies to the west. His soldiers were descending upon Asra from the north, tearing it apart.

Not *his* soldiers, he corrected himself. Not quite yet. There was no king seated on the crystal throne. And there wouldn't be any until he dictated it.

The traitor smiled, recalling the day he'd found his calling, when he was but a child.

The overking had been sick, and the traitor had asked his mother whether he was going to die. He'd wanted that fat, disgusting pig to die. Even as a child, the traitor had been thirsty for the blood of those who'd wronged him.

"Hopefully not," his mother had said.

He had frowned. "Why, Mother? He took you and set you aside like you were nothing. His men did this to you!" he'd roared, pointing to the scar that devoured half of her once-charming face.

"Because for all his faults, if he died today, the world may end up a darker place for it. The realm of crystal isn't a democracy. A leader is appointed by a technological device I don't quite understand. And they all are bound to follow that leader. While it is Orin, the Isle is safe because he demands peace. But if he was to die and another leader was chosen, there could be war. People like us are the first to die in war, my little prince. I may hate fae, but I've seen wars. I hate them more."

The traitor had kept his mouth shut, but secretly he'd wished for war. Suffering. Chaos. He'd wished for the world to burn, and now it was.

She would never admit it, but Devi would have preferred to carry on riding with Valerius. She was a proficient rider, but she'd never been fond of horses. They had minds of their own, and relying on a creature that may very well hate your guts didn't seem wise to her.

But she had a plan. She tiptoed to the elegant, powerful brown and white beast that she was to ride and whispered, "I heard you're called Alarik. Well, I'm Devi, and this shall stay between us." She emphasized this by doing a shushing motion. The animal seemed unimpressed—at least until she pulled out a brown sugar cube and held it up on her hand. "There are a few of those where that one came from, boy. Here's the deal. You don't throw me over or change course, and you definitely don't ridicule me in front of His Mighty Pain in the Butt. Sugar cubes for you in exchange. What do you think?"

The horse whinnied, and she chose to believe it was a sign of agreement. "Good. Here's another one to seal the deal."

Devi knew little of horses, but she was aware that this one was mighty all the same.

Elham was far removed from any other dwelling, standing alone with nothing but open fields for miles, because the principal family of the little town had bought every stretch of land on their horizon.

The Fairfolks bred horses and sold them to the soldiers of the unseelie realm. The horses that pulled Shea's silver carriage had also been born here. In fact, fae came from near and far to this small, otherwise irrelevant little town just to purchase their beasts. Valerius must have emptied a fair part of his purse to acquire three tonight. But they could not have hoped for better steeds, hurried as they were.

Where a normal horse may strain after trotting a mile, the dyrmounts could cover ten before they needed a break.

The horse was eating out of her hand when Valerius came out with their supplies. He handed her a share to store in the bags they fastened to their saddles.

"These will give us a fair advantage," he said, visibly satisfied with the two beasts before them.

"Unless, of course, those who come after us decide to stop and buy horses themselves."

Valerius's smile showed all his teeth. "Aren't you cute, thinking I haven't thought that through." He lifted a brow. "I bought them all, except for the pregnant mares and the yearlings. Express delivery. Three of Thain Fairfolk's sons are leaving at once to deliver the rest of the herd to my mother. We're bound by honor to bring them back three studs by spring."

Devi knew enough of finance to feel a little dizzy. When her agent told her that new horses had to be bought, she always groaned, thinking about the fact that she would have to spend more on one animal than on the food provision of her entire household for a month.

And Valerius Blackthorn had just bought a *herd*. At least fifty horses.

"I'm gonna be sick."

She could come to terms with the fact that they now were at war, but throwing millions away in the space of half an hour was another matter.

"Such a spoilsport. No one likes a penny pincher, you know."

"You're going to ruin this kingdom if it ever becomes yours to rule."

"Now, now. I'll have you know that I didn't spend a penny of the royal coffers. No, this all comes from my pocket.'"

"And you so happened to have a fortune on you?"

He shrugged. "Some of my bonds were in my bag, fortunately. Asra may have fallen, but gold bonds from the Isle's Bank can be cashed anywhere."

She shook her head in disbelief. This male may as well live in another universe.

"Don't you get all judgy, little miss. If you must know, I make a salary, just like you. I've just lived a lot longer. Money amasses when you don't do much with it."

"And *you* don't do much with it?" she questioned doubtfully.

Valerius lifted a brow. "Someday, when we have some time before us, ask me what I do in my home. I may yet surprise you."

She didn't say so, but he was probably right, because Vale surprised her at every turn.

Another thing that she wouldn't say, even under torture: she was glad to have company. Besides, while the elves of Wyhmur might have something against finding her at their borders, they probably wouldn't turn their back on Valerius Blackthorn.

As well as a bloody herd and a coat she hadn't asked for, Vale had bought her a change of clothing, food, more arrows to replace those she'd used, and other resources, paying for her supplies without making a big deal out of it. It was a little weird to her. Normally she was the one who bought things for others, but tonight she had nothing on her except for a few coins. When she was leaving her room, Devi had believed she was just going to spend a normal night at work; she generally didn't need her purse for that.

Surveying everything she was packing away, she realized she'd be set to head to Shea. She didn't need to beg the elves for the essentials, thank all heavens.

But still, whatever way she thought of it, the safest path for her now was through the well-guarded woods.

The dark forest extended from low south to all the way up in the far north of the Isle, slithering along the lands of the seelie and unseelie alike, stopping right at the southern bothers of Corantius. All of it belonged to the elves, and no one with half a brain would enter without their consent. If they let her pass, she could circle the enemy's army and join the queen west of Asra, where her troops had been stationed.

Once he was done dividing their purchases between Alarik and Midnight, the black horse he'd chosen for himself, Vale took her hand, leading her to the horse's flank. Again she noticed how warm it was, particularly when he wrapped his hands around her waist and lifted her to help her on the horse. She was too busy contemplating how stupid she was for being quite so aware of him to protest that she could very well mount a horse by herself.

"Let us make haste," he said, once he'd gotten on his own steed. "Whether those sent to hunt us be of Corantius or the seelie realm, they are day dwellers. We're to put as much distance between us and the city of night by dawn."

"How far are we exactly?"

She was vaguely familiar with the road ahead because she'd looked at maps, but she wasn't quite certain of the distance they had to cover.

"It would be a twelve-hour ride if a horse was capable of covering that distance in one go. We'll have to stop one or twice. These horses may be good, but I'll not have them die on our account."

"We'll get to rest, at least," she said, quite thankful.

Four hours later, Alarik was fine, and the large beast of Vale's was galloping ahead of her at a pace and with an ease that seemed to say, "Pfft, I cover that distance as a warm-up, bitches." Meanwhile, Devi hurt absolutely everywhere, including muscles she didn't know existed. She was as fit as any female—the protectors' rigorous training paired with her time in the basement with the queen had whipped her into shape—but damn, she was gonna walk funny for days.

Still, she wasn't about to say anything, imagining Vale's mockery. To her relief, although he seemed just fine, Vale still slowed down for a break once they neared Shorthaven.

It was close to dawn, and the streets were empty, quiet. Devi wondered if word of the war breaking out had reached the small village yet; she doubted it. From there, they couldn't see the clouds of smoke over the city.

"We announced our presence at Elham. Let us be discreet here. There's an inn at the other end of the village. We'll stop for an hour and pay them to tend to our horses. If anyone asks, and they will, let us say we're headed to the ocean for a getaway."

"In the winter?" She lifted a brow, questioning the hasty story.

Valerius thought it out. "Good point. Did you say you came from a county near my land?"

"Yes, just east of it, along the borders of Graywoods."

"Where Kal is headed." Valerius frowned, weighing his next words carefully. "If we say we've taken the quiet, picturesque roads to head to your home, whoever asks will follow Kallan's trail, I'd wager."

And he didn't want his friend to be in more danger, so that wasn't an option.

"All right, the beach it is." She added, "No one will believe it, but that's a story."

Valerius smirked wickedly, his maddening smile lighting a certain mischievous glint to his violet eyes. "They'll believe it," he stated.

For the first time today, she was a little afraid.

EIGHTEEN
HUNTERS AND PREY

And then I got down on one knee and told her I wouldn't live another day without binding myself to her. We're to wed on the beach and then honeymoon at Castle Creek, at the top of the hill of Sandleham."

There actually was a violin playing deep, soulful music in the background while Valerius served a pile of horseshit to the little crowd assembled around the bar. He never stopped smirking.

Devi wasn't quite sure whether she wished to strangle the male or laugh her ass off. Either way, keeping her expression that of an enamored fool took some effort.

"You're far from the coast, Your Grace."

"Aye, we'll stop again, perhaps at Hemladris in a couple of hours," he carefully lied. "There's a nice little inn, if I recall correctly."

"Oh yes! They'll set you up all right. My missus and I spent our anniversary there not a fortnight ago."

And so it was without invasive questions—other than a few that concerned the manner of Vale's imaginary proposal and their intentions after the nuptials that would never take place—that they set out again two hours later.

"I can't believe you," she said, although by that point she would have actually believed him capable of just about everything, particularity if it was likely to either irritate or embarrass her.

"They certainly bought it."

"Tonight," she concurred. "But on the morrow, they'll know their prince lied to them, and didn't care to tell them that they ought to run for their lives."

Vale shrugged. "Running wouldn't do any good. Act like prey and predators will chase. If they go about their business and are in fact entirely innocent, they'll have less to fear."

Devi thought it through and regretfully had to agree. Vale was an odd mixture of knowledge, silliness, gravity, and solemnity she may not quite get even if she spent years studying him.

"Right. We have another four hours ahead of us. For pity's sake, try to move with the damn beast. Loosen your waist a little. You're fighting it, that's why your lower back hurts."

She needn't ask how he knew it; Devi had done her best to hide it, but each of her steps had been a challenge.

"Here, don't move."

She yelped in surprise as Vale pushed the right side of her coat behind her and slid his hand on her lower back. Then she sighed in relief. He was holding a small, hot object.

"I had the innkeeper warm a water skin. It won't help for long, but it should provide some relief. Let me know when you need a break. We have a head start, and our steeds will be grateful for the reprieve."

She hesitated. "I don't mean to delay you. If you'd be faster by yourself—"

He didn't let her finish. "To your horse, Rivers. We are in a hurry, which means no time for nonsense."

She went to greet the animal, who seemed to have appreciated his rest. "Hello, you. You've kept your part of the bargain, now here's mine."

She gave him another sugar cube, and finding eyes set on her, Devi turned to the intimidating beast Vale rode. "And look who feels left out." She held up a sugar cube to Midnight. The black horse's eyes stared right at her, unflinching. He didn't move, displaying no interest in the treat.

Well then.

"Are we above treats, Sir Midnight?"

Vale laughed. "Above being bought, more like. My mother's dyrmount, Grayshadow, is Midnight's brother. He is worth as much as the rest of the herd, for good reason."

She sighed. "You're telling me you spent the equivalent of a hundred horses, not fifty, then?"

Vale shook his head. "No, he didn't cost me a dime. He's mine by right. Or he will be one day."

Devi frowned in confusion.

"Midnight is the horse I am to claim if and when I become king. His lifeline is bound to mine. He's seven hundred and thirty-two, just like me, and he won't die until I draw my last breath. I only have a right to him when I ascend to the throne. For now, I'm borrowing him."

"How fancy."

"Indeed." Valerius came to stand next to her and held her hand up. "Midnight, meet Devira. She's a friend, and you're to trust her." He winked at her. "For now."

The horse neighed and finally decided that her sugar cube was worth exploring.

"All right, time to go."

It might have been the rest, the hot water skin, or the advice, but the second part of her journey was a little less painful. Dawn was near. On the horizon, the sky, still dark, exploded in reds and purples over the outline of the old woods they were to reach in another five hours, perhaps.

"We'll stop shortly," said the prince. "I doubt the horses can easily ride the rest of the way without some rest first."

Stopping was a perilous business that they needed to consider carefully. Vale saw fit to seek her council on the matter, displeasing and pleasing her all at once.

He was proving himself too hard to peg. One minute, she called him every name under the moon and the next, she found that she respected him. Worse yet: it had grown on her sneakily, without an ounce of volition on her part, but she liked him well enough now.

There was a very limited number of living fae whose company she enjoyed. Shea, of course. Jiya and Rook. And now Valerius Blackthorn.

She had been exceedingly unhappy with him the previous night, about his mocking her heritage, but a few hours of sleep, an attack on their court, and their fleeing together had rendered the whole incident rather insignificant. She recognized that her temper and her being used to prejudice might have colored the whole incident. Vale might have just teased her innocently. He certainly didn't act like he thought her a lesser being.

"We've made good time. If our pursuers had set out directly after us, they would have caught up with us by the time we'd reached Elham. No horse would have beaten our dyrmounts, unless our enemy owns a pair of pegasi. I believe it may be safe to stay put for two hours or so. But not anywhere near the road." Vale pointed south. "We could head that way and reach the coast. There's caves near the seas. But we did tell the villagers we were going that way."

She nodded. "I vote for option two, whatever it is."

She visibly amused him as usual. "Very well. The Valley of Doom it is."

Devi lifted a brow. "Obnoxious. How did it garner such a name?"

"It was well earned. Have you noticed we've not seen a house nor a village, even on the horizon, for a time?"

They'd avoided towns, hamlets, and the simplest houses, but it had been some time since they'd encountered one.

"When I was a boy, we had forces posted not far from here. They stopped any travelers on these roads, controlling the path to the seas. That way, no supply could reach Daryn. The elves didn't take kindly to the embargo. They received regular provisions from the merchant guild of Corantius. So their mages pushed us back, using a plague that spread like wildfire, affecting high and common fae alike. Yet the elves could walk and breathe the air without being affected. Our soldiers were rendered useless; they were not killed, but sick and feverish for weeks on end. The Valley of Doom is what they call the stretch of land which, to this day, remains infected."

"Frightening. One might wonder why they've made no use of their weapon on a bigger scale. They might have won the war if they'd infected the entire seelie and unseelie army."

"But at what price?" Vale asked. "Nothing grows in the valley. No animal goes near it. It is now a land of death and silence."

Devi grimaced. "And that's where you propose to go now?"

Vale slowly bobbed his head up and down. "I believe it might be the safest place to stop, for no one would think to look for us there. I was not infected by the plague as a teen, nor was my mother. And it is my belief that a half-elf such as you would be immune to its evil. The sickness is not sudden. If you redden or start to cough, we'll leave directly. But otherwise, I believe it might be safe enough to think of taking a longer break there. A few hours."

"What of the horses?" she asked. "Would they not sicken?"

Vale shook his head this time. "Animals do avoid the valley, but the plague was designed to infect fae."

That settled it.

"To the Valley of Doom, then."

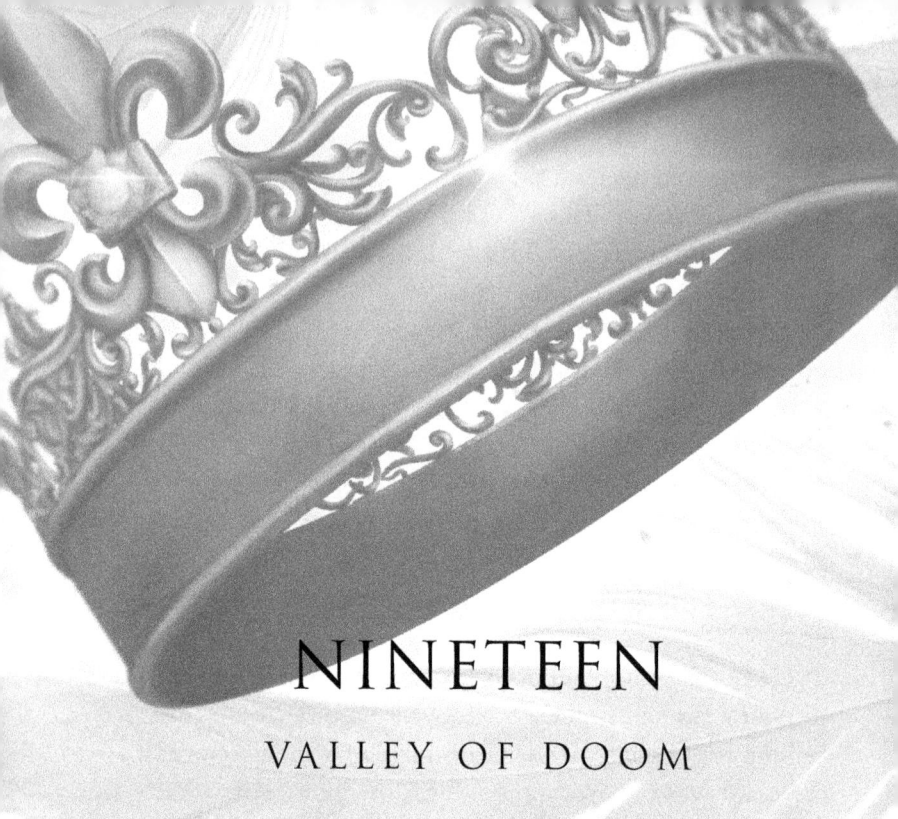

NINETEEN
VALLEY OF DOOM

It had been a long while since Vale had gazed upon these lands. He was glad and saddened to find them unchanged. Saddened, as before his eyes stretched miles of barren wasteland. No plant had grown there for long, other than a brownish moss that had been called elvesbane. Faebane might have been more accurate. Ground into powder, it was one of the most powerful poisons one could use against a fae.

Still, he was glad, because they would be safe—as safe as they could be anywhere on unseelie land in these times of peril, anyway.

Vale turned to his left, to the female who'd followed him without so much as a complaint all night. He could feel her pain, her fatigue, her anxiety. She didn't let them hinder her.

And to think that he'd thought her a pretty doll once, three days ago. A lifetime ago.

"How do you feel?" he asked, observing her closely, because he knew she might pretend to be well.

"Fine," she said. The answer he'd expected, but it sounded true. "Are we in the Valley of Doom yet?"

She tilted her head to look down. The grass at their horses' hooves was still green.

"We're at the borders, but if the air was dangerous to you, I believe you might already have sensed it."

Devi frowned. "I sense something. The air is perhaps heavy, and warmer. I can't quite put it into words."

Vale hesitated. "It may perhaps be prudent to remain here along the border."

The female shook her head. "Not on my account." And already, without paying any mind to him as he called her name, his tone grave and commanding, she pulled on her horse's reins and trotted forward.

Vale stared in disbelief before sighing and following the infuriating female.

"If you die, I get to say, 'I told you so.'"

"I actually can picture it. My body broken, still and frozen, my mouth open yet without breath, and you towering over me, smirking, and saying, 'I am the wisest, smuggest, hunkiest prince of the realm, and you can see the fate of those who'd defy my will.'"

She'd lowered her voice in a poor imitation of his, intending and managing to amuse him again.

"Hunkiest?" he repeated, reaching her side. "I think not. No such word has ever passed my lips before this day."

Their light-heartedness was short-lived. Her smile disappeared, and a frown marked his forehead at the exact same time as they redirected their gaze ahead. They'd now passed the borders of the valley. Vale's senses were on high alert, sensing danger all around them. He'd been wrong before. The valley had changed. Now it truly deserved its name.

Wordlessly, Vale drew his sword, and Devi removed her bow from her shoulder.

"There are…" she thought it out and settled on "things. All around us."

He nodded carefully. Opening his mind to get a reading of the creatures who watched them in darkness, Vale heard whispers in the shadowland, in a tongue he'd never heard.

The Isle had adopted one common tongue long before he'd been born, but still, the ancients recalled the words of their ancestors. Vale understood some of them well enough. Various dialects of Latin and Gaelic. The words around them didn't make any sense to him.

"They're talking. Discussing us, presumably."

"What do they say?"

"I don't know."

"The words. Can you repeat them?"

He frowned but did as he was bid, his crude tongue struggling with the strangely beautiful language of the creatures he couldn't see.

To his astonishment, Devi then spoke, her words flowing in the same strange language.

"What are you saying? What speech is this?

She shrugged, replying, "Dragontongue."

"And you so happen to speak Dragontongue."

"I took foreign language as an elective. Your mother approved of that decision; she speaks various languages herself."

Of course, Shea would have encouraged Devi to learn dragontongue, old elvish, and the harsh tongue of mages and orcs, too. Such knowledge befitted a queen. Every day, the fact that Shea intended for Devi to succeed her became more obvious.

"I chose to do it mostly because I wished to work my way through all the books in your mother's collection someday. I can't say I'm an expert, however. I can't translate the words you've told me. And as for what I was saying, I was introducing myself, and telling them that we only wished to rest a few hours here. Do they have any words for us now?"

But the creatures weren't speaking anymore; they were listening, and watching them closely, curiously.

If Devi was right and these were indeed dragons, Vale knew things could go two ways. They'd either be ignored, or killed on sight. He'd heard at least seven distinct voices; there was no way two fae could battle against so many beasts.

Dragons were rare in the Isle, and often hunted. A forsaken land such as the Valley of Doom was an ideal haven for their kind.

"One of them is talking now. Just one. He seems to be addressing us. His words were something like '*arsh kan deyu darfrak dale*,'" Vale repeated. "Can you make sense of it?"

"I think so. I'm by no means fluent, but it's something like 'and what name has this rider.' I guess they want you to introduce yourself too."

Vale nodded. "Tell them I'm Valerius Blackthorn, master of Carvenstone. Tell them we're chased. Tell them we wish to sleep, let our horses drink at the lake downstream, and be on our way."

Devi pouted. "That's a lot of things to say. Very well. *Gayr deen darfrak Valerius*," she started, but her words died on her lips.

Before their bewildered eyes, a dragon appeared out of thin air, right ahead of them.

It was the stuff of legends, a creature seven times larger than their horses, with shining black scales and long red wings. Its eyes were blood and fire. After the beast had revealed himself, others appeared at his flank, none larger, but each just as imposing.

The dragon grunted, growled, and the next instant disappeared again. In his place, there was a female who looked a little like a fae. Taller, perhaps, and certainly more bestial. She had light brown skin and hair of silver, falling in waves around her bust. Her beautiful skin was tattooed and marked with scars.

To think that the female was less imposing than the beast would have been a mistake. They were one.

"No need to butcher any more of our language, Devira, daughter of water and ice. We know your tongue."

Vale had never heard common words sound quite so sensual as it did in her low, sultry timbre.

He noted that the female was glaring at Devi defiantly. Frowning, he wondered why there seemed to be animosity from either side. Devi had stiffened and narrowed her eyes.

The next instant, the dragoness directed her eyes to Valerius. They softened. "And we know of you, Valerius Blackthorn. We know of your deeds in your carven home. Words of Dayus and Tradora have reached our ears."

The names were familiar to him. Dayus was a male loner dragon who'd come to them defeated and broken after his sister had gone rogue and attempted to kill him.

Vale had sent a dozen fae after the female; a violent rogue dragon at their border wasn't a matter he could ignore. But his warriors had returned with the beast alive. She was in pain and mistrusting, but not beyond salvation.

It had been perhaps a hundred years. Tradora was now part of his guard.

"You may pass. You may rest for a day. We do remember our debts. Ours has now been paid."

And after those words, the female and the dozens of dragons around her disappeared.

After a minute of stunned silence, Devi said, "What the fuck was that?"

"Proof that good deeds seldom go unrewarded. Let's go. They've given us a day. I think we can afford to sleep for perhaps six hours."

"Really?" Her eyes widened in delight. But she was soon sighing. "Is that wise? We ought to get to the forest as soon as possible."

"Sleep is a luxury we'll only seldom be able to afford in the days, months, and years to come. We have to seize it whenever we can. We're in a land others fear, protected by fire-breathers. It would be foolish to let the chance pass."

"Why did they let us go free?" she asked. "Tell me. I'll not be satisfied with vague statements about good deeds."

Of course she'd be curious; he'd seen the question coming.

Valerius found himself feeling strange at the notion of opening up that part of him. "Because their kindred were in need, and I did what I could to help," he said. "Look ahead. We're getting close."

While the borders of the valley had been just as dreadful as he remembered them to be, now they were drawing close to the lake, trees had started growing, and they could hear small animals around them. The dragons had been clever, ensuring that their lands still seemed sick to strangers, but soon the sun rose to shine upon a picturesque dale near the mountains of Frey and Vardas. The river of Eral ran from the top of Frey and fell to the lake where he'd meant to stop.

By the time they'd reached it, it had started snowing.

"We'll camp here," he said, opting for a spot under the shade of a deciduous tree. It offered some protection from the snow as well as the sunlight his eyes weren't used to.

Vale dismounted and moved to help Devi.

"I can get down myself," she saw fit to inform him, all the while taking the hand he offered.

"Of course you can, but I see no reason why you should."

She stumbled a little, then walked just as awkwardly as she had when he'd first met her after hurting her foot. Vale stifled his smile.

"A word about my looking as though I'd been thoroughly fucked all night and I'll shave your hair in your sleep," she warned him.

He hadn't thought anything along that line before, though he certainly did now.

"Nonsense. If you'd ridden me rather than your horse, it would have done something about your prickliness. Go, sit. I'll unburden the horses."

He was surprised that she did as she was asked. She truly must have been exhausted.

Devi sat at the foot of the tree. "For the record, I resent you for still having so much energy after an entire night of riding."

Truth be told, he had very little energy. Centuries of peace had done much to destroy his prior endurance. But if his muscles had faded, his will had not.

"This bag has clothes. Use it as a pillow," he said, throwing a leather satchel at her, and another one a few feet away.

Once their load had been removed, he led the horses to the water and spoke to them low. "Rest, drink, and come back to us," he told them in the tongue of fae horse masters, making each of his words a command they wouldn't refuse. Then he returned to the bags and unpacked some food and water. Devi's eyes were already closed. He could tell she wasn't asleep.

"Do you wish to eat?" he asked.

She shook her head. "No. My one wish is to sleep for the next five days without interruption."

He cut two small pieces of bread, some cheese, ham, and took two water skins. Vale wrapped her portion in a piece of cloth and dropped it by her side before sitting next to his bag.

"Drink. And you'll wake hungry."

The female opened her hazel eyes and set them on him, tilting her head curiously. "You're a caretaker," was her remark.

He shrugged. "I'm a lord. Caring is the beginning and end of our duties."

"And yet I've heard that you were nothing but a playboy and a mercurial bully, often cruel to those who displeased you."

Valerius offered no word, lying on the cold ground, his head on his bag.

"Who are you, really, I wonder."

"A dangerous question. And I wonder what you'd make of the answer." The silence stretched before he finally spoke. "I am everything they say. I am the dark prince. I was called that because I tortured and killed without mercy during the war. Then there was peace. I learned to grow a conscience and found ways to atone for my sins in Carvenstone."

"Like helping the dragon kin."

He acquiesced. "Like that. But to the court, I'll forever be that person. They recall my darker days. I make sure to give them a glimpse of what I am still, so they continue to fear me. That's one effective way of ensuring they don't interfere with my affairs. And when I'm king one day, they'll know better than to question my rule."

Devi considered his words in silence for a time. He wondered if she was going to say anything at all. Finally, it came. "Shea is also feared. Yet I wonder if a monarch could endeavor to be loved instead."

"The love some feel for their lords is fleeting. It lasts as long as the king and queen's actions please them. I choose fear, for it is far less whimsical."

"I see." She smiled as she lowered herself to the ground, lying next to him, turning so she faced him. "Well, you'll be sorry to hear that in our short acquaintance, I've not found you very scary."

"That would be because I haven't attempted to frighten you." After reflection, he added, "Much."

And then she had to ask, "Why?"

He could have said many things: that her opinion didn't matter much, that she was his mother's ward.

Instead he opted for the truth. "I don't know. Now, let us sleep. The time we have to remain idle is going to pass us by before we know it."

She closed her eyes obediently. After ten minutes, a sigh escaped her lips and she opened them again, catching him in the act. He'd been looking at her.

"I can't sleep. The ground is hard, the water is noisy, and the wind is making this damn tree move too much."

"Spoiled little princess. Would it be your first night without a roof over your head?"

She glared at him. "Well, you obviously can't sleep either."

"I'm cold," he said. A truth. Only it wasn't why he couldn't sleep.

Truth was, he'd been thinking. Of the war to come, of the days that had passed, of Devin, the soft and apparently friendly king whose arrival in the court of night had started it all. And above all, of Devi, and the schemes his mother had entangled her in. Then, rather than letting those notions weight on his mind, he'd started to look at her.

"If you can prevent yourself from acting like a jerk, there's plenty of room under my cape. My body heat does tend to be higher than most."

He hadn't seen that offer coming. Before he'd found anything to say, she was withdrawing it.

"Never mind. Dumb idea."

"The best idea you may have this night. Come closer."

He inched forward, dragging his pillow-bag along, and when he was close enough, he pulled her forward. Devi parted her cape in the middle and wrapped the long span of fabric around them.

She was right. It was delightfully, impossibly warm next to her, despite the snow. Warm and fragrant, and soft. Before long, his mind was void of troubling thoughts, and he fell into a restful, dreamless sleep.

TWENTY

A LITTLE ELF

She dreamed that morning. An actual joyful dream she could not recall by the time her eyes opened. One thing was sure, it hadn't involved her drowning or lashing out at anything.

Opening her eyes, she found that she'd set her head in the crook of Vale's neck, and that his arm was wrapped around her waist, holding her so very close. And she also found that she was reluctant to move.

He smelled so very good, damn him. She was sure her scent resembled eau de sweat, but Vale's was woodsy, spicy and enticing.

He stirred shortly after she'd awoken.

"Good day," he mumbled, a low whisper that resonated in her mind.

"Good day?" she repeated. "Are we not still running from enemies and clueless as to what is actually occurring around us."

"Indeed. No better cause to wish you a good day, little elf."

Vale pulled back her cape and got up, calling the horses. She sighed. A morning person. Looking at him was enough to make her yawn.

Reluctantly sitting up and then getting to her feet, Devi blushed when an ungodly noise came out of her.

Vale turned sharply. "Was that your stomach?"

"Not a word."

"I don't think mountain lions growl quite so loud.

"Not. A. Word," she repeated, fetching the parcel of food he'd packed for her from the inner pocket of her cape. She devoured the lot in a few bites, then wanted more.

But of course, they had to ration what they had until they were closer to reaching the end of their journey. She sighed, grabbing their bag from the ground and bringing them to the horses.

Valerius was waiting for her with two small sandwiches in his hand. He handed her one and bit into the other.

Devi watched him suspiciously. "Are we eating more than we ought to?"

"We should reach Daryn by nightfall. If the lords of the dark woods don't opt for killing us on sight, they'll feed us."

She happily finished the food, then helped loading the horses. Her limbs were, if possible, heavier than they had been the previous night. She was aching everywhere, but she hid it well.

Or so she thought.

"After a week or two, your body will be used to the exercise," Vale told her. "The first few days are the worst."

She admitted, "I feel so damn useless. I'm stronger than that."

"You're extremely strong, that much is obvious. But riding at this speed would be taxing to any novice."

"Am I delaying you?" she asked.

He shrugged. "Perhaps. By no more than an hour or two."

Devi opened her mouth.

"If you're about to suggest we part ways, you may as well stop talking now. It was my mother's wish that we should travel together, and so we shall."

That shut her up.

They rode for two hours before arriving at the end of the Valley of Doom. Again there was a wasteland for a few miles, and then they were back on the road they'd left behind, a good ten miles closer to the Graywoods.

Devi had relaxed now that their destination was in view. They were very close to the borders now.

Then her attention snapped to the east and she frowned, wondering why her body and mind were telling her to stay on alert when her eyes couldn't see more than a flock of birds passing by.

"Devira, bows."

Valerius slowed his horse and had his weapon in hand, aiming toward the approaching animals.

She grabbed hers and aimed as well. As they got nearer, her eyes took in their formidable size. The birds might have been as large as her horse, and their form wasn't birdlike at all. They had long tails, hirsute at the ends, sharp-clawed paws, and the body of a feline.

"Griffins," she said in awe and wonder.

So, what now?

The griffins were friends to those who knew their secrets, and redoubtable enemies to the rest of the world. There was no way of knowing which clan they were facing yet.

"With or against us?"

"I don't know."

Fuck. If they waited until they were upon them, it would be too late; they had very little chance against the half-dozen beasts. If they shot now, the beasts would certainly be their enemies, even if they hadn't meant to be at first. Could they risk it?

"If we can't shoot, we can't stay here. The forest is seven miles away."

Would they make it before the griffins got to them?

"You're the one with a crown. Your call."

Vale hesitated half a second before retracting his bow. "Let's go. As fast as you can, Devira."

On that note, Midnight shot out like an arrow, so fast he and his rider were far ahead within an instant, showing them all just why he was worth dozens of his peers. So she *had* really slowed him down.

"About that deal of ours? Catch up with him and you can get as much sugar as you want, got it?"

Alarik tried, at least, hurrying at her urging. Getting the healing charm Beck had entrusted her with out of the pouch at her belt, she helped her steed along using healing magic, making his aches and tiredness fade as he rode. She wished she'd remembered the object sooner; she might have used it on her poor limbs.

Despite the help, Alarik wasn't fast enough. The griffins neared and charged at her, claws extended, crying high.

Vale, already in the shades of the woods, shot at the beasts. Some of his arrows did hit their marks, but none were lethal, only serving to enrage them. In any other circumstance, she might have relished in the fact that she'd finally found something the dark prince didn't excel at. Better yet, something *she* was quite good at.

"Just in case you haven't noticed," she yelled to the prince, lifting her bow, "they definitely aren't friendly."

Devi aimed and released an arrow that hit the closest beast in the right eye socket. She frowned. She'd aimed for the left one. Her aim was off because of the motion. Hitting a moving target was one thing; hitting one while moving herself, in an unstable way as her horse galloped, was considerably harder.

They'd aimed for her because they were too wise to go close to the woods. She had two choices: reach the borders of the Graywoods, which meant going faster, something she wasn't capable of, or she had to keep those beasts at bay.

"Here goes nothing," she muttered before leaping up to her feet, standing balanced on the saddle. This was better. Her knees could move with the dyrmount, granting him some stability.

"You remember our deal, Alarik. Don't let me fall."

And then she pulled an arrow, aimed, and released it. The weapon hit the closest griffin right in the heart and the graceful creature fell. Its peers' eyes landed on him, and silence followed. As one, they redirected their eyes on her, and with a frightful cry, they rushed her.

She didn't even think, her arms repeating the same action five times at high speed. The whole thing took perhaps one minute; four of the arrows killed their marks on contact. The fifth lodged itself in one of the creature's wings as it veered just in time to dodge it.

Devi swore under her breath, pulling another arrow out of her quiver. She was too late; the cruel, sharp talons of the griffin hooked on her shoulder, lacerating the cloth of her cloak and some of her shoulder with it, as the other four griffins hit the ground.

At least he didn't manage to knock her off her horse.

"Fuck!" she yelled, attempting to pull the sword at her side.

The damn bird was smart, though; its talons still digging in, he used his pointed beak to hit her, again and again, aiming for her ribs, and then her neck. Its hinged legs were just as vicious, their clawed paws scratched at her viciously, however much she pushed against it. If the beast had been hooked to her the other way around, it would probably have gone for the heart. She had to get rid of it before it found a way to get to rip something essential from her body.

Over the brouhaha of the screeching bird, Devi could hear hooves approaching; Vale was coming to the rescue, of course. Dammit. He'd never let her live it down.

Devi stopped fumbling with her belt, or pointlessly attempting to keep the creature at bay. Instead, she focused, concentrating, calming down. She forced herself to imagine a peaceful room, bare and white. A room where she was in control. A second later, she opened her eyes. One of her hands reached out.

One little taste. One instant. One simple, short second, and then, she'd rein it in again.

A smile curved at the corner of her mouth as she let go, for the first time in decades. A strand of silver-white and blue energy flew out of her hand and hit the griffin.

She immediately closed the lid back on herself, caging her own power in, as the beautiful creature froze in motion.

It fell and broke into a thousand shimmery shards, like an incredibly realistic and delicate ice statue.

A meter away, his sword in hand, Vale was staring at her, eyes wide.

Devi resumed a seated position. She hesitated briefly before turning her horse away from the border of the forest and heading toward the griffins' corpses.

No sense in wasting perfectly good arrows.

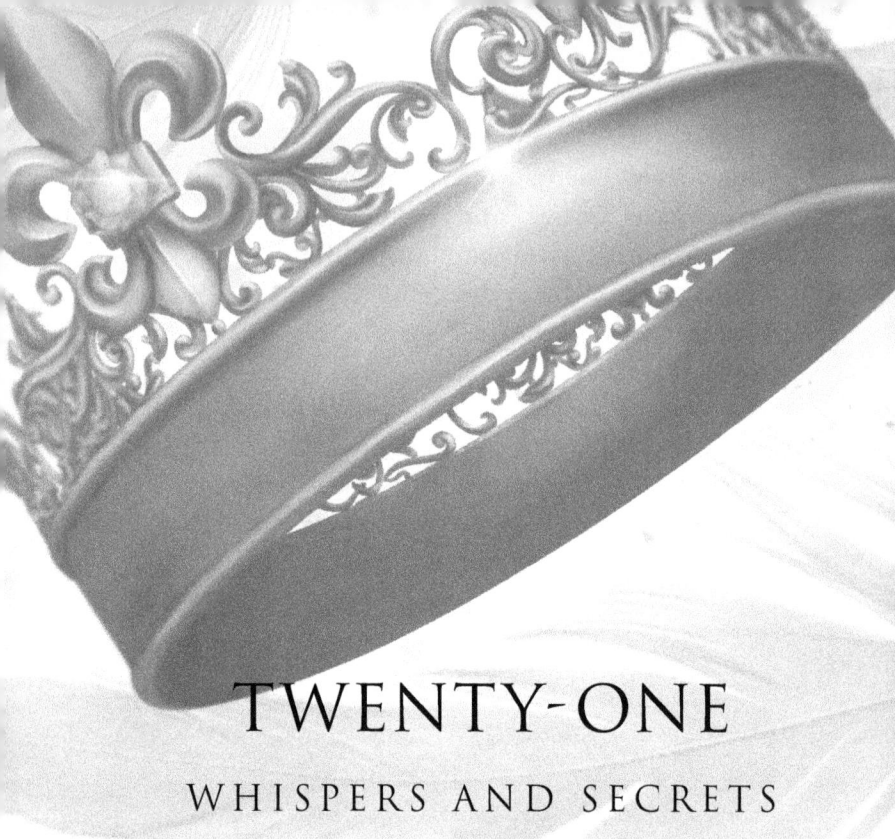

TWENTY-ONE
WHISPERS AND SECRETS

Vale felt strange. He had the instant his horse entered the woods. As if there were things observing him now, watching him closely. Dangerous things he couldn't smell, hear, or see around him.

A part of him wanted to tell Devi to stay out of the shadows of Graywoods, but it was hardly safer out there.

"You just shot six moving targets while racing at full speed on a galloping horse," he stated when the female joined him, spelling it out just in case she'd failed to notice.

Devi just shrugged. "Not my fault if you tend to shoot first, aim later."

He had to let her win this round, because she wasn't wrong, and mostly because he didn't feel comfortable talking in the still, silent woods.

There was room enough for the horses to go, but they needed to advance one by one. He took the lead, watching to the left and right, and opening his mind up to scan everything around him.

Nothing. Nothing but the sound of the dyrmounts' steps on the mossy ground and the wind blowing gently through the thick fog of twisted branches above their heads.

"Something is blocking me," he said.

"Yep."

"I feel like there's a cocoon around me, and I can't hear a thing. Not even a thought."

A time or two in his youth, when striving to shut out the thoughts all around him got tiring, he had wished that his power was taken away from him, if only for a moment, so he could rest. Careful what you wish for, they said. He'd long ago learned to purposefully stop hearing thoughts, but now he was trying, and not a whisper came to him from anything but the female trotting behind him. His old wish had been belatedly granted, and he'd never been so helpless.

Devi wasn't as anxious as he, but now that he was paying attention to the energy around him, he could tell something was making her uncomfortable. Offering words of comfort, or at least distracting her with some teasing, was tempting, but he had to keep his focus on this strange place that made no sense.

"Valerius?" Devi called from behind.

"Hmm?"

"There are twelve arrows pointed at you, and if you go much farther, they'll probably shoot. Unfortunately, these guys will aim better than you."

He didn't ask how she knew this. He'd almost forgotten for a minute that Devi had a parent from these parts of the world. It might prove useful.

Vale removed the hood of his cape and called out loud, "I'm Valerius Blackthorn, heir to one of the fae realms. I request an audience with your king in the north, Elden of Wyhmur."

There was nothing but silence. "Did that work?" he asked Devi, keeping his voice low.

"Can't tell yet. They're whispering, talking amongst themselves."

He had to admit to feeling a little irked, as he heard no whispers at all.

"How come I can't hear a thing?"

"You can. You just don't know it for what it is."

Vale frowned and listened again. There was nothing except the wind.

He frowned. Yes, he heard wind, and yet the leaves around him didn't move at all.

"Ah. Neat trick. Air magic?"

"It's common among elves. And useful, particularly against unseelie."

He didn't question that; some seelie fae might be blessed with an air affinity, but every elemental mage of the Unseelie Court was an earth user, to his knowledge.

Sensing a stronger wind, he asked, "What now?"

"Now they're asking that I present myself."

She sighed before also removing her hood.

The forest stilled suddenly—no more whisper, no more wind. No one in the vicinity was paying him any mind, entirely focused on Devi.

"Look, I'm not supposed to be here, but we've had a long night and a longer day yet. We really, really could use a little break. Let us pass. No drama. We'll head to Daryn, take the portal to Wyhmur, he'll say his piece to Elden, and I'll be out of the Graywoods in no time, I promise."

Each of her words was a plea. Devi had never sounded more nervous. Since they'd met, he'd seen a strong female who didn't care about any shit like rank, status, or caste. He'd treated her like just another piece of ass for all of two seconds, and she hadn't hesitated one instant before showing him what she was made of.

Seeing her like this was very unpleasant. Her sudden lack of self-confidence, self-worth, and her doubt pissed him the hell off.

The elves didn't answer with more whispers in the mists. No, twelve shadows appeared from either side of the road, walking slowly, like the predators they were.

Vale had seen elves of the Graywoods in his younger days, during the war and right after, when they'd gathered to swear to uphold to their peace treaties. They'd struck him as strange, other, but he would have been hard-pressed to explain how, because like high fae, they were tall and long-eared with handsome features. It was perhaps that they were colder, seemed older, and more versed in the arts of killing. The few elves who lived in Carvenstone were softer, more fae-like.

These dozen were all Graywoods, all slow, purposeful movements and wild demeanors.

Three came from their right flank and another three from the left. The elves wore shining armor entirely made of silver, which shimmered in the dim light now that they'd pulled their dark capes over their shoulders. Their bows were hooked on their backs, and their swords were in their sheaths, until they pulled them all out as one.

Vale had his hand on his own blade, eyes narrowed. Then he watched them all thrust their swords deep in the ground and kneel, heads bent.

"Your Highness," an elf said, lifting his head first. "We did not expect to see you here. Pardon our impudence."

Such words were generally addressed to him, but it was Devi they were paying their respect to.

Devi Star....

A humorless chuckle escaped him. "Devi Star Rivers," he said out loud, turning to her with one brow crooked. "Were you planning to tell me you're the daughter of Elden Star, king of all elves, and lord of Elvendale, before or after we'd reached the winter court?"

She was entirely unapologetic. "Well, you didn't exactly ask." To the elf, she said, "I wouldn't be here if I had a choice. The court of night was attacked, and the queen told me to head to Daryn. May we go forth?"

She was visibly relieved when the elf replied that they could.

"Of course. And with your permission, I will escort you through the path so you may not be obstructed again."

The elf ordered his companions to remain at their post and started to walk with them, holding on to Alarik's reins.

"Thanks. Appreciated," Devi said, sweet and charming. "What am I to call you?"

Flirting again. She'd done that with Kallan too; that made two males in as many nights.

Vale had a lot to think about right now. A war, everything his mother had told him the previous night, the fact that he was the son of some sort of god, Kallan potentially pursued in his place, everyone in Carvenstone in danger. But nothing seemed quite as important as the fact that he'd realized she'd never flirted with him. Insulted him? Certainly. Held on to him while he was kissing the fuck out of her? Definitely. But she'd never softened her voice, played with her hair, or smiled that way with him.

"Gallal, my lady," the elf replied.

"Well, Gallal, lead the way."

Yes, please, Gallal, Vale mentally echoed. *Lead the way and stop staring at her like you want a piece.*

Not that he could blame the elf for that. Vale shook his head in disbelief at his own surge of anger, his urge to punch the other male. It wasn't normal. Not in their world.

His own mother shared her bed with a few males. So did most high fae females. Evolution had shaped their society that way. Jealousy wasn't in his DNA. It wasn't natural.

And yet here he was. It had to be sorcery. He liked this theory, clung to it, ignoring the voice that told him it was a lie.

The ride through the woods was slow and punctuated with laughter and more flirting from the two behind him. He did his best to ignore it and failed, listening to every word.

"No, I promise you, the people will rejoice at seeing you safe."

"I doubt that."

"Your father gave us all clear orders from the day you left. We are to give you whatever aid you require of us."

"Wait," Vale interrupted, "didn't you say you grew up in the north? Near Carvenstone? And yet I seem to understand from this blabbering that you lived in the Graywoods."

"I did, on both accounts," Devi replied. "My father took me to the winter court after my mother passed away. I stayed a year. But your mother and mine had arranged for me to go to court, so when I was of age, she called me."

He wasn't buying the tight, neat story. He would have pushed the issue if it weren't for Gallal the Flirt. Whatever secret she had wasn't for the ears of strangers.

Then he recalled that he'd met her not a week ago. Strangers was exactly what they were.

Irritated, Vale forced his mind to focus elsewhere—thinking of the war beat this. He was just wondering why his mother would have sent him here of all places when he caught a swift, unexpected change in the air.

"Devi, watch out!"

The soldiers in red and gold were on them within seconds, circling them.

Once, not so long ago, he would have taken them for high fae. Now he knew them for what they were. Corantians.

Devi drew her bow while Vale and Gallal both pulled their swords. Each passing instant seemed to last an eternity as the eleven scions approached.

The shortest one planted the sword in his hand deep in the ground, before removing his helmet. The creature truly resembled a fae in every way, but he also seemed brighter, as though an inner light illuminated him from within.

"I don't suppose you remember me, Valerius Blackthorn." The face was familiar; he'd seen it in Corantius. He couldn't recall if he'd ever been told whose name belonged to it. "I was captain of the guard for you father, and his father before him. Derveran Jernel. Surrender and you have my word that your companions will be spared. I shall swear to it."

Vale considered it for half a second, but an arrow flew, aimed right between the scion's eyes. Looked like Devi was answering for him now. Oh well.

Derveran's hand moved at an impossible speed, and caught it mid-flight, just as the tip of the arrowhead touched his skin.

The scion smiled maliciously, tilting his head and looking right to Devi.

"My, aren't you delicious. Pray, bastard, do resist. I certainly would love a reason to play with your whore."

Alright, that was enough of that. Vale drew the small knife at his belt and tossed it, accompanying the movement with a slight compulsion. The scion hesitated for one short instant, just a second. Seeing the blade approaching, the scion moved, but not fast enough this time: the knife drew a line of dark blue blood on his neck.

"You'll find no easy target here," Vale warned. Then, because he couldn't lie, he had to add, "except him, maybe," gesturing to Gallal.

"I guess we'll find out."

The eleven scions charged at once. Gallal had the sense to jump on the back of Devi's dyrmount.

"Go!" he yelled, and the two steeds took off.

The mounts barely gave them an advantage: the scions were that fast. One of Vale's hands lifted toward those at his left, farthest from him, and closest to Devi, as the other one lifted his sword to counter the blows coming his way.

Three of the scions slowed down and Devi took the opportunity to shoot at them, making one stumble, and the others take cover. Then she yelled, "Stop this!" Damn female. "Stop the fucking gallantry, I can take care of myself, and you need to stay alive."

She wasn't wrong.

Facing ahead, Vale urged Midnight forward with soft words. It looked as if their pursuers were finally losing some ground. Vale was just starting to breathe a little easier when a cloud of red and gold mist appeared right before them.

Dervan.

Devi's dyrmount spooked, and she was thrown off her horse. Vale leaped from his own, landing in a crouch beside her the next instant. He held two of his fingers to her throat and breathed out in relief. She had a pulse, but remained unmoving.

The flirty elf had his bow in hand and shot at the soldiers, each of his arrows hitting a mark. He was good. Not good enough. The enemies were too swift, too agile and lethal.

Still kneeling next to Devi, Valerius pulled his blade and waited, eyes closed, concentrating.

"A little help may not go amiss here!" Gallal yelled.

"In a moment," Vale replied tightly while repeating familiar words in his mind, carefully removing every one of his shields.

Gallal didn't seem to like his answer. "You'd let me fight alone against a dozen!" he yelled in outrage. "You faithless son of a—"

"I wouldn't go there if I were you."

No one was insulting his mother.

At a distance, Gallal had a slight advantage with his bow, but the enemies were close now. A red and gold soldier launched at the elf, who pulled his weapon. He wasn't half bad with a blade, but soon three other Corantians were upon him.

Then Vale regretfully pulled his hand from Devi's throat. Her heartbeat was strong; she'd only hurt her head.

It struck him as odd that he cared. This wasn't Vale. It was the dark prince. Vale would have expected him to abandon the female's side without a second thought. But the prince abhorrent having to leave her.

He got up, violet eyes set on those who'd hurt her. The next instant, he lifted one hand and all scions froze, hands around their necks, attempting to unhook the invisible hands crushing their throat. But there was nothing there, nothing they could fight against. His fist tightened, and he smiled as they were close to choking. The scions gagged, desperate to breathe. Another second of this and they'd fall.

The dark prince dropped his hand, releasing them from his hold. It was too easy a death. Too neat. Too quick. They'd hurt Devi Star Rivers. For that offense, they would bleed.

The prince pulled his sword and moved faster than Vale could. His blows broke armor, slashing his enemies' flesh at the groin, the arm, the neck. All eleven wounds he inflicted were fatal, but the scions would take a while to bleed out.

Scions were more powerful than ten fae, his mother had said, and the reason why he couldn't contradict her was because he'd never been able to explain to himself how he could move the way he did, with the power of a monster.

"Get on your knees, bastard."

Vale turned slowly.

He hadn't felt this one slip by.

The creature had come from behind and had his arrow directly aimed at Devi.

"On your knees or your whore dies."

"Whore?" the dark prince asked, his voice so much like Vale now, tinted with humor and delight. "I'm going to make this slow and painful. I'm going to enjoy this."

"On your fucking—"

"Hold that thought."

Vale's hand reached forward again, but instead of choking, his enemy screamed as his flesh burned like someone had thrown acid at his flesh.

"I'm certain you'll wish to know that this trick only works on the weak-minded. It means you're a worthless piece of shit."

The lowlife, who'd dropped his bow and started begging now, should be thankful the dark prince had other concerns. After enjoying his torment for a few instants, Vale twisted his wrist and broke the soldier's neck.

His little games hadn't been without cost. His energy had taken a hit, he could feel it. If another volley of enemies fell on them now, he'd be close to defenseless.

"What was that?" Gallal questioned, looking stunned.

The dark prince ignored him and moved back to Devi, pushing her hair away from her face. Her forehead was cut, bleeding.

Bleeding blue.

He added it to the million questions he was going to ask her someday and gathered her in his arms.

"Is she all right?" Gallal stood over them, concern in his eyes.

"She hit her head and got knocked out." Her horse had spooked, but Midnight remained where Vale had left him. He took her to the horse and started walking next to it. "Lead the way. The fastest way. There will be others on our trail."

And this time, he wouldn't have the strength to destroy them with his mind.

As they walked in silence, Vale realized that he hadn't sealed the darker part of himself inside him. He'd not said the words. And yet he was in control now; he hadn't attacked Gallal, and his every movement toward Devi had been careful, almost tender.

He considered reciting the spells just to be safe, so he didn't hurt anyone. But something told him that he would need his baser self again before it was over.

Long ago, in another time, a friend had told him that he would have to reconcile himself with who he was—what he was—for Valerius Blackthorn would never be whole without the dark prince. At the time, he hadn't believed it possible. But he and the prince were in agreement about something, at least. As he watched Devi, still unconscious, both of them had one thought in mind. They'd keep her safe.

Gallal led him in silence until they'd reached a glade. There was a tall polished and sculpted stone carved amidst a high tree.

Vale was surprised to see nothing around it, not a guard or a building.

"Is this your portal?"

He'd believed it to be in the middle of the city of Daryn, not standing alone in the woods.

"Indeed. And it is better protected than you may think. Even in Daryn, not all elves have seen the Tree of Worlds. Those who do not know the way will never find it. They roam in the woods forevermore." The elf gestured him forward. "After you."

Vale frowned. "I've not used a portal before."

"And you shall not again. Walk forward if you would. You'll be led to the winter court. You may trust that I shall send our lady to safety."

Vale didn't know what to make of Gallal, but that, he could believe at least.

"I thank you for your help. If I may return it, one day, I will."

The elf inclined his head in farewell as Vale strode toward the stone, one step after the next, until he'd reached it. Then he walked forward again. The horses didn't like it much, but they did trot next to him.

For an instant, he felt weightless as a strange light engulfed him. Then a heavy air cooled his face, cooler than the snowy wood he'd just left. When he opened his eyes, he stood at the foot of a tall, proud white hill. Unmeltable, delicate ice sculptures had been carved there, and around them were steps cut into the stone of the hill, leading up to a city surrounded by clouds. Each monument was made in shining black stone.

He'd finally arrived at Elvendale, the winter court.

"Master."

The traitor turned to the demigod of lesser blood who'd led the attack.

"Asra has fallen. We have the seelie king in our custody, along with all his advisors. However, we've failed to secure Valerius Blackthorn."

Rage twisted his heart when he heard the name. It had always been disgusting to his ear, but now he truly hated the unworthy bastard.

"We randomly bumped into each other and, well, bumping a little more into each other seemed like a great idea at the time," Devi had said, smiling at him like she was happy about lying with that filth.

Rook Stormhale would gut him, cut him up piece by piece for touching what belonged to him.

"You will bring him to me, Dervan."

Dervan frowned. "Lady Kelina said we needed him dead."

Rook tilted his head. "Are you questioning me?"

Dervan attempted to reply, but before a word came out of his throat, he bent in two, screaming at the top of his lungs, begging for the torture to stop.

The overking might have forsaken his bastards, but he'd been generous in sharing his lethal gifts.

His hunger for pain made Rook consider ending the fool at his feet, but he recalled that Dervan was a useful tool in his arsenal. Regretfully, he let go.

The large soldier got to his feet. "I'll give the order, my prince."

Rook directed his attention elsewhere, already bored. Once he'd ensured his work was done in the city of night, he extended his wings and flew at full speed. Reaching Corantius took him an hour. A dragon might have been twice as slow.

He could have taken the time to gaze at the lands he passed, but they were of no interest to him. Besides, he'd done that commute every dawn for half a decade now.

Rook had spent his nights in Asra, when the court of night was awake, and his days in the court of crystal. He slept perhaps once a week. It was enough, for one of his kind.

"Hello, brother." He hated when she called him that, and she knew it. "Pleasant surprise. I didn't expect you until dawn."

Kelina greeted him at her balcony, wearing nothing but a bedsheet she held at her breast.

He smirked. "Asra fell in less than two hours."

The advisor's daughter laughed. "I knew they were weak, but that's pathetic. But this is good news. You can keep me warm tonight."

She turned on her heels and let go of the bedsheet.

"You know how screwed up you are? Calling me your brother and asking me to fuck you within ten minutes."

The female looked over her shoulder and winked. "What should I call you, then? Pathetic little orphan my father took pity on? Bastard of the overking, thrown out to the wolves before you were even born?" she laughed. "I know. My favorite one: Prince of Worms."

She knew what people got for calling him that. She wanted it. She wanted his rage and his pain and his suffering. He gave her just that, throwing her at the closest wall, spreading her legs, and fucking her like the hateful whore she was until they both came.

Kelina was him. She had his guts, his balls, his disgust, his violence, and powers just as formidable as his. He wished he could love her. She might have been a decent queen to the Isle.

But just as he hated himself, Rook hated her with all his dark heart. She was poison. She'd let him destroy the Isle once she was queen.

Rook had seen what it was to grow up with nothing in this accursed land. He'd crawled his way out, even when he had nothing to eat but worms.

This was why he had another queen in mind.

A beautiful creature of light with golden wings, who'd help him save the world once it was his. He'd be the pillar of strength and darkness. She would be the magnanimous light to counter it.

Just as soon as he had the reins of the entire continent in his iron fist.

TWENTY-TWO
LORDS AND THRONES

She woke up pissed, and with a serious headache, which didn't help matters. It was rare that her kind got any sickness or headaches at all, so when it occurred, it sucked.

Feeling Vale's distinctive presence next to her before she opened her eyes, she kept them closed and groaned.

"Tell me I did not just faint like a stupid damsel."

"All right," Vale agreed, "I won't say it."

She opened one eye to know where her target was and closed it again before slapping his shoulder. "Dick. What happened? How's Alarik? And Gallal?"

"So your priority order is the horse first, then the irritating elf poser. Interesting."

That wasn't an answer. With difficulty, she sat up and finally opened her eyes.

She knew this room. She was familiar with the high stone walls held up by columns, the glassless opening leading to her balcony, and the carved sculptures around the curved doors. The bed was still perfect, firm like she liked, with soft covers of silk.

"The horse is fine." As an afterthought, he added, "And so is the poser. I'm okay too, by the way."

She rolled her eyes. "I can see that." She recalled the last second before Alarik spooked. They'd been surrounded. "We're in the winter court," she realized. She was in the very room she'd occupied in her father's castle some thirteen years ago. "How did we get away? Did we get help?"

Vale smiled. "Aren't you cute, actually believing I need help against a few soldiers. But yes, we are indeed in your father's court."

She frowned. There had been more than a few, and they were more than foot soldiers too. Devi didn't still speak in terms of monsters and dragons. She knew what to call them now. She knew what they were. Shea had taught her many things about the world during their lessons.

"Vale, the Corantians are different. You have to be careful with them."

"Different. What could you possibly mean? Perhaps they can make use of four elements and shoot ridiculously accurately in action. Perhaps they also have blue blood. Wait, that reminds me of someone else." He watched her pointedly as she bit her lower lip. She was not supposed to talk of the scions; Shea had forbidden it.

Devi chuckled. "I'm not one of them."

"I know. You're a seelie unseelie of the elven realm. Everything but them. They come from Corantius. You have the power of every consequential creature of this realm, except theirs."

Her nails were fascinating right now.

"You don't want to talk, so here's what I know. Some sort of gods came to us, settled in the court of crystal, modified our kind and had babies with us. Those babies are powerful and power hungry. They've decided to wage war on the rest of us. And only a few of us are strong enough to fight back. So my mother, in her infinite wisdom, sent us to the relative safety of the elven realm, when she hopes we can find help."

Her gaze was now fixed on his.

Vale pulled a small knife out of his coat and sliced a small cut in the palm of his hand before holding it up.

His blood was dark blue, just like hers.

"It is you and me now. My mother is far to the west. In a few hours, I am to speak to your father, known to be a wise king of a strong nation. I am going in with little knowledge of what's going on. Whatever you know, now's the time to share it."

She'd long ago promised Shea that their lessons were private and confidential. Opening her mouth without her say-so went against everything she was. And yet she did so, feeling like she could trust him.

"Scions. They're called scions. The children of the gods and their descendants. Shea is a scion, so you're one too. And I'm also one, from my mother's side, as well as my father's."

Vale nodded, encouraging her to continue. Nothing she said seemed to be news to him.

"But they... did something to me. Before I was even born. Gave me more power. Only the first generations have blue blood. The direct daughters and sons of gods. I'm not one of them. I have as much power as one though, and my blood is as blue as theirs. Did they do the same to you?"

Valerius shook his head. "No, I was made the old-fashioned way. Daddy dearest's blood colors my veins. I'm the son of the overking. Shea was so good to inform me that he was a divinity just a few night ago."

"Wait, you're the son of the *overking?*" she repeated.

Vale tilted his head. "I'm surprised you're impressed."

"I'm not. It just explains a lot." She frowned. "The overking wanted peace. As it's unlikely that he would have just up and changed his mind, we have to assume that someone else is in charge of Corantius now. That would be someone directly in line for the throne."

"My half-brother, Aurelius." Vale inclined his head, following her reasoning.

"Yeah, well, he might have the power to move the armies, but he doesn't have the throne. He can't."

She saw she'd lost him there.

"Shea and I have spent hours together. Every other night, she'd summon me. We trained sometimes, and she tried to help me control my powers too, but most of the time she gave me history lessons. She said these were tales meant to be told from mother to daughter and only shared with your kin. That writing them was forbidden, but that I had to know. As my mother wasn't here to tell me, she'd taken on the task. I never knew why. Now I do. She was preparing me for this. For generations, our families were preparing us for this. In case the gods decided to wipe us out. So we'd know and we'd be able to fight back. Now we know we have a way to win."

"Well, too bad she didn't see the necessity of telling me any of this. Go on. What's your idea?"

"It's quite simple. We make you overking."

Valerius looked at her for a beat and then started to laugh. "Sorry, I believed you were serious for a second."

"But I am. Look, your mother told me about the throne of the court of crystal. It's not just a fancy chair, it's a piece of technology that controls the walls around their city, and the wall around the entire continent. It can also control the ship their race used to get on our planet in the first place. It *is* power."

"Sounds…" he thought it out before settling on "fascinating. And yet I still fail to see how or why the hell I'd become overking."

"Valerius, the throne will not choose the next leader until all of those who have a claim present themselves in front of it. That's why they attacked the city, why they came after you. You have a claim to the throne, just like Aurelius. And he'd kill you rather than risking that the throne may choose you."

The dark prince seemed lost in thought. Finally, he asked, "You're saying it's a fifty-fifty chance. It might pick Aurelius, right?"

"Would you pick someone who presumably assassinated his predecessor and burned down a city all in one night? The throne chose Orin the Peaceful. It won't empower a lunatic. And as for why would you become overking? Because we need you to be. Because the war that just started ends with your death or your coronation."

His attention snapped to her, looking at her too sharply. "My mother said that. Those exact same words."

Devi shrugged. "Well, she wasn't wrong."

Vale remained there, seated on her bed and watching her, making her feel a little self-conscious.

"What, do I have something on my—"

She didn't finish because his lips fell on her mouth, capturing it in a hot, passionate kiss that neither of them could chalk up pretence. She hooked her hand behind his neck and pulled him closer.

Let the world burn for another moment. She deserved this, and so did he.

End of Song of Night

PART TWO
SONG OF WINTER

PROLOGUE

Elden often mused at the turn of events.
Shea Blackthorn had come to see him some hundred years ago to warn there would be war against Corantius one day. The only reason there was peace at all right now was because Orin, ruler of the Court of Crystal, demanded it.

Shea believed that when the northern kingdom would unleash its wrath against the rest of the Isle, the seelie, unseelie and elven realm would fall. Elden hadn't doubted that fact, but unlike her, he looked upon his demise with a degree of indifference and resignation. He'd lived long enough. Most of his people were also immortals; they'd seen plenty of winters rise and fall. It was all meant to end one day.

"We can fight this."

"A handful of gods. A hundred thousand demi-gods. A million high fae. That's how many enemies we will face when this peace comes to an end. We are doomed," Elden stated.

"A handful gods," Shea repeated. "Let us not pretend that anyone else matters. Seven gods could raze this continent and rule over its ruins."

Another fact. "I fail to see your point. The gods of Corantius will march against us when their overking orders them to."

"The gods of Corantius may. I say we forge gods of our own."

Her scheming was madness, and for a time, he bore her no mind. Then one day, as he walked down the paths to the lakes, Elden spotted a noisy horde of younglings playing in the early autumn snow. Two dozen children of a tender age, laughing innocently.

Did he truly have a choice?

Years after she'd proposed an alliance, he sent his raven to the Court of Night.

"I will partake in your schemes, so long as it causes no harm to my court."

Her reply was swift.

By then, Shea had almost everything she needed to execute her plan. She had enlisted an Ashtar, master of fire, a Winford, lord of air, and the last of Rivers, commander of water and ice. Shea possessed the powers of the earth. The four females would channel their powers to bless one unborn child.

For all their magic, to make a child, they still required a male of some kind. Shea could have called upon anyone, but she'd solicited Elden's aid.

"Loxy will bear the child so that it will have seelie blood. I will take it in and raise it in my court. If you were to father it, the child's very existence would be reason enough for the kingdoms to unite and fight under one flag."

Idealistic nonsense. But what would it cost him? A few nights with one of the most enticing females in the Isle wasn't his idea of an ordeal. He agreed. For three years, Loxy was blessed by the other three females every full moon, and she shared Elden's bed until she was with child.

And here they were now.

Elden Star had seen enough seasons to have learned the value of patience. He'd long ago come to the conclusion that events had a tendency to occur exactly how, and when, they ought to.

That said, the torturous wait had to stop if he was to retain his senses.

He had never desired to father a child. Not once, in five thousand years, had he wished for it. But the cunning, conniving young fae who'd talked him into this nonsense had been persuasive.

Waiting in front of the closed doors and listening to every gut-clenching scream coming from the room where he wasn't welcome, Elden suddenly contemplated the frailty of his sanity. The child was coming.

His child.

Elden looked upon the offending red door before resuming his restless pacing in the corridor. Shea smiled mockingly. It was all her fault. One word from her and he'd happily declare war on the unseelie realm.

Loxy's screaming stopped but for an instant, and then he heard it—a high-pitched cry.

"That's a girl," said the healer from inside the room.

A girl. He had a little girl. A live one with a healthy set of lungs.

Elden resolutely strode to the door. To hell with the propriety, he was going in.

The door opened just as he reached for the handle, and a smiling maiden greeted him with a white linen bundle in her arms.

His daughter.

He looked to the babe and then up to her mother. He frowned. Why was she still writhing so?

"There is another," said a nurse before lifting the precious parcel up to him.

His eyes widened. Was he supposed to hold it?

"Go on. She won't break. And my hands are needed again."

The king of the Wymur and lord of the elves wrapped his arms around his daughter. A child with hair of fire and eyes of grass, like her mother.

"Kira," he said, a smile playing on his lips.

"Hell if you're naming the babes!" Loxy shouted as the nurse rushed back in. "I'm doing all the work. Get out of here, you bastard! You did this to me!"

The nurse shut the door as Loxy threw a pillow at his face.

By nightfall, there was another child. A child with black hair, almost blue. Not his nor Loxy's coloring. She had his eyes and her mother's face, but she wasn't truly theirs; even then Elden could tell. There was so much magic in her.

Loxy held her close. "Devira," she whispered, tears at the corners of her eyes.

No child should be saddled with such responsibility. No mother should give birth to a child made for war. No father should be told to relinquish one of his newborns. And yet here they were.

Shea was smug in her victory. She had her first weapon.

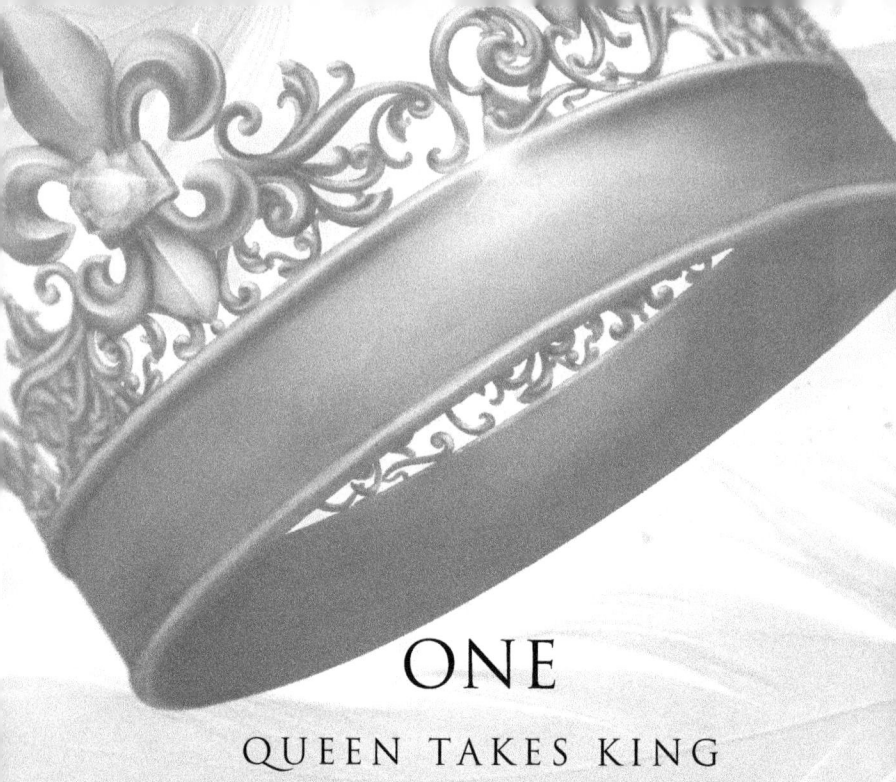

ONE
QUEEN TAKES KING

The common fae hesitated in front of the large green and black tent. It was still strange for a young female of her age and station to enter the quarters of a queen.

"Come in, Jiya."

It had shocked her that Shea Blackthorn knew her name at all the first time she'd said it, and it still seemed surreal now.

Three days ago, at dawn, when hell had fallen on the Court of Night, Jiya had woken to a commotion and found the streets of Asra in an uproar. Jiya rushed to put on pants and grab her weapons of choice, two short swords. By the time she emerged out of her modest apartment on Main Street, the city gates had been taken, most of their defenses pulverized.

She was confused and unsure what to do. Jiya was a protector in training, and as such, her duty was to join the guards in mounting a defense, but she could tell that the Square of Dawn, where the headquarters was located, was burning in the distance.

After a moment, she jumped up the closest wall, propped herself up on a store sign, and leaped onto the roof. She turned toward the castle. The next logical move was to find the head of the protector order, who resided with the queen in Wolven Fort.

Her best friend also lived in the royal keep. If nothing else, she'd find Devi. Devi would know what to do; she always did.

Jiya had been halfway to the brownstone keep when a voice reached her mind. A voice she knew. A voice that had never spoken her name till this day.

"Jiya."

She froze. Was it a trick? Machinations of the hidden enemy? But no enemy of consequence had any reason to pay attention to her, the youngest daughter of the Duniels, an old family of fishermen and traders. Then again, there was no reason for Shea Blackthorn to reach her mind either.

"I have no time to appease your ego, youngling. Follow my orders or don't. Choose."

Jiya dropped to one knee although no one was there to see.

"Good girl. You seem somewhat agile. I have taken the southern gate. Join me."

She turned back and ran across the rooftops to the southern gate as she was told, catching shadows in the smoke down in the streets. She heard screams and cries for help. Many a time, she wanted to climb down and do what she could for the people of Asra, but the first time this impulse arose, she heard the queen's voice again. "Ignore them or die."

And so she ran south.

When she reached the gate, a soldier ushered her to the border of the surrounding woods and gestured for her to remain there before running back to the city to direct another fae who'd just reached the gate.

"I can help," Jiya wanted to say. She was a protector; this was what she was supposed to do. But she realized she could help by remaining exactly where she was.

Others hid in the woods, the old and young, most of them unarmed. She didn't have to butt into the guard's duty to be of assistance.

Jiya unsheathed her swords and started patrolling the woods. That, at least, she could do.

West of the gates, she came to a halt and gasped. From the shadow of the woods, she could see a fight in the distant plains.

There were three dozen unseelie guards fighting four creatures in armor, and at the center of it all, the queen sat on the ground, eyes closed, ignoring all mayhem around her, trusting her knights, protectors, and guards to keep her safe.

Many fell, for the enemies in red and gold were stronger than anyone Jiya had ever seen or heard of, but the three dozen remaining queen's guards kept a circle around Shea and defended her with everything they had. Jiya was frozen in place, watching in horror. Every other minute, another guard was slain. There were only four enemy soldiers, but the highly trained fae of Shea's guard struggled to keep them away from their queen. The enemies' movements were so fast Jiya only saw a blur, and they were powerful enough to bend metal with one stroke.

"What is she doing?" a boy whispered, and Jiya turned to find that some civilians had followed her deeper into the woods.

After a moment of silence, an old common fae with thick, curved antlers replied, "Quite a lot, young'un. Did a voice tell you you'd be safe if you came here? That was our queen reaching those whose minds are strong enough to listen. And if you pay attention to the earth beneath your feet and the whispers of the wind, you'll feel many steps marching from the west and many wings flying from the north. These are the queen's lands, and she is calling on all those who would defend it."

A horn blasted in the distance, and the queen opened her eyes. She rose to her feet just as a large bird of prey descended to hover above her, something shiny flashing in its talons. The bird dropped it, and the queen snatched it in midair.

A sword, too long and too thick for the dainty female, it seemed.

Appearances were deceiving.

Moving with the same preternatural speed as the four males in red and gold but with more agility, she thrust the heavy weapon through the metal breastplate of the first enemy, plunging the blade into his heart. She pulled the sword out, leaped onto the second soldier's shoulders, and shoved her blade through the nape of his neck. The two other males closed in, coming from the front and back. The queen effortlessly lifted the heavy blade, facing one soldier and paying no mind to the other. Her guards rushed to her aid, but Jiya saw the soldier behind Shea draw a throwing star. She jumped out of the woods and ran as fast as her legs could carry her.

Unnecessary.

After beheading the third soldier, the queen lifted her hand toward the last one and tightened her fists. The ground beneath his feet shook, and thick vines rushed out of the earth, winding serpentine around his legs and arms and keeping him firmly in place.

The soldier struggled to break free and winced.

"I wouldn't do that in your place," said Shea conversationally. "The more you move, the faster they'll tighten. They'll break your bones first, and then I suspect they'll detach your left arm from your body. The head usually comes last. You can thank your armor for prolonging your suffering."

The queen turned on her heels to face Jiya.

"It takes great courage to see what scions are capable of yet choose to place yourself in harm's way, Jiya. You will ride with me."

And so here she was, three days after the fall of Asra, with her queen and still alive, unlike so many in the city.

Jiya had never admired Shea more than on the day of the attack. They all heard stories of her great deeds during the War of the Realms, so many centuries ago, but it was one thing to know that the queen was powerful, and yet another to witness it.

Jiya entered the queen's tent to find Shea in her dressing gown, her platinum hair undone. Her hair was usually braided down her back, out of the way; seeing her like this felt strange. The queen looked younger, almost vulnerable.

"Excuse me, Your Grace."

"Do you have news?" Shea prompted, taking a comb and untangling the imaginary knots from her perfect mane.

"We do. An hour ago, we found a male following us. Loralei Night almost killed him, but I recognized him. It's Devin Farel. He's under guard until you decide what to do with him."

The queen nodded, unsurprised. Was she ever surprised?

"Very good. I'm glad you kept the seelie king alive. Lora can be a delight, but she's quick to draw her sword. You've done well."

Jiya blushed at the praise.

"Your orders, Your Grace?"

"Release the poor boy and feed him, too. I'd wager he's ravenous."

Jiya blinked. They'd been attacked right after the seelie's arrival at court.

"He has nothing to do with this mess," the queen continued. "His one sin is having an ass for a father, and I can't very well begrudge him that. Besides, he may be of help. I'll speak to him, of course, but I consider him our guest." She paused. "For now."

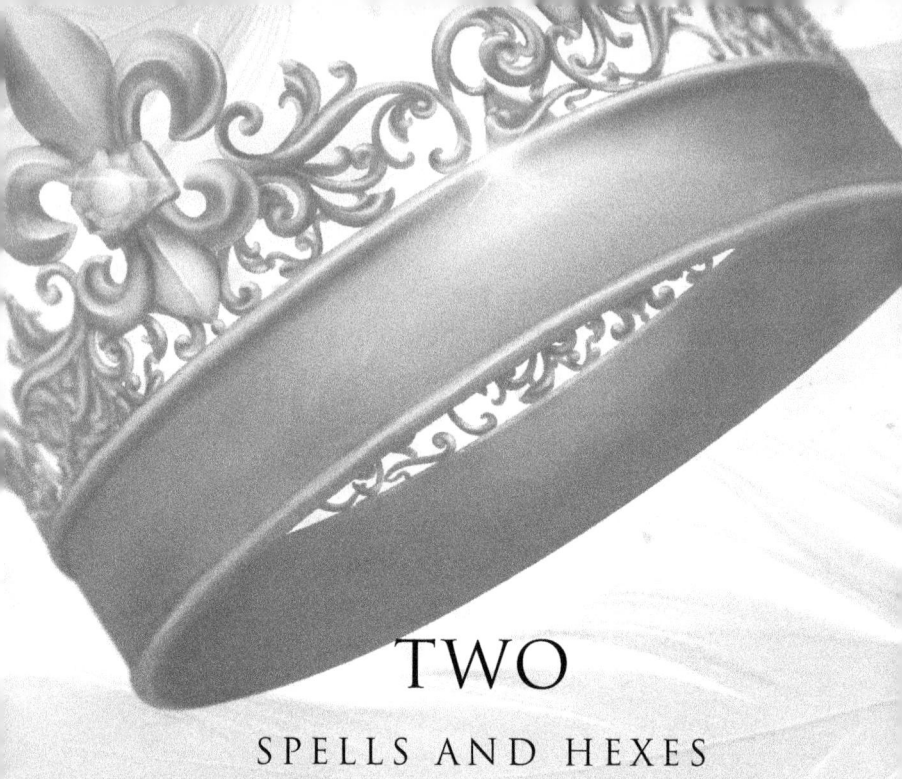

TWO

SPELLS AND HEXES

Just a taste, Valerius told himself. A fleeting touch of Devira Star Rivers's tantalizing lips and then they'd go back to talking politics, machinations, wars, and nonsensical notions such as the absurd idea of his occupying the most powerful position in the Isle, the throne that ruled over all thrones. Ludicrous. She must have hit her head too hard before passing out during the attack they'd just survived.

Him, the dark prince, made king of kings.

Part of him—the part that made people shudder, the part that relished the suffering of others—desired it greatly. But he knew better than to wish this fate upon the world. It was one thing to govern a few thousand souls he cared for in his remote northern home. Calling himself monarch of the rest of the Isle was another thing altogether.

The second his mouth took hers, none of that mattered. He wanted—needed—more. He couldn't have controlled himself if he'd cared to. Vale and the dark prince were again in agreement: their one wish was to keep caressing her delectable, soft skin and savoring each moan, shiver, and wordless gasp. His lips only left her mouth to tease her neck, her collarbone, the curves of her breasts.

Devi held on to his shoulders and ran her fingers through his hair again. That was her thing, apparently. Vale found he liked it just fine, although he couldn't recall the last time he'd let a female do anything so intimate.

Anyone else and he would have pushed away, or taken her hand and shoved it in his pants. Anyone else and he would already have been buried deep inside one of her holes, pumping in and out. Devi he wished to explore and savor every part of her flesh and soul, one exquisite bit at a time.

He lifted his head to reach her throat and ran the tip of his tongue on her golden skin. Devi's flavor was salt, woods, ocean, and sin. He trailed kisses from the crook of her collarbone to her ear, perhaps the single most sensitive part of any fae. Vale wanted to bite her earlobe hard enough to leave a mark. He wanted to demand she extend her wings so he could caress each long golden feather. To claim every part of her—the parts she wouldn't share with anyone. Not his Devi. She was too proud for that. She wouldn't have let herself shudder, beg, or fall into the arms of anyone else.

Fisting her disheveled black hair, Vale inhaled her scent and sighed. Finally, he moved away, putting one foot of distance between them.

"You're bad for me, Devi Star Rivers."

"Oh no," she purred low next to his ear, and playfully nipped at his earlobe. Fuck. If he hadn't been hard before, he would be now. His length throbbed in his breeches. "I'm very, very good. Trust me."

But he didn't.

After their ordeal, he would have trusted her with his life. Vale was mistrustful to the extreme; he'd never actually *slept* with any of his previous lovers. After fucking, he would return to his apartments or ask them to leave his. Yet he had slept next to Devi without once thinking she might take the chance to slit his throat while he was helpless.

He felt confident he could show her his back and count on her to guard it.

Before her, there had only been one person he could say as much about: Kallan. But Devi would lay down her life for him. She'd already done it, back in the Square of Dawn. She hadn't counted on him to help her, and he'd seen the shock in her eyes when he turned his horse back to get to her.

What he couldn't, wouldn't trust her with was this. His intimacy. His feelings. He'd never been fond of the game of affection everyone played in the Court of Night. No one ever won.

It was perhaps why, despite his mother's best efforts to match him, no female she'd ever introduced him to had ever tempted him until now. The ladies of his mother's court had been raised as powerful females who knew their place: at the top of the world. They collected conquests like pearls for a necklace.

Having sex with Devi was one thing. The danger lay in letting her touch his heart. He feared she'd already gotten too close to it.

So slowly and regretfully, he moved farther away from her. Vale got up from the bed, walked to the curved window, and gazed down upon Elvendale, keeping his distance.

Devi seemed confused, and with good reasons.

Under guise of an explanation, Vale stated, "I believe my mother may have spelled me, little elf. Perhaps both of us. This thing between us is…" What was it, exactly? "… abnormal."

Devi frowned and repeated, "Spelled us?"

Yes, well, that was his best theory.

Vale nodded. "I've seen obsession spells in the old days. They're outlawed in the unseelie court now; they have been since the death of Tenaliel Trenar. Do you know of her?"

"I don't," Devi replied curtly.

She was vexed, obviously.

"She was a young beauty my mother singled out. She greeted her and invited her to court often. No one at court sang like the Lady Tenaliel. And it wasn't the only thing she did well: she was a fantastic lover by all accounts, with the appetite of a goddess of sensuality. I had the pleasure of sharing her bed once or twice myself, and I can personally attest to the validity of those tales."

"Is there a point to this…" Devi paused to find her words. "… fascinating story."

"There is. Tenaliel refused to choose mates, although many proposed; instead of binding her fate to a handful of consorts like most females of the court, she opened her legs to whomever she wanted for centuries. In the year 2893 of this age, she took a knight as her companion. She gifted him with something she'd never given anyone else: exclusivity. It lasted for a year, perhaps two. Then Tenaliel went back to what she loved best."

"As was her right," said Devi.

Vale didn't argue, echoing her words in agreement. "As was her right. The knight didn't take it well, however. He paid a sorcerer to concoct an obsession spell and gave it to his lady. At first, all was well. She shunned others, male and female alike, desiring no one but him. How glad he was. How proud. Soon, they were announcing an engagement. You know how rare it is for our kind to bind ourselves to one individual for life. Sometimes, high fae agree to a hundred-year contract, mostly when the rights of succession are of some importance. My mother and father made such a vow. But marriage? That's for the lesser fae, who won't live long enough to regret an eternal oath. But they vowed under the stars that they would love each other until the end of time. The whole court was present to witness the oath and wish them well. It was thought a rather romantic thing at the time. The male's machinations weren't yet known."

"And then?" Devi prompted.

Her irritation had given way to curiosity.

"And then things changed. Tenaliel couldn't bear to be away from her husband, not even for an instant. She screamed and yelled, driving herself mad when he had to go on guard duty, and she sobbed until he returned. Once, the knight had to leave for five days, so his beautiful, melancholic, mad wife climbed up the highest tower in Wolven Fort and threw herself down."

The years hadn't made that memory less heinous.

"My mother cared for Tenaliel a great deal, so she called the knight and questioned him until he confessed to his deeds. He was punished accordingly, and obsession spells were banned from court."

"What a terrible fate. I do hope his punishment was severe."

Vale laughed without humor. "It was certainly fitting. Mother had one last spell cast before her ban took effect. From that day onward, and until the end of his days, that knight is bound to Shea. He cannot survive without her touch, without living by her side. She took care to ensure he'd never love her, yet he's obsessed with her. Sometimes, she denies him her presence for a few days, pushing him to the brink of despair." Vale shook his head. "Some call me cruel, and I tell them I am my mother's son. The court had no love for the knight after his betrayal, but now, five hundred years later, there is no one among us who doesn't pity him."

"You talk of Drake," Devi guessed. "I noticed that he seems to adore and despise Shea. I did wonder why."

Smart female.

Vale acquiesced and finished his point. "You understand, now, why we cannot allow a spell to take root. It is dangerous, for you and me alike."

"I know what an obsession spell is, I've read about it," she told him, rolling her eyes. "It makes you incapable of thinking about anything else but the person it bound you to. If either of us had been hexed, we most definitely wouldn't have been able to talk of Isle politics."

She had a point.

"Besides," Devi added, "it's entirely impossible."

Vale insisted, "I know my mother. Whatever else she may have trained you to be, trust me when I say that what she's turned you into is a perfect uterus meant to grow my seed."

And as he said it, Vale suddenly understood why. Devi had professed to possess every godly power, and she was almost right. She may be versed in the four elements, but there was one divine ability she still lacked. The most powerful one, arguably. His. Power over minds. The one skill she didn't have was the strength to read thoughts, manipulate people, and make them suffer. Shea had bound them because she loved nothing more than power, and if he and Devi were to have a child, the babe could be blessed with all five powers. Mind and matter in one tiny grasp.

Vale wondered if the other part of him had seen it first. Perhaps that was why the darkness inside him, which cared for no one and nothing beyond his own satisfaction, seemed to value her so.

Devi left her bed and walked out of the room. Belatedly, he noted his lady was more than a little put out.

Vale replayed his choice of words and winced. He had been harsh. Vale followed her, unwilling to part ways on such terms.

"Devi—"

She made no response, moving easily in the smooth black stone corridors outside her doors. Tall elves in thin clothing passed them, their dresses billowing in the wind. There was no glass in the thousands of large, curved windows flanked by pillars, yet none appeared to feel the bitter cold. They bent their heads to Devi, hands over their hearts. She stopped and returned each of their greetings. When their eyes slid to him, they were cold but curious. He inclined his head.

After passing through five corridors and two halls, they reached a wet room with dozens of large natural pools. Three were occupied; it didn't faze her.

He understood. She wanted to put an end to their conversation, and so she'd chosen a public venue. No doubt she had a bathroom next to her large rooms upstairs.

Vale went in after her.

"I didn't wish to offend you. I simply know my mother better than you do, although she speaks to you more than I."

She stared at him without a word.

"And I didn't mean to say I'm approaching you because of a spell. You're lovely, as you well know. I would have wanted you without any interference. But my natural inclination might have been more along the lines of desiring you for an hour and then wanting you far away. This is different. It... doesn't feel like me."

Vale sensed a bond tethering them, as if an oath forced his hands. Trapping him.

He decided against saying it out loud. Devi seemed one insult away from kicking him in the balls.

He immediately saw when she changed her approach. There was a glint in her eyes, and she stifled a smile. Vale considered taking a cautious step back. He'd seen that look before—in his mother's eyes a time or two, for one. The night when she condemned Drake to his torment, she'd borne such a look.

To ensure she was comfortable as she rested, Devi had been uncloaked and unbooted, but she was still dressed as she'd been when they'd left Elham, in his shirt, and leather breeches.

Eyes set on him, unblinking, she started to remove her clothing. Slowly, she peeled her breeches from her slender limbs and stood before him in his shirt. It was pure white and thin enough for him to see her nipples through the fabric. The shirt drowned her, but in the dim light of the declining moon shining through the bare window, he could see the outline of each of her curves.

Fucking delicious.

Her undressing was no invitation—her smug look made that clear. It was punishment. Showing him what he was missing.

Remaining where he stood took all his self-control.

"I'm not vexed," she finally said.

Then Devi slid out of his shirt and stood in all her perfect bare glory for one instant, making him watch how delicious she was: firm, toned limbs, golden skin, wide hips. Because of her strict workout routine as an apprentice protector, her body was athletic yet her figure was so feminine. Her breasts—perfect handfuls— belonged in his mouth.

She turned, and his throat went dry. She'd kept the most glorious part of herself for last. Her generous round ass was downright sinful.

She stepped into one of the steaming pools.

"I find your theory fascinating. Be that as it may, it is—as I said earlier—impossible. If you've only heard of scions two nights ago, you may not know that fae sorcery doesn't work on us. It would be akin to attempting to tame a lion with catnip. Spells only work on the weak. The gods and their direct descendants use elemental magic to harm each other by affecting the nature around them. The reason Orin was feared and obeyed among the gods and scions, even before he was crowned, is because his power is the one thing capable of altering their minds. Either of us could drink an obsession spell, or a potion meant to kill us, for that matter, and it might as well be a cup of tea."

He stood there open-mouthed and then protested, "There's little information about our kind at all. I hadn't heard a thing about scions before my mother mentioned them. She may have led you to believe that so you wouldn't suspect—"

Devi cut him off. "I don't suppose you know how my mother was killed?"

He didn't. When he explored her mind an eternity ago, he'd let go after seconds, minutes at most. He hadn't dug for everything. And if he'd heard of Loxy Rivers before meeting her daughter, he'd forgotten about her. She'd been of no consequence.

The female soon enlightened him. "A death potion added to our wine. Everyone died. Everyone but me. Trust me, I asked why."

Further protests died on his lips.

Devi added challengingly, "Do healing potions and salves help you, Vale? In fact, does anything unnatural affect you?"

He thought it out. Nectar certainly affected his mind, as did wine and ale if he drank enough of it. But they were all derived from natural fruits and grains, not hexes and spells.

"Charms," he replied. When he was hurt, only elemental charms, such as the one she'd used on her ankle, sped up the healing process. "You used a healing spell—on your ankle."

"I used a charm that works with elemental energy," she amended. "And all it does is hasten my own healing abilities by stimulating my cells. I'm talking of curses and hexes. You've lived for over seven centuries, and you have a gift for infuriating everyone around you. Surely many have attempted to harm you. Give me one example of fae magic addling your brain, Blackthorn."

As he ran through his memory, none came to mind. Every occasion he thought of he dismissed, realizing the only times magic had worked against him, it had been elemental magic, as she'd said.

How come he'd never noticed before? When a hex had been cast against him, it had bounced off him. He'd assumed the mage wasn't very good at it.

"That's what I thought," Devi said once he'd remained silent for some time. "Glad we cleared this up. You can go now. I'd like to bathe in peace."

He was dismissed, just like that.

She had told him his baffling, potent need for her was real, and now she didn't want to act on it because he'd been stupid enough to question it.

He smirked as he watched her purposefully ignore him.

"My, isn't this quaint? A female who presumes to treat me like a weakling she can control. Have it your way, little elf. Let us play this game of cat and mouse. It has been long since I've had a chase."

On that note, he retreated.

THREE
THE POISON FRUIT

The previous afternoon, when they arrived at this strange, cold, black city carved atop the highest mount in the northern Graywoods, Vale should have directly asked to be taken to the elven king who ruled over these eerie lands, but Devi's condition hadn't allowed it.

The gash on her forehead had healed within minutes, but she'd remained unconscious.

A quick sweep of her mind had revealed there was nothing to worry about—she was simply exhausted. They'd slept perhaps five hours in the Valley of Doom. It seemed so long ago already. Yet he'd watched over her until she opened her eyes.

With her health no longer a concern, he could see to other matters.

Power had a feel, a scent, to those who were blessed with magic. As soon as he'd set foot on the steps leading up to Elvendale, he'd sensed a potent source.

Valerius followed his instincts blindly, his steps leading him out of the majestic residence and down a snowy path. No wonder his mother had told him to wear warm clothing up here. Unlike elves, he keenly felt the bitter cold—less so than common fae, but enough to be grateful for his fur lining. He lived in the north, yet never had he known such dreadful conditions. At Carvenstone, they'd opted to carve their homes under the mountain, and they kept fires through the fall and winter.

The winding path slithered up the snow mountain flank and opened to a garden where a small company had gathered. The snow and wind blew from every direction, making it hard to see despite his acute vision, but the elves hardly noticed the raging storm. They all wore plain tunics, comfortable in light clothing. An elegant male played a viola, and a youngling sat next to him, singing rather delightfully.

Three males and two females in armor stood, stiff and formal, around the gathering, and an older elf with long white hair sat surveying it all. A crow of white plumage was perched on his shoulder.

A little farther, near a bush of white roses that should not have been thriving in this weather, a few elves were engaged in a game of chess while three couples danced elegantly around them. They were all so joyful, enjoying simple pleasures with no worries.

Valerius stood before the high lords of the Graywoods of Wyvern. If that small group, those two dozen creatures, had risen against the army that had taken Asra, they might have been victorious. A fantasy. Those twenty-five elves would never fight for the Isle. They minded their borders and remained indifferent to what lay beyond. They'd only joined the War of the Realms because the fae had been foolish enough to attack their lands.

Valerius advanced and stopped before the guards.

"May I pass?"

"And what purpose would you serve if we let you?" one of the three elves asked pleasantly and mockingly. It was the tone one used with children, as indulgent as it was condescending.

Valerius took no offense, suspecting he spoke to a creature who'd seen at least twice as many winters as he had.

"I'd have words with Elden Star."

"You may, if Elden Star wishes to have words with you."

Valerius's eyes returned to the plainly dressed musician. "Let us ask him when he's done playing, lest we interrupt a beautiful song."

That the humble musician, and not one of the listeners, was master of this court would have been no secret to any decent psychic, but Valerius needn't use his gift tonight. He'd identified Elden by his hazel eyes, which would have better suited a wild cat. Hazel eyes that had become familiar.

The lord of the Winter Court and king to all elves surprised Valerius in many ways. For one, he seemed so young, just like his own mother. An idiot with no knowledge of auras, power, and magic might have mistaken him as a boy of twenty not yet done growing. The energy around him was telling another tale, buzzing, listening to his will as though nature itself feared his wrath. This "boy" might even have intimidated Shea.

Seeing the father explained many things about the daughter.

Elden Star finished his song, and the white crow flew from the elder male to alight on his master's shoulder now that it wouldn't hinder his movements. The elf stroked the bird's back, and then those familiar eyes fixed on Vale, demanding he submit. Vale inclined his head politely but kept his eyes on the elf. Being cordial was important, but he would not look down. Showing his neck to a tiger would be utterly foolish.

A smile curved the corners of the king's mouth.

"I heard you brought me my daughter harmed at dawn."

Vale opened his mouth to reply; the king, however, wasn't done talking. "I hear also that you would follow her and watch over her rather than greet your host. Peculiar, is it not?"

Oh shit. They were having *the* talk.

"Sir..."

"Don't fret. I have no doubt Devira would cut your bollocks off herself and serve them to you in a stew should you do anything to deserve it. I am simply stating my observations and reading your reaction. You care for the child. Good. This conversation shall be fruitful."

Valerius stilled, reading between the lines. He didn't like the conclusion he came to.

"My mother sent me to you for aid. The city of night—"

"Is burning and the rest of your realm, lost. Yes, Byfram here"—the elf king glanced at his bird—"was so good as to bring me the news, along with a letter written in your mother's hand." Elden pulled a folded piece of paper from the inner pocket of his shirt and carried on talking, without much intonation or sentiment in his voice. "Soon, the foolish eastern fae who thought it wise to treaty with the enemy will also fall. We're at the dawn of a new age where seelie and unseelie will be nothing more than slaves used for your master's amusement."

Well, that summed it up, all right.

Vale hadn't failed to note that the king didn't include himself or his people in his grim assessment.

"And you believe you'll fare better?"

Elden laughed softly, a sweet and musical sound. "I know we will. Your enemy fears me and with good reasons. In my realm, I harbor as many scions as he does in the immortal city. A war with us may spell his doom. Besides, I have given him no cause to quarrel."

Vale shook his head. "How do you know he isn't seizing control of the rest of the Isle first? With the three other realms united against the elves, Aurelius's next logical step would be to take his rival out."

Elden's eyes had cut to him the moment Vale had breathed his brother's name. Now the king tilted his head. "And this would indeed have been strategic. However, it isn't your practical brother you will face. It is the wicked one."

Perplexed, Vale replied, "I don't have another brother."

"Alas, I fear this belief is at the root of all evils." Elden flicked his hand, and as one, the gathering moved to leave the gardens.

Soon, Elden and Valerius were alone in the gardens, with the crow that watched him, unflinching and mistrustful.

The king gestured for Valerius to join him in a stroll through the fragrant bushes, some wild, others planted, and all thriving, making for a pretty picture in the snow and ice.

"What do you know of the first war of this age? Not the War of Realms, but the one that shaped the realms at the start."

Why did everyone feel like giving him an ancient history lesson? He sighed. "Little more than what children learn at our academies."

The king laughed. "So nothing, then."

He feared that was only too true. "I've never been one to dwell on the past. My mother told me of the gods from another world who created our kind."

"The enlightened," Elden amended.

"Excuse me?"

"That is what they call themselves. It wouldn't do to go by 'gods.' Rather pretentious, wouldn't you say?" He didn't let Vale attempt a response. "But I'm glad I can skip the basics. Shea might have spoken of the old times, but she's a child of this age. She does not know the truth of the First War. It was brutal."

Vale lifted a brow. "All wars are brutal. I've seen—"

"You've seen nothing, Valerius Blackthorn." His words were sharp. Unyielding. Somehow threatening. "You came into this world during a time when blood flowed more abundantly than water down the River Reine in spring. Instead of songs celebrating the arrival of a prince, you heard screams. They put a sword in your hands as soon as you could walk. And they awoke something in you, something dark."

How the ever-fucking hell did he know that?

Elden closed his eyes and opened them again. "Yet for all you've seen, you have no idea. The War of Realms was child's play. I found it fun. No elf perished. We did not fight you. We made a point, to ensure that the next generations of fae would know better than to test our borders again, nothing more."

Vale didn't doubt that.

"How different was it, then?" Vale asked. "The First War."

"I will not talk of it," the elf stated resolutely. "Know only that wrongs that can never be undone were committed. Wrongs such as burning cities, threatening, torturing, and raping innocent. You only need to hear of one of these horrors. I've not talked of it in the last five thousand years, and I will not mention it again after today."

Elden took a deep breath before saying, "One of the enlightened was ordered to take a young girl savagely to make her father talk. I watched in horror as all of our enemies were slaughtered after we'd gotten what we had come for."

He'd watched? Vale took that in with awe and some apprehension. The male was at least five thousand years old. Most mages Vale knew only grew stronger with time. How terrifying did that make Elden Star?

"Rape and carnage." It sounded like just about any other war. "What of it?"

"I saw it with my own eyes when your father spared the girl he'd taken; out of pity or guilt, I know not. His blade struck her face to make her bleed and pass out, so that none would suspect he'd spared her, but the blow was not lethal. And so the girl lived to birth a son."

Ah. Well that had certainly gotten his attention.

His father had another son? One born of hatred over five thousand years ago?

"I have another brother."

Elden inclined his head. "He has plotted in the shadows since the dawn of this era, and his time has come."

FOUR
THE KING'S DEAL

After a long bath to soothe her tired limbs and wash away thoughts of Valerius Blackthorn, if only for a moment, Devi returned to her room, got dressed, and walked up the path to her father's gardens. She had only lived in this court for a year, but if she recalled anything, it was that Elden could be found in his frozen paradise more often than not. She wasn't surprised to feel Valerius's presence along with her father's as she approached.

On her way up, she encountered a handful of elves that were part of Elden's council.

She greeted them, rather surprised that he'd sent them away. What did the king of elves have to tell Vale that he wouldn't share with his most trusted advisors? Devi certainly didn't wish to miss that conversation, although the words might not be meant for her ears. She approached slowly, tiptoeing and masking her presence.

Close to the winter garden, she heard their voices. Devi halted and listened to the tale her father was sharing with Vale. The first words confirmed their talk was related to their affair, and she needed information as much as Valerius.

She listened as Elden talked of a war, gods, enlightened, monsters, and brothers, her mind storing each detail, until her spying session was rudely interrupted.

"I see you have not yet learned what is said of eavesdroppers, daughter."

Devi sighed and stepped into view. "I can't say I have, no. Don't expect an apology. I'd very much like to know what's happening." Elden had never talked to her of anything of importance in the past, and she doubted he planned on starting now. "So, you're saying the evil five-thousand-year-old son of Orin is yet another contender for that blasted throne up north."

"Evil is a matter of perception, daughter. The son of an abused female, raised in poverty, often starving and without a home, may grow into a person a child such as yourself—born and raised in palaces—cannot understand."

While it had been delivered with as much condescension as possible, she had to concede his point.

"Fair enough. To me, burning a city to the ground, entirely unprovoked, definitely counts as an evil deed, but each to their own."

"Inconsequential. The boy has long plotted, patiently waiting for the right moment. That time is now. He has considered every possibility, every scenario. He's prepared. You may expect to lose this war."

She had to note that her father didn't seem troubled by that perspective. Devi didn't have to think too hard to imagine why. "You've made a deal with him, haven't you?"

Her tone held no small degree of contempt and accusation.

Elden didn't take offense. "A long time ago, when the child lost his mother, he crawled to these lands, dirty, famished, and wild, and aid was offered to him. He came to me more recently, saying that my kindness hasn't been forgotten. He asked for a favor, and I have granted it."

Vale was astonished, which meant that he had no idea who Elden Star was.

"You helped him?"

The king didn't so much as quirk an eyebrow. "It is not in my nature to refuse aid to those who need it." Elden stared at Valerius pointedly. "Be glad of that."

The poor guy was left speechless, and Devi, amused. "You made a deal with him, and now you wish to make a deal with Vale too. That way, whichever side wins, your realm will be safe."

"Indeed." The king kept petting his bird, deaf to the criticism in her tone. "Take note, daughter. This is how rulers ensure the welfare of their people."

She shook her head. "Suit yourself. I hope you'll also agree to a deal with me."

This got the king's attention. He lifted his chin and turned his unnerving eyes to her. "That would depend on your terms."

"I want the location of Queen Shea and the resources to reach her."

He returned to petting his bird. "Denied."

She wasn't even surprised. "On what grounds?"

Elden lifted the folded piece of paper in his hand, holding it in the light. Her eye caught a familiar seal—the outline of a wolf. "A letter from that queen of yours."

Devi stepped forward, hand extended to take it.

Her father smiled. "I think not. These words aren't meant for your eyes."

Her eyes narrowed. "If whatever's in that letter determines my fate, I'll have you tell me."

"And I shall tell you. Reading my personal correspondence is another matter altogether, daughter."

She kept glaring until he finally decided to explain. "Shea has taken what's left of her court, her army, and the seelie king. She is riding east through the Graywoods in the south, with my blessing. Asra is lost; the Elderdale fortress, home to the seelie court, still stands. She will attempt to defend it. She expects to fail, eventually. The old walls around the city will help, for a time, but she cannot hope to last more than a year under siege. Regardless, once the gates are closed, they will not open again, not even for you. She has made that clear."

Fuck. How could she argue against that?

What was she supposed to do, then? She'd never felt more helpless. But Elden was done with her; he'd redirected his attention to Vale.

"You have a quest, princeling. I will give you whatever assistance is in my power. We'll talk details in the morrow. I demand one thing in exchange." Elden stared at Valerius long and hard, and Devi wondered if she was hearing the whole conversation or if Elden was also speaking to Vale's mind. "Should you claim the crystal throne, you will take a female with elf blood to sit at your side. Our kind has long been forsaken in the thoughts of the rest of the Isle. You make agreements and trade without inviting us. I would have your rule end this. I would have us thrive together."

Devi's outrage rendered her speechless at first, then she exclaimed, "Did you just offer me up like a piece of meat? Again!" Her voice had risen to a shout in her indignation. "I can't believe this."

Elden was the picture of indifference.

Vale seemed as unfazed. He pointed out, "To his credit, your father said a female with elf blood. Pretty certain that includes just about every female in this court. Not everything is about you, you know."

For some reason, that only fueled her rage. She unhooked her bow from her back, pulled an arrow from her quiver, aimed, and shot at Vale, who caught the weapon in midair before throwing it aside.

"What did she mean by 'again'?" Valerius asked unsympathetically.

"Devi's mother and I had, before her birth, agreed to relinquish her to your mother's care. In exchange, my court was granted whatever nectar we required at a fixed rate, regardless of inflation. Quite the deal, if you ask me. Devi disagrees."

"Fixed rate?" Vale gasped. "The price of nectar has doubled these last ten years alone! *Quite* the deal," he repeated, impressed. "In any case, I've passed many comely ladies of your court during my short stay. It is no sacrifice to agree to your terms."

Devi shook her head in disbelief and realized an alarming fact: Valerius was a younger version of Elden.

"I'm surrounded by opportunistic idiots. And as his royal pain in my ass pointed out, your stupid agreement does apply to any trollop in this forsaken realm. Let me go to Shea. If I portal south, I can join her before she reaches Elderdale."

The king and Valerius both said, "No."

"And why, please?"

"You're handy with a bow. The boy may be decent with a blade, but projectile weapons are important. He'll need your help if he's to live long enough to fulfill his side of the bargain," was her father's answer. "I pledged to give him power over his enemy; you're part of that deal."

Valerius added, "Besides, my mother made both of us head to Wyhmur. I'd wager she intended for you to accompany me."

The two very logical points pissed her off because she had to concede, begrudgingly, that they weren't without merit.

"Fine," she grumbled, still put out. Then, thinking of her own stipulation, she said, "But you'll send someone along the western borders for me. There's a male riding a dyrmount alone, heading toward Carvenstone. He would have hair dyed dark and a plain cloak. If I'm not to go that way, you shall grant him help. That's my condition."

She'd planned to catch up with Kallan on her way, if she could; but she said that mainly because coming out of this discussion without the king agreeing to one of her demands might have felt too much like losing.

Valerius lifted a brow, impressed she'd thought of his friend, no doubt.

She rolled her eyes. "He's too pretty to let him die."

The prince didn't like that. *Good.* Another win for her.

"Who's this pretty male, Valerius?" Elden asked him rather than addressing Devi.

They were getting along.

This was perhaps her worst nightmare.

"My second. He's indeed pretty, and loyal, too. I'd be grateful if you could lend him a hand."

"Hmm. Very well. I shall send Kira after him."

Devi's eyes widened. "Kira?"

The king feigned innocence. "She's my fastest rider and the best warrior in our ranks."

"And she'll also eat him alive and spit him back out for fun," Devi added.

Elden didn't deny it.

Vale asked Devi, "You know this Kira well?"

Elden answered for her. "Kira is the general of my forces in the western woods. Given the unrest, she's currently at the borders. If your second is alive, she'll find him faster than anyone else."

None of what he'd said was technically a lie, yet he'd avoided revealing anything of importance.

If only to rattle her father, Devi filled in the blanks. "Kira is my twin. And she makes me look like a helpless, delicate damsel. A *reasonable* one."

While Devi had been raised by their mother, Kira had lived in the Winter Court her whole life. After Loxy's death, when Elden brought the fifteen-year-old weakling whose only credit was her modest skill with a bow to Elvendale, Kira greeted her with a snort. They were the same age. She had the same face, although her twin had her mother's green eyes and flaming red hair, while Devi had taken her father's hazel eyes and dark hair. But their main difference was that, unlike her, Kira had already been lethal and fierce.

"You, my twin?" The girl grimaced. "Well, we'll see what we can make of you."

Devi's thirteen years of training with the unseelie queen had never troubled her because it hadn't been nearly as brutal as the one year she'd suffered at her sister's hands.

Kira already controlled her devastating power by then—better than Devi did, at age twenty-eight. And no game had pleased the elf princess more than making boys do her bidding. At *fifteen*. Kallan had done nothing to deserve this fate.

Thirteen years ago, when they were fifteen, the age when both fae and elves were called to train for their higher purpose, Shea sent word to Elden, requesting one of the twins. She didn't say which, but Elden didn't even hesitate before naming Devi.

Devi cried and begged him to stay. She'd found a home here: guarding the borders with her sister. She was *happy*. Leaving for a place she knew nothing about was a punishment like no other.

"Listen to me, Devira," Elden had told her. "You don't belong here. Kira does. We've taken care of you because it is our duty, but you're not wanted in this court. There is no place for you here. Shea Blackthorn has use for you. I do not. Do you wish for civil war when I am gone? There can only be one heir to my crown, and I have chosen Kira. You *will* go."

She'd left with an empty heart and dry cheeks, as she'd already cried all her tears. She'd left cold, expecting to find a darker world.

But the unseelie queen had welcomed her with open arms. Shea, who couldn't lie, had said, "I've always wanted a daughter, Devira. Now my wish has been granted, it seems. We're alike, you and I." And other things, such as, "There will always be a place for you in the unseelie realm. No matter what."

Her loyalty was with Shea Blackthorn because Shea Blackthorn's loyalty had been with her when no one else's had.

Devi hadn't seen Kira since she'd left for the Court of Night, but she could only imagine what her sister had become.

Still, she kept quiet, because Elden wasn't wrong. If Kallan was alive, there was no doubt that Kira would find him. The only question was, what would she do to him when she did?

"Wait, you have a twin sister? How come I'm only hearing of it now?" Valerius asked.

Devi pointed out, "You didn't ask."

"Seriously? Consider this my asking anything of relevance whatsoever about your family tree."

She gave it a good thought. "That's about it. One dead mother, one unstable twin sister, and a pain in the ass of a father. Although, I'd say that's rich coming from the son of Orin and brother to a couple of murderous warlords."

"That doesn't count," Vale argued. "I didn't know about the second brother."

"Children, if you're done with the domestic dispute, I have orders to send and matters to consider. Shoo. Supper is at sundown in the dining room, if you care to join me, and I'll see you at dawn, when I shall uphold my end of our bargain, young Valerius."

They were dismissed. Devi left the garden, marching down a sinuous path to the city of her youth, and Valerius followed her steps.

FIVE

A FAIRY DANCE

All in all, Vale left the king's gardens satisfied with the outcome.

He couldn't deny his surprise that the man had helped their enemy, but at the core, he understood Elden. The unseelie had been attacked and thereby forced onto one side, but there was no doubt that in the same position, Vale would have acted like the elf lord, in order to guarantee the prosperity of his realm.

Devi disapproved, but Vale guessed she also understood her father's decision.

"An interesting scion, your father," he said to break the silence as he trailed after her on the uneven snowy path.

"That he certainly is."

He coaxed a few other words here and there, but Devi was troubled, he could tell. Vale itched to reach out through his mind to see why. The dark prince was still there, right under the surface, and he saw nothing wrong with invading her thoughts. Perhaps the time had come to seal him away again, now they were safe.

Vale balked at the idea. The term *safe* was loosely applicable to his current situation. He was in unfamiliar territory, surrounded by strangers. He needed to keep his edge. Or perhaps he just wanted to.

He didn't seal his volatile alter-ego, but he stopped himself from reading Devi's thoughts, forcing his attention away by observing their surroundings.

As they went farther down the mountain, the surrounding landscape changed. Rocks were polished at first, then also sculpted. By the time they arrived at the bottom of the anfractuous path, it was paved and flanked by graceful statues of elves. Before them lay the city of winter, thus called because it always snowed that high up in the mountain.

Valerius would have imagined empty streets, wood chalets with sloping roofs, and wide eaves poking out of the houses; it only made sense given the weather. The northern parts of the unseelie realm that endured colder winters, like the villages outside of Carvenstone, boasted such structures.

The elven city was the opposite. High columns, flat roofs, open halls with no wall. A crowd of younglings and elders, who conversed pleasantly and sometimes sang or danced, had gathered outside. Was anyone ever displeased in this white wonderland? There were smiles and laughter at every corner.

None of them wore anything half as warm as Valerius's coat, yet they seemed quite comfortable. Meanwhile, Valerius wished he had also worn gloves and a scarf.

Vale had been about to ask Devi whether every elf was impervious to cold when the crowd turned to them and gasped as one. A hush had fallen over the elves.

"The young lady!" they said.

Others cried, "The winter fae!"

The elves approached Devi, who seemed rather awkward but unsurprised.

"We heard of the attack and feared the worst, for a time," said an elf sadly.

"Mistress Kira was furious," someone else announced. "Sir Elden had to send her away on duty, for she talked of joining the war should any harm have befallen you."

By this, Valerius gathered that Devi's mysterious sister had a fiery temper.

Everyone rushed to tell her how glad they were that she was here, safe. Most ignored Valerius, others bowed their heads in salute, but for all it mattered, he might as well have been completely absent.

He wondered if it was how Kallan felt next to him. Invisible. If so, how the devil had his old friend put up with him for so long?

Devi was quick to reassure her anxious admirers, professing she was just fine. In her efforts to minimize the danger she'd been in, she made it sound as though their journey to Wyhmur had been a pleasant stroll.

A young child pulled at Devi's shirt, and the female kneeled to her level.

"Hello, little one."

"Say, mistress, is it true you can ride the fall? Mama says you can."

"And your mama's right."

Valerius had no clue what riding the fall entailed, but the child was impressed.

An elf told her there would be songs at the city hall, and the gathering begged her to attend. She smiled pleasantly, assuring them she couldn't think of a better way to spend her evening; then she was off, following them.

Vale remained where he stood, feeling positively out of place.

The little child who'd talked to Devi looked at him as though he were an oddity. Finally, she declared, "You should come too, you know. You look like you could use some music."

Amused, he asked, "And why is that?"

"Because you seem very grave and grumpy. Dadda says that's how you get white hair. This way, Mr. Fae." With those words, she took his hand and led him after the crowd.

He had received no formal invitation, but no one protested either.

The city hall was a large, open space supported by four columns, not unlike the Square of Dawn. A platform had been erected at the center, and every elf present sat around it. A youngling was perched atop one of the four columns, where he could catch a better view.

Now that she'd led him to the party, the child dashed into the crowd, leaving him alone and, again, feeling awkward. He considered leaving, but an elf on his right asked, "Have you ever heard our songs, fae?"

"Elden was playing just an hour ago. Rather beautifully," he added.

The elf laughed. "The king is known to be a poor performer, although one cannot fault him for practicing. Stay and listen, stranger. It'll do you good to witness what beauty comes when war and malice have no place."

And so he stayed. Without fanfare, a male walked onto the platform and started to sing.

The deep baritone was slow and meaningful. Vale wasn't familiar with the words—it wasn't a language he'd ever heard—but it spoke to his very soul. It was the story of a love lost to time and found again; he sang of hope. The song was over too soon for Vale's liking, although the sun had fallen behind the mountain, which meant the singer had been at it for some time. The elf took a bow, and the crowd bowed back in silence. Other elves stepped forward, either to sing or play an instrument they'd carried into the hall with them; various strings and winds, all played so well that even the dark prince was at peace for a time.

One after another, dozens of strangers took the stage and spoke to his heart. Vale understood why the elf had told him Elden was a poor musician, although the king might have belonged in any unseelie concerto; those performing that evening were all so incredibly gifted.

"What do you think, fae?" asked the male who'd talked to him earlier during one of the breaks.

Many elves were shamelessly eavesdropping on their conversation; he could guess it was a matter of national pride. He didn't disappoint them.

"That I could easily remain here listening to your kind's music for the rest of my days and forget everything else."

They were quite satisfied with his answer and happy to play some more for him. Soon, someone handed him nectar, and another fae thrust a plate into his hand.

Seated a couple of rows in front of him, Devi turned to him and smiled pleasantly.

"You came with the princess," said the elf who'd been the first to welcome him.

Vale could tell everyone was paying attention now. "I did."

"And you live with her in the Court of Night. Is she happy there? We hope she might be."

"I don't know," he had to admit. "I met her recently. My home is Carvenstone."

He had to hold back a sigh as he said it, expecting the usual backlash that came with the admission of living in the Court of Sin, the judgmental eyes and the unspoken accusation.

Every elf within hearing range—most of the assembled—turned to him, obvious awe on their features. Confused, Devi stared at Vale as he shifted uncomfortably.

"Whispers have reached us from Carvenstone. Interesting whispers," said the elf.

Valerius stiffened.

"They say the wild creatures of the world have a home there. They say everyone may occupy whatever office they are qualified for, by order of its lord. There are lesser fae practicing law and children riding unicorns, which would have been hunted and killed for their horns anywhere else. They say the dark fae who rules over these lands is the greatest lord of this age."

Well, shit.

Devi's eyes were the size of saucers, and her mouth hung open.

Valerius sighed. "Who talks of this? There's a reason why what happens in Carvenstone is kept secret. It works because the outside world leaves us alone."

Their world had changed, but if there ever was a tomorrow for the unseelie realm, Vale's duty was to ensure the safety of his people.

"What you do in your land has attracted much curiosity from the old creatures of this world, young master." So, he wasn't "fae" anymore, by the sound of it. "You may have had one or two wandering sorcerers disguised in the shape of fae under your roof. And phoenix have flown close to see it with their own eyes. And the dragons also know of your deeds. We're friends with such folk, and they've brought us tales."

Tension eased from his shoulders. As long as they didn't report his actions to his mother or her courtiers, all would be well.

Shea may not be against his management of Carvenstone—not really. She was good at heart. But she was also queen to a court of bigots who'd rail against his methods and rush to his lands, armed with spears and bows.

"Fear not, word of this will never leave these woods."

"I appreciate your discretion."

"I am Gaer of the high council. You may call me friend."

Offers of friendship were rare from high elves. Vale knew to value it. "I go by Vale. And likewise."

The elf smiled wickedly. "And among other accounts, the whispers also say the lord of Carvenstone plays almost as well as an elf."

"As for that, I can attest that it's a complete exaggeration." Vale laughed with good humor.

Too much time had passed since he'd been able to just talk and laugh freely. War still loomed on the morrow, but the music had washed his cares away for a night, allowing him to find some peace.

"If you think Elden plays poorly, you'll need to stuff wax in your ears to put up with my music."

The elves would hear none of it. Now that they knew he played an instrument, nothing but a performance would satisfy them. In no time, Vale found himself pushed before the steps leading up the platform, a beautiful violin in his hands.

He shook his head in amusement and walked up the steps.

He was no elf, and their soulful music was far beyond his capabilities; instead of attempting to imitate the songs they appeared to favor, Vale chose to show them a peek of his world.

Long ago, according to a children's tale, a lesser fae once scorned had enchanted his song so that all those who heard it would be cursed to dance for an eternity. Vale didn't know where the story had come from, but the song ascribed to it was called "The Fairy Dance." Only those who were proficient enough to play nuances at a high speed and with dexterity were taught it. Vale had learned the song in his youth, and the last time he'd played had been at the end of the war centuries ago, but he recalled it well enough and improvised the rest.

It was a three-step. Vale gave little credence to the fairy tale, but he'd never played the song to an indifferent audience; the fae always danced to it. He closed his eyes as he struck the familiar chords; when he opened them again, he smiled at the two hundred elves on their feet, dancing and clapping to his enchanting notes.

There were no thoughts of war and sadness for the night.

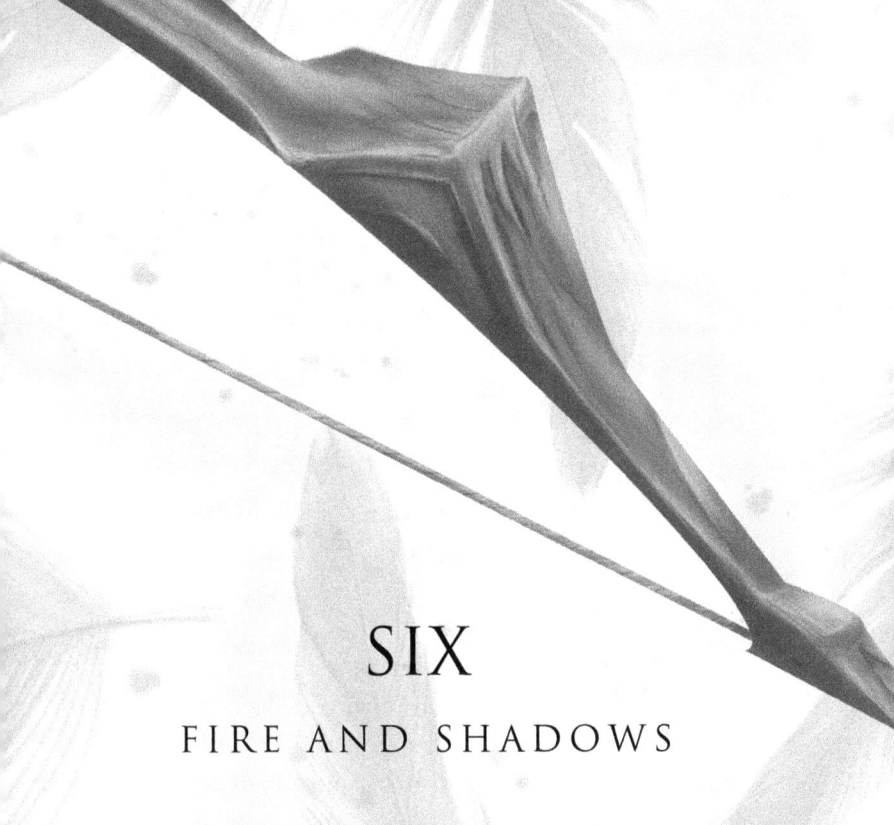

SIX

FIRE AND SHADOWS

Nothing made sense where Valerius Blackthorn was concerned. She'd believed she'd known who he was from the start, but instead of a mercurial beast, he'd proved to be a slightly arrogant, teasing male who treated her like an equal. Someone she'd found entirely impossible to dislike, infuriating as he was.

Back in the Valley of Doom, she'd heard that he'd come to the aid of a dragon in his lands. In the short time they'd spent together, she'd come to understand there were many layers he hid from the world. And now this? What the elves said of the Court of Sin blew her mind.

She was ashamed to admit she'd never seen it coming. Despite everything she'd learned over the last few days, Devi had believed the talk. The Court of Sin was rumored to be a house of depravity and indulgence, home to the dark prince, whose temper was feared throughout the realm. But it turned out Vale maintained a front to protect the despised or hunted.

Nothing he'd ever done or said had prepared her for *that*. She understood why he kept his deeds under wraps. If what Gaer had said was true and Vale allowed any fae to take whatever work they were qualified for, he was going directly against the idiotic laws of castes, which determined the limitations of lesser and common fae. As unseelie nobility, she was familiar with the laws; she'd often spoken up against them, to no avail.

Devi felt rather strange whenever she looked at Valerius now. Confused. A little shy, perhaps. Ashamed of not having looked past the surface when all the clues had been there. She saw it now. He'd never truly put on a façade with her, showing her glimpses of who he was every time they talked, as if daring her to believe in him.

Then the elves had practically forced him onto the platform, and he'd played masterfully, with love and passion, unveiling yet another facet she'd never known existed. She had to admit, if there was one thing she knew about Valerius Blackthorn, it was that she didn't know him at all. And no surprise there, since their acquaintance had been so short.

Devi remembered Healer Beck's warning that the prince was quite irresistible, that he was more than a crown or a handsome face. She should have listened.

Vale was begged to keep playing after his first song, and then the crowd insisted on another, until they'd danced and laughed most of the night away.

Vale and Devi were creatures of the night, but they'd both had trying days; his fatigue didn't prevent him from playing like a virtuoso, but he had trouble keeping his eyes open, so the elves refrained from demanding another song. Devi walked to the platform.

"Hey, I figured you might need a guide to get back up to the house," she said.

Not the best excuse, perhaps. Elden's keep, a fortress of black stone, dominated the city, standing tall and proud higher up the mountain.

She added, "I mean, to the guest quarters. It's a big place."

Valerius was kind enough to cut her rambling short.

"Appreciated," he replied, smiling as he handed the musical instrument he'd borrowed to its owner, a male Devi remembered from her days in the Winter Court.

The elf refused to touch it, protesting, "Such music has never been played on these chords, and I fear my instrument may resent me should I take it from you. You will keep this violin."

Vale laughed. "Nonsense. Besides, I'll soon be gone to places where one does not carry such joyful things."

"It is in the darkest places where music matters most."

Devi intervened, "Know a lost battle when you see one, Vale. Telenar insists."

The elf's expression lifted as he turned to her. "It warms my heart to hear you recall my name after all this time, my lady."

She chuckled awkwardly. Her selective memory never forgot the names and faces that might come in handy. Telenar, as the general of her father's northern armies and a member of his high council, certainly qualified.

They took their leave after exchanging pleasantries. Walking up the path they'd taken earlier, Devi felt infinitely more awkward.

Finally, she forced herself to open her mouth, if only to fill the silence. "Funny how you complain of my forgetting to mention a thing or two, all the while concealing anything of relevance about you," she told him, one brow lifted in challenge.

"Touché. In my defense, I am seven hundred and thirty-eight. If I took to reciting my attributes to everyone I met, I'd be known as Vale the Tedious rather than the dark prince. Doesn't have as nice a ring to it, now does it? Besides, one must retain a certain air of mystery to entirely deserve such a name."

She rolled her eyes. "There's keeping some things private and then there's purposely hiding everything you are." As that sounded too much like an accusation, she was quick to add, "I get it. What you're doing in Carvenstone wouldn't work if everyone poked their noses in your business."

She just would have liked if he'd told her about it. But she'd sooner pull out her own fingernails with pincers than admit to this.

They'd arrived at Elden's keep, seeing it in all its splendor. The limestone edifice stretched along the mountainside, built around a waterfall that started at the summit and dove all the way down to a lake at its base.

"Let us stay a moment, if you don't mind. I didn't take the time to gaze upon this keep on our way in."

Complying with his request was no hardship.

The Court of Night was beautiful in its own way. It looked exactly the way a fortress harboring a queen ought to, with its tall gates, the castle's heavy frame, and the conveniently narrow streets that prevented the army from entering shoulder to shoulder. It was the creation of a queen ready for war. The Winter Court was first and foremost a home. A home that could comfortably house hundreds of guests when it needed to.

Yet the only way into the keep on foot was over an elegant alabaster curved bridge—the only part of the building that was relatively new. It had been built after the War of the Realms, for in times of peril, the fortress had stood alone, impenetrable to those who knew not its secrets. Some might try attacking it by air, but those with any sense knew better: elves were famous for their devastating aptitude as archers.

Elden had sheltered the young and infirm while the able-bodied males and females of age had fought their enemies back across the borders.

"Exquisite, is it not?"

She agreed fervently. Her curiosity piqued, Devi asked, "What is your home like? Carvenstone?"

Valerius shrugged. "My formal keep is but an old, drafty manor with few remarkable qualities. It will, no doubt, be destroyed or sacked in these next few days. Let us hope the seelie and scions do me a favor and raze it completely. I should have rebuilt it years ago, but other projects took precedence."

Devi asked, "If it's of so little value, why did your friend, Kallan, risk so much to get there?"

She must have understood the prince a little better, because Devi wasn't surprised when he replied, "For the people. There's a dwelling no seelie or scion has heard of—an ancient place that used to be sealed. Kal and I found it by accident. Its entrances are concealed and secured by many spells. Those who would be in danger if discovered live there, but there is enough room for more. If Kal makes it back before the enemy reaches it, he means to evacuate the city and the surrounding towns."

Vale's concern was obvious.

Devi gave him what reassurance she could. "He has a dyrmount. The scions failed to reach us on our journey; their Griffins and scouts only found us when we reached the forest. I bet the scions we faced were already posted in the woods to intercept anyone who ran through the eastern gate."

"I think so, too."

"So, your friend will be just fine. Kira will find him."

She said it with so much conviction that Vale nodded. "Now come. Elden wishes to see us on the morrow. From this day forth, we must catch sleep when we can. We'll leave after speaking to your father. Pleasant as this place may be, we cannot linger."

Not with everything else going on in their world. Staying idle would go against who she was.

Devi led Vale to a guest apartment and found their parting uncomfortable when they reached the doors.

"Tomorrow, then," she said before turning away, returning to her quarters.

She'd expected to manage a few hours of sleep, but she tossed and turned until the sun rose in the east. It was too early for one used to the unseelie schedule. Devi didn't think she'd ever been that exhausted. But her mind wouldn't let her rest. Something felt amiss. With a resounding sigh, she got up, got dressed, and headed back to the king's gardens.

Kira Star Rivers wasn't one to welcome a missive telling her what she was supposed to do, regardless of who it might come from.

Elden's words were concise and to the point, relaying a direction that sounded too much like an order. But she was also bored and in desperate need of a distraction, so she opted to comply.

The western border was quiet. Too quiet, perhaps. Kira was certain it would change soon, but she might as well find a way to occupy herself in the meantime.

"Hela, you're in charge in my absence. Kill anything that doesn't belong in these woods."

She liked to keep her directions simple. Her second smirked. "Can I play with them first?"

Kira rolled her eyes. Stupid question. Of course she could.

Elden's letter stated, "There is a fae male riding along our borders. You are to extend him your aid until he reaches the end of his journey. He has Corantians on his trail."

Kira disliked most fae, but her distaste for anything coming from Corantius ran deeper yet, especially now.

She was indifferent to Isle politics because the Isle overlooked the Graywoods of Wyhmur in all dealings, but when she heard the seelie and the Court of Crystal had joined forces against the unseelie realm, her blood had boiled.

She couldn't say she cared about many unseelie fae—or any, really.

Except one.

Her sister lived in those lands, in the very city that had been attacked. She knew Devi to her core. She could take care of herself. Hell, had she wanted to, Devi could have destroyed the entire army single-handedly. However, that would have meant killing every single living thing around her, and Kira's sister just didn't have it in her.

No, the genes for brutality had skipped her twin; Kira had been granted a double dose instead. Devi could be in danger. If the seelie and the Corantians had hurt her twin, she'd not rest till they were all ashes in the wind.

"What are we doing?"

She lifted her eyes to the black crow circling her head. *"Rescuing a boy."*

The crow flew down and stared her right in the eye as if to check that the statement had come from his master.

Kira added, *"And torturing him until he tells us every single thing he knows of Devira's whereabouts."*

The bird beat his wings and returned to his affairs, as if concluding, *Never mind.* That was definitely Kira.

She leaped onto a branch ten feet in the air and propelled herself higher and higher into the thick tree, until the branches struggled to bear her weight; then she jumped to the next tree and the next after that, fast and silent and invisible to the most acute creatures of the woods.

She froze suddenly as a shiver ran up her spine. Kira pulled the long staff strapped to her back as her head snapped to her left, seconds before it came. A wind of shadow and fire moved so fast that it was at the border one moment then passing beneath her in the next, ignoring her entirely and racing for the heart of the forest. She'd barely seen a thing, but she could feel a powerful force.

Her eyes narrowed in the direction the shadow had fled. Thousands of miles away, there was Elvendale. She considered her options. Fast as it was, she'd never reach her home before the foe. She couldn't even send Crow with a message; the bird was swift, but it'd still arrive too late.

She put the staff back in its sheath, shrugged, and kept on jumping from treetop to treetop.

What did it matter if the elves of Elvendale had no warning? She pitied the demons that attacked the Winter Court.

SEVEN

THE SWORD AND THE CROWN

Despite the soft feather pillow and the mattress perfectly calibrated to his taste, Valerius couldn't sleep. After a while, he stopped trying.

He headed to the king's garden before dawn, hoping to catch Elden before Devi joined them. He found the ancient lounging on a chaise, leisurely picking dark grapes.

The three guards stepped aside to let Vale pass without being prompted, this time.

"I'm rather vexed," Elden said while remaining the picture of joy and serenity. "I heard I missed quite the performance last night."

Vale smirked. "I'm certain we'll have other occasions, given that I am to wed your daughter."

They'd spoken as vaguely as possible in front of Devi the previous day, but the king had lowered the shield around his mind for an instant to clarify his meaning. The deal was his help, as long as Vale was to marry Devi.

The king smiled. "If you survive."

That was a big if. "Well, it seems like you have reasons to wish I make it. What support can you grant us?"

Elden was amused. "On one hand, there's a vindictive brat still stuck in a rebellious stage, and on the other, a youthful boy who's never thought of anyone outside his borders."

Valerius couldn't deny that accusation.

"I can't say I find the outcome of this quarrel all that fascinating. Your brother came to me asking for maps and spells. He was granted both. You are unarmed and ill-equipped. I will give you weapons and supplies. My armies will let you pass through my lands and come to your assistance while you're in my territory. That's all I can concretely offer; I cannot support you outside these borders."

Vale understood. If Elden were to help him openly, his brother would see the king as an enemy, regardless of the deal they'd struck. It mattered not. The elf king offered exactly what Vale needed.

He inclined his head and pressed his hand over his heart reverently. "The unseelie realm will know of this. We shall not forget."

"I expect you wouldn't. I'm not done, however. But let us wait a moment, for Devira will make such a fuss if we were to continue without her."

A moment was all they needed; Devi appeared, in armor. Not the brown leather she'd worn in the Court of Night, not even the uniform elf guards wore around the city. She had on tight pants hidden under a long coat comprised of both metal and fabric—a soft gray material like silk. There was a high slit on either side of her legs to allow for easier movement, and the fabric swayed with each of her steps. Vale didn't mistake the outfit as a stylistic choice, although she certainly looked devastatingly beautiful. It was maille, the most pliable, thinnest, and strongest of metals that could be spelled to stop steel, absorb blows, and even repel dragon fire.

The metal was as precious as it was rare in the Isle. Vale knew his mother owned such armor, and perhaps five nobles in his acquaintance could boast to possessing a piece, no doubt gathering dust amongst their treasures.

Devi had braided her hair down her back, and it fell to the backs of her knees, completing the picture of a goddess of war.

Vale hoped he wasn't expected to talk anytime soon—or look away from her, for that matter.

"Daughter."

"Father," she replied with a dip of her head.

"I see you've found your wardrobe."

Devi didn't seem particularly surprised or impressed that an armor worth more than an entire horde of dyrmounts had been waiting for her. She simply replied, "Thank you for updating it. I was glad to find the clothes fit."

"I assumed your measurements wouldn't differ much from Kira's," Elden replied, and sighed. "And like your sister, you choose to wear armor. Two daughters and not one is interested in dresses."

The corner of Vale's mouth hiked up. He could imagine the old king dressing his little girls in the prettiest silk and lace, and despairing the moment they learned to say no and choose pants instead. Such was the burden of fathers who raised strong daughters.

He frowned. No, from what he'd seen in her mind and heard of her past, Devi hadn't been raised here.

Without being privy to the details, Vale could guess at the story between Devi and Elden. The king clearly loved his daughter as much as any powerful lord had ever loved a child, but to the likes of Elden or Shea, children were a commodity. The tension between them was all too familiar.

"Oh, I'm interested," Devi replied. "I'll come back to raid the closet someday."

Then she turned to Vale, missing the glint in her father's eye. The prospect of her returning to these lands warmed the ancient's cold eyes like nothing else Vale had seen since meeting the king.

"What did I miss?" she asked Vale.

"Your father has offered us supplies, and we were waiting for you to hear the rest."

Devi's eyes widened in surprise.

"I was telling your prince the outcome of this war is rather inconsequential to the Winter Court. However, there's one thing to consider."

"The fact the other guy may attack you once he's done with the rest of the world?" Devi guessed.

The king laughed. "No. You."

Devi bit her lip, hesitant and baffled.

"Your alliance is with the unseelie realm, and you are my daughter. As such, I will grant Valerius Blackthorn one weapon I denied his kin: knowledge." Elden turned to him. "Gallal informed me you were good with a sword. Fast, too. But you didn't maintain your speed for long. I imagine you can't."

He was reluctant to divulge too much to the scion whose loyalties were as fleeting as the wind, but he acquiesced. "I can keep it up long enough to dispatch any enemy I've faced."

"But you have not faced any powerful Corantians yet," said Elden. "Scouts aren't warriors or knights. Imagine how well you'd fare against those who were granted gifts like yours."

Vale remained silent. Such thoughts had entered his mind and kept him awake when he ought to sleep. If the throne in the Court of Crystal could choose the next king, as Devi had told him, reaching it was their best chance of survival. He had to force his brothers into starting the selection process, ending this conflict once and for all.

Should the throne choose one of his brothers, Vale would be no threat. He'd bend the knee and swear fealty. It would kill him to surrender after the destruction of Asra, but he'd do it to avoid the slaughter of his people and protect the realm. Vale could ask to return to his lands and live in exile for the rest of time. That was his hope.

If he was crowned overking, however...

Elden didn't give him time to think through that daunting prospect.

"There are objects that may help you," said the elf. "Devices your enemy doesn't know of."

That caught his attention, as well as Devi's.

"The enlightened came to us with swords and axes; peculiar for a race advanced enough to create vessels to travel through space, wouldn't you say?"

It was, and yet it wasn't; guns and bombs were available in the Isle, but they were the weapons of the weak, only wielded by lesser fae. A high fae could outrun the blast of an explosion or defuse it with magic. The strongest chose steel because nothing was as fast and lethal as *them*. Bows were redoubtable to those swift enough to shoot a dozen magic-infused arrows faster than bullets per minute, like Devi. A gun, however, was of little use against fae who could control the elements around them or were nimble enough to move out of the way.

Still, Vale imagined that an advanced alien species would have developed fancier ways to kill each other.

"Their instruments were more than they appeared," Elden explained. "Technological marvels designed to enhance the power of those wielding them. They recharge their wielder's magic like a battery."

"You mean to say that with one of these instruments, I could retain my higher speed for an extended period of time?" That sounded too good to be true.

"For as long as you need to. And a divine device would also exponentially increase the reach of your power. Our limits are defined by our resilience. The first lesson we teach our young is not to overtax themselves, for they could collapse or even die. What if using magic had no effect on you? What if it drained an inanimate object instead?"

Devi asked the one question at the forefront of Vale's mind. "How do the devices work? They can't have infinite power. You say they're batteries. How do we charge them?"

Elden hesitated. Before the words crossed his lips, Vale could tell he was about to lie. "They're powered by sunlight. They absorb it during the day, store it, and redistribute the energy."

Vale opened his mouth, but Devi beat him to it. "Great. Awesome. Now the bit you're not telling us, pretty please."

She plucked grapes from her father's plate and popped one into her mouth before handing one to Vale.

Elden watched her move, confused, like no one had ever questioned him or stolen from his plate before.

He opted to shrug off the slight.

"Like most enlightened devices, the weapons are sentient and can therefore opt not to recognize a bearer."

Of course they were. Despite the warning, Vale's mind raced, seeing all the possibilities. Devastating powers without any limit or effect on him. It was the sort of thing one could only dream of.

"You don't happen to have one hanging around by any chance?" Devi asked.

The king laughed. "I said I would grant you knowledge, not unlimited power, daughter."

Typical.

"In the old days, the enlightened used their weapons freely before my eyes. When I joined my father in combat, they granted me one, and still, it serves me well, but it would be of no use to you. These devices are forged to recognize their rightful masters. Mine only answers to me and shall do so until the day I pass it on. Then you can fight Kira for it, as it will only answer to those of my blood."

Devi pouted and grumbled that her chances were grim in that case.

"And no Corantians know of this?" Valerius asked, doubtful.

If such objects existed, surely they would be the talk of the whole realm…unless the enlightened had purposely hidden them from the masses.

Elden confirmed it.

"After the first war, the enlightened decided to keep the knowledge of these devices secret, for armed with those weapons, their descendants would be dangerous. There is no other scion who bears a divine device, and only the ancients are aware of them. Few still live to tell the tale, and none would, for they were ordered to remain silent on the matter. But there are seven enlightened in Corantius. They own their own divine weapons."

Ah, yes. Those guys. Valerius had conveniently forgotten about them. He was going to have to ask about the actual gods before they left. His mother had told him precious little, and he guessed Elden knew more.

Again, Devi was first to speak. "These gods. What are our chances against them?"

"You have none," her father replied.

Great. Encouraging.

"But you may count your blessings, for the enlightened prefer to remain idle and out of the way. They will not act until a new overking is chosen."

At last, some good news.

"Are you sure of this?" Vale asked.

Elden considered the question. "Fairly. Most of them write to me from time to time."

Great. He was pen pals with the gods. Vale found himself wishing the male could truly be on their side. He might have ensured the outcome of this war.

"Long ago, the god of misrule left this world with dozens of enlightened. Two of the seven remaining live in another land with their court. In the Court of Crystal, only Pallas, Styx, Thea, Hyperion, and Iapetus are left. I've not heard from Pallas and Styx in some time, but the rest of them have contacted me over Orin's demise. They'll stay out of the mess until an overking can command them."

Good. Vale focused on the issue at hand. "All right, back to the weapons. You say they answer to blood. I'm guessing Orin had a device I might claim?"

Elden smiled. "He did, as did his father before him. The two divine devices, a sword and a crown, remain in this realm. Both are now on display shelves, unused. Still, they are well guarded among other treasures and mementos of darker times. Seize one of the two devices, and you may stand a chance. Seize both and I shall formally pledge my allegiance to you as the rightful overking and grant you the use of my armies."

Oh.

Well, that changed things.

Vale turned to Devi. "Fuck the throne. Let's go get the sword and the crown."

"Yep," Devi concurred. "Sound plan. Except, if it were easy, daddy dearest wouldn't have offered such a big payoff. What's the catch?"

Elden blinked twice. Then he turned to Vale for confirmation. "Did she say 'daddy'?"

It saddened him that he had to be the one to explain it. "I think she meant it ironically."

The king was unfazed. "I'll take it. And the catch is that the crown and the sword happen to be in the Court of Stars, home to the Duke of Stormhale, a first-generation scion like me. He's a warrior of the Court of Crystal, and he has a predilection for collecting trophies. They're exhibited in his home, a museum of sorts, open to all Corantians. There will be protections in place against thieves."

Of course they were. Getting in unseen would take no small amount of skills and trickery.

"We'll manage," Devi stated confidently, "so long as you swear you'll have our backs when we do."

Elden inclined his head. "On my honor, you have my word."

Great. Now they had to break into a demigod's stronghold and steal his treasures.

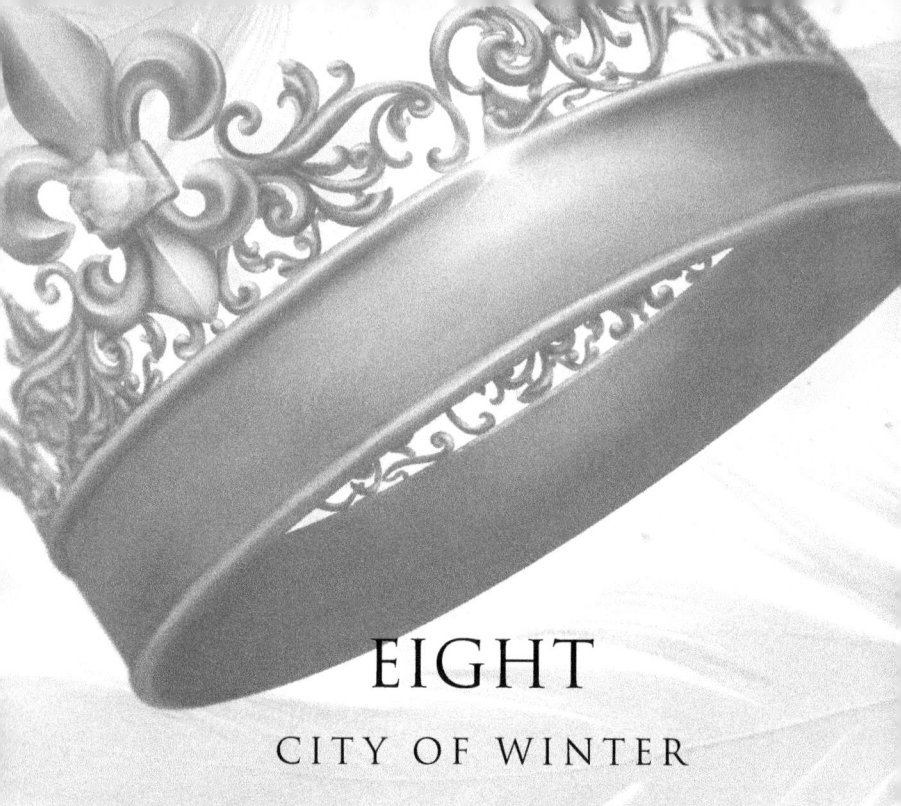

EIGHT
CITY OF WINTER

Alarik and Midnight grazed in the grounds behind the king's keep. The open field was somehow free of snow, and a few horses roamed freely. None were half as magnificent as the dyrmounts of Elham, yet in these strange frozen lands, the shorter, more robust horses might have served them better. Midnight—not unlike Vale—was freezing his hooves. Proud as they were, both fae and horse hid their suffering as best they could, but Vale deciphered enough of the animal's feelings to glean he'd be glad to leave Elvendale.

For once, he wished he had elemental magic, if only to warm the poor horses. He turned on his heels. Devi had made her way down to the town as soon as they'd finished speaking with her father. Vale had let her go her own way, much as he would have enjoyed her company. It wouldn't do to force his presence on her at every turn. When would she have time to miss him if he was always in her face? But he didn't doubt there were others who could care for the beasts.

He asked the first elf he encountered in the bright corridors of Elden's house. "Excuse me, might you know to whom I should speak regarding the care of our horses?"

The tall, thin male's expression was pure boredom. "Any willing elf would do, for our kind know how to treat beasts. But I have much to do today. Try your luck in town. No one in this house is here without an assignment."

The stranger proved as rude as elves could be, but he still bowed his head before resuming his walk.

Vale watched him walk away, somewhat perplexed. Another time, he would have let it go. Another time, the dark prince would have been locked inside him.

He let his mind reach out to the retreating stranger and caressed the surface, getting a taste of his thoughts.

… unworthy. No fae should have claim on a lady of winter. Devira is ours!

Ah. He'd heard enough.

Vale again wondered about Devi's life in his mother's court. No doubt she'd also suffered from bigotry. After a day, he'd had enough of it; he couldn't imagine living that way for over a decade.

Another reason Vale didn't wish to be overking. If he took power in a land that wasn't his, he'd be inviting a lifetime of whispers and curses behind his back. Devi would endure it, too.

Vale headed down to the city of winter, banishing thoughts of the future. He had horses to take care of.

The main path down to the city was familiar, as he'd traveled it while carrying Devi to the king's keep, yet it appeared new, for the paved roads were covered with white flower; an homage of sorts, he realized. Arriving in town and finding a crowd larger than the one in the hall yesterday, he wished Devi were standing next to him; surely her people longed to see her, not him. But they held their hands over their hearts and inclined their heads respectfully.

He was returning the greeting when his mind picked up a disturbance in the surrounding energy. His head snapped left toward the waterfall that tumbled along the mountainside—and he found it entirely frozen.

Considering the low temperature, the water should have been frozen from the moment they'd arrived in the city; Vale had noted the running water and wondered what magic kept it that way the previous day. But now the entire cascade of water, as far as the eye could see, was ice.

Children were laughing and pointing at the peak. He followed their gazes, and his eyes bulged when Devi slid down the ice at full speed with a board under her feet. She jumped down and landed on a crouch. The young child who'd talked to her last night was the first to scream in pleasure; there was applause and merriment all around, entirely confusing Vale.

The elf who'd given him his violin stood close by.

Vale stepped forward to greet him. "Telenar, was it?"

The male inclined his head.

"I'm missing something. What has everyone so enthusiastic?"

Telenar smiled indulgently and explained, "No one can ride the fall. No one can even touch its waters. Master

Elden performed powerful magic, in the old days, to protect us from our enemies. It is death to any who'd dare to drink from it. Those who touch it grow sick. Everyone except the ladies of winter."

"So, their father's magic protects them."

It wasn't unusual. Many spells were crafted to only serve one bloodline. There was even a room in Wolven Fort that Shea herself couldn't enter as the former unseelie king had sealed it so that only one of his kin could open it.

The elf shook his head. "Elden cannot touch it."

Vale's eyebrow rose. "Then how—"

"The twins are born of Rivers and Stars, some of the oldest blood in this world. They've been gifted with powers we aren't meant to comprehend. Say, have you ever seen Devira's ice before today?"

Come to think of it, he hadn't. He hadn't seen her use water magic at all, although she'd used every other element. He'd assumed she was less proficient with that element, but it made little sense. The elves of Wyhmur *were* known for their water magic. Why would she excel in every element save for that of her ancestors?

Watching her closely, he saw, at a distance, that her amber eyes had turned blue, as though the water were part of her, running in her blood. Water wasn't her weakness; it was her strongest power.

"No, she's never called to it."

Telenar snorted. "And with good reason, no doubt. Here, in these lands, she knows there are powers that could stop the devastation should she fail to control it. But it is a force of nature. Fascinating for those of us who dabble in the studies of magics. Water is often used in healing magic for its purifying properties. My first guess is that Devira's ice temporarily cures the toxins in the water. It could be something else; I couldn't say without a thorough course of studies."

Vale's attention snapped to Telenar, catching something in his eyes—a fascination he didn't understand. His speaking of studies and the nature of magic clued him in.

"You're a scientist of sorts, are you not?" Vale asked.

The elf smiled. "Refreshing. Elves generally call me a wizard. Yes, I am the head of the research facilities of the Winter Court. Long ago, I was party to some of the later experiments the Corantians did on your kind."

Ah, so he wasn't an elf after all.

"You created the fae."

Telenar shrugged. "Some, yes. My team finalized the process. We created the thirteen."

Holy fuck. "The thirteen original high fae families?"

"Ash, Fyr, Cinder, Frost, Rivers, Rime, Zephyr, Winford, Gale, Dale, Forrester, Blackthorn, Anima," the ancient recited. "They were code words at the time. We had over seventy experiments on the go, so initially, our subjects were just numbers, but when we succeeded, we named the fae. It was a real triumph—for a time."

The light dimmed in the scion's eyes.

"Then what?"

"Then greed, power struggles, and war. So many wars. When I heard that one of my kind had set up a peaceful community in the forest, I joined him, and together, we built this haven. Not long after, we had to protect it, so I went back to work."

"And created the elves," Vale guessed. The perfected high fae.

Telenar was a higher power who'd shaped entire species. A true divinity. Vale asked the one question that came to mind. "Why don't they have wings?"

He'd startled Telenar.

"In every other way, elves are superior to fae—slightly faster and much stronger—but they don't have wings," Vale clarified. "Was that purposeful?"

The ancient chuckled. "I said I was part of a team. The scientist who came up with fae wings remained in Corantius. It wasn't my area of expertise." He grimaced. "Too fiddly."

Vale had to laugh. How very natural and vulnerable. Perhaps the gods weren't so different from fae after all.

"What of the laws of lies? The penalties for breaking oaths? The costs of magic—"

"Slow down, young one," said the scion, laughing. "As for the first two, they were attributes designed to weaken fae. We were ordered to saddle them with weaknesses so they may never surpass scions. Here, in Wyhmur, we approached things differently. Elves were not weakened. But using magic tires the minds of elves, scions, and enlightened alike. Think of it as a rush of energy, particles vibrating throughout your body. If they were to vibrate too hard, your system would shut down and you could *die*. Our bodies let us know when we're exhausted to avoid such an outcome. I did not set the costs of magic. Nature did."

How fascinating. Were these peaceful times, Vale could have spent hours, if not days, engaging that male in conversation about his knowledge. Now wasn't such a time, however. Remembering his purpose, he said, "I came down here to find help. Our dyrmounts are suffering from the cold, and the weather will not improve as we go north. You're no doubt quite busy, but could you recommend anyone at leisure to help?"

The scion snorted. "And you believe 'anyone' might help as well as the mind behind the evolution of fae and elves? I think not," Telenar said proudly. "I'll care for the beasts. I'll need perhaps two hours. Enjoy the city of winter while you can, young prince."

Perfect. Elden had promised their supplies would be ready by midday.

"I do not know how to thank you for your time."

In his world, elders with such knowledge often kept it jealously.

"And no thanks were asked of you," were the ancient's parting words as he retreated toward the road that led higher up the mountain.

Vale glanced toward Devi, and finding her watching him, he waved pleasantly before making his own way, aimlessly wandering the cheerful streets.

Elvendale didn't feel like a city the way Asra or Carvenstone did. It was but one long, sinuous avenue carved along the paths of the highest mountain in the Graywoods. Houses and monuments lined the path. Vale noted that every building, small and great, was of exquisite craftsmanship. He couldn't discern whether there were richer and poorer neighborhoods. All elves wore the rich fabric only nobles could afford anywhere else, and their fashion, lavisher and subtler all at once, was quite different from that of the fae.

"What are you up to?"

Devi.

Vale managed not to smile. He'd known she'd come to him if he gave her a moment to herself.

"Presently, nothing. Our horses are being tended to and your father promised us supplies in a moment. We have a luxury we will rarely be afforded in the coming months: free time."

"Perfect. Have you eaten?"

All of a sudden, with its existence acknowledged, Vale's stomach was curmurring. No, he hadn't; he'd only had a few bites of food the previous evening, and the grape Devi had given him.

Devi laughed at the obnoxious sound. "Apparently not. You should have said something. My father would be horrified at the thought of a guest going hungry under his roof."

"I seldom notice hunger."

Growing up in a time of war often had such consequences.

"Well, I was on my way to Deissa's when the children accosted me. I would have brought you a bowl, but as you're here, you may as well come along and get your broth hot."

As it turned out, Deissa was a beautiful elf with silver hair who sat on a chair in front of her house and served hot soup from a large cauldron to any who asked for it.

At least a dozen elves of all ages waited to be served. They parted to let Devi go first, but she protested, "None of that. We have time to wait in line."

Vale said nothing, although his stomach greatly disagreed. The scents emanating from the pot almost had him whimpering. He detected rosemary, mushroom, garlic, and other equally delicious flavors. The next few instants were physically painful, but at long last, he stood with a steaming wooden bowl of stew and a roll of white bread in his hands.

Devi thanked Deissa and was told to bring the bowl back.

As they walked toward a nearby tree, Vale asked, "Are we not to pay the female?"

She snorted. "Many have tried and failed. Deissa accepts leeks, parsnips, squirrels, and the occasional deer in winter."

He shook his head. "I don't understand the economy here. I haven't seen any money exchange hands."

Devi nodded. "Money isn't needed inside these woods. Don't get me wrong, Elvendale and the rest of Wyhmur wouldn't function without imports from the other realms, so the elves need money for that, but they earn plenty from their main export. Here, the hunters hunt, the builders build, the tailors make clothing, and everything gets distributed. Riches such as jewels and other treasures can be earned, but few elves value such things."

What a strange and enchanting world. "And what if an elf wants to purchase goods outside this realm? Your father talked of purchasing nectar from the unseelie realm, for instance."

"Ah, well, there's plenty of work. Most elves serve a function and they get paid with gold marks, like everywhere else in the Isle. They don't need to use them here. And people like Deissa, who doesn't wish to have an employer bossing her around, do well enough from trade."

At the tree, Vale leaned against it and grinned as Devi pocketed her roll and hoisted herself up onto the first branch, feet dangling in the air. So very elvish of her.

Vale took his first sip of the broth and closed his eyes, moaning in delight. It was a lamb dish, potentially the best he'd ever tasted, although his hunger may have biased him. Deissa deserved all the deer, rabbit, and parsnips she could wish for.

"Lend me your bow. I need to go hunt something for that master in the art of cookery."

"Great, right? But we have no time to pay her tribute now. Rest assured, I've often hunted for Deissa when I lived in the city. And a good thing too, considering your lack of skill with a bow."

He let her tease him. Valerius was no worse than the average fae at shooting, but he certainly didn't excel in that department.

As his mind traveled back home, he mused, "This broth, paired with Dorrel bread."

The roll was good, still warm, crusty, and fluffy inside, but nothing compared to the delights Elar fashioned in his kitchen.

Devi groaned. "Oh, by all gods, please!"

Of course she knew Dorrel, as anyone who'd ever passed through Asra should.

They ate in pleasant silence before heading back up the mountain.

Elden had kept his word.

Bags of supplies were already attached to their horses' saddles. Vale opened one and froze, finding a familiar shimmering fabric inside. He pulled it out and discovered it was a dark cloak not unlike the one Devi was wearing. While hers was blue and silver, the colors of the Winter Court, his was embroidered with green filigrees around the sleeves and collar and lined with white fur. He could tell it would fit, although he was taller than most fae and broader-shouldered than most elves. It was as though it had been made for him.

"Maille, again," he said in wonder. "There's no better armor in the world. It takes much skill, and plenty of magic, to turn the metal into fabric. This coat rivals my mother's."

"Don't think the kingdom ruined itself on your behalf. Most maille clothing is made here," Devi said, confirming his suspicion: someone had crafted the garment for him overnight. "Where the fyriron comes from, I have no idea, but artisans specialize in tempering it in the court. That's the elves' main trade."

No doubt the kingdom could thrive solely on the income from that one export. Fyriron was priceless. Vale wondered why he'd never heard that it was tempered here.

Vale tried the cloak. Perfect fit. And for the first time in days, he wasn't cold.

The other bags contained provisions, healing charms, unlocking keys to open any coffer, well-carved knives, and handcrafted arrows.

"We have everything we need and more. If this quest should fail, it wouldn't be for lack of supplies. Your father has been very generous."

Devi rolled her eyes. "My father has had several thousand years to amass his riches. He can part with *things* easily enough."

"The fact he can afford it doesn't diminish his kindness. He was not obliged to have magical armor worth more than all of Carvenstone combined made for me. Elden is very kind. Probably because I accompany you."

"Stop supporting him. He never wished to be a father to me before, and I don't see why he'd start now. Besides, you assume he had anything to do with your armor. You forget you're popular around here."

Devi had a point. He searched through the bags and found other things the king of elves might not have thought of: sleeping draughts, warming charms, and even sweets. Everything was small and light so as not to overburden the horses. And, of course, someone had added his violin to the lot, safely stored inside a case.

"So are you," Vale said. "What did they pack in your bags?"

"Food, a change of maille, soap, charms, girl stuff—"

He stopped her there. "You know what? I don't think I need to know."

She laughed and opened her mouth to speak, but no sound came out. Her attention, like his, had been called far to the west.

Something approached, a thing of great power moving too fast and heading right to Elvendale.

Vale drew his sword, Devi lifted her bow, and they mounted their horses.

The city was under attack.

NINE

DIVINE INTERVENTION

The enemy rushing toward the city of winter was a mile away and barely perceptible one instant, and then at the base of the White Mount the next, too close to the city. In all his years, Vale had never seen such celerity. The enemy would reach Elvendale in moments.

Without discussing their options, he and Devi were on their horses, heading back down to the city.

They were too late. Five minutes, that was all it had taken. They'd gotten on their horses and ridden down the mountain flank in less than five minutes, and a dark fog already engulfed the streets. Elves were confused and coughing. Many shouted, "I can't see."

Vale motioned to Devi to cover her mouth and nose. "Poisonous gas."

Though they were likely immune to it, there was no point in taking chances.

A scream from the lower section of town pierced the darkness.

"Wait," Vale told Devi as she motioned her horse forward. "I feel fire." She seemed determined to advance until he pointed out, "Alarik will panic, and we cannot afford to dismount our horses."

"What, then? The only path down the mountain wide enough for our horses is through the city, in any case."

He hesitated, reluctant to ride into the fog, although taking one of the many footways down the mountain and getting lost in the woods also presented many dangers, even with the king's blessing to travel his lands.

Another scream stood out among the rest, for it was unmistakably that of a child. Vale dismounted, got to his feet, removed his coat, and tore off the shirtsleeves before putting it back on.

"We're the reason for this attack. We leave, it stops. We can blind the horses and push through."

He tied the fabric around Alarik's and Midnight's eyes, whispering reassurances, before grasping their reins and guiding them forward.

Devi remained on her horse and lifted a bow, eyes narrowed. "Vale? Touch me."

A stunned chuckle escaped his lips. "You certainly have interesting timing."

"Get your head out of your ass and touch something—my leg, my foot, anything. Skin to skin if you can."

He did as he was told. If the last few days had taught him anything, it was to trust Devi. She wore long boots, tight pants, and maille; no part of her skin lower than her chest was bare. Vale removed his glove and slid his hand under her tunic, lifting it to her waist. She was unexplainably warm.

"Videmus," she said.

His vision instantly cleared. He could see the streets and the elves. Some were shielding children, keeping them out of the way. Others blindly rushed forward, determined to find the intruders.

That was a neat trick Devi had up her sleeve. Air magic, he guessed.

Regretfully, he removed his hand from her waist, put his glove back on, and resumed marching toward danger with the reins in hand. The sooner they got out of Elvendale, the sooner they'd cease to endanger its people.

Now that he could see what was in front of his nose, Vale advanced much faster. As they passed by the open city hall, he stopped.

A female lay on the ground, unmoving. She'd fallen face first. Some coward had attacked her from behind, leaving gouges in her back. She was cradling a newborn in her arms. Vale crouched beside her and checked the child's pulse, although he already knew. The child was now lifeless, its body broken.

He turned to Devi. "We can't leave."

She nodded.

The enemy was cowardly, hiding behind the mist and only attacking the vulnerable, suggesting that for all its speed and theatrics, it was weak.

"I am Valerius Blackthorn," he bellowed, "son of Shea, son of Orin. You're here for me. Come out!"

Vale walked forward, away from the horses.

"I'm alone. One on one. You'll not have a better chance to please your masters. Come now and face me, you coward!"

Vale could feel the creature stirring in the shadows. It was prideful. Good.

"Are you only strong enough to slaughter females from behind and kill children? You're a disgrace. They'll tell tales of your great cravenness after I've gutted you from stem to stern."

He purposely put distance between himself and Devi. If he was right, the creature was a beast of fire and naturally feared elemental mages.

Something moved in the shadows, and Devi angled her bow.

Vale lifted his hand. "Stay out of this. That thing isn't going to come out and play if you're backing me. The recreant fears you, little elf."

She snorted, and the creature stepped forward.

All pretense of humor disappeared from Vale's expression. As he'd guessed, the beast was of shadow and fire, with thick, dark mist for fur. Beautiful blue flames surrounded it, but it was not a thing of evil. It resembled a young fox but for the magic trapped inside it. There was a silvery collar around its neck and binds on each leg. Vale had seen such restraints, infused with magic. Some barbarians tamed beasts by inflicting pain until they knew nothing but obedience.

This thing was nothing but a pawn.

Thinking back to the female on the ground and the child in her arms, Vale lifted his sword. "Come at me, coward."

The beast sneered and leaped forward, fangs exposed. A jet of fire rushed out of its mouth. Praising himself for not caging his stronger self, the dark prince, Vale used all his speed and jumped back fast enough to avoid the fiery stream. The beast attempted to leap at him, all its fire magic ready to strike. It didn't fight like a fox, relying entirely on its power rather than its claws and fangs.

Vale stood his ground. The fox breathed fire, and the roaring flames hit Vale right in his chest. The fox tilted its head, confused, and spun around to strike him with its blazing tail.

Poor creature. It had never encountered something it couldn't burn, but a plain cursed canine was no match for a cloak meant to withstand dragon fire. The beast should have learned to bite.

In another world, another time, Vale would have done what he could for the creature—removed its binds, taught it the meaning of kindness, and released it with its peers—but this was war. There was a chance that the fox would return to its master, tail between its legs, and report everything it had seen: the horses, the maille clothing, Devi's presence. So Vale thrust his sword through its neck. The least he could do was make it quick.

The dark fog didn't lift. Vale frowned as Devi trotted forward.

"It wasn't alone. And this isn't about attacking the city; you made the beast come forward by gloating, but I'd wager they were told to stay out of the way, create panic..."

"And draw us out," Vale guessed.

The enemy didn't want to attack the Winter Court head-on, so instead, it was trying to force them to leave it while spies watched every road.

"I say we stay and kill them all."

"You'll do no such thing," a stern voice said from behind them.

Vale turned to find Elden standing behind Devi at the head of a small contingent. The king waved his arm, and a wind blew all traces of the thick fog away, clearing the air.

"We'll take care of the vermin and protect our borders," the king stated.

The elves behind Elden lifted their bows and swords and disappeared between the buildings on either side of the street.

"You have a quest to undertake, if I'm not mistaken. Our city will fare well whether you fail or succeed, youngling. But the fate of the rest of the Isle is in your hands. If you value the lives of the few over the many every time you have a hard choice to make, you are doomed."

On that note, Elden pulled his sword from its sheath on his back.

Vale and Devi froze as they took in the strange weapon. What it was made of, he couldn't tell. The blade was too shiny, its edge so sharp it shimmered in the light. The basket hilt curved like an incredibly smooth dragon tooth. Blue strands ran along the sword, through the blade and hilt, like veins. It almost seemed alive.

This weapon was Elden's divine instrument; Vale would have bet anything on it. The king had always been a silent force of nature, quietly stating his dominance and power. Now, he looked terrible and magnificent—a beautiful, devastating nightmare come to life.

Then, Elden disappeared, and the beasts started screaming.

Vale removed the horses' improvised blindfolds and hoisted himself onto Midnight.

TEN

PURSUED

Devi and Vale traveled the road north, so far in peace. She guessed the elves had cleared out whatever spies might have been lurking in the woods, for she sensed none.

They came close to wild beasts and things of darkness, but the creatures only watched them carefully without wishing them harm. With no present danger, they let the horses canter so as not to exhaust them on the first leg of their journey. The heavens and hells knew that they might have to gallop through the lands again.

At the base of the White Mount, the temperature improved considerably, and for a time, Vale kept his long cloak open, but by the afternoon, as they rode north, he'd closed it again. As day turned to night, the air chilled further, and it started to rain. The horses bore it well, unlike their masters. Vale was back to cursing under his breath, muttering about the "blasted weather."

They'd gone most of the day without bickering, perhaps because of this morning's incident still fresh in their minds.

Few had suffered in Elvendale, and less than a handful of elves had fallen, but their presence had endangered the safety of the Winter Court. It was lucky Elvendale was such a well-protected city, but ancient scions would not be guarding the next place they visited.

They could not linger anywhere.

And then there was the poor fox. Devi had no idea how to bring up the subject, although she had seen the light in Vale's eyes dim when he'd struck it.

The creature had not been evil.

She wanted to tell Vale she'd killed small game for no other reason than they made good targets and tasted delicious in a bowl of stew. Tell him he'd done the right thing. But the words failed her utterly.

But teasing him she could do; it was as natural as breathing.

"Shivering again? Who knew the dark prince was so delicate."

"It's literally freezing. The only reason it's not snowing is because it's too wet. The rain is biting."

"You live in the north, farther up than where we are now, right?" Carvenstone was close to the west coast of the Isle, right at the border between the lands of Corantius and the unseelie realm. "Surely you're used to such weather."

"I'm used to staying home with a fire in every room and drinking a warm brew in such weather. We rise for hunts in the winter, of course, but it seldom rains."

"A cat," she said.

Vale, riding ahead of her, twisted on his horse to look at her, a brow lifted in question.

"You remind me of an old, grumpy cat."

He laughed. "Careful, now. One might take it as an invitation to share what I think of *you*."

"Do you think I care?"

Devi's attention was drawn away as the wind whispered around her, indicating her father's troops were nearby. None approached.

"We have company?" Vale guessed.

She nodded.

Devi half wished Kira were in the woods so they might have seen each other again. But a little more than a day had passed since she'd asked Elden to help Kallan. Kira would have reached Carvenstone by now.

"Good. If your father's troops are nearby, we should rest here," Vale suggested. "The horses cannot go much farther without a break, and if I'm not mistaken, we're but half a day from the border. It'll be harder to find a peaceful place to lay our heads once we're out in the open."

Devi looked at the darkening sky and frowned. "Our internal clocks have changed in the Winter Court. The problem is, the scions and the seelie are day dwellers. Carrying on during the night while they sleep is one of our only advantages."

Valerius took a moment to think through what she'd said. "Fair point. However, I don't like the idea of exhausting ourselves or our steeds. I couldn't so much as close my eyes last night. You can't have had more than a few hours of rest. It does not improve our odds of defeating any foe we encounter."

He had a point.

Devi sighed. "Fine. But we could push forward until midnight, at least, and find somewhere to sleep near the border."

Vale countered, "Let's compromise. We can sleep four hours here and then carry on until dawn."

Sleeping now was tempting, so she agreed.

"I'll take the first guard," Vale offered.

"No need," Devi said. "We don't have much time, and these woods are as safe as anywhere for now. Let us both sleep if we are to do it here."

He wasn't inclined to argue. The horses were grazing at a small patch of grass near a stream; Vale spoke to them, whispering words Devi didn't understand as she'd yet to pass her animal care courses. These were old spells fae had taught the beasts they were on friendly terms with—horses, dogs, and birds. Spells each beast knew the meaning of from the day they were born, just like they knew how to stand and gallop as young foals.

Devi listened absentmindedly while she set up their makeshift beds of clothes and bags under a willow so they would be mostly shielded from the rain.

"Almost perfect," said Vale as he inspected her work. Then he pushed his bag-pillow so it rested against hers. "Except you happen to be a furnace, so I'll keep you close, if you don't mind."

She glared at him. "What if I *do* mind?"

He shrugged. "You may not need extra warmth, but I know you enjoy it, Devi Star Rivers, and I have a cloak we can both fit into."

He was starting to understand her too well for her taste. "Fine. Just keep your hands to yourself."

Valerius rolled his eyes. "The goal is to rest, not use up our energy. You're perfectly safe from me for the foreseeable future, little elf."

"I'm safe from you for the rest of my life, Blackthorn," she countered.

He laughed, actually laughed, like he truly believed she was joking.

She wasn't. He made her feel uncomfortable and out of control. She might not have seen it at first, but hearing him accuse her of consorting with his mother to ensnare him had been a wake-up call—because it had hurt.

She should have just laughed it off and feigned indifference. Had it been anyone else, she would have. What did it matter what he thought of her? He was a stranger who would disappear from her life the moment this mess was over.

She could have dealt with her attraction to a sexy male conveniently there to scratch an itch. This was all she, and anyone in the Court of Night, knew. But however short their acquaintance had been, Valerius Blackthorn had somehow bulldozed his way onto her short list of people who *mattered*. If she wasn't careful, she may even grow to care for *him*, ignoring the fact he was a playful, indifferent royal whose only concern was for his borders and his people. She knew better than to touch him. She knew he'd flirt and even attempt to seduce her on their journey; she would be the only warm hole to fit his dick in until their quest was over. She would shut it down time and time again until they parted ways.

Her resolve was firm. Then she lay down on the bed of grass, and Valerius pulled her against his chest.

Oh, dear. This wouldn't be easy, would it?

She jolted awake, violently ripped from an unusually peaceful, dreamless slumber. Two hours had passed at most; the night hadn't yet conquered the sky. Right away, she knew something was wrong. The forest was too silent. The wind carried no talk, not even a whisper.

Sometime over the last couple of hours, Vale had wrapped his arms around her waist. She found she didn't dislike the feeling. At all.

She shook her head, focusing on more pressing concerns.

"Vale!"

"Mmm?" he moaned sleepily, and pulled her tighter against his chest.

Devi did her best to fight her desire to curl up beside him and let him hug her until the end of time.

"Something's wrong. We need to go—now."

Just like that, his eyes snapped open, alert. He released her and, crouching, moved to gather their belongings. She joined him, rushing to fasten their bags to the horses.

"The elves have either left their posts or they're dead," Vale stated. "I can't feel anyone alive around us."

Her father's army never would have abandoned their post, so they were all dead, yet Devi felt nothing menacing near them. She could usually sense elves and fae, or any other creature of note, particularly if they had magic.

"I don't feel anyone."

Still, the silence perturbed her.

"You wouldn't. You've never come across their filth before. On your horse. We may yet outrun them."

She hopped on Alarik, asking, "'Them'?"

Vale grimaced. "You cannot sense life or magics around us, because there's none, but trust your nose on this."

Frowning, she tentatively sniffed and noticed a nasty rotting scent she couldn't place.

"Orcs," Vale said before mounting Midnight.

ELEVEN
ICE AND SNOW

Devi had never encountered orcs. They didn't venture deep enough in the unseelie realm to reach Asra or Farj up north. Shea had troops stationed all along the coasts, so the foul creatures met their doom as soon as they set foot on land.

By the smell of it, she didn't wish to get any closer to them.

"How could they have ventured so far into the woods!" she shouted.

"Not without guidance," Vale replied. "But the guard posts along the coasts are likely unmanned after the attack on Asra. More orcs will invade the lands soon!"

To her knowledge, orcs were repugnant but not particularly powerful. "Why are we fleeing? If we don't get rid of them, they'll attack the weak and pillage villages."

Orcs were no threat to the likes of Devi and Vale, but they could destroy the small villages of defenseless common and lesser fae.

"Their one strength was in their numbers, and we don't know how many are coming. If they've overthrown your father's forces, I'd say there are many."

Blast! Devi cursed. She wasn't fond of running, and they'd done nothing else in the last week. She pulled on Alarik's reins, calling to Vale, "Wait! I have an idea. Follow me."

"What idea?" he asked, unmoving.

She considered sharing the details of her plan, but he'd only argue with her. She lowered her voice and said, "We should remain quiet, lest they hear us. Come on."

Vale sighed but complied, letting her take the lead.

She dismounted and led Alarik off the path, carefully navigating between the trees. Away from the well-trodden path, the woods were very different, eldritch and menacing. Devi knew of some of the creatures who lived there, and many were to be feared by those who were unwelcome in the woods.

Once they'd put some distance between them and the path, Vale asked, keeping his voice low, "Where are we going?"

"I remember a cave on a hill not far from here. It's out of the way and big enough for the horses. If the orcs keep following Elven Way, we'll ride on their tail. If they manage to track us, even better: the woods will take care of some, and when the others reach us, we'll have the high ground."

"Not a bad plan, little elf. Of course, should the enemy overwhelm us, they'll have us trapped and we'll die in a ditch."

Yes, there was that, hence the reason she hadn't outlined her plan before heading toward the cave.

The march was long and unpleasant; they were knee-deep in mud in no time. Between the sinuous trees, Devi had to start slashing through thick spider webs to make her way forward. She did so with grimaces of disgust. If the fire and smoke would not have exposed their presence, she would have burned them all.

"What a wonderful walk. Clearly, we should follow your plans more often."

"Clearly," she echoed grumpily. "I came in the summer. The way wasn't so mucky and grimy then."

"That, or you're lost. It doesn't look like anyone has been through here in a decade."

Devi snorted. "I'm not lost."

She wasn't sure whether she was lying. She'd been rather confident of their course, but Vale had a point: it didn't look like any elf had walked here in eons.

"It wasn't a well-traveled road back then either," Devi explained, for her benefit as much as for Vale's. "My sister took me. She used to come here when she wanted time to herself." Seeing an opening through the thick trees, she beamed and pointed. "There! Cheer up, we're almost at Hillsides! And if Kira has left her supplies, we might even find a way to make a fire."

"Otherwise known as a great way to announce our location to anything tracking us."

She rolled her eyes and turned to him. "I'm not as stupid as you'd like to think I am. A blackfire, Blackthorn."

Vale's expression brightened. "You can make blackfire? Why do I hear of this only now?"

Blackfire didn't create smoke, emitted no light, and did not burn, but it was a powerful source of heat used by scouts during harsh winters.

"I can't without supplies. Another reason to head to the cave now."

"I might have looked upon your scheme more favorably if you'd opened with, 'Valerius, you'll stop freezing your balls off if we head over there.' Keeping my extremities intact is high on the list of things I'd risk a potential orc raid for."

She laughed. It wasn't that cold, was it? Devi's armor had a low-cut neckline and ended above her navel, yet she didn't feel the need to wrap her coat around herself. She was a child of winter.

She let go of Alarik's reins for a moment and walked back a few steps to stand in front of Valerius.

She put her hand on his chest over his cloak and pushed a small amount of fire energy through.

"There." She lifted her eyes to his face. "Better, you big baby?"

Gazing deep into her eyes, he observed, "Your eyes always go blue when you use magic. Even fire."

Oh, standing so close to him had been a terrible idea. Now she had to put up with the full force of his violet eyes on her, and the way his very presence set her core on fire.

"I can't say I've ever noticed," she mumbled, and stepped back. "I don't typically train in front of a mirror."

"Thank you, Devi. But now I know you can do that, I may have to request it a time or twenty."

"I think not. I have to preserve my energy."

At last, Devi spotted a narrow bridle path to their right and sighed in relief, glad she hadn't led them astray.

"There. A stranger to these woods might follow that path, but to get to the caves, we need to stay in the woods and hike up the hill from the other side."

"The orcs might still follow our footsteps or scents if they're led by a half-decent tracker."

Devi chewed on her lip as she thought it out. Her mind made up, she asked Vale, "Can you take the horses and go forward at least five hundred feet?"

"And why, might I ask?" Vale said, disinclined to obey again without the details first.

"I can make it snow, I think. To cover the tracks." Reluctantly, she admitted, "But I can't control that very well, and if things go awry, I'd rather not have any living things around me."

Her lack of control over water and ice frustrated her greatly. Had Vale mocked her, she might have taken it to heart, but something in her tone must have clued him in, because he made no remark other than, "Whistle if there's trouble. Can you imitate a bird?"

She winced. "Badly. But I can try to talk to you through the wind. Either way, go ahead, I won't be long."

Devi waited a furlong away and muttered, "Let's try not to mess this up."

She closed her eyes and did her best to concentrate.

Devi didn't have to strain to find the element as she had as a child. She focused to keep it in check, and when she believed she had a hold of it, she opened her eyes, looking up at the sky, and let go. Just one moment, not even a second.

The sky roared, enraged, and a bolt of lightning flashed, almost hitting her. The heavens came down harder, soaking her through with ice-cold rain.

That wasn't what she'd intended. "I said snow!" she muttered, eyes cast skyward.

She tilted her head, measuring how much of her power she could reasonably use.

This time, she pushed her energy outward for three whole seconds, her attention fixed on the clouds. She smiled when the first snowflake landed on the tip of her nose.

Devi looked down to find the ground frozen beneath her feet. Horror seized her chest, and she ran forward. Everywhere around her, there was ice. No. Not again! Not him...

She stopped in her tracks.

Five hundred feet into the woods, Vale was waiting with the horses as he said he would. The ground was frozen all around him, but her ice had stopped in front of his feet, as if it had hit a wall.

Her gaze moved from the patch of frost, to the muddy ground under his boots, and then to his eyes as she tried to comprehend what had happened.

Did he have a protection charm on him? Nothing else made sense.

"Neat trick with the snow," he said, pointing up. "And the ice, too. The snow might not have stuck to the ground without it. Our tracks will be hard to—"

"Do you have a spell against elemental magic? A charm or something?"

Vale shook his head. "I might own one or two at home, but none in Asra, and besides, we left in a rush. Didn't exactly have time to pack. Why do you ask?"

Because her out-of-control ass could have killed him and the horses, too.

She looked away, bashful. "I lost control. I could have hurt you."

Actually, he *should* have been hurt, as he'd been standing within range of her powers. That line on the ground made no sense; her ice never just *stopped*.

Vale shrugged indifferently. "You obviously didn't."

She lifted her eyes to him, confused.

He specified, "Lose control, that is. This looks like an intentional barrier. Glad to know you care, little elf." He winked, so nonchalant even though he could have died a second ago. "Besides," Vale added, "don't think me a weakling. I've fought many elemental mages long before you were born. Strong as you are, you're no danger to me."

Devi blinked. "You don't consider being frozen in place dangerous?"

Vale smirked, smug as ever.

"You're so full of shit it's a wonder you don't stink of manure."

"Fine. Let us prove it. Come at me."

He was seriously insane.

"Go on. Freeze me. Give it your best shot."

Devi huffed. "You have no idea—"

"No, you have no idea, little elf. And you're frightened of yourself because you think too highly of your little tricks. So, do it."

She walked to Alarik, grabbed his reins, and started her walk uphill, ignoring him entirely.

"All right, not ice, then, if you're such a craven. Burn me. Use whatever wind you may command. Make the ground shake beneath my—"

She didn't let him finish; Devi spun round, hand outstretched, and blasted air right into his chest. The wind was strong enough to put any grown male on his ass. Wasting her energy in that way right now was foolish, but also so very satisfying.

She grinned, looking forward to watching him eat his words. Then her smile dimmed.

One instant, Vale had been right in front of her, in the path of her magic, and now, there was nothing there.

"As I was saying…"

Startled, she stiffened and turned to find him right next to her.

"You're not that dangerous, Devira. Not to me."

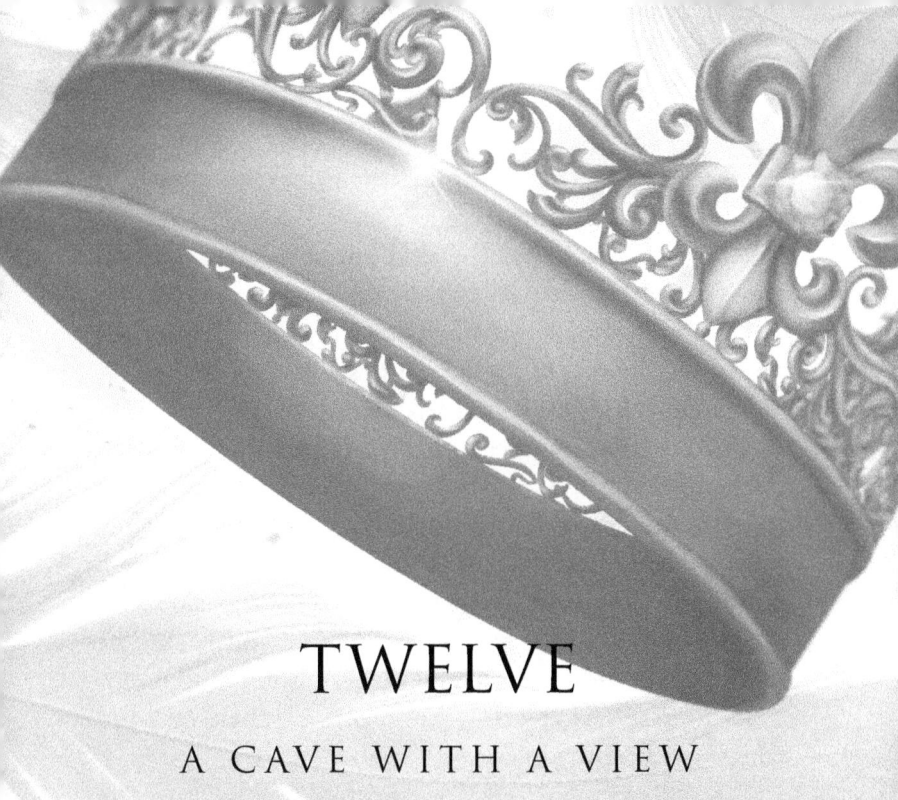

TWELVE
A CAVE WITH A VIEW

Devi served him the silent treatment for all of three minutes before giving in. "How did you do that, anyway?"

He kept his smirk in check. "I'm fast, that's all. How far up is that cave of yours?"

"We're close. It's tucked out of sight, right below the ridge."

The cave was ideally situated, its entrance narrow and inconspicuous. As the hill towered over the forest, one could see for miles without being spotted.

Vale had to admit the chit had been smart tonight. Without guidance, orcs were of little consequence, but someone had led the horde straight to them, and until

Vale found out who controlled them, he didn't wish to face his enemy unprepared.

If the orcs followed the road out of the Graywoods, they wouldn't cross paths; if they tracked them, despite the five inches of fresh snow covering their trail, they would see them coming from miles away.

They would not be surprised.

Vale entered the cave carefully, scanning it with his mind. He found no soul worthy of note, only small animals and the occasional snake or spider. As they walked deeper into the dark entrance, the cave expanded, growing large enough for them to march side by side with the horses in tow. The ground was uneven and sleek. The smell and humidity weren't pleasant, but it would do for a few hours. Perhaps they could resume their rest and take turns keeping guard.

Devi beamed when they reached the back of the cave. His eyes had adapted to the darkness; someone had crafted wooden shelves and two stools of rock. The craftsman's skills were rather rudimentary, but they'd made it work.

"She obviously hasn't come back here in many seasons, but her supplies are here," Devi said, moving to stand in front of the shelves.

Small flasks, potions, stones, and charms occupied the shelves. After some rummaging, she exclaimed victoriously, "There it is!" and took a dark stone in her grasp.

She held it in both hands and closed her eyes, concentrating for an instant. Then, Vale exhaled deeply, contentedly, as a wave of heat radiated from the female.

He and the horses stepped forward, eager to get closer to the source of warmth. She threw the stone over her shoulder, and he caught it in midair.

"Set it on the table, would you? It won't damage it."

Vale carefully placed the blackfire stone on the wood table and sat on one of the two stools. They were considerably too short for him, evidently made for children.

"Your sister is handy."

"She had to be, here. At Elvendale, many eyes constantly observed her. When she found this place, she resolved to tell no one. She made me swear I would never betray her secret hideout to any elf. It's lucky you're a fae—or a scion-fae thing, I guess—or we would still be outside."

Curious, Vale asked, "Are you bound by your oaths in the way of the fairfolks, or can you break your word?"

She grinned. "Wouldn't you like to know."

He would, actually, very much so.

"Devira, can you lie?" he pushed. She was elf and fae, a combination he'd never encountered.

"Can you?" she countered.

Vale frowned. "No, I..."

"You've been told you can't lie your whole life. Have you ever tried? You're the son of Orin; that makes you a first-generation scion like my father. I'm not sure how it all works, but with your mother a strong scion herself, your blood is over fifty percent on the godly side. So, can you lie? Or are you bound by oath?"

He opened his mouth and closed it again. The thought had never crossed his mind. In one breath, she'd challenged everything he knew about himself.

"I don't know."

"Well, try. Tell me something untrue."

Having never lied in his existence, he hesitated, stumped.

"Say my hair's golden or that you're a lesser fae."

"You're an idiot." By all gods. The words had actually crossed his lips. "And you're annoying. And I quite detest provoking you."

Lies, lies, and more lies, all coming right out of his mouth. He blinked, astounded at his newfound power.

"There you go."

"So you can lie and break your oaths."

"I can lie," she confirmed. "And as for breaking my oath, I will never find out."

Never. An easy word on such young lips.

"Will your sister be angry if we keep her stone?" he asked to change the subject.

"Hopefully not, because we're taking it either way, along with this," she said, pocketing a flask.

Vale saw a dark red liquid within and asked, somewhat hopefully, "Wine?"

She rolled her eyes. "That's a healing draught. This, however," said she, picking up a much larger bottle from the ground, "is cider. We weren't too fond of wine at fifteen."

The bottle was still full and sealed, so there was a chance it hadn't soured yet. She opened it, took a tentative swig, then downed a quarter of the liquid in three healthy gulps.

He watched with his arms crossed over his chest, refusing to beg for a share. If she was playing a game, he'd make her regret it on another occasion.

After another taste, she laughed. "Don't look so grumpy."

Devi bent down to retrieve another bottle and chucked it his way. He opened it and tasted the drink.

Fruity and a little dry, but agreeable nonetheless.

"Thanks," he said gratefully before standing up. "I'll take the first guard. You should try to sleep."

Devi shook her head. "There's only one blackfire stone. I'm not so cruel as to withhold it when the weather cannot actually hurt me, but I don't like being cold. I'm coming."

Vale didn't argue against an outcome that suited his fancy. They each carried a stool to the cave entrance and sat side by side, watching the horizon. Devi had insisted he keep the blackfire in his grasp, and for a time, he did. Then he took her hand, tugging at it until she understood his intent. She got up and came to sit on his lap. Vale wrapped his cloak around her shoulders. If she was to speak, she would have to protest, mock, and insult. If he was to say anything, he'd have to tell her truths she wasn't ready to hear. They remained silent, sharing their warmth. Alarik and Midnight soon joined them, attracted to the heat.

Devi stiffened just as he noticed trees moving. It looked so close to the hill, but he knew it was at least ten miles away, back where they'd left the Elven Way.

"Is that…?" she whispered.

Vale nodded. It could only be orcs. No other creature was so disruptive and unrefined. The tree was shaken and broken, and branches fell. Animals stirred and ran, their cries of concern reaching Vale's attentive mind.

The tumult moved north.

"Your plan is working," Vale noted. "They'll be out of the forest by morning, and we'll ride behind them. Since we're much faster with our dyrmounts, we should spend the rest of the night here."

He'd expected a fight, but Devi, head tucked under his chin, nodded against his chest and yawned. The poor female was exhausted.

"Sleep. I'll take tonight's guard."

THIRTEEN

ENERGY

For the first time in days—actually, for the first time in over a year—Devi slept soundly and longer than necessary. When she opened her eyes, the sun was high in the sky, indicating it was close to midday.

"How long was I asleep?" she asked groggily, blinking.

"Long enough to render my legs entirely numb. You're heavier than you look."

She punched Vale's shoulder and got to her feet, stretching happily. Not even he could dampen her mood. She hadn't felt this refreshed in years.

"You shouldn't have let me sleep for so long," she admonished without much conviction.

"Well, I hope you're well rested now. I came to a decision overnight. We're to approach Corantius from the east."

Her eyes bulged. They were but half a day's ride from the fourth realm if they headed directly north, but from the east, it was two or three days away at least. Yet she knew where that suggestion had come from, and she couldn't find any reason to object.

Both she and Vale came from the west; Farj was nestled directly against the Graywoods, and Carvenstone, on the coast. Anyone looking for them—and by now, they likely knew the pair was traveling together—would think to double their spies on the west coast. That they would head to the seelie realm would be unexpected.

Instead of arguing, she groaned.

"If we go east, straight to the seelie borders, we'll reach Rhionhave by nightfall," said Vale.

She tried to remember what she knew of seelie lands, which wasn't much. Until recently, she'd been banned from their realm under the penalty of death, so she'd never expected to visit their realm. Devi hadn't paid attention to any geography lesson about the kingdom of her ancestors.

"That's a port, right?" she asked.

Vale nodded. "The largest in the north. They receive shipments from Corantius and the southern seelie realms. On any day, there are dozens of strangers in the streets of the town. Some don't wish to be known—pirates and traders of illegal goods. I suspect there'd be little chance of two more foreigners under cloaks attracting much notice. We might sleep with a roof over our heads tonight."

That notion was less appealing than it should have been, but the two nights she'd actually gotten some rest had been under the stars and in Vale's arms. And she'd rather die a thousand painful deaths than confess that to the egocentric jerk with whom she traveled.

They broke fast with bread, dry meat, and cheese before setting off on their new path.

Riding west felt less perilous. They'd journeyed for a handful of miles when the wind started to whisper again, and to Devi's surprise, they encountered two elves in maille armor.

"Hello," she said politely, yet also somewhat awkwardly, for she recognized neither.

She'd met so very few folks during her year in Elvendale, particularly not those who were regularly posted outside the city.

Both had taken a knee, and they remained silent for a time.

"Our apologies, my lady. We bear ill news."

Her mind flew to her sister first, then to her father. "Well?"

"A legion of orcs attacked yesterday. They were led by scions, and our scouts perished at their hands. Many were tortured. We cannot know what they might have said to end their torment."

Ah. And that was why Vale had altered their course.

She dismounted and extended a hand to the elves to help them to their feet.

"No apologies. Not to me. I can only imagine the sorrow of losing your peers. Mourn your friends and cherish their memory. They have not betrayed you nor I."

The elves pressed their hands over their hearts and inclined their heads. Devi returned the show of respect. It wasn't until they'd disappeared that Vale felt compelled to point out, "Well, technically, they might have betrayed us. Rather likely, in fact. But as they knew nothing of importance, it's of no consequence."

"Valerius? People died. You're heartless."

"On the contrary, my dear. I certainly have a heart, and it's been beaten, battered, used, crushed, and spat out by unfortunate demises a dozen times, all before my twentieth winter. I am an old acquaintance of death, and I regard her with indifference when I can."

She ignored him, annoyed he'd so easily slipped his mask back on. Vale wasn't indifferent to death. He abhorred it. She'd watched his eyes while he'd taken in the elf female on the ground in Elvendale. She'd felt his rage when he'd seen the lifeless child she held. This was just posturing. The fact he'd waited for the soldiers to disappear before spouting his nonsense was proof.

She remained silent for hours, ignoring his attempts at casual conversation.

As the hours passed, the surrounding trees grew thinner and younger, and they could see the sky between the branches. They reached the border of Wyhmur right after dusk.

Devi bit her lip as she took in the large sea town in the distance.

"We need a story. A believable one this time," she amended. "Names, a purpose, a destination, a ready answer to whatever questions strangers might ask."

"Our story," he replied, "is that we are elves of the unseelie court. We've escaped the war, and we hope to catch a boat to Corantius."

Simple and, under the circumstances, highly believable. Devi doubted they were the only ones with such a tale, although she imagined few had crossed through Wyhmur.

"I'll let you come up with names."

"Won't they ask how we got through the Graywoods?"

"They will, and we'll say we asked the elves for their blessing. Weaving an unlikely tale and looking suspicious as we attempt to recall its details will not serve us well."

She saw his point, but one issue remained. "What if the guards in town have been told to watch out for you? What if you're recognized?"

"Look at me, little elf."

She shifted her eyes from the port town to him and gasped. Instead of Valerius, a blond male of his height and stature, with piercing green eyes and familiar, almost effeminate features, sat astride Midnight. He'd turned into Kallan.

"A simple illusion. I'm hijacking the signal your eyes send to your brain, so to speak. I've also altered your appearance a little, and that of the horses. Nothing but a parlor trick, but nevertheless, it'll take some effort to maintain the illusion over a long period and with so many people around. We need to be fast and intelligent in our dealings with the folks of Rhionhave."

She acquiesced. "Are we to sail north, then?"

He shook his head. "I don't much like the thought of entering Corantius by port. It will be well guarded against intruders. We'll let the seelie think that we intend to sail and leave at first light. Our business is to publicly purchase tickets, find an inn where we might spend the night, and rest." He hesitated. "I must sleep tonight."

Devi winced, feeling guilty for having rested so well when he had confessed to not sleeping the night before. It was a wonder he could remain upright and use his mind mojo too.

He didn't look tired; his expression was neutral as usual, but his eyes had lost some of their brightness.

"I'll take the first guard this time," she promised. She then realized: "We'll have to share a room."

Neither of them would sleep if they had to worry about someone breaking down their door while they were unconscious.

"We should," he replied without so much as a teasing word.

By all gods, the poor male must have been at death's door if he couldn't flirt.

Devi removed her glove and extended her arm toward him. He was riding Midnight beside her, keeping to her pace. Noticing her outstretched hand, he took it without question.

Devi meticulously removed the pesky mental shields around her mind. They both knew he could push his way through them whenever he wanted to, but she let him pass through openly.

"Channel me," she told him.

The fake Kallan watched her with an expression that definitely belonged to Vale.

"Your entire plan depends on your ability to keep up this illusion, and you're about to fall over. Riding might be hard on my body, but my mind is well rested, so channel me. Use whatever strength you need until we're out of danger."

He gave her a moment or two to change her mind, and when her resolve didn't waver, Vale called her energy to him. She let it flow out of her freely. It felt rather strange; all the masters of magic at the Academy had taught her to prevent enemies from sucking on her energy. A mage could die, drained of power. She'd been instructed to resist it with everything she had.

Letting Vale take her strength was an intimate experience. For a moment, she felt him all around her—not his hand, not his presence, but his very spirit, his soul. She saw glimpses, just shapes, colors, and sounds she couldn't make out. Some happiness, a lot of pain, and above all else, isolation. Not quite loneliness. It seemed more purposeful than that. Vale hadn't been rejected; he'd stepped away from everyone, everything, keeping them at a distance.

Something else dwelled underneath it all. A dark desire that overshadowed everything else. This male only cared about one thing. Only one thing he'd gladly kill and give his life for. A light in centuries of darkness. She wanted to push further, walk toward the light to get a glimpse.

Vale let go of her hand, closing the connection just as she'd stepped toward it.

"Eavesdropping is rude, little elf."

She cleared her throat. "Sorry, I don't know what—"

"No matter. No one can control mind-reading powers at first. It took me years to learn how to shut the voices off. From time to time, I still find myself doing it without any volition on my part."

Devi nodded awkwardly and apologized again.

"How come I could read your mind?"

He snorted. "I doubt you could *read* very much. That also takes skill and practice. But channeling is a two-way street. With your energy in me, I could probably use elemental magic for the next few moments if I knew how to."

She beamed, glad to hear about another thing the dark prince couldn't do.

"Thank you, by the way. I feel much refreshed. Young people are incredibly energetic."

"You've never succeeded in sounding so ancient before," she retorted.

His reply died on his lips. They'd arrived in the town, and malevolence hung in the air.

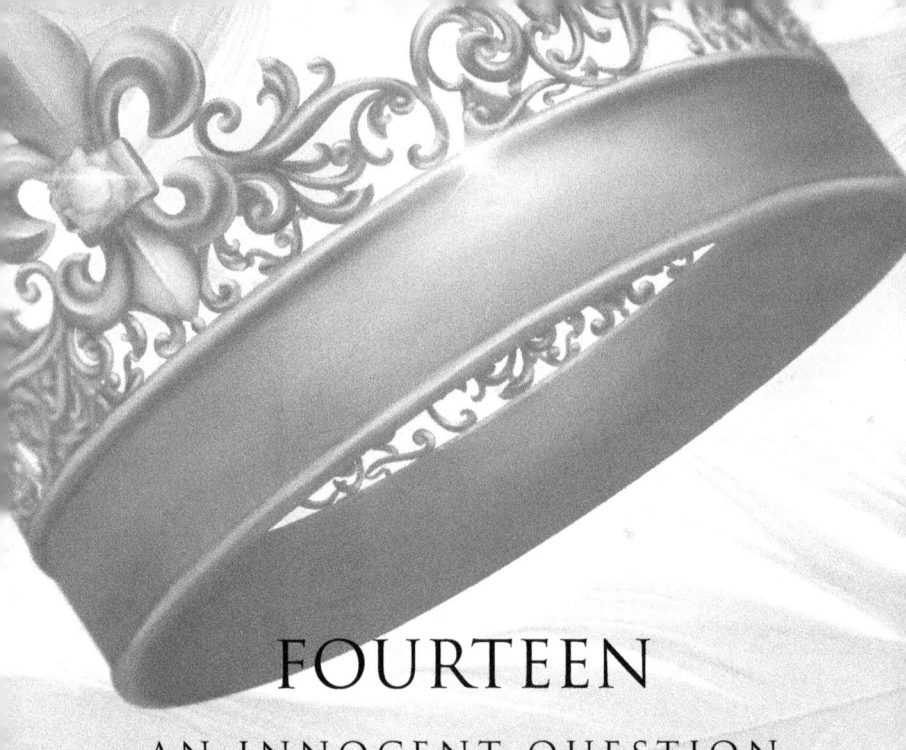

FOURTEEN
AN INNOCENT QUESTION

Over half a century had passed since he'd set foot in the seelie realm, and perhaps two hundred years since he'd passed through Rhionhave, but he recalled it being a cheerful town. The harbor had flourished from the wealthy tourists passing through, so every night there were dancers and musicians in the streets and vendors at every corner.

Now, the town was quiet and dim.

Devi and he slowed their horses and advanced in silence, eyeing either side of the avenue. Where was everyone?

Vale's eyes narrowed as he passed a sign to his left. In bold red letters, someone had written "curfew," and underneath, there were words of warning and promises of barbaric punishments to those who broke it.

"Sundown," Devi read out loud. She frowned and turned to him. "What now?"

He remained silent, feeling the approaching presences before he heard their steps. Five men in blue and silver came into view. The colors of the realm house, meaning they were soldiers.

They rushed to them, one soldier roaring, "You! What are you doing out here at this hour? Identify yourself immediately! What is your business here?"

Vale's darkest instinct reminded him that there was a sword at his side that could take care of the problem in no time. Instead, he said, "Peace! My wife and I have been traveling for days. We're visiting family in the north. We hoped to spend the night at the Sailor's Inn? I recall they made the most delightful clam chowder."

The soldiers' shoulders relaxed with each word. Now that he had more energy to spare, he dared to brush their minds.

Obviously unseelie, they thought, but the soldiers didn't blame them for fleeing their land, what with his wife's condition. He'd been right to conjure the vision of a pregnant female, although Devi might have had a thing or three to say about it, if he'd shared that piece of information. All high fae respected children and saw them as precious treasures, for they were too rare among their kind.

"The inn is closed," a male grumbled. "It accepts no strangers after sundown. Order of the King Father. There's a nationwide curfew."

The King Father. Kravin Farel. Vale couldn't say he was surprised.

"We can sleep at the docks if we have to," said Devi sweetly in a convincing impression of a mild-mannered female that would have had him laughing at any other time.

One of the soldiers scratched his head. "I know ol' Thomson well. We can make an exception, can't we? Given the lady's condition."

Devi's eyes narrowed and she flashed Vale a glare. Then, she clutched her tummy, playing along.

"Aye, I say we can. What did you say your names were?" the male in charge asked.

Ah. They hadn't sorted that out yet.

"Naelynn and Ruven Norfiel, sir," she improvised.

Well played. The Norfiels were a minor high fae house, mostly inconsequential and without much money. There was no risk of their being recognized outside of the unseelie realm. And yet they were noble, for even with his visions, Vale couldn't hide the strength of their auras. Had they pretended to be common fae, they might have seemed suspicious.

"I'll escort you to the Sailor's. Name's Wyn, my lady, my lord."

The seelie grasped the reins of their horses and led them through the dark streets.

Vale had so many questions, but asking any of these strangers, right out in the open, would not be prudent, so he kept them to himself. What had Kravin done with this realm? What deal had he made with Corantius? It all made no sense to him.

The Sailor was a modest inn near the harbor, known for its excellent food and its jovial owner. Thomson was as common as any fae and so very unlike most seelie that Vale liked him well enough.

The soldier led them to a back door and knocked loudly. The man who opened wasn't the smiling, round, loud host he remembered. Thomson was thinner and much older, and there was fear in his eyes.

"What is it, Wyn? I've not done a thing, I swear."

"Quiet, now. I'm not here on official business. We found them two in the street, and what with the lady being fat and all, we wondered if you could put them up."

His eyes shifted from Vale to Devi, then back to Wyn.

"Yes, yes, of course. There's room in the stable and I have several rooms free tonight. Come on through. Let's get you out of the cold. I'll send Pip to take care of the beasts."

Vale did not relax, not after walking inside the inn, and not after the doors had closed behind him.

His illusion hadn't worked on Thomson. Somehow, the common fae had seen right through it.

But he hadn't said a thing.

Yet.

After Wyn had left the alley, the host turned to Vale, his deep voice almost threatening as he said, "Whatever business you're into, I want no part of it. You will keep this spell of yours in my house, understood? As far as anyone is concerned, I've housed a random stranger in need and his pregnant wife."

Vale nodded. "Thank you."

"Arr, none of that, you old bastard. Go on, you know where your damn room is. No one else has the coin for a master's these days. You better pay me well—and tip, too!"

He grinned, breathing a little easier.

They walked through the back kitchen, where Thomson's team was busy.

"Are we too late for food?" Devi asked, hopeful.

"No one's ever gone hungry under my roof, young lady. I'll bring your supper up in a few. Gotta serve those who ordered before you first, so you'll have to wait. We had plumbing installed since the last time you were in. You can take a bath if you want while you wait. Go on, then."

He stayed back in the kitchen, letting them walk in by themselves.

Out of the service corridor, Vale passed the common area, which had always been lively, with a full bar and a musician playing every night. An old lady played the piano beautifully, and a couple of customers were gathered around, but no one talked, no one laughed, and no one smiled.

What had happened to this place, this town?

Vale made his way up three flights of stairs to the principal suite. He opened the door to find it mostly unchanged.

Devi burst in, threw her coat on the floor, and jumped on the bed, groaning in pleasure as she stretched her back languorously. Such a kitten.

Smiling, Vale walked in, checked every corner of the room, and looked out the window.

The harbor was dark and empty.

"You get to sleep first, but I'm claiming the bath!" she said.

"Not yet," Vale replied, still looking out the window.

The bedsprings squeaked as Devi sat up behind him. "Why, what's the matter?"

He reluctantly walked away from the window, itching to see what was wrong with Rhionhave. He felt like he was missing something important that might serve him well later, but remaining at the window through the night wouldn't get him answers.

"Nothing," he replied, joining her. "You've done well for a new rider, but we both know how much you're hurting."

He hadn't realized it until he'd channeled her and felt her pain. Vale had been a seasoned rider from a young age, and over the centuries, he'd never lacked practice. He hadn't understood the toll the journey was taking on her.

He sat next to her on the bed and put his hand on her shoulder, pressing hard with his thumb.

Devi whimpered and groaned the harder he pressed.

"Lie down on your front," he told her.

She obeyed immediately, eagerly. Vale removed his wet cloak, straddled her back, and kneaded her shoulder with both hands, pushing into every knot he found. She yelped once or twice, and practically purred too.

His hands worked her back, spine, sides, hips, and then the curves of her firm ass and her legs; every part of her body, every corner. He pulled her boots off to massage her calves and feet, and then he started on her arms and hands.

"Turn around," he told her.

She flipped onto her back, and he propped her head on his lap to massage her head first. He undid her braid and threaded his fingers through her hair to get to her scalp. She smiled, eyes closed.

"This should be your profession."

Vale chuckled, working on her neck.

At long last, he stated, "I'm done for now."

She opened her eyes and asked, "Can you carry me to the bath? I don't think I can walk."

"Don't push it, Rivers." Nonetheless, he got to his feet. "I'll start the bath. Rest now. It'll be my turn in the bath after the food gets here."

Finding eucalyptus oil on the shelves above the large dragon-claw tub, Vale put a few drops in before drawing a warm bath. Back in the room, he found Devi lying exactly where he'd left her. He walked to the bed, wrapped his arms under her back and knees, and lifted her.

"Hey, I was kidding! I can walk."

Unlike the first time he'd carried her that way, she wasn't struggling to get out of his arms. Vale set her down on a plush velvet stool in the bathroom and walked out with a parting, "I trust you can manage now? Or do I have to change your diaper too?"

Moments later, there was a firm knock on the door. Vale opened it without concern; tired as he was, he'd identified the presence long before it had reached their door.

Thomson had come up himself, probably to limit their run-ins with his staff in case things went awry.

"Thank you, old friend. Come in," Vale said, taking the tray of clam chowder, mashed potatoes, and stewed venison and setting it down on the coffee table.

The owner reluctantly stepped inside the room and closed the door.

"What has happened here?"

The fae sighed. "They came just yesterday, a bunch of longcoats from the city. Not the local guards, those are just fine. The longcoats said we're too lax, that war's coming to our doors and we can't afford to have them pirates, them strangers, them children running around. We ignored them; we always do, you know? And then they started shooting. Everyone who said a word, who disagreed. Some kids, too. They've imprisoned people. Some got a whipping in the town square; others we'll have to bury. I dunno what's going on, I really don't. They say you're wanted for a lot of money and harboring you is treason. I say they've killed townsfolk for sport. I'm not giving them nothing. You do your thing and keep causing them trouble, you hear?"

Vale assured Thomson he certainly intended to, before going to his bag and withdrawing a bond. The silver sheet was among his smaller ones, unlike the thin gold flower he'd used to purchase a horde of dyrmounts, but it was worth the entire inn five times over.

"You're taking a huge risk for me. I will not forget this," he said, and handed him the payment.

Thomson shook his head. "Can't take that. What will they say if I popped it in the bank, hmm? They'll certainly know where it came from."

"Perhaps, but in ten or a hundred years, you may make use of it. I'll pay you the usual gold coin, too, so you can deposit it now."

After some convincing, Thomson accepted the money.

"I have people to take care of here, good people, so you keep the curtains closed, and you use that magic of yours outside the room," Thomson warned as he left.

Vale assured the man he would and went to close the curtains.

He remained seated in an armchair for a long time; how long, he couldn't tell. Vale had much to think of.

What was happening in Rhionhave was revolting. He wanted to lash out, but he remembered Elden's wise counsel. Slaughtering the longcoats would serve but a few—just the people of this small town and only for a time. Then there would be whispers that he had been here, and someone would reveal the direction he'd left. He would not endanger the entire quest for his personal satisfaction.

But this had to stop.

For the first time, Vale realized there was no easy way out. He could not let either of his brothers take power; he could not bow to them and disappear, not if this was what would happen under their rule.

Vale didn't just have to survive. He had to *conquer*.

He didn't hear Devi come out of the bathroom, but suddenly, she stood in front of him, wearing breeches and a loose shirt that fell to her mid-thigh. Her long hair was loose and fell in waves down her back.

"I need to become king of the Isle," he said out loud, stating a simple fact he'd only just accepted.

A fact she'd known from the start.

"You do."

"I'll suck at it. Really, I'll be terrible. There are millions of things I don't care to deal with at Carvenstone, and I get Kallan to do them—open my mail, check the perimeter in the cold mornings. I *hate* the cold," he confessed. "Carvenstone is all right, but the Court of Crystal is fucking freezing year-round. And I'm a bastard in the eyes of the scions. They'll never accept me. My rule will end in a matter of days. They'll slit my throat in my sleep. And they should. You remember how I bought a fortune's worth of horses on a whim? I may ruin the realm. The *realms*."

To his astonishment, Devi laughed. "The fact you're so worried about failing is why you will be a great ruler, Vale. You'll listen to your council and delegate tasks you aren't good at. As for keeping your neck on your shoulders, literally every monarch has that concern. That's why they have guards posted at their doors. You'll call Kallan and whoever else you want to stand by your side."

"You," he told her.

Devi blinked.

"If the day comes when I am seated on that blasted throne, I will call upon you to stand by my side. How will you answer?"

She hesitated. "I will tell my king I'm his to command. Unless he's being a dick. Then I'll kick his ass first."

Vale smiled, letting her lighten the subject. He'd asked a question she wasn't yet ready to answer. No matter. He'd ask again.

"Let's eat before the food gets cold," he proposed, and served the two bowls of chowder first.

She sat on the opposite armchair and accepted the food with thanks.

"I feel very refreshed, by the way. Ready to take first watch."

"Good. I need to rest."

The likelihood that he might sleep, considering the many concerns that filled his mind, was rather grim, but he had to do his best to rest while they had the chance. The War of the Realms had taught him that, during a conflict, there was no way to know when they might next eat or sleep safely.

They ate both courses in silent appreciation, and then Vale moved to the bathroom, undressed, performed the simplest of ablutions, and returned to the room stark naked.

"Oh!" Devi said, eyes wide open to devour him from head to toe, before turning around with a blush. "A warning would not have gone amiss, you know."

Vale laughed. Retrieving his bag, he pulled out the soft pair of breeches he wore to bed when he had company. He got dressed and lay down under the cover.

He might have passed out had he not channeled Devi earlier, but as he wasn't as drained, he failed to succumb to sleep, ruminating over what he'd learned this week: tales of scions and gods, the fact he had a second brother, the death of his father, the existence of the divine instruments, and, above all, Devi, daughter of Elden, master mage, dear to all elves, redoubtable, and perfectly suited for him.

Just when he'd been ready to abandon all pointless attempts to rest, Devi joined him on the bed and sat up next to him.

"You're tossing and turning. We can't keep using the blackfire stone continuously, lest it loses its power, but if you're cold, body heat might help. I can stay awake and alert so long as I remain seated, I think."

His heartbeat slowed, and his mind focused on the moment. Having her right next to him allowed him to stop thinking of anything else, anyone else. Just her.

And then he was asleep.

FIFTEEN
WISER

Vale was a heavy sleeper. She'd gathered as much in the Valley of Doom, but he'd passed out on the cold, hard ground then. Now, on a bouncy, supportive mattress, wrapped in warm, fluffy covers and furs, with a feather pillow under his neck, he had no inclination to rouse.

Close to dawn, Thomson knocked on the door with breakfast. She thanked him and tried to wake Vale for the first time. "Vale? Breakfast is served."

To leave at daybreak as he wanted, they needed to eat and get ready.

There wasn't a peep from the silent, unmoving male tucked in bed. He'd fallen asleep on his side and remained that way for hours on end.

She returned to the bed and shook his shoulder.

He shifted onto his front and placed the pillow on top of his head, decisively shutting her out.

"We should eat and get going before the town awakens. That was the plan, right?"

"Plans change!" he mumbled.

She had to smile. After considering her options, she chose to let it go. He'd let her sleep all night; surely he deserved the same courtesy. He'd get up soon enough.

Two hours later, she sighed. Dawn had come and gone. The town was awakening. They'd considerably complicated their exit now, unless they opted to remain another day.

Four hours later, she checked his pulse.

"I'm alive."

"And awake," she noted.

He hadn't moved at all.

"I refuse to acknowledge that fact yet."

So, he wasn't a morning person. She chuckled at the entirely unexpected characteristic.

"You woke up before most back in Wolven Fort, the first time we met."

"Yes, in Wolven Fort," he repeated. "I never could sleep well among a swarm of hypocrites, thieves, and butchers."

Devi rolled her eyes. "It wasn't that bad."

"Or you didn't know them that well. A dozen years of acquaintances does not make you an expert, little elf."

Finally, he lifted his pillow from his head, emerging with a bird's nest of light brown curls atop his head.

"Breakfast was served around five. It was delicious. Yours is now cold."

"I'll live," he replied, sitting up on the bed, barechested, his very hard muscles on display.

Devi had to look away. He was exquisite from the moment he rose! How infuriating.

"So, what's the new plan, Sir Sleep-a-Lot?"

"I'm not sure yet, but it absolutely depended on my recuperating first, evidently."

"Evidently," she echoed.

He went to the coffee table and attacked his cold porridge with gusto, no complaint crossing his lips. Vale was the opposite of precious.

She realized she was noting his attributes, as if trying to define him, understand who he truly was. Intelligent, sometimes kind, often rude, always arrogant, and a heavy sleeper who didn't need luxuries to be content, despite his rank.

"I say we leave publicly, heading south, then turn back as soon as the town is out of view and walk north. Once we reach the sea, we can return to Wyhmur and make the rest of our way through the woods to Cor's Gates."

Devi frowned.

North of the seelie realm was a mile-wide stretch of water called the Arched Sea; it ended where the forest of Wyhmur and the southern border of Corantius met. Even in times of peace, that pass had always been guarded by elves south of the border and by Corantians north of their fences. Arriving by Wyhmur was dangerous. It would be expected, and the gates would be watched closely.

Fae avoided the Arched Sea, for it was known to house many ancient spirits.

"Wouldn't it make sense to cross into Corantius by water?"

Vale shook his head. "Not with the horses, and I'm not inclined to part with them if it can be avoided."

She bit her lip. "Are there not areas where the Arched is narrow?"

Vale inclined his head. "Yes, west of Cor's Gates, there's a point where there's only a hundred feet of water between the seelie realm and Corantius, if I recall. There is even a bridge that traders can cross, but it is well guarded and far from the Court of Stars."

Ignoring the second point, she asked, "As well guarded as Cor's Gates?"

Vale took a moment to think it through. "It will add many miles to our journey, but it may prove less perilous. Very well, we'll make for the Low Crest Bridge. Do you mind if I take the bathroom first?"

She'd already washed earlier, and he hadn't bathed the previous night. "Go ahead," she said, somewhat awkwardly.

The innocent exchange had reminded her that they were sharing a room, a bed. At least now she was sure that, for all his teasing, he didn't have any serious intentions to seduce her; he might have been too tired the previous evening, but he could have tried his luck this morning. He hadn't.

Good. It *was* good, she told herself resolutely.

Neither of them had unpacked. Vale had left his shirt out, and she'd washed it, along with hers, and left them out to dry next to the fireplace. Now she folded his and put hers back on.

Vale didn't take overlong to bathe; he came out wet, with a towel around his waist.

"Would it kill you to show some degree of modesty?"

"I cannot show what I do not possess, little elf. Thanks for washing my shirt."

"Don't get used to it," she retorted, fiddling with the handle of the bag just to have an excuse to look away as he dressed right in front of her.

The infuriating male was probably flaunting his body on purpose, aware of the fact she was moments away from turning into a puddle of lust. It was unfair that nature had created a male who was so irresistible and exasperating all at once. If he'd been a full-fledged god of old and his worshippers had named him for his gifts, he would have been known as the god of temptation.

"I am decent. You may stop pretending to avert your eyes."

"You're aware that the world doesn't revolve around you?"

"I'm psychic, Devira. It's not my fault your mind screams obscenities every time you watch me undress."

"Don't confuse your dreams for reality, Blackthorn."

He might have a point, but her shields were up, and she hadn't felt him invade her mind. She doubted he actually *knew* she inwardly drooled when she saw him. "Ready?"

Thomson was busy in his office, but Vale paid for their board at the bar while they waited for the horses, leaving a generous tip.

With one glance, Devi confirmed all their belongings had been brought along with Alarik and Midnight. Then they were on their way.

The moment they walked through town, she tensed, feeling eyes on her from every corner. Her grasp on the dyrmount's reins was perhaps a little too firm. She itched to ask Vale if his illusion was working. Thomson had seen through it. What if others did?

They crossed paths with many villagers who watched them with mistrust and too much interest. She was glad they'd planned to go south first. People would talk. There was no doubt about it.

Vale pulled on Midnight's reins, stopping him. His expression was unreadable but so very cold. She halted next to him, but in no time, he was trotting forward again.

Devi opened her mouth to speak, but Vale's words entered her mind. *"Say nothing. Do nothing. For the love of all gods, keep trotting."*

She had so many questions. They were answered as they advanced and the cobblestone town square came into view.

She couldn't process what her eyes were seeing. She couldn't move or talk. Vale leaned toward her and took Alarik's reins to guide her away, prying her out of this living nightmare.

A silent and terrified crowd was assembled in front of a newly built wooden scaffold. Up on the platform, there were a dozen fae in pillories, and fae in long coats with whips were lashing them, each strike drawing blood.

Some of the prisoners were youth, no older than fifteen or sixteen—children, even to her eyes.

"What is—"

"They broke curfew," Vale stated simply.

She froze. They were getting *whipped* because they'd been out after dark?

"Vale..."

"Recall what your father said."

She didn't have to ask what he meant. She remembered Elden's parting words: *If you value the lives of the few over the many every time you have a hard choice to make, you are doomed.*

Devi had taken them as sage counsel. She'd believed them. She'd promised herself she would consider the consequences before acting rashly. The wise course of action was to keep going with their heads down and ignore the plight of these people. So what if they were tortured? They'd learn tomorrow. Eventually, no one would break the rules.

And their spirits would break; they would live in fear without hope.

She got off her horse.

Devi had not been raised to stand by and watch such horrors. She was a protector, and that word meant something. Before serving the unseelie realm, she'd chosen to serve the weak, the poor, and the defenseless. To be the dragon slayer her mother had said she was so many years ago.

"Elden was wrong, Vale."

She turned, hands lifted toward the longcoats on the platform.

Elden was wrong. The few were many, and each one mattered. She would not turn her back on them.

And then there was fire.

SIXTEEN
FROM ONE BEAST TO ANOTHER

Vale sighed. In all fairness, the moment he'd felt the despair emanating from the town square, he'd calculated their odds of getting out of Rhionhave without bloodshed, and they hadn't looked good. He'd known there was a high probability that either he or Devi would attack the longcoats. He was glad to attest that, this time, he'd been the voice of reason. But now that she'd attacked, they had no choice but to kill every single longcoat.

Oh well.

Devi killed one with her first jet of fire and wounded another two, then a mage among them erected a blue shimmering elemental barrier. Water magic. Smart and efficient against her fire. Devi drew her bow and started picking them off left and right.

The longcoats launched forward. Vale got down from his horse and told the dyrmounts, "You will stay here and trust that young little elf to protect your flanks. She may be rather foolish, but she's not inclined to carry your load for the rest of our journey, so she'll ensure you both come out of this contretemps in one piece."

The horses neighed their agreement—or their doubt, Vale couldn't tell—and he walked away.

"Where are you going?" Devi shouted at his retreating back, visibly surprised he'd leave her now.

"Cleaning up your mess," he replied.

Devi was as smart and caring as she was beautiful. She lacked only one thing: experience.

This town had not been terrorized without cause. Vale guessed that most coasts, ports, havens, and hamlets they passed on their way to Corantius would be thus occupied by strangers who were there for one reason.

To draw him out.

They'd revealed their presence, and all he could do was delay the inevitable to ensure no message reached their enemy.

No doubt, the longcoats had been told to check in often, and when they remained silent too long, the Corantians would know to look for Devi and Vale here.

It was his fault. They should have left at dawn.

Vale jumped up onto a low roof and removed his coat and shirt. His wings painfully tore out of his back.

Damn, it was cold. Warmer near the coast than it had been in the forest, but it definitely wasn't the kind of weather he liked to parade half naked in.

He leaped in the air and extended his rusty limbs, beating them in the air. He glided in a circle, eyes and mind scanning the horizon. Within an instant, messenger birds were released from a house near the town square, and they flew in every direction.

Vale flew after them, sword at the ready. How he hated having to slay beasts over the deeds of their masters. Some stained his sword with blood and feathers; others he concentrated on, only relinquishing his hold on their small simple minds when they fell. Soon, only a small falcon with a white throat and warm brown feathers was left.

Its black eyes were fixed on him somewhat expectantly. That bird knew it was looking at its death.

Vale rarely saw the minds of animals clearly; they had very simple needs, a limited range of emotions, and that was it. But that spoke to him, in its own way. He understood it.

The bird was young and would have liked to have seen more of the Isle. It had been bred in captivity and trained to do specific tasks it did not like. Death was a prospect it wasn't entirely set against.

"And what if you never see the far south of the highest mountains whence your peers came? What of your dreams?"

The bird gave no answer. One did not answer death.

Vale tucked his wings in and landed in a crouch atop the roof of a tall dwelling in Rhionhave. He lifted one arm in a wordless invitation.

The bird circled him thrice, crying high, before racing toward him at full speed, talons extended. It landed on Vale's bare arm, drawing blood.

"I will not slay you as long as you do not betray me."

The falcon screeched.

"Good. Now go. I still have work to do."

He lifted his arm, inviting the bird to fly away, but the falcon wasn't so inclined to leave. Sighing, Vale ran, the beast still perched on his shoulder. He headed to the house where the birds had been launched from. There were a dozen longcoats still inside. Vale made short work of them. The home had evidently served as their headquarters.

He paged through letters on a desk, rummaged through their pockets, and inspected whatever belongings he saw on shelves, cupboards, and drawers.

A man with a weathered face and his arms held open like a cross adorned their coins. Corantians. Not scions, evidently, as they'd been easy pickings. None of their correspondences were worthy of note.

He smiled right before the door of the house was kicked open.

"Twenty-seven soldiers!" Devi screamed, glaring and pointing at him accusingly. "You left them all to me and got me to take care of the horses too!"

He shrugged. "That was your call. And forgive me for ensuring the Corantians didn't send word of our being here to every corner of the four realms."

"You're a lazy-ass rake, Valerius Blackthorn!" She calmed down long enough to ask, "And why is there a falcon on your shoulder?"

"Ah, yes. Devi, meet…" He hesitated, turning his attention to the bird. It probably needed a name. "How do you like Vulen?"

The bird screamed angrily. "All right. How about Dain?"

The falcon tapped his head with its beak. "I get it. Not Dain. Adris."

This time, it cooed merrily.

"Adris, this is Devi," Vale said. "She's not usually this crotchety."

"Crotchety!" she roared, outraged. "While you were out bird shopping, I was dealing with a bunch of idiots and then an entire crowd that wouldn't leave me alone."

"And why would they?" Vale asked with a smile. "That's what you get for playing the hero. I trust the horses are tended to?"

"I left them with Thomson while I came looking for you. Come on, we need to go."

"Not quite yet," he replied, taking a seat at the longcoats' desk.

A stack of blank paper was piled at one corner. He took a sheet and placed it in front of him.

"You're catching up with your pen pals? Now?"

Vale lifted his eyes to her. "It could be hours or days, but eventually, the realms will learn of our position, thanks to your heroics. So yes, I must write, now. I'll tell my mother we're to join her in Elderdale, and I'll tell Kallan we're to join him in Carvenstone. With some luck, either or both letters will be intercepted, winning us back a semblance of an advantage."

She sighed. "All right. Then we need to go. Seriously, the people here are all being weird and annoying."

Vale smiled. Before she left, he called, "Devi?" She turned to him. "You wanted the people of this town to believe they would not be forsaken, left under the talons of a tyrant. You were right to act. Do not let my teasing convince you otherwise."

She grinned. "Contrary to what you believe, your opinion doesn't matter that much to me, Blackthorn."

He laughed and returned to his writing.

SEVENTEEN

FIRE

Kallan breathed in and out hard. He couldn't recall struggling this much since his days spent training during his youth. He was a seasoned horseman, and his daily exercise with Valerius Blackthorn had ensured he remained in top form.

And for all that, his body felt like he'd taken a relentless beating. Three days of riding without so much as one stop. If he'd ridden anything other than a dyrmount, the beast would have died of exhaustion by now.

After the griffins came the seelie archers, and then the orcs.

Fucking orcs, dozens of them.

His horse, Falkr, outran most, and his bow and arrow felled the rest. Kallan used the shade of the Graywoods to confuse his assailants, riding right at the border and under the trees when he wished not to be seen. But he didn't remain in that godsforsaken forest longer than necessary. He didn't know if the Graywoods were haunted, possessed, or worse, but they'd always frightened him.

Not to mention, there was the fact he could be cut down by an elf at any moment for daring to enter their domain uninvited.

Yet he did so anyway.

After three days and as many nights, he needed rest and so did Falkr, if only for an hour.

The world seemed to stop once he entered the woods. Time was a strange notion under the shade of the thick trees, where one could not see the sky.

Kallan hated how unnaturally quiet his surroundings were. There were many creatures in this forest. Why weren't any of them making a fucking noise?

He knew the answer, of course. Because of him. Because he was a stranger who did not belong, and they didn't trust him.

He listened closely, eyes closed, searching for one specific sound. At long last, he opened his eyes.

"Come on, Falk. I found water."

They advanced slowly and carefully, tension heightening as they got farther into the wood, but at long last, they reached a small pool. He dismounted Falk and approached, cupping water in his hands to taste it with the tip of his tongue. It was freezing but tasted pure. He'd heard that some streams coming down from the White Mount were poisonous. The last thing he needed right now was to fall ill, but he'd run out of water early that morning. If he did not drink, he'd die regardless, and more painfully.

Kallan got to his feet to return to his horse but stopped dead. Between him and Falk stood a female. Not the sort of female one might encounter by chance and forget someday. Not the sort of female who'd become nameless and faceless with time. A female made of dreams and sorrow. Hair red as blood and eyes of emeralds, so intense he could not look away from them. She wore form-fitting gear, a warrior's attire befitting a goddess of death. In her grasp was a staff—a long, thick piece of carved redwood with a stone embedded at its tip.

Her face was familiar, although he couldn't place where he might have seen its likeness.

"Am I dreaming?" he asked.

A fair question, really. The female tilted her head and stepped sideways to stand closer to his horse. The hand that didn't hold her staff was bare, and a leather glove that ran up to her elbow covered the other.

She lifted her gloveless hand to Falk's head. "Tired," she stated.

Her voice was honey and barbed, a mixture of sweetness and ire. Kallan instinctively knew it reflected her spirit. She was all fire or the very opposite.

"We rode far," he explained. "We are being followed. I'm sorry we entered the Graywoods uninvited, but I'd hoped—"

"Shhh…"

Her eyes returned to him, and he felt as if he were standing in front of a great beast that hadn't decided if he'd make for a decent dinner.

"What is your name, stranger?" she asked.

And there it was. Fire and ice. Softness and strength. If he gave her the wrong answer, he would encounter the beast. He *would* give the wrong answer because he was fae, and he couldn't lie.

"Kallan, my lady. Kallan Blacks. I was on my way—"
"To Carvenstone."
His eyes widened. "How did you—who are you?"
"Kira Rivers Star."
"Devi's sister!" he realized.

That was who she reminded him of, although they had a different presence, aura, and coloring. Everything but that face.

Her eyes flashed, becoming brighter yet more menacing. "What do you know of my sister?"

Kallan smiled. The female seemed so cold and larger than life, but for all that, she was worried about her little sister. There was something comforting about it.

"She made it out of Asra with me and Vale, the lord of Carvenstone. They were headed to Elvendale."

Kira scoffed. "And they made it, or I would not have been told to babysit the likes of you."

Babysit?

"You're here for me?"

"I've been sent to aid you, yes. I'm to deliver you home."

The prospect did not enchant her.

Kallan shook his head. "Not a good idea. In three days, I've had orcs, griffins, and fae after me. Who knows what will come tomorrow. I'll make my own way."

"Funny," she said without a sliver of humor in her tone or composure, "I don't recall saying you had a choice in the matter. Go to sleep, weakling. You're barely standing up. I'll stand watch."

At least the weakling was pretty enough to look at, despite the stinking dark dye in his hair.

Had he been stingy with information, Kira would have gladly gutted him where he stood—and stolen his horse. That was a great horse. But he'd willingly divulged what she'd wanted to know. Devi was safe and home. Some of the ire that had blazed in her soul since they'd heard words of the attack on Asra dissipated.

So, Kira had a temper. And no wonder, given the power running in her blood. They always said fire mages were volatile.

She assumed Kallan Blacks was a friend of Devi, or her father would not have bothered sending *her*. And so she'd deliver him safely to his border before returning home.

Too much time had passed since she'd seen her sister. Thirteen years. They'd been but children the last time they'd spoken in person.

Kira and Devi wrote to each other regularly, but she placed little value in pieces of paper.

"You're a beauty," she told the horse.

It neighed contentedly, obviously concurring.

"You don't belong with the likes of him. Come home with me."

The horse didn't like that suggestion. It shook its head and kicked its front hooves.

"And loyal, too. You're too good for him."

Again, she could tell the animal disagreed.

Kira turned to the weakling, frowning.

Horses were seldom mistaken. Was there more to this Blacks fellow?

Blacks wasn't a name of note among fae, as far as she knew. From his appearance and his presence, she could tell he was a high fae, but she felt no power from him. Yet a horse he'd almost ridden to death showed him devotion.

Tired as he'd been, the fae slept no more than four hours. He awoke alert.

"Kira," he called with a familiarity that grated on her nerves. "I thought I might have conjured an illusion."

She tsked. "You don't have the creativity to invent me. Ready?"

He got to his feet. "Almost. I just need water and—"

He stopped, his eyes going to the small fire she'd built on the muddy ground to roast two rabbits, a squirrel, a duck, and a fish.

"You hunted and fished?"

She shrugged. "I was bored. They should last until Carvenstone."

He nodded. "It should. It's just a day's ride from here. But, Kira, I am chased by—"

"If you're about to make me sound like a helpless female who cries when she breaks a nail, I'll kill you myself. My father says I'm to take you home, and to your home I will take you. The end."

"Your father may not have understood the danger he placed you in when he gave you this assignment."

This time, she laughed. "My father," she said, "is Elden fucking Star, master of Elvendale, ruler of Wyhmur, king of all elves. Please, tell him to his face that he doesn't understand things. Go on. I'll watch."

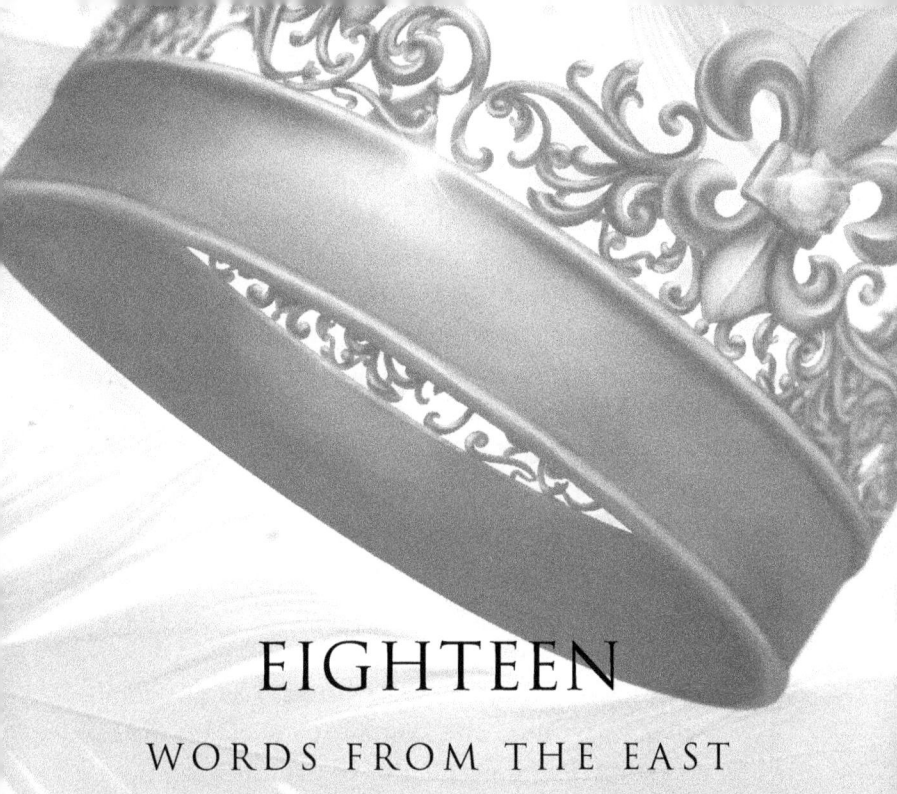

EIGHTEEN
WORDS FROM THE EAST

Kallan hadn't been overly troubled by his fate the last three days. He'd ridden as fast as he could and done his best to fight his enemies and survive. If he died, he died. Now, there was another concern. The thought of endangering a female who had nothing to do with his fight troubled him greatly.

He could tell she was strong. For one, he'd seen her sister in action, and Devi had revealed devastating powers at the eastern gate of Asra when they'd fled the city. Things started to make sense. He'd wondered how a youth who had yet to see her first century could possess such power. Now he knew. Devi was the daughter of Elden.

He had many questions. Why had she been in the unseelie realm and not with her people in Elvendale? But he knew better than to ask Kira.

Kira did not speak unless she wished to. Kira did not stop unless she so desired. Kira would not mount his horse behind him when he'd offered. She preferred to run beside him.

The fact she could effortlessly keep up with a dyrmount was a testament to her strength, but after ten miles, Kallan had to reiterate his offer.

He extended his hand. "Come on up! It'll do no one any good if you're too exhausted when the next attack comes."

She glared in silence. He knew he was risking a feral attack when he pointed out, "You were noticeably faster when we set off. I've slowed Falkr so you can keep up. I didn't know pride thus blinded the elvenfolks."

Kallan stiffened, expecting a blow, given the disdain and anger in Kira's eyes, but she ended up sighing and taking his hand. He hoisted her up. She sat behind him.

"Thanks," she muttered, a little vulnerably.

Kallan smiled. The simple expression of gratitude seemed so out of character.

"You're welcome."

He rode as fast as his mighty beast could go, feeling increasingly anxious as they approached his home.

What if Carvenstone was destroyed? What if their friends, their people, their way of life had been obliterated? The notion made him feel sick.

"Wait!" Kira said as they approached the semicircular chain of mountains that marked the border of Vale's principality.

Kallan pulled on Falkr's reins, but Kira wasn't the patient type. She leaped down before the horse had stopped and rushed south to hide behind a haystack in a small field.

She gestured for him to follow, and he did so.

"There are eyes on the mountains that are careful to remain unseen," she whispered. "Is there another way into Carvenstone?"

The first chain of mountains was called the Fortwall, and it was just that: a fortress carved into nature herself. The only way in was through the well-guarded gap twenty miles north. They had guards patrolling the ridge day and night; the ability to see travelers from miles away was invaluable.

"Not by land," he replied. "If we head south, we can catch a boat and land behind the mountains…"

But the seas were perilous, and there was a high probability there were also eyes on that road.

"All right," she said. "Stay here."

Kira stepped out of hiding. Without thinking, Kallan seized her hand and pulled her back to safety.

"What are you doing?" he demanded.

Kira shrugged. "They're looking for you, not me. I can probably go in without a problem."

"Probably," he repeated. They could also blast her into oblivion the moment she came within range. "Even if they don't have orders to kill anyone on sight, let's say you go in, then what?"

"Well, I expect there will be a lot of screaming, blood, and fire; then I'll open the gates and signal for you to come through. Why, you have a better plan?"

"We don't know how many soldiers are waiting at the bridge. There could be an entire army! Literally any plan is better than that one."

She groaned. "Fae are so boring. Look, I get it, you're a coward. Nothing you can do about it. But I'm the opposite. Not knowing what I may face is what makes this fun."

Stunned, Kallan watched her. How had she survived this long? "How old are you again?"

She yanked her arm back, glowering. Obviously, he'd hit a sensitive chord.

"I am the general of the western armies of Elden."

"That's not an answer, and commanding daddy's army doesn't count for much."

This infuriated her. Good.

"We will wait here until the cover of night, then hike the Fortwall from the south and enter the breach discreetly when I see an opening. Get onboard with the plan or get out of here."

He would not let her get herself killed. She glowered, and he resolutely met her eyes, refusing to give.

"That will add days to our journey," she said.

"Get onboard, or get out," he repeated.

Kira scoffed, but she dropped to the ground, sitting with her back to the haystack. "You're no fun," she told him irritably.

Kallan sat next to her and did his best to prevent himself from smiling victoriously. He guessed the beautiful brat rarely lost an argument.

Soon, it started to rain. Kira scowled pointedly without a word.

"What's a little water?"

"I *hate* water," she retorted.

He shrugged. "So, how old are you, really?" he asked again, curious. "I can't tell at all."

Weaker and more dissipated, youth were usually easily identifiable. By her power alone, Kira was as consequential as any high fae he'd ever met. She might have held her chin high in front of Shea Blackthorn herself. But then there was the ill humor, the pouting, and the temper.

"Why does it matter?"

"It doesn't. I'm just making conversation." As she made no reply, he continued. "I'm seven hundred and thirty-eight. I think I stopped aging around twenty-three—young, for a male of my kind. My friends find it an endless source of entertainment."

"Why?" she asked.

He snorted. "Lack of facial hair. General air of youth. When they wish to be cruel, they use words such as *effeminate*."

"They're idiotic," Kira stated. "You definitely look like a dick."

Was that her idea of a compliment? Probably not.

"Twenty-eight," she finally said.

He lifted a brow.

"I'm twenty-eight. Devi's my twin."

Kallan asked, "Why was she in Asra, then?"

Kira's shoulders lifted and dropped. "Royal politics. What do I know of such things? Your queen asked for her, and so my father gave her away." The corner of her lip hiked up. "She was so distressed when she heard she had to leave, you know. That only shows we're never happy with our lot. I would have given anything to travel. See the world." The ghost of her smile disappeared. "Why are you being chased, anyway? You don't seem that important."

Kallan laughed. He could have made himself seem worthy of notice. Told her he was the captain of Valerius's guard, his first advisor, and the lord of a duchy in the south—a crumbling land of no worth, but he still had a title and that meant something to some.

Instead, he pointed to his hair. "Brown dye," he said. Then he gestured to his cloak. "Vale's cloak to confuse scents. They're chasing Vale."

Revolted, she asked, "He's using you as bait?"

Kallan laughed. "Hardly. Vale doesn't use people. I volunteered. If we'd stayed together, their entire forces would have attacked us; splitting up made sense. And I'm not as weak as you believe me to be. I'm alive, after all."

She was entirely unapologetic. "You have no magic. At the end of the day, it doesn't matter how well you can hold a sword or shoot a bow if your enemy can kill you with a wave of their hand."

Kallan laughed. "So certain, are you? Yet here I am after over seven hundred years, having survived the War of the Realms and battled against many mages, including elves."

Kira blinked, startled and confused. "You're kidding."

"There are several forms of power, Kira Rivers Star. Do not let your strength turn to arrogance. It's as unbecoming as it is dangerous."

After a pause, she conceded, "All right, fair enough."

"We should spar someday. See who comes on top."

She chuckled. "Oh, I can *guarantee* I'll come on top, Kallan Blacks."

His turn to be startled. He hadn't expected her to *flirt*. He hadn't been prepared for it.

Kallan praised the gods when a high-pitched cry interrupted them. He looked high in the sky and spotted a bird.

"It carries a message—for you, I think," said Kira.

Few fae talked to animals, but Kallan had heard that the skill was still taught to elves.

And indeed, when the bird saw them, it flew straight to him.

It landed on his forearm and extended its foot. A small scroll was attached to its leg.

Kallan frowned as he opened it.

The message was written in Vale's hand but not in his usual tone. The note was full of gibberish. *"I shall join my mother as is my duty. You may meet me south in the land of our forefathers."*

Valerius had never uttered or written anything quite that pretentious in his life. There was more to this message.

"What? What's the matter?"

Kallan lifted the note. "This. It comes from Vale, but it's nonsensical. There's a meaning behind it, I just need to figure it out."

The female snatched the paper from his hand and read it. Then, she said, "No one with half a brain would give their intentions away in such times."

"Indeed. It also sounds nothing like him. He says south to his mother because of his duty. Vale only acknowledges the duty to his people in Carvenstone. I believe he means he's headed north to the lands of his father. The opposite." He petted the bird's head and fetched a piece of butter biscuit from his bag to share. "Where do you come from, little one?" he wondered out loud.

"Rhionhave," Kira replied automatically.

Kallan watched her pet the bird. "Are you sure?"

She inclined her head. "This kind of raven comes from Wyhmur, northwest of Elvendale. We trade them to fae from time to time. He smells of fish, manure, and fuel. Definitely Rhionhave or somewhere near it."

Kallan looked west to the mountains of Carvenstone.

If Kira was right, Vale was heading to the Arched Sea to cross into Corantius.

He could join him, or he could return to his people.

Kallan rolled the message and put it back on the raven's leg.

"Are you ready for another trip, little one?" he asked the bird, which cooed merrily. Fae may have forgotten the words of beasts, but beasts still remembered theirs. "Then keep flying west. Someone will try to catch you. Just let go of your message and fly away."

The note hadn't been meant for him, and although he had deduced his friend's real destination from it, he knew better than to follow. Vale had contradicted himself throughout the message, and he'd told Kallan to join him. It meant he wanted him to stay put.

Besides, Kallan knew Vale would never forgive him if he didn't try to help their people.

"What now?" Kira asked.

"Now we stick to the plan."

NINETEEN

TRUST

"So," Vale said without preamble, "how do you like it?"

They were on their fourth day of riding since Rhionhave, and for the last few hours, Devi had been silent. She wasn't one to beg, but she was ready to ask nicely if he could be so good as to massage her from head to toe again because everything hurt. Her ass was getting blisters. Her blisters were getting blisters.

"What, the hundred hours on the road, the cold, the lack of food, or the rain?" she asked.

They hadn't stopped for more than a couple of hours here and there. Vale didn't think it wise to go near a town, and as the countryside of open fields didn't provide much cover, they hadn't dared to make camp.

He promised they could rest at the base of the Low Crest to recover their strength before they attempted to pass the bridge. Devi mentally ticked off the miles they crossed; unless she was mistaken, they'd see the hills on the horizon soon. Finally.

"No, the Rillriets, home of the Rivers. Your lands."

Her eyes widened in surprise. No one had ever told her the location of her mother's home in the seelie realm. Despite her exhaustion and low spirits, Devi forced herself to pay attention to the landscape before her eyes.

She took in the bright patches of purple and green fields and the golden roofs atop the small houses in the distance. They could not have arrived at a better time, for where the sun set on the horizon, fire met water and shone upon the dozens of nitid streams of water. Devi blinked and discovered she wasn't so shattered after all.

"It's rather picturesque, I'll admit," she breathed in awe. Noticing the blue hood of her cape had fallen on her shoulders, she pulled it back atop her head. "But it is not my land."

She leaned forward and patted Alarik's neck. "Go on, old boy. If you get us to the damn hills before midnight, I have more sugar for you."

Thus prompted, the horse drew upon his last reserves of strength.

As they rode past one of the purple fields, an unfamiliar scent assaulted her nostrils, making her dizzy. No other flower had ever thus compelled her attention. She eyed them closely. It wasn't a field at all, but a pond of dark water, and the flowers looked like lilies, only with black leaves and mauve petals.

Unexpectedly, and without stopping Midnight, Vale leaped to the ground, picked one up, and jumped right back onto the moving horse. He always rode a few steps ahead of her; she'd watched the whole thing, amused and reluctantly impressed.

"Show-off!" she yelled at him.

Instead of replying, Vale threw the flower over his shoulder. Devi caught it and lifted it to her nose. It smelled even better.

"What are they?" she asked.

"Godslilies! The main trade of Rillriets. The seeds are medicinal, the petals are poisonous, and the leaves are used for many binding spells. From one end of the Isle to the other, these flowers have value, and they only grow here because they thrive on water magic. The Rivers have blessed these lands."

She could see that and feel it inside her.

"So, what happens now that there are no Rivers?"

Vale shrugged. "It might take a century or two, but these ponds will die eventually. Many things are lost to this world because their guardians forsake them. We Blackthorns grew golden roses that never withered. According to what I've read, ground into powder, they can prolong the life of anyone or anything. But somewhere along the line, we decided we preferred wielding swords to gardening, and the roses are no more."

A sad story, but she laughed nonetheless. "I can't picture it, sorry. You, with a cute spade and a water can, tending to your roses."

"I do have a garden in Carvenstone, I'll have you know. And it is rare that a day goes by without my spending time in it."

That surprised her, although fae were fond of nature. "With a spade?" she asked hopefully.

"With a book. The gardener would not have me mess with his domain even if I'd wanted to."

She tried to imagine him resting in a flower garden. But to her, Vale was the male in the traveling cloak, with a sword at his side. Vale was known as a dangerous, overgrown boy with too much power, and he'd played the part well at first. She could still remember him being casual and flippant in his court finery, but it had not suited him.

Her history classes painted a different picture. Right after the War of the Realms, in the days when they'd had to rebuild the court, there had been little provisions, and little enthusiasm. The Academy teachers had spoken of a prince who led his people with an iron fist, a leader who accepted nothing short of extraordinary. That she could envision.

"I don't think I can see it. You, at peace, reading quietly."

"Let us hope the time will come when you can see it with your own eyes. You would like Carvenstone. The caves in the mountains were built in another time, sculpted like great halls meant to survive a thousand wars. It is a magnificent court. The first unseelie king made it his home, but later, his successor conquered the lands of the wolves in the south and found Asra a better position; easier to defend, no doubt. If Carvenstone were ever under siege, there would be nowhere to run, as it's right on the coast."

She asked, "Don't you have boats?"

"Aye, many," Vale replied, "but most fae of the unseelie court have earth magic in their blood. They'd rather die on firm ground than live on the water. Look ahead. We're almost there."

Their horses had just crested a hillock, and they could see a chain of hills only a few miles away. None were tall, but they extended as far as the eye could see from the west to the east.

"Low Crests," she guessed.

"Indeed."

"Whoever named it had no imagination."

"That, or too many places to name. Come. There are old tunnels dating back to the war west of here. If memory serves, there is water inside. I don't believe they're occupied. Our enemy may not have thought to post guards there; they may not know of them at all. They lead nowhere, and they're unpleasant. We'll rest there until dawn."

"How do you know all that?" she asked.

That question had been on the tip of her tongue for days, as he always had an answer at the ready, whatever the question, but she'd never said a thing. The male's ego certainly didn't need further stroking.

Vale winked at her. "Reach my age and you're bound to have learned a thing or two."

"I'm sure, but don't you forget things eventually?"

"No," he replied simply.

She blinked. "You don't forget anything?"

"I used to, in my youth, but it is possible to acquire certain skills if you're willing to pay the price."

Ah! She'd known it. "So, it *is* magic."

Vale nodded. "Yes. A sorcerer was in need of a youthful, foolish adventurer stupid enough to steal a treasure from a water nymph, and in exchange, he offered a blessing. What can I say? I was but eighty-three, and it sounded like fun."

"I'm twenty-eight, and I'm not stupid enough to do that."

"You forget: I have testosterone."

Fair point.

It took perhaps two hours to reach the tunnels at the foot of the hills. The entrance was concealed between mounds, hard to spot for anyone who hadn't been there before. Vale dismounted his horse and remained at the entrance, perplexed.

"This place isn't empty," he stated.

Devi scanned the area with her mind. "I don't sense anything alarming, but I will defer to the psychic among us."

Vale stepped forward. "They do not have enough magic or strength to be perceived by you. You can only sense power. But weak or strong, all fae have thoughts of their own. Come. I think we will be in no danger in such company."

And so they advanced.

The tunnels were dark and pungent; that was what he'd meant when he'd said they were unpleasant. It stank of petrol and damp.

They walked in silence, and before long, they heard terrified whispers.

Vale paused and extended his hand, reaching out to Devi. She stepped toward him and took it. He guided her ahead of him, inviting her to take the lead. As she passed him, Vale lowered her hood.

"Leave it down, if you don't mind. They will want to see your face."

His words made her guess that the fae hiding here were of the Rillriets, but nothing could have prepared her for their greeting.

Two dozen common and lesser fae were huddled together, shivering in fear.

"Hello," she said, inching forward so as not to frighten them. "We're not here to cause you harm. We were hoping to rest for a while."

Her vision worked well enough, but lesser fae weren't gifted with the same senses as her kind, so she lifted her hand, calling a small flame to her so she could be seen in the darkness.

An old, wrinkled female with branches in her silver hair gasped and turned to her people. "A Rivers," said she.

She was a lady of Farj, a princess of Elvendale, and the ward of Queen Shea, but in all her days, no one had ever thus received her.

All heaved, gulped, and choked before falling to their knees in prayer.

Downright *praying*, chanting, begging, and praising their gods.

Devi looked to Vale in horror. The asshole seemed amused.

She mouthed a desperate, "Help me."

"There, there," he said, more pleasant than she'd ever heard him. "Tell us of your plight. What are you fine people doing in this hole? The place isn't fit for a rat."

All right, almost pleasant.

The old female spoke for her people. "Creatures came to our homes, not fae or elves; things of horrors." Orc or scions, she guessed. "They killed all our guards, all our lords, and they took what they could. We ran as fast as we could. I led my family here. Others went to the woods. Oh, please, Lady Rivers, we have nowhere to go."

Devi glanced to Vale again, but this time he was silent.

"West," she told them. "You will go west to the woods. There, you will find elves. Tell them Devira has sent you." She undid the blue ribbon binding the braid running down her back, hands moving so fast her hair got tangled in the process. "Show this if they demand proof."

The elves would recognize the elven silk and her scent.

"Elves!" The female gulped in horror.

Devi nodded. "You will be welcomed there. I am half-elf," she said out loud. No fae had ever welcomed these words, but they needed somewhere to go, or they'd die.

Instead of cursing and panicking, the old female lowered herself to her knees and kissed Devi's hands. "Thank you. Thank you," she repeated like a chant.

Devi attempted not to grimace and stepped away as soon as she could politely do so.

"What the *hell!*" she whispered to Vale.

He snorted. "You're the River in River-lands."

She rolled her eyes. "Are you saying your people worship you like that in Carvenstone? No wonder you like it so much."

"No," Vale replied. "But Carvenstone isn't the original home of my kin. We Blackthorns ruled in the Darklands before they were destroyed."

She shook her head. "I don't get it. They're acting like I'm…"

"The sort of creature who brings water in a drought, giving life to barren lands? The last of one of the lines who created the fair folks? These lands will forever remember the deeds of the first high fae and its people will always believe in us. It is up to us to be worthy of their fealty."

A daunting prospect.

"How does one go about earning such blind faith?"

Vale smiled kindly. "Running for a week without much of a break to sleep, eat, or rest and heading toward an enemy that outnumbers us a million to one, with the smallest chance of success, all in order to ensure the freedom of our lands, is certainly a promising start."

TWENTY
IN THE NAME OF THE GODDESS

Exhausted as they were, Devi and Vale caught little rest, for the peasants continuously whispered and prayed among themselves, their eyes on Devi at all times. She bore it well, although she was self-conscious.

"I'm leading the horses to the stream farther into the tunnels," Vale announced. "They need water."

Her eyes widened in panic. "I'd better come," she said as casually as she could.

In other words, *"Don't leave me alone with them right now!"*

Vale was deeply amused.

When they were out of hearing range of the common fae, he immediately took it upon himself to tease her. "I believe we may have found one thing you fear."

"I'm not *afraid*," she protested. "Just creeped out. I'm a person. I sleep and drink and use the latrine just like them. No one should be revered like that."

"No one should," Vale allowed, "but we live in a world where those who possess advanced strength and technology are called gods, even though they sleep, and drink, and use the latrines too. We cannot change the ways of this world. Careful," he warned, pointing to the ceiling.

It had grown lower.

Vale frowned. "I'm not sure the horses can pass here. I do not recall this path. Last I was here, the horses could walk comfortably to the stream."

Were they lost?

Devi beamed. "So, you aren't *always* right."

Ignoring her, he told Midnight to remain where he was and stepped into the darkness.

He felt no other minds, no thoughts from beasts, scions, or fae, yet as he advanced, his skin prickled and the hair on the back of his neck rose in alarm.

"If I were to ask you to remain behind, would you listen?" he asked Devi, somewhat hopefully.

"Nope, not a chance."

Vale sighed, unsurprised. "Very well. Stay on guard, then."

He pulled his sword and strode for half a mile. Then he stopped.

Fallen rock blocked the path forward, and right in front of the debris there was a girl—a young thing with skin of mahogany and eyes of fire.

"Hey! What are you doing here all alone?" Devi asked.

Vale lifted his sword to bar her way and shook his head. "This is not what it appears to be," he told Devi.

He couldn't feel her mind at all; it was as if there was nothing there, which meant her shields were stronger than anything, or anyone, he'd ever encountered.

The infuriating female rolled her eyes. "What, it's not an ancient female who can pulverize us both without breaking a sweat?" she challenged. "You, typical male that you are, have missed the obvious: she hasn't harmed us."

Reluctantly, Vale lowered his weapon. It took all his self-control to let Devi approach the thing whose red eyes were so fixed and unmoving.

"You seem cold out here. Can I help?" Devi asked.

The thing smirked. "I do not feel the cold. No mortal may help."

That didn't discourage Devi. "Well, we certainly can't if you don't tell us what's wrong. I doubt you're stuck here of your own volition."

The red eyes flashed and remained fixed on Devi for the longest time. Finally, it said, "You have ice in your veins."

Devi shrugged. "That's one way to put it."

"Then perhaps you may be of assistance." The thing lifted its hand and touched its own shoulder. "Behind my back. An arrow of fyriron. If I move, it will reach my heart."

All they had to do was make her move, and the goddess would die.

Vale marched toward the thing, but he only made it three feet before his boots got stuck to the ground. Glancing down, he found them a foot in muddy sap. He turned to Devi, whose eyes were bright blue.

"Really?"

He'd seen earth magic traps before.

"Yes, really. Don't you even think about hurting her."

"There are seven gods who stood by and did nothing when our lands were taken. Seven gods who will join whoever is crowned overking. I say we get rid of her and reduce their numbers to six."

"And I said don't you *think* about it," she repeated, practically growling.

Vale glowered at Devi. "You're making a mistake."

"Following our instincts and showing kindness are never mistakes," Devi stated before approaching the enlightened. "I can't control ice very well, but I can try. What can I do?"

"Freeze my heart," said the goddess.

Devi blinked in confusion.

"Ice is the purest of the four elements. The strongest. It'd kill a mortal, but it'd just protect my heart. I'll pass out, but I'll live. Dig the arrowhead out of my shoulder blades before I awaken."

Devi winced. "I'm not sure I can freeze your heart and nothing else."

The goddess eyed her. "You're a young thing who has yet to learn control." She lifted her hand ever so slowly and placed it on Devi's chin. "Take mine."

Suddenly, Vale felt the female as she lowered her mental defenses. He took in thousands of years. War, death, hunger, rage, and sorrow. Styx—that was her name. The goddess wasn't just taking a trip down memory lane, though; Vale could feel her purpose. As a youth, Styx had been volatile and quick to anger. With time, she'd learned the various stages of control. First, how to direct her mind, then how to command her spirit, and finally, how to dominate her power.

Nine hundred and seventy-four years. That was how long she'd remained in his tunnel, keeping its entrance hidden so no one could find her. She'd remained perfectly still, without eating or drinking a thing. She had borne many names and many functions, but above all, she was a goddess of will. And she shared it all with Devi, through a slight touch that didn't last longer than a minute.

Devi gasped as Styx removed her hand. Then she touched the goddess's chest and pushed a rush of energy into it.

Styx collapsed; Devi caught her before her head hit the ground and turned her onto her stomach. She plunged two fingers deep inside the flesh of her back. Blood oozed out of the wound—blood of the brightest blue.

"I got it!" Devi exclaimed victoriously and pulled out a fragment of silvery metal.

Then she removed her cloak and wrapped it around Styx's bare shoulders. She carried the female past him, stating a simple, "You're free."

Vale looked down and discovered the sap had disappeared.

"I get to say 'I told you so' when this whole thing comes back to bite us in the arse."

TWENTY-ONE
A LITTLE DETOUR

At the nearest intersection, Vale led them down another corridor; a few hundred feet into the belly of the hill, they reached a source of clear water. Midnight and Alarik were so good as to drink without protest, possibly because they were parched and exhausted.

Devi was furious with Vale, who had so unapologetically been willing to condemn Styx without knowing whether she was friend or foe, but she kept all accusations to herself. Truth was, she'd taken a risk. Again. This wasn't Vale sparing a cute bird and sending it on an errand. If Styx proved to be an enemy, she'd be redoubtable, no doubt about that. But helping her had been worth it, considering the gift she'd bestowed upon Devi.

Never had she felt so calm, in and out. She was utterly at peace and in control of her fate. She'd always felt inadequate among elder fae, perhaps because something about them had seemed superior. Not their power, but their knowledge and wisdom. She possessed those now. She may not have experienced the ten thousand years of Styx's life, but she had most of her memories and all her acumen.

And the goddess had gifted her more yet: control over her own mind. Over her powers.

Perhaps half an hour after Devi had frozen her heart, the goddess stirred on the ground.

"Do you need water? Food?" Devi asked.

Styx got to her feet and patted the dirty rags that clothed her. "I can do without either. I thank you, young one. I will not forget what you did here today."

Styx then left the way they'd come in.

"I won't apologize for helping her, Vale. I don't regret it."

"And I hope you never will. No matter. What's done is done. Now, you likely won't sleep well among the river folk. What do you say we borrow Styx's chamber for the night?"

She grimaced at the thought of sleeping in such a gloomy place, but it certainly did beat the alternative. "All right. Let us fill the water bottles first."

They settled in the narrow corridor, glad that at least it stank less than the rest of the tunnels.

"I'll take the first watch," Vale offered, sitting on the hard ground. "Come here. Sit and give me your feet."

She eagerly obeyed and arranged her cot next to him. She then removed her boots before handing him her feet. His fingers pressed on all her sore spots. She moaned in pain and delight.

"You're so very sore, and the skin is broken in many places. Do you ever complain?"

She shrugged. "I heal the blisters whenever we make a pit stop. They come back, but it's not that bad."

"Such a little warrior."

"Excuse me, there's nothing 'little' about me," she retorted, succeeding in making him laugh.

Vale pulled something out of his bag and held it in front of her lips. Devi tentatively darted her tongue, and her eyes widened in wonder. Sweet and citrusy deliciousness. She opened her mouth and he popped the candy inside it.

She smiled, ridiculously happy. "I'd ask how you got a sour apple hard-balled candy, if I didn't know it came from Elvendale."

It had been her absolute favorite in her youth, and the confectioner had regularly sent extra to Elden's home when he'd found out. Thirteen years ago, she'd left Wyhmur with a bagful of such delights.

"I don't know if I should be mad you kept these to yourself for a week or grateful you decided to share."

"You're too tired to be mad. Just go to sleep."

She shook her head. "No, first, give me the blackfire stone. It's cold, and I can imagine it'll only get colder during the night."

"The temperature doesn't vary as much in the tunnels. And you're basically a furnace. Stay near me and I won't freeze."

She was relieved he'd declined her offer; she was too tired to move, let alone cast spells.

Devi was asleep by the time he was done with her feet, moving on to her calves. As daylight didn't penetrate this far in the tunnels, she had no idea how much time had passed before he woke her, but she was well rested and ready for her turn standing guard.

Vale slept with his head on her lap. Devi found herself caressing his hair. It truly was as soft as it looked. He didn't stir, sleeping as soundly as ever for hours on end.

And then, it was time. He woke up, they ate in silence and suited up with their strongest equipment. She checked her arrows, he polished his sword, and they both donned their maille.

They would cross into Corantius today—or die trying.

Devi tensed as they headed out of the tunnels. There was no avoiding the chamber where the river folk were assembled, and she dreaded any form of interaction with her worshippers. When they arrived in the chamber, the river folks were packing and getting ready to leave. A smiling little boy pointed to her and pulled on his father's leg, betraying her presence.

"Lady Rivers!"

To her relief, they seemed busy and there was no bowing and praying.

"Might you also be traveling west?" asked the older woman who'd spoken to her the previous day.

Uh-oh.

"Well, I...We—"

"—would be delighted to have some company," Vale cut in. "We are headed west, and it would be no hardship to see you through to Wyhmur before going on our way."

Devi managed not to grimace. Vale would pay for that later. "Yes. That."

"Thank you, my lord, my lady. Thank you." And so the bowing started again.

"None of that, please. You may call me Devi. And this is…" She hesitated. "My traveling companion, Ruven Norfiel."

The strangers did not seem to be the kind of folks who would prove untrustworthy, but tongues ran, and the fewer people who knew of Vale's whereabouts, the better.

"An honor. I'm Telda Finch, and these are my little Finches and their loved ones. We're but Godslilies farmers," said the female, as they started to walk out of the tunnels.

Remembering the flowers brought a smile to Devi's lips. "We saw some on our way here. They're delightful."

And so the Finches proceeded to give her a comprehensive account of all there was to know of their trade, their flowers, and their enchanting land.

Devi hadn't questioned how she'd been recognized; even if Devin Farel and others hadn't commented on it, she remembered enough of her mother to know she was her likeness.

Telda revealed there was more to it. "Yes, all Rivers, from the very first, have borne an uncanny resemblance. I've seen the portraits in your ancestors' great halls. You all have the same face, them bony cheeks, sweet mouths, and pert noses. Even the boys. There were only five Rivers: Tulmen of the Gorge had a daughter, and though he died young, he discovered these lands and brought them to life. His daughter lived to be seven hundred years of age, and then one day, she disappeared. Some say they see her in great white gowns on windy nights. Her husband was killed, you see. Very sad affair. But she had twins: two boys. The oldest had a daughter, your mama, Loxy. We were all sad when we were told she passed away.

There was talk of a child, however, and we're mighty glad you're fine."

"Two," Devi revealed. "Two children. I have a twin sister. I haven't seen her in some time, but she's a lot more like our mother. Red hair, green eyes, and all."

This was further cause for rejoicing among the Finches.

As they walked toward Wyhmur, following the hills, Devi relaxed. These people may be overly enthusiastic about her mere existence, but they were nice enough. By midday, they'd entirely stopped curtsying and bowing.

She rode ahead with the matriarch and Vale had taken the back. Every time she glanced at him, she saw him scanning their surroundings, his expression one of careful concentration. She smiled. Vale was very much a protector, too, although he'd never admit it. He'd wanted to get the river folk to their destination safely, although it added a few miles to their journey.

Devi felt her muscles, chest, and shoulders unwind when they reached the shade of the familiar white trees with red leaves of the northeastern woods.

"How much did that delay us?" Devi asked as Vale approached.

He didn't appear to be concerned. "Four hours, perhaps? They slowed us down, but the Low Crest Bridge is just five miles north of here. I thought we might remain here, wait for the cover of night."

She smirked. "Smart. But let's face it, that's not why you offered to escort these people. You, sir, are a softie behind that tough exterior."

Vale laughed. "Right. My offer had absolutely nothing to do with the fact we'd look more inconspicuous to any spy, by air or land, while traveling in such company."

Devi snickered. "I don't buy it. You wanted to help them."

"Of course I did. But my desire to do so wouldn't have mattered had the detour not served our cause. We've established that I do have a heart hiding somewhere, but do not mistake me for a"—he grimaced before repeating her choice of word—"softie."

She laughed. "I hit a sore spot, didn't I?"

"You would have me relinquish all pride, vanity, virility, and mystery, cruel female," he replied, amused.

"I would have you be yourself rather than playing that dark prince persona of yours for all it's worth."

Still mounted on Midnight, Vale directed his horse to circle hers, and leaned forward until his mouth was but a breath away from hers.

"I am the dark prince. Don't ever doubt it."

"So, you're saying you'd turn your back on me and leave me to die if it was convenient? That you'd kill all these innocents to get your way? That the heart you profess to possess is frozen?"

Amused, he replied, "I fear you misunderstand the term entirely. They don't call me dark prince because I'm a gutless, worthless coward. They call me so because I will do anything, *anything*, to protect what's mine, regardless of the cost."

TWENTY-TWO
LOW CREST BRIDGE

They waited for dark. Devi had the time to see that her people would be welcomed on her father's land, and he, enough time to think. What he recalled of the Low Crest Bridge was dated; things may have changed in hundreds of years. South of the bridge, on the seelie side of the land, there had been a small settlement of fae paid by the Corantian crown to guard the bridge and control who crossed it. As common fae, they were of no consequence. If they couldn't be bribed, they could be disposed of easily enough. They were but the first point of control. North of the bridge was a small Corantian outpost. A modest manor inhabited by a noble of low rank, it housed two dozen soldiers along with the staff, at most.

During the War of the Realms, when Corantius had wished to stay out of the conflict, they'd destroyed the bridge. Enemies could still cross the sea —sailing, swimming, or flying—but the twenty-some Corantian soldiers on the other side could pick off intruders one by one with their bows and arrows; hence why Vale had decided to rely on the cover of night. They'd rebuilt the bridge a decade after the war, but there was no telling whether it'd still be standing. Fae could see in the dark, but darkness would help, regardless, if concealment became necessary.

If nothing had changed with the Corantian outpost, the success of their crossing depended on those twenty-four soldiers on the other side of the bridge. If they were fae plucked at random from the masses, there would be nothing to fear. If they were twenty-four scions, however...

Vale glanced at Devi, again grateful that fate had delivered her to him, but also cursing the fucking timing.

Seven hundred and eighteen years ago

"I can't be your son. I'm... just Vale."

The incredibly beautiful creature was looking away from him at her bookshelves. Her long silver-white tresses were braided down her back, with flowers threaded through, and in her billowing backless dress, she didn't seem to be of the same species as he. Vale couldn't comprehend what she'd announced to the court. Shea Blackthorn couldn't be his *mother*.

"Oh, but you are. Trust that I'd recognize the fruit of twelve months of aches, followed by eight hours of painful labor."

"Kallan—" he said.

"Made a good substitute, I'll allow you this. I found the boy south, close to the old Blackthorn lands. His domain was in ruin. His family had perished, but even then, as a child of five, he had a fighting spirit. And so I asked him if he wished to protect his prince. For the last fifteen years, he's done so faithfully. Kallan may be a son of my heart, but he is not of my flesh. You are, Valerius."

Valerius—a name he did not know, given by a mother he'd barely seen in his twenty years.

"I don't understand. Why hide me?"

Then, she turned to him. "Your father was made for me; his soul completes and defines mine. And for all that, we may never be together, because my duty is to this realm, and his to the north. But after one night together, we had you. For a thousand years, I attempted to bear a child and failed—until I met him. I know it's unlikely I'll ever be with child again. You were hidden, protected, because you're my only heir. When a monarch perishes without a child, chaos and civil war follow. I have fought for peace since I was younger than you are now. I do not wish for destruction to be my legacy."

At the time, he'd concentrated on so many other aspects that a part of what she'd really said had entirely escaped his notice, but decades after that conversation with Shea, Vale was researching soul mates, out of curiosity, perhaps.

So many reports mentioned it. From his research, he knew that mortals and immortals alike were destined to one soul, but it was rare that they ever found their mate. Mortals lived too short a life to seek it, perhaps. Immortals rarely recognized it when they saw it. Vale had pitied his mother for having found and lost such a treasure, but he now wondered if he hadn't secretly desired to find it himself.

Could it be the reason behind his reluctance to settle with anyone?

He'd known from the start, from the moment her mind had called to him in a crowded hall, that Devi was different. He'd convinced himself that the irresistible attraction had simply been some machinations of his mother. Now he knew it wasn't, there was no doubt in his mind that fate had tied Devi's soul to his; she was the only female who could ever matter to him.

Indeed, fate was cruel. How was he supposed to let her place herself in the way of harm when she had the potential to be everything?

The only reason he could was because of who she was—what she was. Devi, his little elfling and potentially the most devastatingly powerful unseelie alive. At twenty-eight, she had more power in her little finger than anyone he knew, and immortals only grew in strength as years went by. He wondered when his posturing would stop working; eventually, she'd realize he wasn't her superior.

Vale was her equal.

"I want you to promise me something," Vale said. "If I fall, you'll turn back. Your father and my mother—they'll need to know what happened so they can prepare for the next attack."

I need you to live.

Of course, she was flippant. She waved her hand dismissively. "Come on, it's not that bad."

Potentially not, but he'd needed to say it anyway.

"Your word, Devi."

She sighed but complied nonetheless, vowing, "If you die, I'll get out of here to warn our parents. Happy?"

He wasn't, but he nodded.

"But that would majorly suck, so please don't die."

"I'll try."

They dismounted and hid the horses out of the way at the base of a nearby hill. Vale told them to keep out of sight until they were called. It wouldn't do to have them get hurt if they were ambushed.

A ravine between the west and east hills of Low Crest led out to the seaside hamlet. Vale and Devi scaled the five-hundred-foot ravine and walked across the top, keeping low to the ground. They could have walked through the gorge to preserve their energy, but then they would have been sitting ducks. It turned out, however, that their efforts were wasted, as there was no one guarding the pass.

On the other side, Vale and Devi crouched at the edge to observe what they faced.

The bridge was still intact, and the manor on the north side was occupied. Lights glowed in the windows on each level, and Vale felt energy, movement. From across the bridge, he couldn't tell whether the enemy was of consequence; if he extended his powers too far, they would feel his intrusion.

On their side of the bridge, he felt and heard nothing.

Two guards walked along the bridge and another two patrolled the northern coast. Vale sighed. The guard posted on the bridge was too light. The set up clearly felt like a trap.

"Do you smell that?" Devi whispered, risking no other sound.

Concerned as he was with what he saw and felt, he had yet to pay attention to what his nostrils told him.

He took a whiff.

Orcs. There would be no avoiding them this time, not if they wanted to cross with the horses. They weren't leaving the dyrmounts behind.

Vale frowned. How were Corantians directing orcs so well? Corantians were no friends of orcs; they'd hunted their kind and banned them from the Isle. He was missing something fundamental.

"We'll need to clear the field before we cross the bridge," Vale whispered.

"Or I could freeze them all."

He shook his head. "I can't have you passing out on me. We don't know how many there are, and we don't know what sort of Corantians we're dealing with on the other side. Now isn't the time to lash out."

She nodded. "All right, so what's the plan?"

Vale scanned the beach town south of the bridge with his eyes and mind and found nothing. The horde was hiding. Good. It meant they relied on an ambush. They wouldn't have bothered if they had the strength and numbers on their side.

"We poke the wasp's nest."

He picked up a stone and threw it as far as he could. A dozen vile creatures shot out of a cave in the rocky hill to the west. Vale lowered his head and watched them closely.

He counted thirteen orcs. Leading them was a great beast of alabaster skin. It was entirely bald, with a pointy nose and a jutting chin.

Vale could take care of this lot without breaking a sweat, but he remained still. He doubted that this sorry lot was alone. It was risky, now that the orcs were alerted, but he picked up another stone and threw it to the east.

Close to two dozen orcs came into view closer to the ravine. The creatures shouted in their vile tongue and pointed in different directions. One argued that the disturbance had come from the sea, and others showed the bridge or the water's edge. Only one pointed up at the cliff.

The giant in charge clicked his fingers and gave an order Vale wished he could comprehend. The creatures dispersed in various directions—to the bridge, the beach, and the ravine. Two went up the cliff.

Vale grasped his sword. "When this starts, we will have one, perhaps two minutes before the Corantians on the bridge alert their people," he told Devi, speaking as low as he could manage. "Just two minutes to kill all the orcs, using as little energy as possible so we have enough strength for the second wave."

"Got it. Kill them all but act like we're taking a midnight stroll."

That was the gist of it.

Vale gestured at Devi to be quiet and concentrated to mask their presence.

The foul, chalky brutes lumbered up the hill on their thin, uneven legs. Their torsos were large and muscular, but apparently, orcs weren't into squats.

When they got to the top of the hill, close to where Devi and Vale were standing, they spoke in their rudimentary grunts. One sound Vale could identify: they sniffed eagerly as if smelling a nice dinner.

They'd caught their scent.

Quick as the wind, Vale ran to stand right behind the first; he placed one hand on its slimy forehead, the other across its shoulders, and snapped its neck. As the second started to scream, he thrust his sword into its chest.

The attack hadn't gone as silently as he'd hoped, and the other orcs would soon realize their companions weren't coming down from the hill.

Vale stood at the edge of the cliff and saw a line of enemies rushing into formation. One dozen, and another one, and another one after that. He counted a hundred strong.

"How many arrows do you have?" he asked Devi, not bothering to lower his voice. They knew where they were.

"Seventy-two."

Vale's gaze went across the water. The manor had started to stir; he could feel it. He unhooked his quiver, which contained as many arrows, from his back and dropped it at Devi's feet; he then held out his hand to her. Without needing a word, Devi handed him her sword.

"Save as many arrows as you can. The orcs are cannon fodder."

"Sure thing. I'll let you do your thing and cover your back."

She crouched, extending her right leg to the side for better balance, and aimed down at the path leading to the hilltop.

"Don't die," Devi told him.

"Like you'd let me!"

He glanced back to see her smile before launching himself at the horde of orcs.

Vale couldn't recall ever entering a fight without worrying about protecting his own back, not even with Kallan, but soon, he entirely stopped minding to his own safety, focusing entirely on the offensive. If there was a sword, arrow, or ax headed his way, its barer found a sculpted arrow planted inside their skull before they could follow through with the attack.

He wasn't used to fighting with two blades, and his left side was considerably stronger, but against orcs, swordsmanship hardly mattered. Orcs were all brute strength and instincts without any finesse. He slashed at thighs and calves, arms and knees, his blades always finding unprotected flesh.

He'd killed half the horde when the Corantians crossed the sea, some over the bridge and others by air.

Fuck.

He hadn't been able to tell before—perhaps the water had interfered with his senses —but now he knew. Every single one of them was a scion.

"Shit! Devi, shoot them! I can take care of myself."

He hadn't used his speed or mind power until now to preserve his energy, but he could tell it would not be enough. Better to pick off as many scions as possible before they were on them.

His head snapped up to the cliff when he felt a push of energy. Air. Just enough to destabilize the flying scions. As they swayed, at the mercy of Devi's unnatural wind, she shot arrows straight into their hearts or between their eyes.

Had they not been scions, all would have perished. There were twenty-six scions, with eleven approaching by air. Only three of them fell, and Vale could tell they'd survive.

He grimaced. What now? They needed to stay on the high ground for as long as possible, but they also had to push forward and cross the bridge at the first chance.

Devi took their choices away by leaping down the cliff and landing right behind him. He handed her the sword.

"I've got something, but it's a terrible idea," she said, staying behind him and guarding his back as she ruthlessly slashed orcs with her bloodied sword.

"I'm open to all ideas, terrible ones included."

It was easy to adapt to her style, as she was using a textbook Shea method—efficient and unpredictable to those who hadn't studied it, but second nature to Vale.

"Great, so, first of all, you have to touch me."

He groaned. "Again? You truly have the worst timing."

Why did she always suggest touching when it definitely wasn't about *touching*?

"Then open your mind to me like you did when you channeled me. We have to wait until they all get close, but I *think* I can freeze them all *without* murdering you if you're part of *me*."

All things considered, it wasn't the worst idea, and they were flat out of options.

"What's your range?"

"I don't know, a mile?"

Too close. At that distance, the twenty-six scions would have their skin if their plan failed.

But it wouldn't fail. He trusted Devi, and he'd seen her use her gifts.

"All right. Let's do it."

TWENTY-THREE
THE TRAITOR

Devi had never felt more uncertain about anything. The odds against them were too great. What if she hurt Vale?

You won't.

She hadn't killed him in the forest, before Styx had helped with her control, and she wouldn't now. She had to believe that.

When he'd channeled her, she'd been able to reach into his mind, using his power, and he'd said he might have gained some of hers in return. That meant there was a good chance that he'd be fine; elemental mages couldn't be harmed by the element they mastered.

For a little while, she put the scions out of her mind and focused on the vermin they had to cut through.

Pungent, slimy, and sickly pale, orcs truly were vile. She barely breathed, but their odor still disgusted her. She doubted they had toothbrushes wherever the hell they came from.

Unfortunately, their insides reeked worse than their outside, so every time they slashed one open, Devi had to fight against the need to retch.

"Oh, stuff that!" she cursed, before screaming, "Get down!"

Vale obeyed, and she threw a jet of fire from her left hand. The line of orcs rushing at them panicked. Some jumped down the hill, and others stumbled; the first few were burned to a crisp.

Devi coughed. Shit. Crispy orcs were not an improvement over lacerated orcs as far as the smell was concerned.

"Mile-range warning," Vale said.

About freaking time. She turned and lifted her hands to Vale's face. Devi expected him to touch hers in return. Instead, he pulled her close and said, "Don't kill me," before kissing her mouth deeply, openly, and with abandon.

He'd dropped all his defenses, all shields, just like she had when she'd let him channel her. Devi tasted his bright, powerful soul. She could have gotten lost in it, savoring each memory, every part of him. But she was more interested in surviving this, so instead, she concentrated on her primal, fundamental power.

Elden was a scion—the very first, he'd said. But his father had been a water-wielding enlightened, and like him, Elden controlled currents, seas, and oceans. Loxy had been a Rivers—the fifth River. Devi wasn't sure how or why, but she understood that power did not weaken with each generation in her family. She was the daughter of two elemental forces, and she'd ended up being twice as strong as either parent. She always controlled, measured, and used little of her strength to ensure she harmed no one by accident. Now, she let it go.

The ground shook, the sky roared, and the Arched Sea rose to engulf the shore. Then a wave of energy vibrated out of her, and froze everything and everyone.

No, not everyone. Not Vale. She certainly wasn't hurting him or the horses. She felt them and created a shield around them. She didn't freeze the curious fox scratching its ear near the gorge or the falcon returning to Vale after his travels to Carvenstone.

She felt them all. After truly embracing the power, she found it was entirely hers to mold, hers to command.

Devi stopped her energy flow and let go of Vale. She turned to the sea to watch her handiwork, and then she laughed.

Everything was ice—the sea and the town, all the elves and scions.

"You've not killed them," Vale noted, frowning.

"I haven't," she replied proudly, ecstatic. "But they'll stay in my power until I release them."

Her ice was eternal; it would only melt if she demanded it to.

She attempted to take a step, but her legs gave out from under her; Vale caught her before she fell, holding her upright.

Oh well. Apparently, she wasn't invincible.

"Tired?" he guessed.

"Exhausted." She yawned. "Call the dyrmounts. They're fine."

She felt Vale whisper through her mind, although his lips didn't move. He was talking in horse speech. Being back in his head was satisfying and comforting.

The horses ran down the icy hill, light on their feet as usual, passing what some would mistake as realistic ice statues of orcs and fae. Alarik and Midnight stopped at the bottom of the hill and waited for them; the first neighed as if trying to explain what he'd had to endure in their absence, while the elegant black dyrmount seemed as unperturbable as ever.

"You're doing so well on the ice," Devi noted. She'd been prepared to have to charm warmth into the poor beasts, despite her wariness, but they seemed indifferent to the weather.

On closer inspection, she saw their horseshoes had a certain shine. She bent down to take a look at one and traced it with her fingertip.

"Maille," she said, "and something else, too."

She trailed her hand up the length of Alarik's leg. The horse had something she hadn't noticed inside him, something new.

"Telenar looked at them before we left Elvendale. In our rush, I must have forgotten to mention it."

That explained it. Kira had once told her that Telenar could not encounter a thing he did not wish to help or improve. Whatever he'd done to the beasts, they hadn't suffered for it, and they seemed better off with it.

"I'll have to thank him someday, if we meet again."

Smiling, she was holding on to her saddle, about to leap onto the horse, when Alarik released a blood-curdling scream and tore through the still-silent night.

The horse stumbled and struggled to keep on his feet. She rushed to his side and found a golden arrow protruding from his flank. She yanked it out, and thick red blood soaked her clothes. Vale lifted his bow and scanned the sky in the direction the hit had come from. She paid him no mind, rummaging through her bag. Her hands shook in her panic. Why the hell had she stuffed her healing charm in there? That had been stupid. Who needed to be healed "in a while" after she wasted precious minutes fumbling through a large traveling satchel? Finally, her shaking hands clasped the precious charm; she applied it to the horse's flank and pushed as much energy as she could through it. She was already drained, and the effort threatened to bring her to her knees, but she persevered until the wound had closed. Then she pulled her bow from her back and joined Vale in his search for their enemy.

"Can you feel something?" she asked desperately, knowing the answer.

She was still in his mind, and there was nothing. Just him and her.

"No. Let us go forth and cross the bridge. Now."

Remaining here in the open was of no use.

Devi mounted Midnight at Vale's prompting, and Vale took Alarik's reins, remaining on foot; the last thing the dyrmount needed while recovering was to carry extra weight. She'd done her best, but the internal wound needed more time to close.

"Come on, beautiful boy. You're the bestest. You can do this," she coaxed.

The words were unfamiliar on her lips. Horse speech—a language she'd never learned. Strange, she shouldn't have picked up this power from Vale—he'd only opened his mind to her for a moment—but she didn't have time to question it.

"I'll give you all the sugar you want if you make it a little farther, Alarik. Just a little…"

But it was too late.

They were halfway across the bridge when, on the Corantian coast, a battalion of soldiers in red and gold appeared.

Or maybe they'd been there all along, hidden from Devi and Vale's senses.

It shouldn't have been possible, but they hadn't appeared out of nowhere, so they must have been there. Which meant that there was a telepath among them. An incredibly powerful telepath, strong enough to mess with Vale's mind.

Devi stiffened.

Dawn rose in the east; the clouds overhead dissipated, and she saw them clearly. Devi's eyes widened, her mouth fell open, and she dismounted Midnight, taking a step forward.

For the second time in as many days, Vale lifted his sword, barring her path to halt her in her tracks. This time, she let him.

In front of the forty-seven Corantian soldiers stood a male dressed in black leather pants, with his chest bare and dark wings folded behind his back. A familiar male with a familiar face and a boyish grin that had never looked so cruel.

"Rook."

The name fell from her lips, full of questions.

He held a bow in his hand. Had he shot Alarik? Why? No, that was probably the least important concern right now. What was he doing here, with the Corantians?

His smile grew. "Go on, Devi. I'm sure you can work it out. As for that beast of yours, I figured it would get your ass moving. You were taking an awful lot of time, and I'm on a schedule."

She hadn't said a thing out loud; he'd plucked her thoughts from her mind. Even in her worn-out and confused state, she'd understood what it meant before his eyes shifted to Vale. His smile vanished, giving way to something colder than her ice.

"Hello, brother."

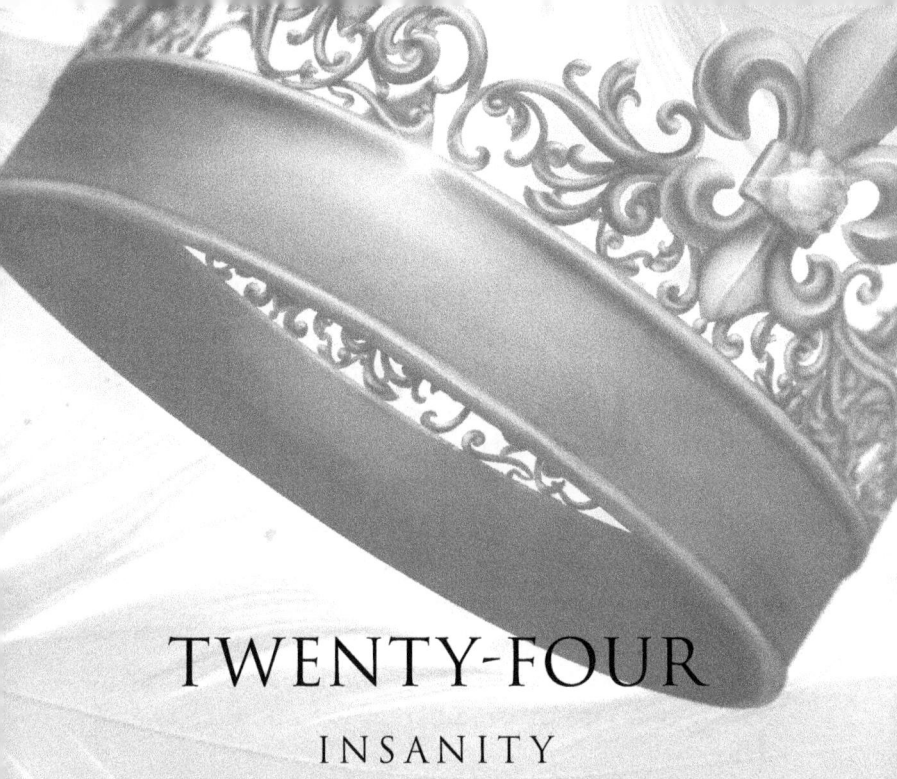

TWENTY-FOUR
INSANITY

Vale kept his mind blank, a skill he'd learned from his father. Their father.

Five hundred years ago, after the war, after learning he was the son of Orin and Shea and taking the better part of a century to process the knowledge, he'd expressed an interest in knowing his progenitor.

Orin received Vale in the Court of Crystal, at Staren, his stronghold. He was dark of hair and grave. Vale found that he didn't like his eyes, or his mind, or his presence, for that matter. The overking made him feel weak.

"That is because you are not foolish, son."

Vale always kept his mental shields up, but Orin effortlessly penetrated his barriers. Vale didn't like that either. Not one bit.

"Then I shall teach you how to keep even the strongest of minds out of your thoughts before you leave my court. Your mother learned it. As will you."

And so, every morning, he'd meet with the titan and practice—another word for psychological torture, which wouldn't end until he could stop the mental attacks of the overking.

Orin always looked bored, disinterested, indifferent to everything. Vale didn't understand why at first, but by the time he left, he knew. To truly keep a mind free of thought, one had to stop wanting, needing, being. One had to be no one and nothing.

Vale was glad he seldom had to rely on that skill, as it stripped away a part of him every time he practiced it, shaping him into that indifferent person he pretended to be.

With Devi right in front of him, using that particular skill had never been more difficult.

His brother sucked at it, thankfully. As every second passed, Vale understood more and more about the scion before him—if *scion* was even the accurate term in his case.

Vale looked through his half-brother's past. The male had taken centuries to piece it together.

Rook, as Devi had called him, as he called himself these days, hadn't been born of a human, or a fae, or a scion. His mother had been something else entirely.

Long ago, after the humans had created the deadly virus that spread through the lands, spelling their doom, the enlightened traveled to Eartia and fought to keep humanity in check. They needed to. The enlightened had a low birth rate, even lower than that of the fae, and they mostly produced males. Human females were the only other creature in the universe with whom they could reproduce. The first generation of enlightened who'd traveled to Eartia tweaked human evolution to ensure they'd resemble their race and that they could bear their heirs. So, keeping humans alive was crucial to the gods.

First, they combated the virus itself. To an extent, they succeeded. The disease rendered humans undead, killing them first, then turning them into mindless beasts that were entirely useless to the enlightened. The cure they developed returned the undead to life, giving them back their sense and thoughts. But they remained what they'd been reduced to: vile creatures who only wished to destroy the living and eat every life form they could get their hands on without any notion of creating.

The orcs were created.

The battle that followed was ruthless, for the orcs were many, and the enlightened, mighty as they were, were too few to protect the rest of humanity. They built strongholds under energy walls, and kept the survivors safe. Then, the enlightened targeted specific targets—the orcs who'd risen into power among their kind.

An orc who had surrounded himself with many wolves took Achdrak—modern-day Asra. Since the cure had spread, their kind had been able to reproduce. The lord of Achdrak had a harem at his disposal, and he'd impregnated many females. When the enlightened took the fortress, Wolven Fort, they were disgusted by what awaited them within.

The orc lord was fond of his children, so when the time came to make him talk, the enlightened threatened, tortured, and did worse things to the young orcs.

Eiulr was such a child. The overking, Cronus, ordered his son, Orin, to rape her right at her father's steps. The ultimatum they gave the orc lord was simple: all orcs leave the continent in boats and never return. The orc would hear nothing of it, not even to spare his children.

All were killed in Achdrak and in many orc cities. Finally, once the powerful had been dealt with and the vermin left alive had been chased behind the walls of the Isle, there was peace.

But in Wolven Fort, Orin had looked at the poor female he'd defiled and he'd pitied her. So when his father ordered the enlightened to kill all orcs, he slashed her face with his sword, leaving a scar that would never fade, pretending to slay her.

Eiulr lived to give birth to a son she called Makrs, a boy born in the Isle to a creature who could find no reputable work and who had no home. They erred through his childhood until his mother perished one cold winter at the edge of a forest. The boy had no skills to talk of and nowhere to go. To sate the hunger that never quite went away, he ate anything he could find, mostly worms.

Then a beautiful male found him. He laughed and called Makrs the prince of worms. A name the boy still loved and hated.

"Come," he said. "We will feed you at our table."

Elden Star took pity on the famished, lost creature and brought him to the small settlement he'd recently founded in the heart of the Graywoods.

"Marcus," he was called for a time, a strong name that fitted him well, but as the boy grew, he asked himself questions. Dangerous questions, such as why he only had one name. Who were his people? Who had fathered him? He asked Elden, one day, because Elden knew all things. Never had he seen the king turn so grave.

"I cannot speak of it. I will not. If you wish to learn of your past, go north to the lands where our kind still dwells behind their walls."

At twelve, Marcus went north. He observed and listened with his mind and ears. He spied in the shadows. After a long time, he finally saw him: a male of great consequence who looked like him and had the same powers of the mind.

Orin, son of Cronus, now overking of the Isle.

Marcus never knew hatred until he saw his father. So, he began to plot.

Over the centuries, he rallied many creatures, many fae and scions to his cause. He seduced the Duke of Stormhale with promises of riches and the Stormhale daughter, Antera, with promises of crowns. Once she was his, he whispered into his half-brother's ear until he found Aurelius's weakness.

Aurelius had long wanted a child of his own. Easy enough to provide one, when one knew what to look for.

Finally, it was time. In the middle of the night, Marcus hid his spirit, sneaked into the overking's chambers, and struck Orin in the heart.

Vale pulled himself out of his brother's mind, disgusted by every word and vision he'd read.

Cronus was a monster. Orin was a weak waste of space, and Vale was glad of his death. Aurelius had had no spine. The Stormhales should rot in hell. And as for Marcus…

Makrs had been innocent, without evils, without greed or vices. But sometime over the last two thousand years, his brother had been consumed by something else entirely. Marcus, Rook—whatever name he chose—was a cancer that needed to be cut out for the good of the Isle.

Vale was certain of it, now he knew his brother's endgame.

Rook was obsessed with one thing: destroying the walls around the Isle. He wanted to let his brethren once again roam freely on their land. He believed that coexisting peacefully with the orcs was possible and that they deserved a chance to leave the undead seas. But Vale knew this would only unleash chaos on all the realms.

If he succeeded in his endeavor, fae, elves, scions, and even the gods would all be doomed. Even the dragons had reasons to fear that outcome.

Vale gleaned all this information in less than one minute, as his half-brother stared into his eyes with unadulterated hatred. Beneath the loathing was something else. Clear jealousy. The male fancied Devi. Vale almost smirked.

Good luck with that, asshole. Devi was his.

Rook signaled to the Corantians, and two men walked forward with chains.

"I wouldn't resist if I were you, Blackthorn." Rook lifted his bow, the arrow aimed right at him. "I'm a fairly good shot."

Devi was exhausted. Rook had tricked her into using her power too early; Vale wouldn't make the same mistake. He had no clue about the extent of Rook's powers, but he wouldn't underestimate a two-thousand-year-old demigod with a chip on his shoulder and an arrow aimed at his face.

He lifted his hands and let the soldiers chain them in front of him. The moment the manacles snapped shut, all strength and energy left him. Vale struggled to stay standing. Another pair of guards advanced with similar devices, and Vale almost snarled. No way were they similarly crippling Devi in her state.

Rook lifted his hand, stopping them in their tracks. "No need. The girl is exhausted. Besides, she and I are going to have a pleasant chat, are we not?"

Devi's glower suggested that her idea of a pleasant chat consisted of carving his entrails out with a teaspoon, but if he noticed, Rook didn't take it to heart.

"Come on through. You're just in time for dinner."

TWENTY-FIVE
DINNER AND DEALS

Two soldiers, one male and one female, escorted Devi. They stood right behind her and nudged her with their swords whenever she slowed down.

They followed Rook through empty rooms.

The manor was old and decrepit. It looked strange, with walls too plain and symmetrical, columns, round-top windows.

Devi let it distract her. Better she muse over the architecture than try to understand how Rook—Rook of all people—was Vale's psychotic elder brother.

She remembered the first time she'd met Rook at the start of her protector-in-training courses. He'd seemed nice. He'd been nice, self-deprecating, kind to anyone he encountered, and quick to laughter. It just didn't compute in her mind.

So, she focused on windows, doorways, and wood flooring.

Rook turned to find her glancing at the walls. "Do you like this place?" he asked conversationally. "It survived an age. It was built before the war. The owner renovated it. A lot more effort than razing it to the ground and rebuilding, if you ask me, but it has a certain charm."

"I didn't ask you," she replied.

Rook laughed. "Fair enough. You're angry, I get it; trust me, I do. Hence we're going to sit down, have dinner, and talk. We're friends, aren't we?"

Her head was going to explode.

"We were. Then you turned out to be an evil bastard. Literally."

The anger that flashed in his eyes gave her pause. It wasn't annoyance or vexation, but pure, undiluted, murderous rage. Others would have shivered. Devi had always poked the bear; it was in her nature to have a snarky retort for anyone who deserved it. Her instincts told her to be cautious with this male. He wasn't rational. He could, and would, see her suffer for crossing him and laugh with glee. Nice Rook was a facade, a shadow.

But the anger was gone as fast as it had come. He had some self-control.

"Careful, now. That wasn't very nice."

"Shooting my horse wasn't very nice either."

She recognized his laugh well.

By all gods, how she hated him.

"Fair. All right, come on through. I bet you're parched and famished. That was an impressive display out there. For a minute, I wondered if your ice would reach us."

She wished it had.

Rook shrugged. "Of course, it would not have affected me, but I would have had to replace my guard. That would have been a shame. I like those guys."

"Please don't say another word. I won't listen to another word, unless what's coming out of your mouth is some sort of an explanation about what's going on here."

Rook smiled. "Always so focused and dignified. That's what I like about you, Devi. Come, sit. You eat, I talk."

She walked into the formal dining room, set for two with golden candelabra, porcelain dinner sets, and silver cutlery.

A candlelight dinner? She attempted not to recoil. She'd always known Rook fancied her, and the fact had been nothing more than a slight annoyance; now it was downright repulsive. He'd better not have designs over her.

"Oh, but I do," he answered her thoughts. "But you're quite safe from me for now, don't worry. I never have and never will touch a female without express consent."

She wasn't surprised that he could reach her mind; she'd left most of her walls down, making her an open book to anyone with mental skills. Most. All her energy was focused on keeping one small piece of information to herself, just the one. She hoped she had enough willpower to keep it hidden.

Rook couldn't know about the devices. If he did, all would be over. She'd seen him fly. He was faster than any fae she knew. He'd rush to the Court of Stars and take them before the night was through. She couldn't let that happen. She wouldn't.

Devi sat, looking at the delicate, fancy food on the plate before her. She'd take dry meat on the back of her horse in Vale's company over this anytime, but she grabbed her knife and fork.

"Is it poisoned?"

Rook chuckled. "No poison can affect you—or me. But you know that. Go on. I have a chef traveling with me. He's quite talented."

She ate, partially because she was ravenous after using her strength, and partially so he'd explain himself. The food was nice. Okay, it was fucking delicious, but she gave no outward sign of delight, because fuck him, his fancy dinner, and his chef. At the tenth mouthful, she reminded Rook, "You said you'd talk."

He grinned from the other end of the table. "That I did. Long story short, Orin raped my mother, cut her with his sword, and never again thought of her for the rest of his miserable existence. I killed him for it."

He said it with little feeling, as if they'd been discussing sports or the state of the finances of the realms.

Rook was amused. "Come on, you know me better than that. I take the finances of the realms very seriously," he said, answering to her thoughts. "Orin's life was of no worth to me."

She took another bite of food. "Okay. I get it. I'm all for murdering rapists. Can we skip to the part where you decided it'd be cool to attack the unseelie realm, hunt your brother through three realms, and terrorize villages for kicks?"

Because there was no doubt that he was behind what had happened at Rhionhave.

Rook sighed. "It's complicated."

"Try me, or get out of my face."

Why was she pushing him like this after realizing how unstable he was?

"Because you know I'll try my best to fight my instincts with you. I will not harm you."

The moment he said it she knew it to be true. Despite everything, she would have sworn that Rook would rein in his rage when it came to her.

"Of course, you should be aware that I will redirect my anger on my brother, should you displease me."

She froze and lifted her eyes to look into his. Had she understood him correctly?

She dropped her cutlery.

"I took over the management of Corantius, with the blessing of my other brother. A charming male. Very fond of family and entirely focused on his newborn. He and I agree that one race has been too long forsaken in this world. We intend to open the wall surrounding the Isle and welcome them here, in our haven."

She couldn't have heard him right. Surely not.

"You're insane. Orcs! Billions of orcs, here?"

Rook shook his head. "Not billions, no. We'll only open the wall in one point and let through a few of them; the children and smarter ones. It's only fair."

"There were five continents, and the two that weren't protected are now barren wastelands because of what those creatures—"

"Don't you dare!" he screeched, getting to his feet. "Don't you dare talk of them that way, you spoiled, selfish little princess, coddled from birth. You know nothing."

She closed her mouth, and her eyes widened. He was one of them. A half-orc.

Devi's heart tightened in her chest.

"This," he said, "this is why you're here. No pity. No disgust. Just empathy. You know what it's like to be different from the rest of them."

"I'm nothing like you," she told him.

They might both be hybrids rejected by half of their kind, but Devi had never—would never—use that as an excuse to destroy them. She could have. So many times. She could have annihilated the Court of Night without effort.

"Yes, you're kinder than I am, which is why I need you. When I am overking, I will be cruel. It is in my nature. My queen will need to balance that."

She closed her eyes to suppress the rising wave of nausea. "And if I refuse?"

He smirked, showing all his white teeth. "Well, then, I guess I won't need to keep my brother around as leverage, now will I?"

She seriously wished she'd read him wrong earlier, when he'd mentioned that her displeasing him would affect Vale. Apparently not. He was truly that disgusting.

"I'm done eating—and talking."

"But you're not done thinking. I'll give you until the end of the day. There are matters that cannot be avoided today. Your friends are making a nuisance of themselves in the west. Make up your mind before dusk. In the meantime, get comfortable. There are forty-seven soldiers, all scions and more experienced and better rested than you. Try to leave and they have orders to bleed out the Blackthorn boy. Slowly."

On that note, Rook got up, and as he left the dining room, he addressed the two guards who had stood behind her the whole time. "Show the lady to her chambers. Keep an eye on her until I return."

TWENTY-SIX
THE GREAT HALLS

Kira was never going to admit it to the annoying male she'd accompanied west, but she was glad to be here. Glad to have aided his purpose. Kallan Blacks had changed her mind about fae.

After dusk, on the day the crow had brought them news from the Blackthorn prince, they started to follow Kallan's plan. They sneaked to the Fortwall and commenced the long, miserable hike up to the ridge.

Kira did not like hiking. The next day, however, they reached a thin gap in the mountains—the entrance to Carvenstone. Then they got to have fun.

There were a hundred guards. A hundred against two were the sort of odds she liked. This would be a story worth telling when she returned home.

"Are you laughing!" Kallan screamed over the brouhaha of clashing swords and smashing skulls.

"If you're not having fun, you're not doing it right!"

She had to give the male this: he was pretty handy in a fight, better than she would have believed. And he also happened to always ensure to be positioned behind her so no one could hurt her. At first, it was disconcerting, as Kira was used to watching her own back, but she got used to it fast enough.

Kallan was all bow and arrows when he could, but he switched to his sword when an adversary got within range. Similarly, Kira used her fire for long-range attacks, when she could hit a few enemies at once so as not to waste her energy. Up close, she used her staff or the daggers tucked in her sleeves.

It took them perhaps an hour, but they found themselves back to back with a hundred fallen bodies at their feet. Kallan was breathing in and out hard.

She rolled her eyes. "Someone shouldn't skip cardio." She tilted the head of a corpse with the toe of her boot to get a good look at its face. "They aren't seelie."

"Corantians," Kallan stated. "Let us hope that's the last of them."

Kira doubted it. If these weaklings had come here alone, the gates would not have fallen, not if the rest of the folks of Carvenstone were half as well trained as Kallan.

"How many soldiers were patrolling the Fortwall?" she asked.

"Two dozen," he replied. "Not our strongest. They'd be in the city, closer to the shore."

Kira snorted. "Great strategy. Let's leave our gates unmanned and hope for the best."

"We were at peace. The purpose of the guard here is to warn us of unwanted visitors. Hopefully, a scout reached the city before the Corantians made it through the gates."

Kallan called his horse, and they ate while they waited for him to join them; then they rode all night until they reached a magnificent mountain, taller than any mountain in Wyhmur. There was moss, grass, and thin trees along its slopes, and a wild waterfall cascaded into a beautiful lake. The light of dawn shone through its clear water, and Kira, for once, had nothing to say.

"Beautiful, is it not?"

She just nodded.

"Come on through." Kallan carefully led the way through a path circling the lake until they arrived at the waterfall.

Kira grimaced as he walked forward, under the water. "I don't like getting wet."

"Such a fussy princess."

Nothing else he might have said would have made her move as fast. Discountenancing that he knew how to manipulate her so well after just a few days.

Shivering as the water drenched her to the bone, she warmed herself by calling to her fire. Without thinking, she lifted her hand to Kallan's face and pushed some energy through him too.

He lifted a brow. "Useful trick. Thank you."

She was ignoring him, her gaze taking in everything. When they'd been before the waterfall, she'd felt nothing but wildlife—the occasional deer, a bear perhaps, some wolves—but now, she sensed so much more. Looking at the opposite end of the cave, she found an impasse.

Kallan walked forward and put his hand on the dark, damp stone. Its dull gray surface came to life; the rock changed, smoothing to reveal the shape of a round door so large three dragons could have passed through side by side with ease. Kallan pushed it, ever so gently, and the wall entirely disappeared, revealing great halls with impossibly high hammer-beam ceilings meticulously carved into the stone.

They were greeted at lance-point by three dozen armed soldiers in formation. The moment they saw Kallan, they lowered their lances. Two soldiers, a male and a female, detached from the formation and rushed to hug him, laughing.

"I knew you were too stubborn to die!" said the female.

The male turned grave. "Valerius?"

Kallan smiled. "Alive and traveling north to end this madness."

Everyone relaxed, their shoulders dropping, and sighed deeply.

"Come, our people need to see you and hear you and…" The female stilled. "You've brought a girl."

Kira couldn't recall the last time anyone had called her a girl. Probably not since she'd learned to wield all kinds of weapons at the age of eight.

She stiffened, wondering if she might encounter some animosity, but the female yelled enthusiastically and rushed to hug her, too.

Shit. Kira did not hug.

"Calm down, Nyx. Kira, meet Nyx, head protector of Carvenstone, and Kit, her brother. Guys, meet Kira. She bites."

They were led down the halls, which grew in grandeur the deeper they walked inside the intricate network of caves.

"This is the Court of Sin?" Kira asked, baffled.

Kallan snorted. "An ominous name, I'll allow, but it keeps strangers out of our business, and that's all that matters."

"I heard you take in folks of all races here. That your master is attempting to be less barbaric than the other fae."

"Don't the elves kill anyone on sight without asking questions for crossing their borders?" Kallan retorted.

Kira wasn't apologetic. "Anyone? No. Fae in armor, bearing ill will? Certainly."

They passed many doors that led to smaller chambers. Most were empty, but as they went farther into the belly of the cave, Kira started to see light, hear voices and laughter, feel warmth.

They reached a hall so large Elvendale might have fit inside it twice over, yet it was almost full.

At least five hundred thousand fae were assembled in the hall, some cooking on one side, others chatting in circles around a fire, and others sleeping on the side. They'd set up beds on the floor along the walls; some of hay, some of feathers, others made for fae with covers.

"So many children," Kira noted as she watched, confused.

It was rare to see a child for a thousand elves; from her understanding, the same numbers could be applied to high fae, yet there were thousands of little ones running around. Only a few had marks of lesser fae, with parts of nature on their features, such as branches, hooves, and antlers.

Kira turned to Kallan, frowning.

"That's what you get when no one restricts what casts you can wed. There are many lesser fae married to high and common fae here. Our population has grown considerably as a result. There may be more folks in

Carvenstone than in the rest of the unseelie realm combined."

"Less inbreeding is always a good thing, I say," Nyx helpfully piped in.

The children weren't the only things worthy of note. They played with a foal of pure white fur sporting a small upturned horn in the middle of its head; other unicorns rested around the room, napping peacefully or walking around the fae, at ease.

Kira had a way with beasts, yet even *she* could not approach a unicorn that didn't bolt. Their race had been hunted to near extinction over many generations, but not here.

There were other things, on the ceiling, in the corners of the room, or mingling with the folks of Carvenstone. Bears, wild beasts, phoenixes, and, if Kira wasn't mistaken, a few dragons. She could feel them; like her, they were creatures of fire.

She'd heard of this place and dismissed its beauty. Now she got it. It was precious and worth preserving.

It was also powerful. Very, very powerful.

"Why haven't you joined the fight with the rest of your people? This… the warriors among you are an army."

"An army that shall defend this place, our home. If we go, who will protect our children?" Nyx asked. "We'll only march to war if Valerius Blackthorn asks us to."

Valerius Blackthorn, the lord of these halls. Kira had held little curiosity about the elusive prince before seeing the Court of Sin for herself. Now she started to understand why Devi traveled with him and why she had sent her to his companion's aid. This was another

Elvendale. A court forsaken by most, different and strong.

It had been a week since they'd arrived in Carvenstone, and although her mission was complete, Kira had not yet left. No one questioned why she was still there, and they let her take a turn standing guard.

She would have to go soon, but for now, something was keeping her here, anchoring her.

She'd been sleeping on a cot when the noise started. From where she was in the hall, it sounded like knocking. She leaped to her feet and ran toward the entrance of the cave. The noise grew louder and louder as she approached it. She found Kallan and Nyx and twice as many guards as usual.

It wasn't knocking. Something was hammering at the mountain relentlessly.

"They don't know how to get in," Nyx whispered.

Far from a reassuring statement; it meant the intruder was no friend to Carvenstone.

"Will they get through?" Kira asked.

Kallan shook his head. "Not this way. There are many ancient spells keeping this place safe, and Vale and I added all the protections we could; the main door is sealed with all the elements. An enemy would need to have a mage controlling each one to get through. But they may dig their way through the mountain."

Even if they dispatched this assailant, they would still have to deal with a brand-new hole that wasn't as well concealed or well protected as the entrance to the cave.

"Show me another way out," Kira said. "I'll get rid of them."

Whoever was attacking them needed to die, or they would reveal the location of Carvenstone and more enemies would come.

Kallan protested, "We don't know how many—"

"One," Kira stated. "I feel one power, one aura. It'll be a piece of cake."

Though he knew she was strong, he still hesitated. Kira expected more nonsense, but after a moment, the male nodded. "Not the worst idea, but you're not going alone. Nyx, can you manage things here?"

The warrior snarled. "I managed just fine while you were out galivanting through the countryside."

He laughed and then tilted his head to show Kira the way. "Let's go."

Whoever was out there, they'd kill them in an instant and come back in time for breakfast.

TWENTY-SEVEN
THE COURT OF STARS

The Corantians led Devi to a frilly room—lace, ruffles, pink and white cushions. She might have puked had she not had more pressing concerns at hand.

The guards made no move to leave.

"Can I have a minute? I'd love to freshen up."

They didn't so much as twitch.

Got it. Better save my breath.

Devi headed to the door on the left side of the gaudy bed that could fit half a dozen. Finding a bathroom on the other side, she entered it and shut the door firmly behind her. At least her guards didn't insist on following her there too.

Devi closed her eyes and scanned the surrounding area frantically, desperate to locate Vale. She'd felt his strength diminished, drained by the strange chains they'd wrapped around his wrists. Somehow, they were stopping him from using his powers, weakening his mind and body. No doubt an enlightened tool. Fortunately, the device hadn't affected her; she could still access his power, but for how long, she didn't know.

Vale had been right. She had no clue how to use his gift, but the focus Styx had given her helped; she thought of Vale and nothing else, expanding her mind, eyes closed, trying to scan her surroundings. Below, left, right, down…

There he was. Under her, somewhere to her left. She recognized his presence. Devi bit her lip and reached out.

To her surprise, it was easier than she'd expected. Almost as soon as she tried to communicate with him, his mind opened to her, as if there had been a bond she'd just needed to tug on.

"Where are you?" she asked, cutting to the chase as she was unsure how long she'd be able to pull that off in her state.

"Dungeons. One guard in front of me, another two at the door. How are you?"

Only three people against Vale. Rook was far too cocky and sure of his device.

"I'm fine," she said. "Gonna try something. Don't die."

She opened her mind up to her ice and tried to direct it the way she had earlier. She thought it was worth a try, at least. Though she was used to relying on contact or at least visual connection to use her powers, there really was a solid link between her and Vale right now; she concentrated on that connection and did her best to visualize Vale. He was sitting up on a cot, one leg folded, the other extended, with his hand resting on his lap. Devi fixed her mind on the metal restraints around his wrists. The lit screen in the middle displayed the picture of a closed lock. She zapped the bindings with small doses of ice and watched through Vale's eyes as they turned light blue, then white, as if covered in fresh snow. Soon, the restraints were covered in ice. Vale tugged on his wrists, and the metal cracked just as someone pounded on the bathroom door.

Devi let go of the connection and went to open the door. She found the female guard waiting, obviously irritated, with her lips pursed and narrowed eyes.

"Can't a lady freshen up in peace?"

"You weren't. The tap isn't running and you're dressed. What are you up to?" the Corantian demanded.

Devi opened her mouth to answer, but a cold breeze swept into the room, and the next instant, the guard's head cracked against the wall. Devi winced, then smiled at Vale. "What took you so long?"

"No time. Come."

"Not without the horses."

"They're waiting," he replied, before kicking the closest floor-to-ceiling window open and grabbing her hand.

Devi leaped out of the opening without hesitation and landed painfully on a crouch. A one-floor drop shouldn't have hurt quite so much, but she was drained.

The horses were right before them. Vale rushed onto Midnight's back and offered her his hand again; Alarik couldn't be mounted yet, not with his injury still healing. She took his hand gratefully and let him hoist her onto the horse behind him. Then the dyrmounts rode at full speed through the snowy road and up a steep hill.

"How much of a head start do we have?" she asked.

An arrow flew past her ear. She hadn't even heard it.

"About twenty seconds, apparently," Vale replied. "And I don't have our weapons or any of our supplies."

Great. Perfect, in fact.

"So, we're screwed," she summarized.

Vale laughed. "I think not!"

She had been about to ask in what universe weren't they screwed when Vale pulled on the horse's reins to halt its course and turned to watch dozens of their former captors rush toward them by foot, horseback, or wings.

Had he lost his fucking mind?

The ground shook under Midnight and lightning bolts zapped across the sky. A blizzard lowered onto the hill, and all the snow slid down toward the enemy. After lightning struck the first flying scion, the others landed, and now either fled downhill, away from Devi and Vale, or erected shields to protect themselves from the wrath of three elements.

An avalanche, a storm, and an earthquake.

"You've borrowed my powers for an hour and you're already better at controlling them than I am," Devi lamented with a sigh. "But I guess a thank-you is in order."

"The only thing in order for you is sleep. Come, move to the front so I can carry you."

Only a fortnight had passed since she'd declared she couldn't sleep on horseback. Now, cradled between Vale's strong arms, she passed out within mere instants.

The moment Devi destroyed the bindings sapping his energy, his strength was restored, but to get out of his cell and break them out of the manor, Vale used up most of his energy. He considered halting, but opted against it. Now, more than ever, getting to the Court of Stars fast was paramount. Rook would be on their trail in a matter of hours, if not sooner.

He rode as fast as he could with Devi in his arms, avoiding all towns and settlements. Seven hours later, the sleeping beauty stirred; by then, he'd covered half of their journey.

"Rise and shine, sleepy," he whispered.

She moaned, reluctant to admit she was awake. He understood that feeling completely, but they had no time for it. "Come on, lazy. The horses need a break."

As did he. Devi opened her eyes and straightened. Vale missed her warmth against his chest.

"Morning," he said.

"Morning," she repeated groggily. "Where are we?"

"About two days south from Staren, and perhaps six hours away from Stormhale, the Court of Stars. We're approaching a village. I don't feel anything alarming emanating from it, but it could mean we're facing someone with powers greater than mine, as well as the opposite of mine, north of the borders. Still, we have to risk stopping."

She wrinkled her pretty nose. "Do we?"

Vale nodded. "It's essential. I'm not well known in these parts, but these clothes are recognizable. We'll need to change if we want to blend in at Stormhale."

She sighed. "Well, I certainly wouldn't mind new clothes, but it'll pain me to remove the maille."

"We'll search for something to put over it, if we can." He didn't like the thought of shedding their defenses either. "Time for Naelynn and Ruven Norfiel to come out and play again."

"All right, but don't make me pregnant this time," she said. "I don't want to have to buy maternity clothes to keep up the ruse."

"Fair enough. I'll change our appearances now. Let us hope the fates decide we've had enough ill fortune for one day."

The fates concurred, as the trip to the small hamlet of Gyl-Elworth was fruitful and devoid of incident. Having left their bags back at Low Crest, Vale had little resources, but Devi again came to the rescue.

"Thankfully, my father's folks recalled I like pockets. The coat has two, and my pants have four."

She'd stuffed her pockets with various things; she had to remove three flasks, the healing charm covered in dried red blood she'd used on Alarik, and many such things until she found a purse with gold. Not much, but enough for cloaks, warmer boots, food, drinks, and care for the horses.

They stuck to the story of the Norfiels from the south who wished to find refuge with relatives, and the people of Gyl-Elworth looked no further.

"I certainly do not blame you in such troubled times. May you go in peace," they said.

Listening and reading between the lines, Vale noted that the common folk of Corantius were as worried about the fate of the realm as the seelie they'd encountered. They'd heard of the war in the south, and though the south was far, war was never good for simple fae such as they.

Vale and Devi spent two hours in town; Vale sat at a dining table in an inn, regrouping whatever energy he could in such circumstances. He would have loved to sleep, but they could not afford such luxury now, so they were on their way by nightfall.

Devi healed Alarik a second time; with rest and her help, he was good as new for the second leg of their journey. They rode faster now that she was on her own horse, and they reached the edge of the city in five hours.

Vale and Devi stared wordlessly at the tall, translucent dome on the horizon, and inside it was a golden castle, its walls higher than the peaks of Carvenstone.

Devi broke the silence. "Looks like the Duke of Stormhale is compensating for something."

TWENTY-EIGHT
WHISPERS AND PLEAS

They arrived in the middle of the night, dressed in their new finery. Devi wore a red and white cloak over her maille and over-the-knee boots that served to hide most of the garments she wore under the Corantian clothes.

She liked the boots, and Vale had eyed them with keen interest. She couldn't deny his look had pleased her.

"So how do you propose we break into Stormhale's place? The dome—it's an energy wall, right?"

Vale nodded carefully. "I recall your father saying the Stormhales exhibit their treasures, however."

"*A museum open to all Corantians,*" Elden had said. If he'd been right, they had a way in, at least.

"You're a scion, and I'm something close to it, and with these clothes, we look like Corantians, so maybe entering their domain will be easy enough."

That wasn't much of a plan to go on. For one, they also needed a way out.

"I say we spend the night at an inn in town and play tourists?" she suggested. "We could ask questions, and you could rest."

Vale shook his head. "Staying in a small village was one thing, but we cannot assume I won't be recognized in a city. There are too many high fae and scions who might have seen me when I came to Corantius a few centuries ago. As for my illusions, they'll be useless against anyone of consequence. It's too risky."

He had a point.

"Well, they might recognize you, but no one knows *me*. I could go and ask questions."

Devi could tell he *loathed* that suggestion. Somehow, their bond was still solid; she felt his mind brushing up against hers, and his power still flowed through her.

Despite the fact that she could hear his thoughts vehemently arguing against it, he carefully nodded. "It's the best solution. You can do the talking, and I can act like a monk or perhaps a servant. But you can't book a room with unseelie coin."

"I have coins from all three realms in my purse," she replied.

Devi had found it odd until today, but the elves must have been thinking ahead, anticipating their needing Corantian money across the border.

"Perfect."

Vale removed all his finery, from his maille to his boots, placing it all in a bag they'd bought at Gyl-Elworth.

He kept his newly acquired cloak, lowering the hood over his eyes, and wore only his shirt and breeches beneath.

"How cold are you?"

"Very fucking cold," he grunted. "Words can't express how much I regret having left the damn blackfire stone at Low Crest."

Devi tried her hand at sending warmth through the bond.

Vale sighed in delight. "Thank you. I forgot. I might have been able to do that myself."

She frowned, musing out loud, "Strange that we're still channeling each other. It didn't last long the first time."

Vale made no reply, but he was hiding something. She could tell. His mind had shut down, keeping her out.

She narrowed her eyes. "What is it?"

"Nothing I wish to discuss. Trust me, I'll tell you when I can, but we can't afford the distraction."

She was intrigued and frustrated, but she let it go.

Many inns populated the main street alone; all had signs at the front, with their prices and food options displayed. Devi examined a few; while her purse was heavy with coin, most of it was seelie and unseelie. She didn't want to waste what little Corantian money she had on her.

Her indecision was also calculated. If anyone was observing her, they'd see a tourist shopping around like any other innocent traveler.

She settled on a modest but busy inn that served food day and night. Inside the cheery establishment, Devi saw a merry group of scions at the bar, all in various stages of drunkenness.

"Hey there, pretty lass! How can Vera help?" a small, beautiful, and buxom lady with green hair greeted her.

The place was called Vera's Roof, so she was apparently talking to its owner.

"I would like a suite, with a bed for my male servant next door, if it's available."

The sign had shown the pricing for such a setup.

"Aye, it's available. No one coming here ever has the coin for that room!" Vera laughed, then turned to Vale. "You, boy!"

Devi hid her smile. When was the last time anyone had addressed Vale like that?

"The stables are left of the inn. Take the service entrance and pop by the kitchen on your way up. The staff will give you meals to take up to the suite. They're included in the rate." She turned her attention back to Devi. "We take payment in advance for strangers."

She'd prepared the right amount of coin, plus an extra one to engender goodwill; she gave it to the innkeeper.

Vera gave her a toothy smile before calling to her staff, "Jeryn! Come here, girl."

The "girl" in question was also an adult. Friendly as she was to Devi, Vera was awfully condescending to her staff.

"Take the lady to the suite upstairs for me, then see that her boy doesn't get lost at the back, hmm?"

"Yes, ma'am."

Jeryn led the way in silence.

The suite was large, elegant, and tastefully decorated, at least compared to the last bedroom she'd stepped into. There was a sitting area with a chaise longue, an armchair, and a low table next to a fireplace; a liqueur cabinet, a writing desk, and a door leading to a bedroom with white and yellow furnishing. Someone had picked wildflowers and put them in vases on both bedside tables.

"Will this do, ma'am?"

"Very well, miss. It's a lovely room. I love the flowers."

Jeryn blushed.

"You brought them up?" Devi guessed.

The female nodded. "Aye, ma'am. I think they cheer the room right up. There aren't enough flowers in the city. Too much pollution, what with them cars up in the castle."

Devi lifted a brow and repeated, "Cars?"

She knew what they were, but people had ceased to use them long ago to protect the environment. Only a few vehicles remained, powered by sunlight rather than finite resources.

Jeryn looked down. "The Duke of Stormhale has several. Old ones, you know. The ones that run on petrol. He has a race every other day up in his tracks."

The conversation couldn't have flown in a better direction.

"How extravagant. I hear the duke is very much into treasures. Is it true he opens his doors to strangers who may wish to gaze upon them?"

Jeryn nodded fervently. "Strangers, aye, ma'am. Not the likes of me or any common blood—but it's plain enough there's blue or gold in your veins, so no doubt they'll let you in."

All right. Apparently, the duke was a jackass, and any guilt Devi had felt at the thought of stealing from him had evaporated.

"I think I might try my luck," Devi said.

Vale appeared at the top of the stairs, holding a tray of food.

There were two servings; the same food, but one meal was exquisitely presented on beautiful plates, while the other was served in a wooden bowl.

Devi made a disgusted moue.

"Do they treat the common folk well here?" she asked Jeryn, curious.

The female looked around and lowered her voice. "As well as anywhere in these lands, miss. You know what it's like. Us fae aren't the same as you gods. We don't have the same rights and all. It wasn't all that bad under the overking 'cause he said, 'No torture, no blood, no bruises!' And so the servants were treated fairly well. Now he's dead, though…" She closed her eyes. "We can only hope the next king is a decent fellow. They say the bastard prince might claim the throne." Her voice fell to a whisper. "And I hope he does, ma'am. That I do. I'd take a bastard treated like us over a pampered prince any day."

Devi smiled. "I hope he does, too. Thank you, Jeryn."

Jeryn gave a small and awkward curtsy before heading to the door. "I wish all them lords were as nice and polite as you, lady. You don't even talk down to the likes of me."

And then she was gone, closing the door behind her.

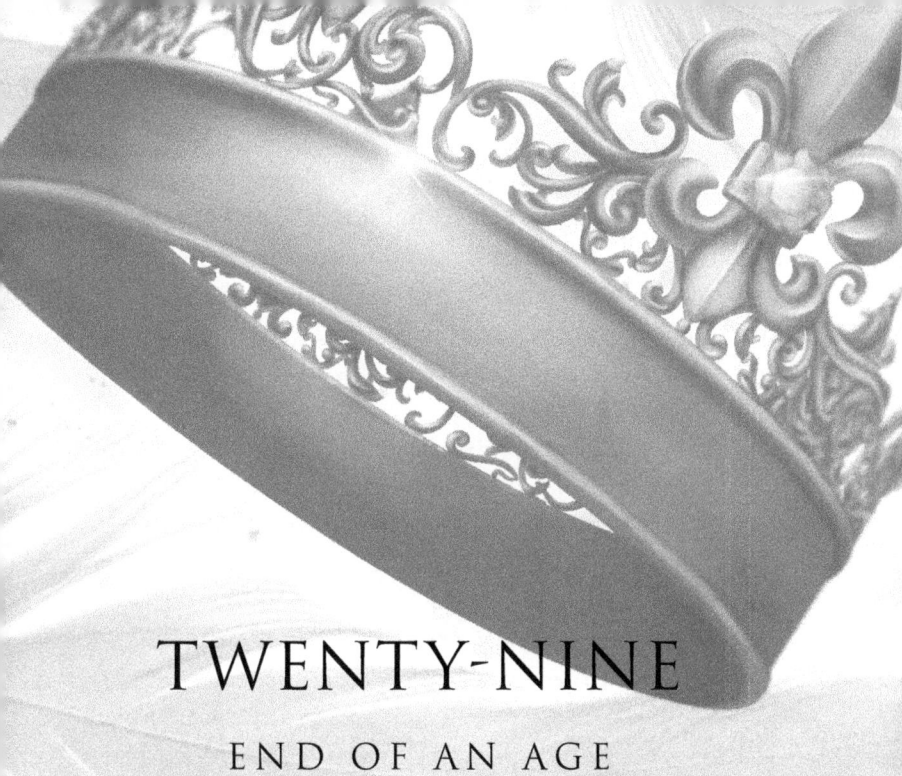

TWENTY-NINE
END OF AN AGE

Vale was not surprised by the state of affairs in Corantius. Why would he be? High fae preyed on the weak, and high fae were the creatures of scions and enlightened. The beautiful, sweet girl who would have had a thousand suitors south of these lands was little more than a slave here.

They say the bastard prince might come and claim the throne... and I hope he does.

Was she alone in thinking that? Or was he the secret hope of many oppressed fae like her? Vale understood why Devi had been so uncomfortable with the river folk. Having such trust and hope put on his shoulders was overwhelming.

"I can't believe these people," Devi grunted, grabbing the wooden bowl and attacking the mashed potatoes and meat pie that smelled succulent before she even sat down. "What a hypocritical bitch! Vera was smiling at me and barking orders at you and that poor fae like you were—"

"Shush," Vale interrupted. "I didn't mind. It certainly put things in perspective."

Vale had never snapped at the help, but now, he'd make a point to always treat them with respect.

He sat next to Devi and started to eat.

"I'll take the first watch," she offered. "I've slept more than you of late."

"Thank you. You were talking of the duke's keep when I got to the stairs?"

"Yes. According to Jeryn, he lets in any scion. No fae. I think it'll be easy for me to get in, but I don't know about you. And I'm not sure how we're supposed to get out with stolen treasures, either. The energy field around the domain makes things a little complicated. That and the fact he has racecars that could catch up with us, even with the dyrmounts."

Vale smirked. "I have an idea."

Vale would have preferred to study the surrounding area, evaluate the risks, and fine-tune their approach, but it was only a matter of time before Rook found their trail. They needed to act and soon.

His plan only held a minimal risk if it failed, so they decided to attempt it the very next day.

Devi left in the morning, after giving the innkeeper coin for another night.

"I'm going up to the castle to see what all the fuss is about."

Vera beamed. "Oh, you'll see treasures like none before, and spoils from hundreds of wars! Don't forget to visit the south wing. There are dragon claws and fangs."

Devi didn't know in what universe anyone would want to see a collection of bones, let alone collect them, but she thanked the innkeeper nonetheless.

She walked the main street up to the gates. A black fence with golden finials surrounded the energy dome.

A small group of people waited by the gate, and two severe guards spoke to each individual before letting them through.

Devi froze. There was more to this security, she was sure of it.

An instant later, the guard asked, "Are you of enlightened blood?"

The tourist nodded confidently.

The guards unsheathed their swords and pointed them at him. "We do not suffer lies, vermin. On your way, unless you wish to taste fyriron in your guts."

They must be Truth Seekers, Devi realized. Thanks to Vale's power, she had known the male had been lying, but the guards weren't psychic; she would have felt it if they were.

Truth Seekers were creatures blessed with an uncanny ability to hear, see, and *feel* lies.

Shit.

She bit her lip. Should she retreat? What if they asked a sensitive question? But she was in a queue, and there were already four people behind her. Leaving now would only make them suspicious.

It was her turn within ten minutes.

The guard on her left, a tall and bulky female, snarled down at her, "Your name?"

Devira Star Rivers, her true name, was the answer, but she'd also chosen another one and made it hers. She said confidently, "Naelynn Norfiel."

The guard narrowed her eyes. "Your age."

"Twenty-eight."

"Humph. A baby, then. What is your purpose here, child?"

"I heard the Duke of Stormhale has many treasures and that he opens his home to the curious."

Circling around the truth had always been second nature to her, but she had no idea whether Truth Seekers could detect lies by omission. Was she sweating?

The scion shrugged. She practically breathed out her relief.

"And do you have enlightened blood? The duke does not tolerate rascals on his land."

"Yes," was her reply.

The female stepped aside and let her pass.

Devi looked up at the sky. She had an hour to waste.

As it turned out, wasting time wasn't as problematic as she had thought. Inside, the long golden tower was a maze with many chambers and corridors. The first ten floors, she was told by a guide at the doors, were open to the public; upstairs housed the family quarters and the rest of the duke's home.

Devi acted casual, admiring each treasure with equal interest. There were many paintings, ancient sculptures of marble, and the most beautiful tapestries. Other things weren't to her taste: stuffed animals and the pelts of bears, lions, and gryphons.

She found the armory on the seventh floor. There were short swords, long swords, curved sabers, and thick blades meant to cut enemies down in one blow, horse and rider. As she started to fear she might never find what she was looking for, something caught her eye. In a display with six other armors practically identical, all modern and impressive, with cream plating of flexible material threaded with golden fyriron, just like maille, and red filigree running through, one item in particular made her pause.

It wasn't a sword so much as a dull, bladeless hilt at the base of the display case. She might not have noticed it at all had she not felt Vale stir on the other side of their bond. It was as though the simple, plain hilt called to her, whispering temptation.

One instrument out of two. Now she just needed to locate the crown.

She walked through each floor faster, mentally keeping track of the time. If Vale managed to execute his part of the plan, she didn't have long to find the second device.

On the tenth floor, she found the dragon fangs, as promised, as well as many other gruesome things, such as unicorn horns and a dying phoenix in a cage, fated to wither, burn, and come back to life, although it was never fed or allowed to fly. She felt it. Felt the creature's distress, his call for help.

This disgusted her more than anything she'd witnessed since arriving in Corantius, including Rook's advances, and that was saying a lot. The poor thing. Devi was boiling with anger. These people were barbaric.

She was looking at the fiery bird when all the lights went out. A high-pitched alarm blared, and Devi smiled.

It had worked.

Vale had located the power generator outside the dome and pushed as much energy into it as he could to overcharge it until it failed. Vale had doubted that the generator would be on the grounds, inside the dome; these things were noisy and ugly. A man such as the Duke of Stormhale would prefer to keep the nuisance out of sight. Vale and Devi had taken a chance that there would be no backup generator ready to kick in. If there was one, Devi would simply exit the building with the rest of the tourists. But as the lights were still out, she knew their risk had paid off and it was time to act.

She prayed the energy dome around the domain had also been blasted when the generator had been destroyed; otherwise, she was on her own. Either way, she had no time to spare.

Devi grabbed the closest heavy object available—a five-foot-tall statue of a winged scion in flight—and smashed open the phoenix's cage.

"Go, little one!" she told the bird, and then rushed down the stairs to the seventh floor.

At the armor display, Devi froze the case's glass and kicked it in. As she grabbed the hilt, the lights came back on. Shit.

She was alone in the room, so she hid the hilt behind her back, under her coat, and rushed to the exit.

She collided into someone's chest and leaped back. Then she breathed out a sigh of relief. "Vale! Is the dome down?"

"Not for long, as the lights already came back. Let's go."

"I don't have the crown," she replied.

Vale led them toward a service elevator to the ground floor. When they were inside, he pulled a circlet adorned with a red ruby at its center from his pocket.

"I felt it call to me when you were watching the jewelry upstairs," he explained. "As I got the impression you recognized the sword, I figured I'd go find the crown first. Come, now. I found a passage a fae was taking earlier. She was dressed in an apron; it was a servants' way, so hopefully, we won't—"

He opened the door leading outside and froze.

Two dozen scion guards stood in front of them, their bows aimed at the door—at them. Each arrow was expertly aimed, each tip deadly.

"Fire!"

The arrows armed with elemental magic and all the strengths of scions traveled so fast Devi had just enough time to register that they'd been fired, and they were already on them.

What a dumb way to die, Devi had time to think.

At least Vale would live. He was fast enough to evade them.

At least...

And then, the arrows hit their mark.

Devi blinked, bewildered as to why she was alive, why nothing hurt, and why a heavy weight had her pinned to the ground.

And then she screamed, and screamed, and screamed, so loud everyone in the Isle might have heard her.

Vale was fast—fast enough to get away from a volley of arrows fired by scions—and he'd made use of his speed.

He'd covered her with his body, taking ten arrows through his chest to save her.

Devi was mindless, soulless, hopeless—a simple body moved by basic needs. She shifted the body above her carefully to get up. Her left hand clasped the dull hilt at her back, and the moment she pulled it from her belt, a blue, flamboyant blade extended from it. She lifted her sword arm and swung it once, in a downward motion from right to left, cutting through seven warm bodies. Blue blood sprayed out, soaking her chest. She rotated and swung it again, this time from right to left. Three scions dead, dead, dead. Heads rolled. The others pulled their swords. Some advanced on her, and others retreated. It didn't matter. They didn't matter. Nothing did. She thrust the sword high overhead and screamed, calling the sky to her.

Her next blow froze the bodies it didn't slash, incapacitating the rest of her enemies. She kicked the ice statues, breaking them into a thousand pieces on the paved ground of the courtyard.

Devi didn't spare them another gaze, another thought, to return to Vale. Ten arrows. Four inside his heart. He was still breathing, only just.

She could barely see him through the blood and tears.

"Don't. You can't go. You can't leave me," she pleaded.

He chuckled but choked on blood. "I have to, but we'll meet again, you and I. Fate…"

Fate. Just like that, she knew what he'd been hiding from her, what he'd kept to himself until it was time. She was his, as declared by fate. His mate. The legendary, impossible, one in a billion occurrence that Loxy had read to her from children's fairy tales.

He was hers, and he was dying.

She was dying. She would be no more the moment he left this world, not now that she knew what he meant to her. How could she survive such darkness? How could she fight in a world without hope or light?

Devi hadn't even realized her hands were tearing at his clothes and pressing on his chest. When she became conscious of what she was doing, she'd already removed three arrows and frozen the wound to stop him from bleeding out.

She wouldn't let him go. Not now. Not ever. She'd give everything she had first.

"Ice is the purest of the four elements. The strongest. It'd kill a mortal, but it'd just protect my heart. I'll pass out, but I'll live. Dig the arrowhead out of my shoulder blades before I awaken."

She'd saved Styx. Surely she could do the same for Vale?

A little voice at the back of her mind reminded her that Styx's arrow hadn't pierced her heart. She told it to shut up. She could do this. She *would*.

The only arrows left were the ones in his heart. Devi heard enemies approaching and tuned them out. They didn't matter. And they would not disrupt her. *They would not see her!*

A guard ran past her, talking in the communication device affixed to his ear. "Nothing to report here. All clear."

Devi removed all four deadly arrows successively, as fast as she could, and froze Vale's heart. Then she gathered him in her arms, extended her immense golden wings, and leaped skyward. She remembered a time when she'd been too weak to beat them. It had been too painful.

She'd had no idea what pain meant then. Flying through the sky, she ignored the ache every time her wings lifted and fell.

With the city out of sight behind her, she descended and landed in a small forest. She laid Vale's body on the ground, ever so gently. She refused to say "corpse," although his heart wasn't beating. He wasn't moving. He was alive, and that was all that mattered.

She removed the charm from her pocket and pressed it against his chest, but found it useless. It was meant to mend flesh, not ice.

She'd find someone who could heal him. Anyone. There was still hope.

She lowered her head onto his chest, and she cried and cried until there were no more tears to shed.

Night had fallen when she lifted her eyes and found a silhouette standing before her. She hadn't heard anyone approach.

Someone had followed her, of course. Death had come for her. She almost welcomed it.

"Well done, little princess. Quick thinking on your part, with the ice. Nothing else would have saved him."

Devi's mouth opened, then she blinked and pinched her own arm to check if she was hallucinating. Of everything that had occurred to her in her entire life, this was the most astonishing turn.

The female standing over her was of her height, her weight, and her very image, except for the red hair, green eyes, and the unique, enchanting voice she hadn't heard for close to fourteen years.

"Mama."

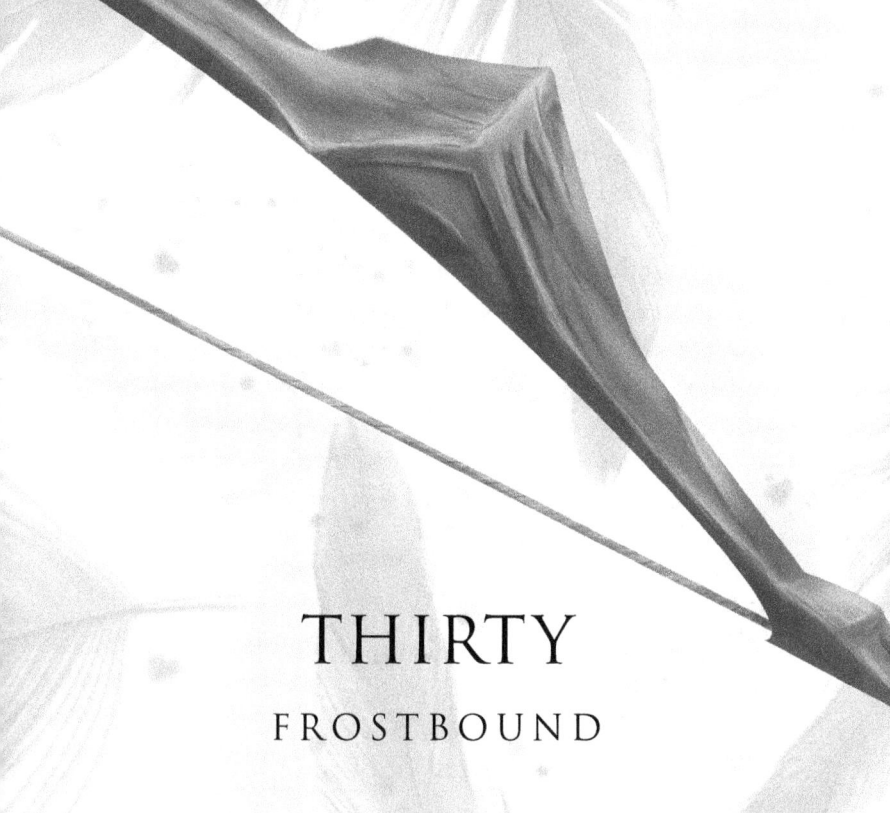

THIRTY
FROSTBOUND

Loxy knelt next to Vale, her hand on his forehead. "If he hadn't been bonded to you, he certainly would have died, but he's hanging on. Not for long, though. We have to act quickly."

She was dreaming, right? That must be it. She'd passed out from shock and this was just a strange dream.

A group of elves stepped up on either side of them, weapons in hand as they surveyed the area, protecting them.

Tearing her eyes away from Vale, Devi glanced around them long enough to see that they weren't alone. Not by a long shot. There were hundreds—no, thousands of elves in formation.

"I don't understand."

She didn't understand anything at all. How was her mother alive? What was she doing here, with all these warriors?

"Your father is a man of his word. He said you'd have his support if you retrieved the sword and the crown, and so you have it."

All right. That she could wrap her head around, but it didn't explain one thing. "How are you here?"

Looking up from Vale, her mother's green eyes cut to her. "Are we having this conversation or are we saving the overking?"

Oh. Yes, of course.

"Hand on his chest, like—"

Devi was quick to obey, pinning her hands flat on Vale's chest.

"That's it." Loxy nodded. "You already share a soul. He opened his mind to you and you to him. Was the bond sealed with a kiss?"

Devi bobbed her head.

"A near perfect bond. We should be able to link your hearts. I need you to reach through to him and make him hold on. Do you understand? I can perform the binding oaths, but you must keep him in this world."

Devi had no clue how to reach him, but she'd move mountains to save him. "Hey, Vale. You remember when we first met? You said I'd tell my grandchildren about our meeting one day. I want to, but you have to help me. You have to help me reach you."

There was a tug on the other end of their bond. A flicker of life. She focused on it, reaching for it through her mind.

"Vale?"

"*I'm here.*" Just a whisper, through her mind.

"My mama's alive and she's doing stuff. Chanting. It's weird. I don't care because she's going to keep you here, with me."

"*It's cold.*"

The ice all around his heart. "It won't be cold forever, I promise. Just stay with me a little longer…"

"*I'm tired.*"

No, no, no.

"Me too. I'm tired of fighting, and riding, and everything, but we need to hold on. You know that. For that girl, Jeryn, and for everyone like her. For your mother, and my father, and their people. And for Carvenstone."

"*Carvenstone…*"

"Your home. I want to see it someday. Not without you."

"*My home. It's beautiful, Devi. You* should *see it.*"

"We should. We will."

"*Great halls. Laughter. There's so much life…*"

"And Kallan is there, with my sister. No doubt they're bickering like children. I'm the nice one, you know."

Vale laughed. "*Poor Kallan.*"

She could have cried. No more whisper. He was here with her.

Then there was nothing but sharp, devastatingly cold pain, and Devi passed out.

Vale awoke in a great room of pale stone with a circular bed of silk, feathers, fur, and wool. Devi lay by his side.

He looked down at his naked chest. The arrow wounds had all healed, but on the left side of his chest, right over his heart, there was a mark, inside his flesh and beyond. The sign of a binding oath.

He recognized the runes. They stood for love and forever. He pressed his hand to his chest. His skin was ice cold, but a heart beat inside him.

Not his.

His eyes shifted to his left. Devi stirred in the bed, flipping over in her sleep.

She wore a nightgown with a distractingly low neckline he might have appreciated more had his attention not been on other things.

Her left breast bore the same blue mark.

Their heart had been frostbound, forever beating as one. Now, if they ever died, they would die together.

She stretched languorously and opened her eyes, beaming like he was the best present she'd ever received.

"Vale."

"Devi."

There was much to discuss, so many questions to ask and answer; they needed to plan their next step. But none of that mattered as much as tugging on her hand to pull her close and lowering his face to her neck.

"I want you so much it fucking hurts," he whispered, kissing her collarbone, her neck, then the corner of her jaw.

She sat up on his lap and wrapped her arms around his shoulders. "Then take me. I belong to you, and you to me."

"Until the end of time," he whispered, reciting the vow Loxy Rivers had engraved on their skin.

Devi rubbed her heat against him while taking his lips, deep, hard, almost desperately. He slid his hands up her thighs, on either side of his lap, and lifted her nightdress. He caressed her torso, then the curve of her breasts. Finally, he removed it and set it aside before plunging his head to her nipple and sucking on it. She moaned in pleasure, and between her sweet cries and the incessant movement of her hips against him, Vale grew hard as steel.

He would have loved to savor her, taste every inch of her, and soon, he would. But not tonight. Now he needed to be inside her and claim his mate like the beast she'd reduced him to.

"Please, I need you inside me now," she begged, shredding the rest of his self-control.

Vale flipped Devi onto her back. He opened his breeches, pulled out his thick length, and plunged it in her heat, his mouth seeking hers and muffling her shriek of pleasure as he pulled in and out of her tight pussy over and over. His vision blurred. All the sounds coming out of them were wild and frantic. He was so very close to the edge, but he'd take her with him when he came, even if it killed him.

His right thumb found her clit and his left hand massaged her breast. Vale sucked on her ear, teased the sensitive bundle of nerves at the apex of her thighs, and caressed her chest until she clenched, impossibly tightening around him. Then, finally, she let go with a mindless scream, and her release triggered his.

He kissed her shoulder, and her neck, and her mouth, keeping her in his arms until the night ended.

One night of love. Tomorrow, there would be war.

End of Song of Winter

PART THREE

SONG OF HEAVEN
AND ICE

ONE
WHAT MATTERS MOST

Something felt wrong. Kira could tell as soon as they emerged out of the network of sinuous corridors crawling out of Carvenstone.

When they'd been alerted of an intrusion at the borders of their hideout, she had felt confident. Especially when she'd clearly sensed that it was just one person. Whatever it was, whoever it was, Kira knew she had a fair chance.

Her entire life she'd trained against the elf lords of the Graywoods—gods and demi-gods. Some were stronger than she, certainly, but it was rare that she ever met a match outside of the borders of their lands.

And now as they approached the gates hidden under the waterfall, she felt warier with each passing moment.

She had to force herself to take one step after the next. She knew then: whoever this was, whatever it was, it was different. Stronger. Fouler.

She kept going all the same. Running away wasn't in her nature.

The male at her left had grown quiet, his expression betraying the same concern. It only served to increase her anxiety. Had she ever seen Kallan Blacks afraid?

She wished she could communicate with him without risking being overheard, but they were too close to the hidden entrance. They had to remain silent, lest they betray their position.

"Oh!" a stranger exclaimed, appearing out of nowhere, without so much as a noise or a shift of energy in the air.

Kira's eyes widened as she took him in. He looked quite handsome, all things considered. Or pretty, perhaps. There was something almost feminine to his delicate features. His build was lean, though muscular. Kira couldn't even feel magic emanating from him. The male should have looked and felt like an irrelevant weakling.

He didn't.

There were two sorts of people whose aura didn't betray their power. The weakest, most innocent creatures in the world. Hopeless babes, tiny lesser fae as harmless as bumblebees.

And creatures so strong they could suppress their very selves, their presence, and their powers.

This male was terrifying.

"Two of you," said he, conversational. "Marvelous. I do love a merry duo."

Then his eyes narrowed as he watched her.

"What's your business here?" Kal demanded to know.

A slow smile formed at the corners of the intruder's lips as he redirected his attention to the Carvenstone commander.

Somehow, it made him appear even more intimidating.

"Tell me, do you care for each other?"

His tone was curious and casual. His eyes weren't. They were cold. Colder than ice.

"Never mind," said he. "Let me check."

Then Kira screeched, louder than she could recall ever yelling, but the sound was drowned by the heart-wrenching scream erupting from Kal.

Her entire head started burning white hot, as if the creature had placed a helmet right out of a forge's fire on her scalp. Except he wasn't touching her. He looked so very calm he might not have been doing anything at all.

Just as suddenly as it had started, the torture stopped.

"Apparently, not really. You're practically strangers. Shame. Still, we can play a little game."

He reached out for her, his fist approaching her throat. Kira twirled her staff in her hand, ready to strike if he got anywhere near her. Instead there was nothing to strike at, and all the same his grasp closed around her neck, tightening around it.

He was choking her with his mind.

A psychic. A quakingly powerful mind manipulator. He turned to Kal.

"You seem like the noble sort. Are you noble enough to save a pretty damsel in distress? It's simple. Open the doors. Open the doors, and she will be spared."

Kira knew then she was dead. Kal would never agree. He'd never betray his people, the thousands sheltered within Carvenstone, for her sake.

"My offer expires in ten seconds, good man. I'm not the patient sort. Eight. Seven. Six."

Kallan launched himself at the stranger, who smirked, before avoiding each of his blows, moving like swordplay was a dance he enjoyed, a dance he excelled at.

"One," the stranger said.

Then he lifted his other hand and Kallan was propelled backward, crashing against the wall of the mountain so hard the ground trembled.

He fell to the dirt, coughing up blood as he got up.

What was this thing?

It didn't matter, in the end. Kira tried to find peace. She even considered closing her eyes. But she was too furious. Instead, she summoned all of the fire locked inside her and launched it at the monster.

It was a weak blow, for her. He hadn't released his invisible stranglehold around her throat, and with each passing instant, she was fading. Still, even her weakest fires were deadly to most.

The monster didn't move. He let the burning wave hit him right in the chest, without making a sound, without a reaction at all. A strand of jet-black hair caught fire, and the male wet two fingers with his lips before putting it out.

Indifferent.

Then he took a step toward her.

Kira stumbled back with a yelp.

"Well, I suppose that particular bluff didn't work," the monster said nonchalantly.

He waved his hand and his hold on her dissolved instantly.

"I can't kill you. You're too good a hostage. Devira's cousin, I'd guess? You rather look alike."

He knew Devi. Her eyes widened.

"I know you," said Kallan. "I know you from Asra. You're a…guard."

"Protector, if you please," the thing replied with a genteel nod. "Well, in training. It was moderately fun, for a time, posing as a servant to the fae royal. If anything, it showed me how conceited and disgusting your entire race can be."

His voice had lost its insouciant intonation, becoming darker, deeper. Hatred, barely veiled, emerged.

"Which makes me think, you're no valuable hostage. You, I could have my fun with," he said, approaching Kal.

Kira tried to retrieve her baton from where it had fallen when she'd hit the ground, finding she couldn't move at all. The sudden paralysis made her heart beat a thousand miles an hour. Never, in her entire life, had she felt quite so helpless.

The fact that Kal could move at all meant that he was amusing the monster. No predator enjoyed immobile prey. She wanted to scream, tell Kallan to run, warn their friends to get away while they could.

Regrettably, her lungs and voice, like everything else, were under the monster's control.

Kira was nothing.

Death might have been a preferable fate.

Suddenly, and entirely unexpectedly, she felt a surge of power light up within her, exploding, destroying and redefining her very self.

No, this didn't come from her. It had nothing to do with her power, her strength, her fate.

It felt cold. Cold as ice.

Devi. Something had changed in Devira, her twin. She felt stronger and weaker all at once. As though a part of herself had been lost in the process—the part that used to be innocent and delightfully optimistic.

If she didn't know better, Kira would have believed that her twin was dead. But she did know better. She could feel her heartbeat as surely as her own.

Devi wasn't dead. Just altered.

And if she'd found that kind of strength buried inside her, maybe Kira didn't have to give up just yet. She didn't have the strength of her sister, but perhaps she was a little more than her fire or her staff.

Kira closed her eyes, attempting to let go of her fear, and concentrated, digging as deep as she dared.

She could do this. She had to.

The intruder lifted his fist and Kal gasped, out of breath. At the back of the thing's silk tunic, two velvety wings extended, flapping merrily, suggesting he enjoyed nothing more than torturing minds.

Kira couldn't move? Fine. She didn't have to.

She felt her eyes burn as she stared at her enemy's back, directing every ounce of the fire inside her to her target.

She would have grinned if she could, watching the tips of the bat-like wings burn.

The monster swerved, watching them with utter horror, and she had the pleasure of seeing him spin on his heels, trying to put the flames out. It only served to stoke them.

Kira felt the moment his concentration snapped; she fell forward on all fours, finally master of her own body.

The monster leaped into the lake. They had only instants.

She turned to Kal.

"No time to argue. He won't kill me. Go. I'll keep him busy for as long as I can. Everyone needs to be warned to get out of here."

She could see Kal, the protector, recoil against the very idea of leaving her here. Too bad it came down to helping her or all of Carvenstone. He nodded.

"Stay alive," he told her, before rushing toward the main gates. There was no time to take the secret passage again.

He'd only just reached the waterfall, when the enraged monster leaped out of the lake, landing right in front of Kira.

Stay alive.

Easier said than done.

But she'd try.

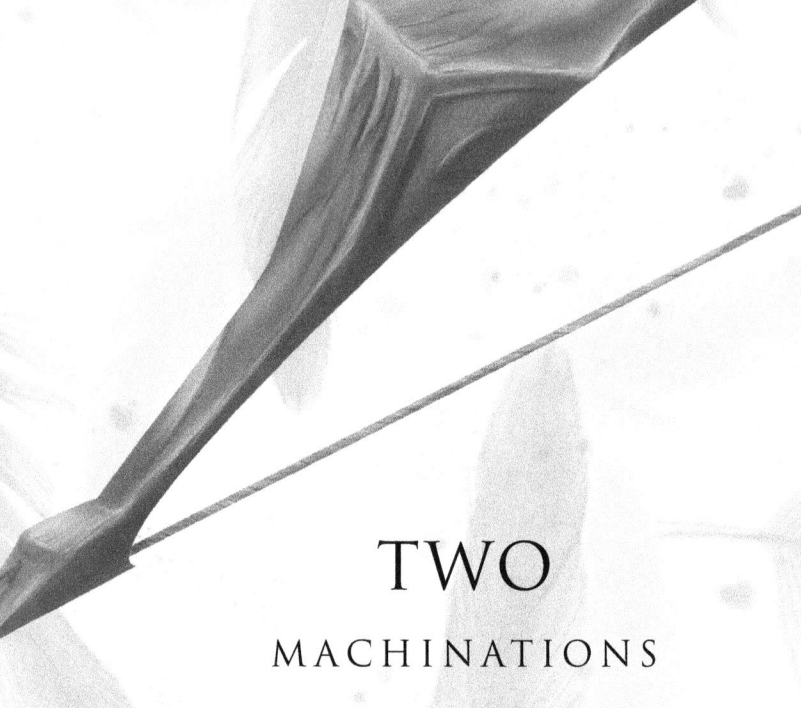

TWO

MACHINATIONS

At the northern tip of the Graywoods, right next to the borders of Corantius, there was a single guard tower carved from great white stones. It was abandoned for the most part. The guards of these woods favored homes built in high trees, where they could watch unseen.

Nevertheless, the tower had been swept and dusted, the silver, polished, and each room was decorated with freshly picked wildflowers.

A little excessive for Devi's taste. They were staying a day, two at most, while they waited for the bulk of her father's forces to join them at the border. Then, the army would head north, crossing into enemy territory. Again.

The prospect of entering Corantius was daunting. The last time she'd been beyond their border, she'd lost…

Something. A heart. Hers, or Valerius's. She couldn't tell.

When Valerius was shot by several arrows, something snapped inside her. She wasn't sure it was back to normal now that they'd saved him.

They.

She and her mother.

Devi wasn't ready to even think about the fact that her mother was alive. That she'd lied to her, abandoned her. That everything she knew to be true was a fantasy constructed to manipulate her.

Thinking of war was easier.

When the elven army arrived, they'd cross the northern border. Which direction they took would be determined in council now.

Devi and Vale were last to arrive in the highest room of the tower, where the meeting was going to occur. Her fault. She had a terrible habit of being late. This time, she had to admit her tardiness wasn't entirely accidental. She dreaded coming face-to-face with Loxy again.

The chamber was devoid of any furniture save for a wide table and seats around which a notable crowd was assembled. Among them were Elden Star, the elven king, his generals and advisors, and a beautiful brown-skinned woman with silver-white hair and a memorable presence. She was an ambassador to the dragons living in the Isle—a small but mighty community. That Elden had invited her here was no surprise; her father rarely passed up an opportunity to broker deals with the powerful figures of their world.

One high fae stood out from the others. A face so much like Devi's it was like staring in a mirror. A tainted mirror that changed nothing except the color of her eyes and hair.

Her mother.

She ignored her.

Other faces weren't familiar, though all felt and looked like elders. There was enough power in this room to redefine the order of the world.

A good thing. That was exactly what they needed to do.

The lords had left two places vacant, side by side. One, a chair just like everyone else's, the other, a seat made of vines and driftwood.

No, not a seat.

A throne.

There was only one in the room; the others were chairs. When they'd walked in, Valerius Blackthorn, the dark prince of the unseelie realm, one of the heirs to the overking ruling their entire Isle, walked right to it. Then he pulled it out, dragging it over the grass, to let Devi claim it.

She smiled. It was a little forced, and didn't last long. The change in her features was noteworthy all the same.

A day ago, she hadn't believed herself capable of smiling ever again, but she did so then. Because he was alive, because he was hers, and because for now, they were safe.

As safe as anyone could be when their home had been razed, their country invaded by the descendants of gods, and were about to discuss breaching enemy territory.

"Good of you to grace us with your presence, daughter. Son?" Elden said, somewhat questioningly, turning to Valerius.

Devi's mate smiled.

"That might take some getting used to."

It was neither a confirmation nor a disagreement. Trust Vale to make his mouth formulate words that ended up meaning nothing at all.

As a scion, the son of a god and a fae, he could lie, but he'd spent centuries bending the truth, and he excelled at it.

Devi and Vale were bound by all the laws of nature, but they sure as hell weren't going to discuss their relationship with a room full of quasi-strangers.

There would be another time for celebrating their union. A time of peace. The subject wasn't going to become a tangent to a war council.

"Well, Valerius Blackthorn, overking of the Isle, you have my armies. Where will you lead them?"

It sounded like a trick question with no real answer.

"He isn't overking, no matter what you call him. Until the throne chooses Orin's successor, Corantius will not recognize any true leader. Which means that until then, Roo—" Rook. She was going to say Rook. Devi caught herself in time. Her friend Rook didn't exist. He never had. "Marcus can order them to attack the rest of the Isle. And Aurelius can, too, if he feels like it. We've already learned that Marcus wants to open the wards around the Isle and let the orcs in. That's a madness that would consume our world. And their soldiers, as well as the gods of Corantius, can choose to be loyal to whoever they want to, because they'll have no actual authority figure. There's only one thing to do to stop Marcus..."

She caught Vale's gaze, and he nodded his agreement, finishing for her. "We take the throne."

The lords around the room started to talk all at once—everyone other than Elden, whose gaze was fixed on Devi.

The elven king lifted his hand and the cacophony fell silent. "How?"

Vale said, "Not with your army, that's for sure. The immortal city is surrounded by wards as strong as the ones around the Isle."

Their continent was walled off, to protect it against a sea of undead monsters—the orcs. The one true threat, the enemy they could never vanquish. Not that orcs were all that powerful, except their numbers made a fight entirely unbalanced. There were billions of them, against less than two million fae and scions on the Isle.

"We could lay a siege at their door for decades without success. Attacking them upfront is stupid. The other cities of Corantius don't have that sort of protection, and to my knowledge, their stationary troops won't rival the elven army."

Now, Elden was smirking. "I'm listening."

"Take the cities. Take them in the south, in the east, and above all, in the west, as far from the immortal city as possible. Corantius will have to send soldiers to protect their lords, and to push you back beyond the borders. Their eyes will be on you. A small strike team will then infiltrate the crystal court—Devi and I will lead it. As soon as we're certain both Rook and Aurelius are in the immortal city, the bulk of our forces can turn to the court and start a siege. They'll barricade their doors, locking us all in. Once that happens, we'll force the throne to select a ruler."

Or die trying.

They'd discussed the stratagem together the previous night. It wasn't faultless, but it would limit the casualties on both sides.

They were optimistic the throne would choose Vale, but in case Aurelius was picked, there would still be hope. Vale could beg for mercy, ask to return to his land, exiled and tethered or cursed to remain in Carvenstone.

There was also a chance Rook—or Marcus—the first bastard of the overking, would be chosen. In that case, they were all as good as dead.

But one way or another, it had to end.

THREE
DARKEN PATHS

Krea was cradling Surin when Kallan Blacks burst into the main hall of Carvenstone, flanked by the captain and commander of their guards. He shouted orders.

"We're under attack. Don't take anything with you. If your name starts with A to F, take the north path, back to the forest, with Nyx. G to M, the western way, toward the sea. Dayus and Tradora, can you take them?" The brother and sister nodded. Blacks promptly moved on. "N to Z, head south with Kit, to the valley leading to the Fairfolds estate."

Krea was too stunned to move. That was it? They were leaving the safety of their most sacred home? If they were in danger here, how would they survive in the woods, in the dreary old Fairfolds estate even Valerius

Blackthorn, their lord, hated? And the very thought of going to the sea was enough to make her feel sick.

But Kal looked terrified. She didn't think she'd ever seen him even remotely rattled before. His expression was enough for her to leap into action without question. She shook Surin until the little boy woke up.

He wasn't that little, not compared to her. Still, she was in charge of him today. There were many children in Carvenstone, and not enough grownups to take care of them today, when anyone who could fight was armed and protecting the gates. So, she'd been asked to look after the six-year-old.

Krea made sure he had a woolen cloak before taking her own. She placed his favorite toy—a stuffed cat—in his arm, and after a moment of thought, she grabbed her doll, too.

It wasn't a very pretty doll. She'd made it in class, and sewing wasn't one of her strengths. The doll's smile was a little crooked, and her eyes weren't even. But she was hers all the same.

Blacks had told them not to take anything, so she hoped she wouldn't be told off for taking her doll.

Krea hesitated. Her name made her part of the second group, and Surin was part of the third.

She steeled her resolve. She was in charge of Surin—their professor had said so. Which meant that west or south, they'd go together.

Krea thought things through. She liked Kit well enough. He was one of the strongest knights of Carvenstone. However, Dayus and Tradora were actual dragons. If there was danger, she decided that having fire-breathing monsters on your team wasn't the worst idea. She rushed to the west opening, part of a long line of people walking as fast as they could.

Surin's hand in hers, Krea tried to keep up.

Soon, she started to feel tired. It wasn't an easy path. She knew it kept going for miles and miles. And though she was strong, she wasn't a grownup .

"I'm hungry, Kreeeeh."

Surin couldn't pronounce her name right yet.

She smiled. "I know. I'm hungry too. If we try to get there as fast as we can, we can eat when we arrive."

"Where? I'm tired."

Krea tried to hide her frustration. What could she do to alleviate the little boy's tiredness and hunger, when she couldn't even appease her own?

They were almost at the back of the line. She looked around, hoping to find a familiar face. Carvenstone was a large estate and not everyone knew each other well.

No one stood out. They'd dropped back with the weaker, slower fae, and they didn't seem to have a care, save for reaching the exit.

They all froze as one when a piercing scream resounded through the corridors. The network of labyrinthine paths was narrow and dim. It sounded like it was so close.

Krea's eyes widened, and her grip around Surin's hand tightened.

Unexpectedly, a stranger stopped in front of her. Krea looked up. A male with cat-like eyes and furry ears.

"I'll carry him," he offered.

Surin protested, while Krea looked at his long legs. She nodded, releasing the chubby hand.

Sometimes, the responsible thing was to let go. The grownup would get him out of here faster.

He strode away, Krea watching his back. She didn't think she'd ever forget Surin's glare. The betrayal in his eyes. Or his sobs.

He'd get out of the tunnels a lot faster without her.

The child ran as fast as her feet could carry her. The floor of the path carved in the belly of the mountain was damp and cold, freezing her bones, and she knew she couldn't stop.

More screams echoed, all sounding so very close. She could smell blood in the air.

The monsters were approaching.

She forced herself to face forward, always forward, and keep going.

Her legs were attenuated, shorter than most. She couldn't catch up.

Moments ago, she'd been glad that a grownup had offered to take care of Surin. Now, a nasty part of her was wondering, what about her? She was nine. Why hadn't anyone stopped for her?

Krea tripped over the smooth, slippery gray stone, and a yelp came out of her mouth as she fell forward, scraping her knees.

Back up.

She had to get back up.

But she couldn't. Her limbs suddenly weighed a thousand tons. Her heart beat at a thousand miles a minute and she cried.

Carvenstone was supposed to be a safe haven for people like her.

Now it would be a tomb. She could hear the monsters' approach, so very fast and strong, their blades and teeth whetted by fae blood.

This was the end of their world.

She cried where she sat, hopeless and defeated.

Through her blurry vision, she could barely detect any features as a tall figure approached at high speed. Krea got back to her feet and lifted her small knife.

This, she could do. Fight till her last breath. That was the way of her people, the only way she knew.

He moved so fast she couldn't see, let alone act against him.

Before she could do or say a thing, he'd grabbed her by the torso, right under the armpits, and thrown her over her shoulder like she weighed nothing more than a sack of potatoes.

Krea stilled, gasping. She may not see much, but she knew this scent, under the blood and the fear. Sea, lilies, and curses. Burning wood.

It smelled of home.

Kallan Blacks, the commander of their forces. He'd led soldiers to the doors when the enemies had come.

"Where are the other soldiers?" she asked.

Suria, her training master, and Baen, the silent man who played the lyre. Aessa, Fauken, Vyssers. They were all heroes to their people, male and females she'd admired her entire life.

Blacks didn't say a word, and then she knew.

Dead.

They'd all been killed protecting Carvenstone.

FOUR
DYRMOUNTS

Jeryn kept her head down, as she always did. She was a pretty female, and bad things happened to pretty females who were noticed by the males of Staren. Anyone with half a brain knew that. Besides, no one watched their mouth in front of an invisible servant, and Jeryn was desperate to hear news of the world outside of the stinking city she couldn't afford to leave.

That day, she heard many whispers.

They said he'd come to Corantius—the southern fae with a claim to the throne. They said he had a winged goddess by his side, and that he'd stolen treasures from right under the scion knights guarding the Court of Stars.

"They say the bastard prince might come and claim the throne...and I hope he does," she'd said to a stranger, a female she'd never seen before.

A female who hadn't come back for her things or her horses after the incident up in the Stormhale residence.

Jeryn kept her mouth shut, served ale, and listened some more.

Armies, elves, had come to Corantius. So many whispers, and all meant the same thing: war.

War was never good for the common folks, she knew that. Yet the current way of things had made her little more than a slave from the moment she'd open her eyes. Although she had magic, she was no scion, and in Corantius, that meant she was nothing at all.

Jeryn remembered the women she'd shown to a chamber just the night before. She'd been kind and respectful, despite the fact it was plain as day that her blood ran as blue as any of the scions she'd ever met. The female had been a scion at the very least, perhaps even an Enlightened, but she'd looked straight in her eyes and spoken to her as if she mattered.

At the end of her shift, Jeryn stretched her neck out in the kitchen. There were just as many whispers here, among the maids and cooks, and they talked of the same thing.

"You should have seen her. Wings as large as a dragon, bright as gold. For a moment, she hid the sunlight."

Jeryn wished she'd seen it—she'd been working the previous day.

"They killed a dozen scions, just the two of them!"

"I heard it was a hundred."

She smiled, took her things from her locker, and left the inn through the back door. She lived half an hour away, in the poorer part of town, with the other fae. Jeryn rented a room in a decrepit female's home, small, but clean and safe enough.

She took two dozen steps before her feet stopped and her head snapped left. She tilted it and frowned, listening with more than her ears.

Since she'd been a little girl, she'd had one gift—one small, useless gift that no one valued in this realm.

She took another step forward, and the buzzing troubling her mind grew louder, bolder.

After checking her right and left, Jeryn ran as fast as her feet would carry her. Not home. She headed to the stables instead.

"Dammit," she cursed, lifting the latch of the main door.

The door flew open, kicked in by the most magnificent beast she'd ever seen. It was larger than any horse, slender and powerful, and fierce.

"Well, you certainly know how to command attention."

She snickered as the horse proudly marched past her, ignoring her entirely.

If she was right—and something told her that she *was* right—she'd served a goddess the previous night, and seen a glimpse of a prince. A prince who didn't mind passing for a servant. There would be no song, or banner, or trophy for her, but she'd also let his horse go.

Horses. After the great black beast, a chocolate-brown beauty with a white mane followed, lowering its head to hers as he passed her by. This one wasn't quite as self-important.

Jeryn watched them go for a moment, before checking her surroundings again and heading east, toward her home.

She'd only taken one step when the beast neighed, demanding her attention again.

The black horse looked right into her eyes, his mind reaching out to hers.

"Come on, you have more magic in that mane of yours than I do from head to toe. I'm sure you'll find your way."

The beast nickered.

"Go, before Vera's horsemaster realizes you're missing."

The beast did not move, staring intently.

Jeryn knew what the animal wanted of her. The only question was, what did the horse of Valerius Blackthorn, unseelie prince, heir to the overthrone, want from her, a simple servant?

In the end, she decided that it didn't matter.

Jeryn walked to the black horse that bowed to her like she was a great lady. She laughed as she mounted its back, and they set off into the night.

The Fairfolks lived by their oaths. Horse masters or nay, they were noble folks of high fae stock. They'd long since sold their keep in the north to pay the debt of some careless ancestors, but they were respected throughout the Isle.

So, this situation just wouldn't do. Rehar, Marek, and Gaios, heirs of Thain Fairfolk, simply couldn't fail to deliver goods.

The fifty-three horses bought and paid for by Valerius Blackthorn for his mother's use had to reach their destination. They just had to.

For days, they'd followed her tracks, and for days they'd found nothing. First, they'd gone east of Asra, then as south as south went in the Isle, to the very tip of the unseelie kingdom, and still, they found nothing.

They stopped at the border of the woods.

"Are you sure they passed through the elven realm?" Rehar asked.

There was no track to speak of, not so much as a footprint in the sandy dunes.

"Aye, I'm sure. Who's the air mage among us?" Marek was grumpy, and no wonder. It was the first time he'd failed to locate a client.

Following the unseelie queen, when she didn't wish to be followed, had proved most vexing.

"So, what now, then?"

Never had any Fairfolks crossed the forest. Fae didn't cross the forest and live to tell the tale unless they'd been given leave to do so by the lords of the Graywoods.

No such lord stood at the border to invite them in.

Gaios said not a word. He wasn't the most vocal of the three brothers, but his actions spoke for him. He tugged on his mount's reins and marched forward.

They had a herd to deliver, and they would do so.

The fifty-three dyrmounts followed the lead, and with great sighs of frustration, so did his two brothers.

"If we die, it'll be your fault."

"If we die, it will be known that the Fairfolks keep their contracts."

"Only there would be no Fairfolks to speak of left."

Again, Gaios said nothing. He believed that the fate of his family, and the rest of their realm, was linked to their queen. If the dark prince believed their dyrmounts might help in the war, he would bring them to Shea Blackthorn, whatever it took.

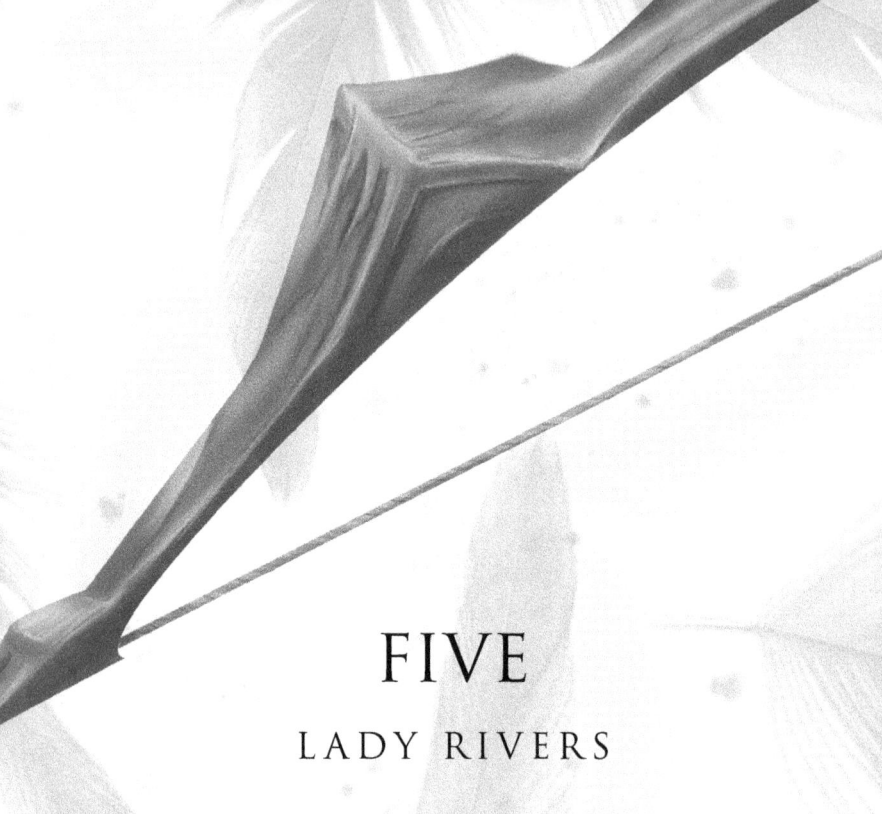

FIVE
LADY RIVERS

Loxy Rivers's eyes were fixed on the borders far ahead to the west. She couldn't see the incorporeal energy barrier separating their Isle from what lay beyond, but she could feel it, slowly humming, simmering. A shiny film protecting their world.

Since the purpose of Orin's third son's quest to claim the throne had been revealed, she'd found herself trying to reach out to the walls, checking it was still in place. The prospect of opening their world up was terrifying.

She'd seen orcs. A lesser fae had little chance against one of them. A common fae could take one or two before finding themselves outmatched. High fae greatly varied in strength. She could kill a hundred, maybe. A little more, a little less. It depended on their power as much as hers.

It wouldn't be enough. If the gates were opened and those creatures swarmed the isle, they'd be outmatched a thousand to one.

The gates had to hold. Marcus couldn't become overking.

For now, the wall was still in place. And as long as it remained in place, there was hope.

She didn't move when she heard the footsteps heading toward her. She'd expected them at some point.

Her daughter was avoiding her, speaking to her in short, curt sentences only when she had to. A rejection she'd earned and deserved. Now Devi had questions that needed answers, whether she liked it or not. Hence why Valerius Blackthorn was joining Loxy now.

"I don't believe I've thanked you for saving my life."

Loxy attempted a smile. "I didn't. My daughter did the heavy lifting. Literally."

He didn't smile back. The dark prince wasn't one for civilities when he didn't care to play nice.

"You want to know how I'm alive. My little princess has told you I died of poisoning when she was a child, I'm sure."

He remained silent and focused on her.

"I love my daughter. Daughters," she corrected. Kira was just as precious to her.

Not to the rest of the world.

"The very reason I bore them in the first place was for this. Because this war was always coming, sooner or later. It might have been in our time, or in a thousand years, but anyone looking at the signs knew the Corantians would eventually seek to rule us. There was going to be an enemy greater than ourselves, an enemy we'd need a shield against. Devira was a sweet, innocent girl in my care. Had I not sent her to your mother, she would have remained that little girl. Taking what she knew, teaching her the meaning of loss, honed her into a weapon."

Vale didn't protest. She had known he wouldn't. He was old enough and wise enough to understand.

"Did her twin know?" he asked her.

Loxy shook her head. "Fair is fair. Letting go of one child and doting on the other would have made me quite the hypocrite. I punished all of us equally. Kira was raised in the Graywoods with her father, Devi in Asra with your mother."

"And what did you do, in all this time?"

He enunciated each word slowly, entirely calm, but Loxy heard the threatening edge dripping. She'd hurt Devi. She'd hurt his mate. She'd pay for that in due time. The Blackthorns weren't known for their forgiving hearts.

"My daughters aren't the only ones who needed to be honed, Your Highness. I trained, so that I might be of use when the time comes. I trained in water and ice magic. I trained in spells and hexes. I trained in shields. I trained in binding spells such as the one keeping your heart beating."

She'd trained in anything that let her forget what she'd given up for the greater good. Anything that kept her mind occupied, forgetting that she had two daughters mourning for their mother.

"Your actions took courage. You also hurt Devira. Worse, you distract her."

Loxy nodded in agreement. "Yes. I don't intend to get in the way of your progression. I'll march east with the army heading to the coast."

"Good." Vale started to walk away, then hesitated. "And then, when this is all over, we will talk. All of us."

Because, for better or worse, they were one clan now. One family. He didn't say it. Loxy understood all the same.

She smiled. "I'll look forward to that."

Just as he turned his heel, movement caught their attention from the southwest. Just a rippling of leaves, but anyone who knew these woods realized what it was.

The part of Elden's army posted on the western borders of the Graywoods had reached them. The eastern front had already arrived a few hours ago. Next there would be the southern knights, who'd cross through the portal of Daryn leading directly to Wyhmur.

Their march north was imminent.

"You'd better get some sleep while you can," Vale recommended, not unkindly.

His tone reminded her that while the male was to be her daughter's groom, he was half a millennium older than Loxy.

In her time in the unseelie realm, she'd seen him perhaps twice. Each time he'd been drunk, kissing one stranger and torturing the next. The male standing before her now couldn't be more different. Loxy didn't know him well—he seemed warmer than his mother. A caretaker. She hoped that this side of him was the real Valerius Blackthorn. For the sake of her daughter, as well as the rest of the Isle.

If their plan worked out and he was crowned, the fate of all four realms would be in his grasp. No one should have that much power, but if someone had to sit on that throne, Vale was their best option.

At least he'd have Devi by his side.

Provided they all survived the march north.

SIX

KING OF SAND

Devin Farel awoke to the smell of ashes and steel that night.

He knew. Right away, he knew. He'd suspected that something had been amiss for weeks.

Two weeks before the solstice, his father unexpectedly abdicated the throne. Almost immediately, his advisors pushed a visit to the unseelie realm. Devin saw the sense in it, though he wouldn't have chosen to do it so soon. Wouldn't visiting his own realm, getting to know the lords of his lands, be a more pressing issue? The members of his council argued he could meet lords on his way.

They took the scenic road. Instead of requesting to cross through the Graywoods—which would have made their travel a five-day ride—they went north, spending one night in each of the seelie countryside territories. Lords drank to his health and all was well, for a time.

Devin didn't understand why more men had joined them when they reached their northern borders. But he did find his advisors' explanation satisfactory. Yes, it did make sense that they needed a larger escort traveling through Corantius, and then riding down south to Asra, than they had in their own land.

He ignored the feeling in his stomach, attributing it to his inexperience and anxiety.

When he heard the explosion and rushed to his window in Wolvenfort to find the city of night under attack, he knew it was his doing. He may not have planned to wage war on the unseelie realm; instead his naivety had spelled doom.

Devin rushed out of his quarters to find Shea Blackthorn. He had to explain himself and ensure the famed queen didn't take this as his will. If he managed to convince her, there could still be peace between their nations.

His path was soon barred by a dozen soldiers in gold armor. Now that they'd changed their clothing from the seelie blue and white to their true colors, he knew them for what they were. Corantians. And he knew he was in over his head.

Corantius was not a realm of fae; more than half its lords were demi-gods. Scions. Devin didn't attempt to fight his way out of custody. They took him down to the throne hall where the unseelie court had greeted them just a night ago.

He and his advisors were detained, watched by two guards. No handcuffs, no curses or spells. The guard was too light. It felt like they were being protected, rather than imprisoned.

As though they were complicit.

Devin knew his decision that day would define his future. Define who he was, and perhaps what his realm would become.

Another fae may have remained next to his council and let their machinations unfold. Instead, he called to his powers, gathering as much energy as he could while the city screamed.

The Farels were folks of the air, whimsical masters of illusions. Devin had to admit he'd never been fond of his power. The Rivers in the north were known to call the powers of the sea to the shores and bring rain in the middle of droughts. The Ashes, Fyres and Cindres could burn their enemies where they stood. The Zephyrs were able to fly without even extending their wings. In the face of such legends, what was his legacy? Nothing to boast about, simple parlor tricks.

Devin had always favored his blade over his magic. Right now, he was grateful that his stringent education hadn't allowed for any gaps in mastery. His power was air. And he finally understood just how valuable it could be.

Devin gave his mind and body to the air, letting it move him, all the while maintaining the illusion of his presence in the hall for precious seconds. By the time the vision faded, he was in the empty kitchens. Ignoring the confused, angry guards shouting upstairs, Devin took a shabby cloth cloak left on a bench and slunk out into the service corridors, where no one thought to look for him.

The fighting had stopped in the streets. Corantians patrolled, but they never spared a glance for a poorly dressed fae looking down, walking unhurriedly. The cloak smelled of fish and onions. Devin used what was left of his energy to make his ears appear curved like a common fae's, his hair, graying. None of the shouting guards looking for the king spared him a glance. They let him leave the city with the forest workers fleeing at the doors. He was invisible. Common fae were invisible in this world. A fact he'd never felt resonate before.

Devin walked as far into the woods as he could before collapsing. He'd never maintained an illusion for more than a minute at a time. His escape had taken five hours. He didn't think he'd ever even understood what tired meant until this day.

Devin didn't know how long he slept. Hours, day, a week? He only came to when his mind alerted him to imminent danger. Devin opened his eyes to see four spears and a sword pointed at his chest.

A dark-haired beauty dressed in fyriron drew her weapon back, preparing to strike, but before Devin could get to his feet, a familiar figure placed herself between him and certain death.

"Wait!" It was the girl he'd danced with that first night in Asra. A lifetime ago. "That's the seelie king."

The warrior female bared her teeth. "And why would that warrant my waiting, exactly?"

A pertinent question. To her, he was the enemy. All clues pointed to him.

Jiya Duniel remained stubbornly between him and the blade. "Because the queen will want to decide if he lives or die."

At long last, the knight lowered her sword. "Fine. Bind him. If he escapes, be it on your head."

Devin was better rested. He might have been able to escape, perhaps even without magic: Jiya was a youth, and a common fae. She tied ropes of vines that felt loose and comfortable around his wrists. He could get out of them without straining.

He didn't. Betraying a female who had come to his aid wasn't in his nature.

They reached the unseelie queen's army south of Asra, and within the hour, Jiya came back with a knife. He looked up at her unblinking. She stepped forward and cut his bonds.

"We will feed you, if you're hungry."

"Thank all the gods. I'm ravenous." And surprised. Mostly surprised. "Shea told you to release me?"

It felt like a test of sorts.

Jiya nodded. "She'll receive you later. There are matters of greater importance to her now."

It indicated just how little regard she had for him, if there were matters more important than seeing the king of the seelie realm. Devin awaited his fate.

He still remembered their first meeting. He'd half-believed his life would be forfeit within an instant.

She received him in her tent after a long march east. His bonds had been cut hours ago, but he felt more trapped than he had in the throne hall or at sword point. Shea's very presence felt like a threat.

She sipped from an iron goblet—an action that would have rendered him violently sick immediately, perhaps to emphasize just how different they were.

She needn't have gone through the trouble. He understood that well.

"I must congratulate you on getting out of Asra alone. When I located you in my keep, under guard, I believed you were lost. Not many manage to surprise me."

Devin wondered if there was a veiled accusation, if she believed he'd been released to be used as a spy.

"I believe no such thing."

He blinked. "You're psychic?"

Shea smiled. "No. I was mated to a psychic, however. There's also seer blood in his bloodline. Quite the useful arsenal."

Devin hadn't realized Shea had ever had a mate. Consorts, certainly, but a mate? And she said so in past tense.

True matings were never dissolved. The only way to break such a bond was…death.

Then, he knew. Somehow he knew.

Shea had been mated to the overking. Which made her the most terrifyingly powerful thing on the Isle right now. Mates could access each other's' strength in their lifetime, and upon death, they could absorb it, make it their own.

If they survived the loss of the one person made for them.

An earth mage. A psychic. A seer. Devin couldn't even imagine how strong an adversary the queen was.

"Oh, there are worse things in this world. You lack imagination. And strength," she added, cold and regal. "You slept five days after a little bit of magic. I know youths of ten with more inner fortitude. That won't do. We need you to become more."

He'd believed he might greet death in the tent. Instead, he found a worse fate.

Shea Blackthorn's training.

Devin Farel had never had any reason to consider himself a weakling. He'd spent half a century navigating the most severe, austere court of the Isle. In Elderdale, nothing short of excellence was demanded of the prince and heir. And even when he had reached excellence in his schooling, his craft, his swordplay, his father showed nothing beyond contempt. So, he trained harder. Became stronger.

And for all that, he was spent. A month of traveling with the unseelie queen was all it had taken to break him.

The traveling itself may not have proved problematic, though they walked many miles in the dry heat of the southern unseelie deserts every day. But the queen took to training him. He could not devise a greater torment.

After their limbs were exhausted, they walked. Long after his toes pinched at the tips of his boots, they kept walking. And at last, a halt was called, the cooks on duty prepared meals with what they could find or hunt, tents were erected, a guard was set up, and those who'd performed these duties at their previous stop got to rest till morrow.

Not Devin. This was when the queen called him to spar with her.

Another word for beating him senseless while pointing out everything he did wrong. A lesser man would have begged for the mercy of a quick execution. Then, there were the nights when she wanted him to use his magic. Those were tormenting. Creating an illusion, keeping it while he attacked on another front, then doing it all over again for two hours nonstop.

The next day at dawn, he was expected to keep walking.

One month of this changed everything he knew about himself. Mentally and physically.

Devin had always been tanned. The seelie court were day dwellers, and their royal city was set in the south. After his time in the desert, his skin had never been so dark or dry. He barely recognized his reflection now. The growing beard couldn't have been more out of character. He'd never had facial hair before. Few fae of his line did. His once-slender limbs were bulkier, more defined, not unlike the seasoned knights who'd once been his guards.

But what had truly changed beyond recognition was his mind.

Once, he'd allowed tutors and professors to tell him how far he could go, how fast he could cast his spells, how strong he was.

Now he knew the truth. He was the only one who could define his own limits.

Devin turned west, listening to the shift in the air. He frowned.

"Anything of note?" Shea asked.

She was walking next to him for once. Devin knew it for a test, like everything else she did, or asked. She always knew everything—or so it seemed.

"I feel a shift at the border of the woods."

After roaming the desert for weeks, never staying still, retracing their steps, they'd finally crossed into the Graywoods two days ago.

Devin guessed they'd been moving to avoid a direct confrontation with the scions. What had changed, he wasn't sure. He didn't sit on the queen's council. Now they were finally heading toward Elderdale.

His home.

His attention had been easily caught because the woods were silent and still, watchful and unmoving. What he'd heard had been nothing of the sort.

Riders. At least a few dozen.

"Yes, and what do you make of that shift, king?" Whenever she called him "king," it felt like a joke.

"I..." It was hard to put into words the whispers he caught in the wind, but he tried his best. "I'm not sure it feels like pursuit. They're too slow. And I can't feel any real power. Just...purpose."

Shea watched him intently, before inclining her head. "Indeed. You have good instincts. Trust them." Her voice carried through the woods as she called, "Halt!"

All stopped at once, obeying their queen unfailingly.

Devin doubted he'd ever inspire such trust.

She turned to him now. "Let us wait for the horde."

"The horde?" Devin was confused.

She smiled.

He wondered if he'd ever seen her smile before.

"Yes, Devin. I'd wager you've had enough of walking for a while."

That was putting it mildly.

The unexpected halt was a treat in itself, especially since Shea didn't demand they train while they waited.

They'd stopped in a clearing near a river. Devin sat with his feet in the water, enjoying the simplest of pleasures.

"How are the blisters?" Jiya asked.

He grinned. The fae had become a friend of sorts—at least, he liked to think she had. She was always in Shea's shadow, and Devin had noticed subtle changes in her.

She wasn't suffering through the queen's training as he was, but she was learning all the same. Her stride had changed, becoming quieter. She held herself differently—more alert perhaps.

"I'd kill for a healing," Devin admitted. "Or a pair of knitted socks."

"Typical of a male. Killing rather than learning how to knit."

"Who's to say I'm not a proficient knitter? I simply lack materials."

Their easy exchange was interrupted by the sound of hooves at first, then by shadows approaching. Finally, they appeared. Horses taller than any he'd seen, slender and muscular and almost too beautiful to behold. Three males rode in front of them, leading the four dozen gorgeous beasts.

Fifty horses or so. And there were thousands of soldiers in Shea's army.

Devin's heart sank.

"Never mind socks," murmured Jiya. "I'd kill to get one of *those*."

SEVEN
ONE MOMENT

Devi listened to Vale's explanation, eyes fixed on the map of Corantius just in front of her. She'd spent the better part of the day poring over their plan, analyzing every possible way it might fail. Five minutes ago, she'd believed a distraction might be helpful. Now all she wanted to do was to go back to the map.

Vale had fully recovered, and so had she. They were back on their feet, full of energy, stronger than ever. Their bond had changed something deep rooted inside her, inside them both. What, she couldn't tell. Regardless, Devi knew it had increased her strength.

In the morning, three out of the four parts of her father's army had arrived, and when the southern forces joined them, they'd head north, edging back into enemy territory. They would be outnumbered on unfamiliar lands. Making sure their plan was perfect was paramount to their survival.

The plan had been discussed with the general, and with Vale, and with her mother just that morning. She doubted a youth of her age would miraculously find a flaw seasoned commanders had overlooked, but she couldn't help it. Checking out the map was comforting, easing her ragged nerves.

Until Vale came to tell her about her mother, anyway.

Devi listened without a word. Vale was playing with her hair. He'd taken to doing that of late, rolling a strand of hair around his index finger, curling it before letting it go, and starting all over again.

She didn't dislike it.

Then he was done. Devi laughed.

"You think I didn't glean as much the moment I saw her?"

That her mother had staged her death for her betterment had been obvious. It didn't mean Devi had to forgive her for it after a day or two, even if the timing and circumstances of her return had done a bit to endear her to her.

Devi had called for help, with everything she was, begging anyone who'd listen to come to her aid and save her mate. And Loxy had answered the call, tugging the bond between those who shared blood to locate her. They'd already been on their way, leaving the Graywoods for Corantius the instant Vale had recovered his father's heirlooms, as Elden had promised. But without Loxy, they might have wandered for days before finding them. And by then, Vale would have been dead.

"I thought you might value the fact that she isn't attempting to lie. She seems nice enough. Nicer than my mother, for one."

Devi grinned. "There isn't a female alive who isn't nicer than Shea Blackthorn. The unseelie queen doesn't need to be nice. She needs to be respected."

"Spoken like a true sycophant. She'd be proud."

Devi might have laughed, if her mind hadn't just caught on to something.

Thinking back to Loxy appearing in front of her had triggered a new idea.

Their plan was simple. As soon as they were sure Rook was in Corantius, the elven army would provide a distraction outside the gate of the Court of Crystal, and while the scions focused on them, Devi, Vale, along with a strike team they'd yet to form, would sneak into the city and make their way to the castle.

The hows of getting into the Court of Crystal weren't clear, but once they were inside, Devi's mission was to lure, or drag, or even seduce Rook into heading to the throne room. Vale would do the same with his other brother, Aurelius. There also was a child of Aurelius to think about. Devi hated that a newborn had to be part of the war effort, even as she knew there was no other choice. Without all heirs present, the throne wouldn't activate—Gaer, her father's best scientist, had said as much.

Once all four males were in the throne room, they'd start the coronation ceremony, at long last forcing the throne to pick a new overking.

And hope against all hope that its choice wasn't Rook.

Devi knew Vale wanted his brother to be chosen. If Aurelius was overking, he could beg for mercy, then return to his land, and they'd have harmony for another thousand years.

Assuming Rook didn't kill Aurelius and start this mess all over again.

Devi didn't think the same way. Vale needed to take the crown. Not because she wanted him to be overking. Far from it. Her mate, becoming lord of a foreign land he didn't know or care for, ruling over his enemies because a divine device said so? It was a recipe for disaster.

It needed to happen regardless. They wouldn't be safe otherwise. She knew Rook too well to think differently.

"Blood," she whispered. "You're linked to Rook by blood. It might just be your father's; you're still brothers, however different you are otherwise. That means we could find him through your blood. Same for Aurelius, and even the child. We'd need someone specialized in tracking spells with us."

"Smart. So, a tracker—plus someone who can operate the throne to start the selection, and the two of us."

A group of four was ideal. Small enough to fail to garner attention. Four friends touring the world was a common occurrence.

Devi bit her lip. Before their trip in the Court of Starlight, she would have said that was all they needed. The two of them, and two specific individuals to carry out the tasks. Now, her priorities had shifted. The mission still mattered. Nothing mattered more. But as well as doing what they could for the Isle, she wanted to survive. She wanted both of them to come out of this upheaval in one piece.

"And a healer." Devi had learned the basics. She could take care of flesh wounds and some minor ailments, but someone actually versed in the art of healing would have been invaluable in the first leg of their journey. She'd been uncomfortable riding for days on end. Both she and Vale had grown weak at one point or another. Good specialist healers could brew potions out of herbs—natural draughts that could affect even their kind.

Scions such as she and Vale could not be addled by fae curses, spells, or hexes, although natural ingredients worked well enough. She wasn't versed in the art of potions, and there was no time for her to learn now.

Vale smiled at her. "A healer," he acquiesced. "Now come here. We won't have a chance to rest safely for some time."

He tugged on her hand. The moment their skin touched, her anxiety dissolved in a cloud of mist, giving way to something very different.

She grinned back at him. "Rest?" she echoed, palm on his chest. She looked into his violet eyes. "Is that what we should do now, old man?"

Devi knew they should sleep. Their travels had taught her just how valuable a good night of sleep in a bed was. But right now, nothing felt quite as important as taking her mate's mouth. So, she did just that.

Vale wrapped his arm around her waist and practically flew them to their bedroom, moving so fast he was a blur. He pinned her on the soft feather mattress and peeled his shirt off his delectable chest.

"Fine. We'll rest when we're dead."

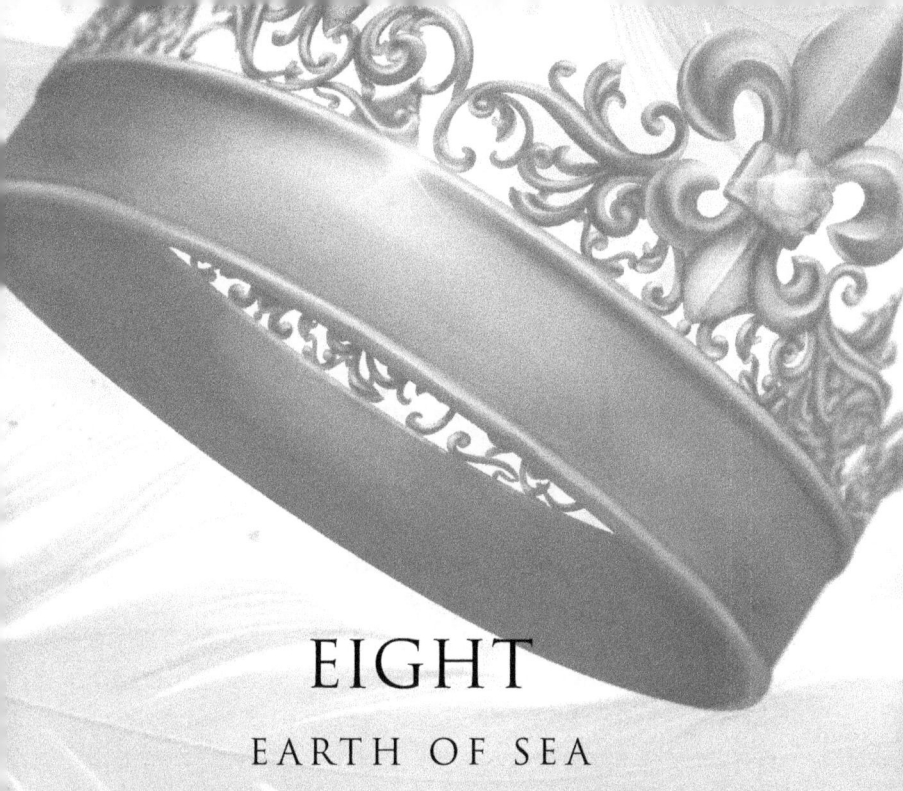

EIGHT
EARTH OF SEA

It had been some time since Kallan had boarded a ship. He didn't enjoy it, albeit his dislike of sailing was nothing compared to that of the fae who wielded earth magic. To them, the sea wasn't just uncomfortable—it was also a punishment.

At all times on firm ground, they could feel their connection to the earth, even in great halls of marble—they only had to reach down to get to the roots of their power. On the sea, there was another element blocking their path, muddling their access. Fire and water mages might be used to it, but there was nothing more unnatural to an earth mage.

Or so he was told. Kallan had no magics to speak of. Unlike the little girl with her head between her knees, reeling each time a wave hit the vessel.

He laughed. That kid was tough. Krea, one of the few orphans of Carvenstone. Orphans were everyone's kids, everyone's responsibility. Seeing her so vulnerable wasn't usual.

He was still angry when he remembered seeing her alone at the back of the procession heading out of the tunnels. He got that she wasn't the kind of kid to ask for help—she'd probably hidden the fact that she needed anyone. Someone should have noticed her all the same.

She was here, safe among the survivors. That was all that mattered.

All of this group had made it out of the caves in one piece. Kallan hadn't received word from the procession heading to Fairfolds, or the one going to the mountains, yet he was hopeful. He'd remained in the caves until all civilians had been evacuated, and he'd helped seal their path with rocks.

Kal wasn't deluded. He knew that would only hinder a thing like the one who'd come after them for moments.

Moments were all they'd needed to protect their people.

Kal didn't think he'd ever forget this day. He'd wanted to remain with the guards who'd volunteered to stay at the doors. He'd wanted to remain with Kira.

All had told him to go, for the sake of their people.

Their screams would be forever branded in his mind, haunting his every nightmare.

It should have been him. He should have died with them.

He hadn't, because there was no other lord of Carvenstone. No one else their people would turn to. No one who could fight for them.

There were warriors among them, like Nyx and the dragons. They could defend them, and would do so to their last breath.

But none were thinkers. None were leaders.

It wasn't Kal's place to lead anyone. Oh, he knew how. He'd shadowed Valerius for long enough to know what it took. Kallan only had to think for one instant, and he could practically hear Vale speaking next to him. Telling him what to do next.

He'd separated their people for a reason: in the event one of their three groups was trailed, the two others would survive. And if all three groups made it to their destinations, they would be surrounding their enemy on all fronts. They'd observe Carvenstone from the sea, plains, and forests, and when the time was right, they'd take back their lands.

One person couldn't hold Carvenstone forever, mighty as he might have seemed to be. Eventually, the monster would leave.

Kal walked down to the cabin in the belly of the ship. They were in *The White Wings*, Vale's vessel. While their lord had only used it once, to inaugurate it right after the ship had been built, Kallan had ensured that the prince's cabin remained well stocked.

He went to the study and found a small red chest next to the desk and a captain's chair stuck to the polished wooden floor.

Kal opened it and smiled. It was stocked with herbs, as he'd instructed. He opened identical square pots, checking their contents. A blackfire stone, several healing charms, roots of midnight lilies and crushed bluclydes. He'd almost given up when he found what he was looking for: plain old ginger.

Kallan headed to the kitchens next and troubled the self-assigned cook for a pot and some fresh water.

The male in charge, Tulor, didn't appreciate the intrusion—Kallan caught several nasty looks as he infused some water.

"I'm not cooking my own food, Tul. Any idiot would die for your seabroth." The cook's expression morphed into a much friendlier one after Kal had appeased him.

"What are you up to, then, my lord?"

Kal borrowed a ladle and scooped the drink into a ceramic mug.

"Making a sweet ginger infusion. My mother used to take it when she felt sick."

The cook's eyes widened, and Kallan could guess why. High fae females seldom were sick.

"She was common fae," he clarified. "Do you mind if I borrow the ladle?"

Tulor snorted. "You're in charge."

Kallan paused.

His entire life, he'd envied Valerius. He hadn't resented his friend for his birthright, despite wondering what it would be like. To have his orders carried out without question. Not having to answer to anyone in the land—just a distant queen who sent no directives.

Now, he had his answer. It was terrifying. Every instant, he wondered if his decisions were right. If his people fell, it would be because of his ineptitude.

The fact that seasoned warriors laid down their lives so that he made it, in order to ensure that the folks of Carvenstone had one lord left, made it exponentially worse.

The responsibility for so many lives was a burden like no other.

But he'd shoulder it. He'd shoulder it, and no complaint would cross his lips. For the fallen.

Kal wondered about Kira. The monster had clearly stated that he wanted to keep her alive as a hostage, so there was hope she'd made it.

He closed his eyes. The girl was tough. If anyone could survive the black-winged demon, it was she.

"Thank you, Tulor. For your support."

"We're behind you, you know. All of us. Wherever you lead. If you say we must return home and fight the invaders, we will."

Kal shook his head. He hadn't gotten them out of Carvenstone to send them to their death the next day.

"We'll see that our people are safe first. Then, there's only one war that matters."

The monster who'd taken their home could only have been sent from Corantius. Alone, the soldiers Kallan had wouldn't make a difference, but they could join Vale, where their actions might tip the scale.

It was time for Carvenstone to make a stand.

He emerged from below stairs and headed right to Krea. Kal hated seeing the girl so defeated.

"Here, drink this."

She lifted her pale head from between her knees. Her eyes were unfocused.

Kal laughed. "You're green."

"Being on the sea is unnatural," she grumbled, reaching out for the mug and sipping it without question. Krea moaned appreciatively. "It's nice. Thank you."

"It might help with the sickness. Maybe."

He'd been a child of five when his parents had been killed in an orc raid, so his memory of that time wasn't clear. He might have messed up the amount of ginger or honey—maybe there had been other ingredients. Still, it did smell nice.

"Cheer up, Krea. You'll be climbing the mast in no time."

She snorted as he walked away to share the drink with the rest of the kids on the ship. By the time he'd made the rounds, Krea looked decidedly less indisposed, standing on her two feet.

Kal returned to the kitchen to infuse another pot.

One thousand soldiers had died today. Thanks to their sacrifice, five hundred thousand Carvenstone folks had been given a chance. Kallan's group was composed of a third of them, sailing aboard a hundred ships.

Ninety percent of them were earth folks.

He was going to need a bigger pot.

NINE
INSANITY

Kira was starting to regret her recent life choices.

She should have returned home as soon as she'd dropped Kallan off to Carvenstone, as planned. Then she wouldn't have been dragged into this mess.

To say that the monster was pissed about her burning his wings was an understatement. He'd held his punches earlier; as soon as he emerged out of the lake, he used his immaterial hold to crush her ribs one by one, and made her head burn, her skin freeze.

She'd believed that she was going to die, that it was the end for her. After an interminable moment she couldn't even begin to measure or quantify, he let go, freezing her body in place again, before following Kallan through the waterfall.

Kira heard him punch and kick his way through spells that couldn't, shouldn't have been destroyed by brute force. He did it all the same.

Then there were screams. Screams of agony and torment as he tortured his way through the guards of the peaceful community. He tore down a utopia. Hearing without seeing it was worse. Kira tried to gather her strength again, break out of the magical binding, but she was spent.

The monster walked back to her, blood marring his features and clothing.

"Well, now that that's over with, we can go."

She couldn't believe her ears. Just like that? He'd killed hundreds of thousands, just like that?

"You're a demon."

He smiled as though she'd paid him a compliment. "And here I thought you were going to applaud my restraint. Aren't you glad I didn't pursue the little children, or your pretty lord?"

Kira blinked. Then she realized she could blink now. He'd released her.

She knew better to think that she was free. One move, and he'd freeze her again. Or worse.

"What I heard suggests otherwise."

"What cause could I possibly have to lie to you?"

A fair point, even if Kira felt like he was the type of male who lied simply because he could.

"True, I disposed of the soldiers. The civilians, I spared. I don't care one way or another what becomes of them. It is the land I need. I claimed it, they took it back, I'm claiming it again. Next time they push me, I may not be so kind."

Finally, the penny dropped. It was him. He'd sent the scion army. Everything that had happened since the destruction of Asra was his fault.

Kira wanted to lash out, as was her way.

At her best, she wouldn't have won against him. And she was as far from her best as she'd ever been. So instead of calling to her fire, she asked, "Why? Why are you doing this? Taking Carvenstone, attacking the unseelie realm."

"A complicated question. One I don't have time to discuss now. This can go two ways. Am I carrying you home and finding you a nice room to stay in, or shall I tie you by the ankles and drag you to a dungeon? Your call."

Her fists tightened at her sides. Everything about him infuriated her. He wanted her to submit voluntarily. That was his demand, his meaning barely hidden beneath pretty words. She was either going to be a good little prisoner who heeled well, and get thrown a bone when her master was pleased with her, or she could retain her self-respect.

The man underestimated her. She was a lady of Elvendale, a princess of the Graywoods, not some bitch.

"Drag me then."

The monster grinned. She regretted her impulse almost immediately. He liked this. He liked the challenge. "Oh, you're definitely related."

He was speaking about Devi again. How did he know her sister?

"Sister," he echoed, plucking the information out of her brain, no doubt.

Kira was too tired to maintain efficient mental shields. "Devi's my twin. What's it to you?"

The monster grinned. "Why, she's my future bride."

Kira grimaced. Great. She was stuck with a monster, and he was clearly deluded. Just what she needed. "Sorry to break it to you, we Star Rivers like our males sane." She looked at him, taking him in from head to toe. "And attractive."

He actually was handsome, but hell if she admitted that out loud.

Kira expected a blow, or another mental attack, when he strode to her and lifted his hand. Instead, she immediately fell into a deep dreamless sleep.

When she woke up inside a red and gold room, tucked into a bed with soft pillows and a velvety comforter, she realized with horror that the monster always got what he wanted. One way or another.

TEN
GREAT HOUSES

Devin could practically feel Jiya's glare as he climbed up the dyrmount assigned to him. She hadn't been awarded one, unsurprisingly—there were only a few, and Shea had ensured they went to her general, her consort, her best healer. And him, of course. He may not have many skills compared to her entourage, but he was seelie king, and they were entering his realm.

Devin sighed in relief as he got off his boots. "Good boy, that's it. Turn around, Wysted."

The horse didn't need much direction, responding to the slightest tug along his reins. He trotted to the river where Jiya was still sitting, waiting for the company to resume their walk.

"Are you going to gloat?" She glared at him, arms crossed over her front.

Devin grinned, leaning forward and extending a hand wordlessly.

She looked up from his palm to his face. "Really?"

"You saved my life," he reminded her. "I can save your feet from blisters for a few days."

A second rider would have slowed him down in most circumstances, except the bulk of their company was on foot, so they weren't likely to ride fast. Besides, the fae was light enough to not be a burden for his beast.

She didn't make him repeat his offer, taking his hand and hopping up behind his back.

The east border of the Graywoods was two days' ride away from Elderdale on horseback—a two-week walk with everyone, young and old.

Two weeks and he'd be back home. On his throne.

And he had questions.

The late winter air was kind under the shed of the woods, but as soon as they left the borders of the elven realm, they returned to the sweltering heat of the South.

"Is your country always so hot?" Jiya asked as she sipped from her water skin.

"Seasons mean little here. It's either hot and wet, hot and dry, or hot and...hotter?"

The protector-in-training grunted. "And you aren't bothered?"

"The men of the South are used to the South." Devin tilted his head, admitting, "In this case, it may have something to do with elemental magic. Take your friend, Rivers. I'd wager she is rarely cold."

"Devi?" Jiya snorted. "Yeah, that female could literally bathe in a frozen lake's pool."

"Elemental mages are known for having a greater tolerance for extreme weather, in general. Though I can't say I liked the northern climate when we passed through Corantius. I suppose we get accustomed to our environment as much as any beast."

Jiya was silent for a time. Then her voice was soft. "How could you not suspect anything, after passing through Corantius and gaining soldiers you didn't recognize? Didn't the situation strike you as odd?"

Devin would have preferred to avoid spelling the answer to that question out. No matter how he spun it, it didn't paint him in a favorable light at all. "It was arrogance, I suppose? I didn't think it possible for my advisors, lords who'd served my father for a generation, to betray me. Besides, I can't say I spared much thought for foot soldiers."

"So, what you're saying is that we're in this mess because you're a dismissive, elitist prick?"

He had no answer to offer. She wasn't wrong.

Devin had thought of servants, low-ranking soldiers, common and lesser fae as minor. Folk unworthy of his time and notice. A ruler had greater concerns: politics, matters of state, taxes, preventing catastrophes and wars. Servants were tools designed to facilitate his office.

Observing Shea had considerably shifted his views. She commanded her force with an iron fist. Her orders were law, promptly executed, never questioned. Conversely, she knew each of her soldiers' names, and the names of their children. She ate among them, talked to lesser fae as if they were high-ranking officers. Even now, she walked among them beside her horse.

Little wonder the unseelie queen was the most respected monarch in the Isle, now that the overking had passed away.

"My noticing the oddity of the soldiers' presence wouldn't have changed the fate of Asra," Devin said after a time. "Your enemy had a plan. I doubt it relied solely on my oblivious character."

If he'd questioned the Corantians, would he have been killed? Whatever way he ran the events of the last few weeks in his mind, there was only one conclusion he could reach.

He wasn't meant to survive his trip to the unseelie realm. The question was, who'd plotted his demise, and that of the rest of the Isle?

"You're probably right." Jiya sighed. "Shame. It would have been nice to have someone to blame for this whole mess."

Someone was to blame. They only had to figure out who, and why. And when they did, Devin would gladly step aside and witness all the reasons why the dark fae of the west were called unseelie.

They'd proceeded on the long march—or ride, for the more fortunate among them—out of the Graywoods for half a day when a spec of gold and red shot through the sky. Jiya—along with most of the unseelie—gasped as they lifted their gaze to the flock of gryffins flying overhead.

"Don't you see them in Asra?" To Devin, they were as common as rabbits and deer in the woods.

"Never. Gryffins don't fly anywhere near the City of Night. I think I read that back in the day, during the War of the Realms, they attacked the city. The Battle of Wings and Blood, they call it. Our soldiers were posted along our borders, leaving the city defenseless. Then, you seelie arrived on the back of those beasts. Our soldiers shot you by the thousands with fyriron arrows, but still, many passed and managed to raid the city. There were mostly children and vulnerable common and lesser fae left. I suppose your side thought they'd be easy pickings. They underestimated our children. There were many losses on both sides."

That explained it. Gryffins had a long memory. They lived a thousand years or more. Some among the flock might have seen the war.

"They're on the sigil of my house," Devin told her. "For as long as I can remember, they've landed in the grounds of the keep. Some even played with me as a child. My father could order them around as well as any hounds."

He grew quiet, realizing what it meant. During the War of the Realm, the seelie, unseelie, and elves had all fought one another, until the king of Corantius intervened, making them bend the knee and crown him overking, ruler of the rulers in the Isle, to ensure that a world war wouldn't break out again.

If the gryffins had attacked Asra, it was because his realm had ordered it.

Why was he feeling guilty? It had all happened six hundred years before he'd even opened his eyes. And his family had come to power after the war. Back then, their monarch had been the Ashes, often married to the Rivers and Windfords.

Nonetheless, he felt guilty, knowing that no Ash, Rivers, or Windford could have commanded a race as wild as the gryffins. They were bound to one line only: the Farels.

Devin had been taught that his great grandmother had been crowned after the monarch was killed in battle in the War of the Realms. It hadn't occurred to him to question how a family such as his ended up on the throne, rather than the descendants of the seven founding lines. If they'd proved powerful and cruel enough to pass through the unseelie blockage at the borders, of course the other families would have bent the knee.

He felt dirty.

"We learn our side of the battle, you learn yours, I suppose. Still, it was a great achievement for your side—I'm surprised you didn't know that."

There were many things Devin didn't know.

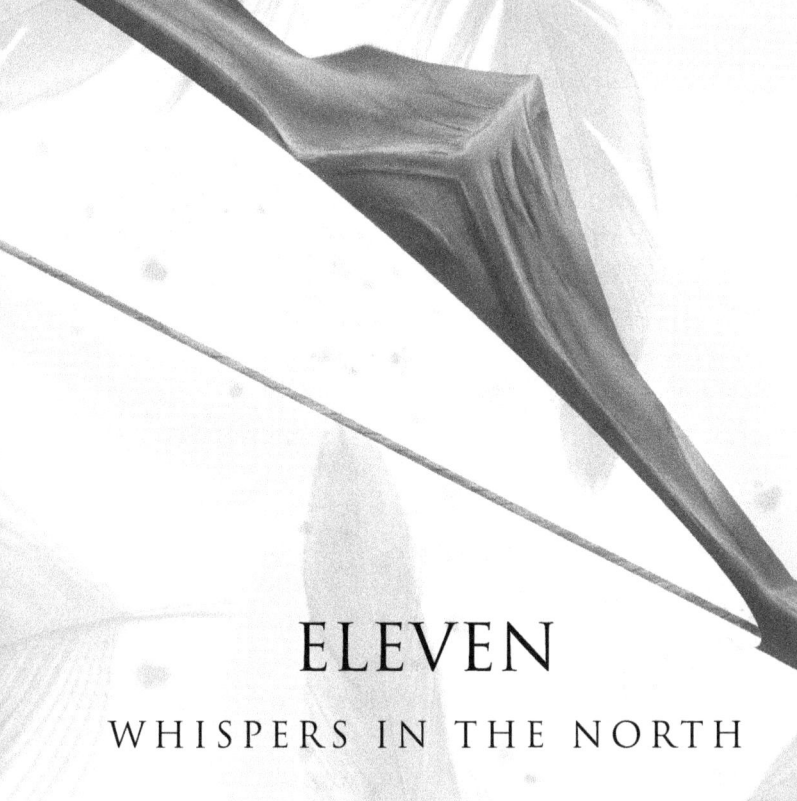

ELEVEN

WHISPERS IN THE NORTH

The female tightened her grasp around her little boy's hand and urged him to run faster. She dared to look behind her shoulder, panic widening her eyes and gripping her heart. Moments ago, they'd seemed so far away; now the army of elves and fae drew nearer. They were armed with bows, arrows, swords. Mounted on horseback they rode with a devilish agility. There would be no hope for her, or her child, unless they reached the gates of Deretus, the city nearest their village.

Mallea had grabbed her boy and nothing else, not even food or shoes, before running as soon as she'd heard the army. They were getting close. They only had to cross the bridge and then the gates of the city would come into view.

"Faster, Ren, please." She didn't think she'd ever begged before, but to all the gods, she prayed that they made it on time.

Mallea had a simple life outside of the city. She wove and sewed dresses she sold at a weekly market, though she'd opted to live in Hers because everything from rent to food was too costly in the city. If she'd lived in Deretus, she would have been poor, and struggled to feed her boy. She knew of women who sold themselves just for loaves of bread. In Hers, they could barter, fish in nearby rivers, and Ren had even learned to hunt, despite his tender years. Mallea had showed him how to use a bow, and well…seven or not, the boy was a fae. She wished she could accompany him in the woods, but she didn't have time. Her dresses paid for their rent and his education.

Now, Mallea was questioning why she hadn't chosen the poverty, the smell of sewers, the leery scion guards. All the woes of living in a Corantian city would have been worth it, for her safety and that of her boy.

Finally, they crossed the bridge. She breathed out in relief.

"Mama?" Ren stopped running.

Mallea turned to him. His gaze was directed forward, to the city. She followed it, and her mouth fell open, horror striking as she watched.

Hundreds of fae just like her, village dwellers from around the city, were gathered at the fortified walls, banging on the doors so hard their hands were bloody, trying to climb up the hundred feet of white stone.

All they found was that the lords of Deretus had closed their doors to them, forsaking them, leaving them out to die, killed by the fae.

The forest was a mile away, but Mallea couldn't bring herself to move, her knees giving out. She buried her head against her boy's shoulder. "Close your eyes," she whispered, though hers stayed fixed on the approaching soldiers. "It will be over soon."

Dying while running for their lives, terrified, desperate, wasn't a fate she wished on her child. Her heart beat a thousand miles a minute, and she winced in anticipation of a blade or an arrow when the elves reached her.

Instead, the horses passed. One after the next, they passed by her, ignoring her as if she were invisible. They kept going for a timeless lap, tens of thousands, riding fast till they reached the gates.

Mallea returned to her feet, completely shocked.

A fae turned his horse back, and yelled, "You!"

She froze, horrified at being addressed by one of them. What did they want now? Were they going to hurt her?

"Tell your people to return to their homes, a siege is no place for civilians. If they're stranded, food'll be served at sundown. We can't spare tents, but there'll be cots for those who need them."

And then, without another word, the rider kept going until he'd reached the gates.

"You're lying."

"I kid you not!" Borr protested. "My own kin is from Deretus. She wrote and said they don't touch us fae, or common folk. They just opened the gates, killed the soldiers, captured the lords, and asked the rest to elect a mayor. Elect, Frej!"

Frej knew better than to believe tales. War was bloody, especially for the people.

"I wish they'd come here," his daughter said with a sigh.

"Genna, don't you let anyone hear you say things like that! We're not traitors."

Traitors were hanged publicly as entertainment for the scions, so they were definitely not that.

His teenager pouted.

For all his words, Frej did wish something would change here in Tress. For his people, for his daughter, and her daughter after.

The fae had always been treated like scum in Corantius. If you didn't have divine blood, you were less than nothing. Servants, if you were lucky—slaves and whores, most of the time. He worked in a kitchen. He'd been there for two hundred years, and he still got paid two coppers per week; not nearly enough to take care of himself, let alone a family. So Frej, his wife, and daughter lived with four other families in one little house. The daughters shared a room, so did the sons, and the four couples took turns sleeping in the barn, sitting room, garden, and the one bedroom left.

They were better off than most.

He sighed. Sometimes, he thought of going south, moving his family to the seelie or unseelie realm, even knowing the cost of a move was something he couldn't afford. Beyond the cost, he'd no doubt be stopped at the border and told to turn right back unless he could prove he had cause to move south. And so they remained.

There was no hope for people like them in this world.

Frej enjoyed his one night in the bedroom, sleeping like a log next to Vanna, the love of his life. It was no wonder that they'd had only one child in one hundred and fifty years. They slept every night, too exhausted to touch each other often.

The next day, he showered in the backyard and dressed to go to work bright and early.

The streets were unusually quiet. He kept his head down, watching the pavement as he usually did. A good thing too—he could barely see ten feet ahead. There was mist in the air.

Frej wrinkled his nose.

No, not mist.

Smoke.

He lifted his head, and first noticed the red sun rising in the distance. There was something ominous about it.

He looked around, hurrying through the street to get to the inn where he worked, when he stopped.

There was a rider ahead, in green and gold, holding a flag with a raven on it.

Frej wasn't versed in grandiose flags, but he was sure he'd never seen that one before. He frowned.

"Are you lost, sir?" He regretted his impulse to speak the moment he formulated the words.

From his pretty, expensive armor, the man was clearly a noble scion. What if he considered his being addressed by a lowly fae insolence, and he dragged him to some dark dungeon?

"It would appear so," the rider said politely. "I was told to gather the people of Tress, yet I don't seem to see anyone at all."

Hair rose at the nape of his neck. He lifted his eyes to the windows and doors, and saw shadows hiding from the stranger.

"For what purpose would you have us gather, sir?" he asked, his tone laced with a courage he hadn't known he possessed until now.

"For the vote up at the lord's keep," he said. "You're to elect a leader before we go on our way. Tell your people, would you, man?"

Frej shook his head. "I've a job to do. I can't be late."

He couldn't afford to be fired. His family would starve within a month if he was.

"No one has a job today, sir," the rider replied. "By order of Valerius, heir to the throne."

Frej blinked and watched in awe as the rider turned back, leaving him to choose his path.

He could go to the inn—it was just half an hour on foot. Or he could call the low town folks and take them to the lord's keep.

It could be a trap. It probably was a trap. It had to be.

Then he remembered Borr's claim that his own kin had voted after her city had been taken by fae and elves.

Nonsense. It had to be nonsense.

That, or hope.

TWELVE
PROMISES

A few weeks ago, Devi remembered dreading the thought of riding a horse for an extended amount of time. Now, she would have killed for Alarik. Walking *sucked*.

"I can't believe we left the dyrmounts in Staren."

It wasn't the first time she'd brought up the horses. Devi had instructed her father, who was supposed to attack the Court of Crystal sometime over the next week, to retrieve them from Vera's Roof. And to kill the owner if that old harpy had mistreated them in any way.

"You. Technically, *you* left them," Vale reminded her. "I had no say in the matter, being unconscious, and—you know. Dying."

Devi glared at him.

"Too soon, Valerius," Telenar told him. "I believe that particular jab may be a little too soon for our lady."

The ancient scientist had joined their expedition north, along with Gallal. Telenar was well versed in Enlightened sciences, but he also could enchant blood tracker stones for Vale when it would be time to find his siblings. Many elves were well versed in the art of healing. Of them all, Devi had picked the charming southern warrior, because Gallal had been friendly, courageous, and eager to help when they'd met on their way to the portal of Daryn.

Valerius hadn't seemed fond of the guy at first, but as it turned out, he was quite a skilled cook. Their first dinner out in the wild had considerably endeared Gallal to everyone. Only the truly gifted could turn a couple of squirrels and some herbs into a delicious stew.

The last member of their party was Rula, a silent scout. She was the only one on horseback. Rula rode ahead to scout their path every day. A single rider brought little attention. When they woke up from a safe hiding spot—woods, a deserted village, fields—they sent Valerius's raven to her, and she found them to discuss their itinerary.

They'd only been on the road for five days so Devi couldn't say she knew the elf well. She was beautiful and dark of skin, with silver strands tattooed around her limbs. Her head was shaved, highlighting her annoyingly perfect bone structure. Devi didn't think she'd ever seen a female as beautiful as she. Which only made the way Vale focused on Devi, as though he couldn't even see Rula, more exhilarating.

They were marching northeast, following the edge of woods so that they might have shelter when needed.

However, the further north they went, the less coverage they had.

Fae loved nature and never settled far from woodlands, but the topography of the northern part of Corantius was wide-open plains, covered in a soft dusting of snow, although it was already spring.

Devi charmed three of the ten blackfire stones in their supply. Three, they used to cool, one was always with Rula on her ride north, and the others were scattered in their luggage, so that they always had at least one in case they lost a bag along the way.

She handed one each to Gallal and Telenar, who took them gratefully.

Vale hesitated. "Is this taxing your energy?"

"Not even a little bit," she assured him. "I just have to ignite the spell inside. The hexer who created it did the hard work."

Her mate nodded, taking the stone. "I get what you meant, finally."

She lifted a brow.

"Back when I wanted to buy you a coat? You said while the cold didn't hurt you, you prefer to be warm all the same." He smiled. "I guess we have that in common now."

They had a lot of things in common. How much, Devi couldn't tell. She felt his mind, and that of everyone else around her. His felt different. It was part of hers. She barely had to stretch, reach out to access it. The others? Their minds felt like a book she could choose to pick up, or to ignore.

Devi didn't dare touch that part of his power. Her power. After hundreds of years, Vale was still known as the dark prince because of what he could do. Learning how to control his gift had taken centuries. It was still a work in progress. She didn't want to imagine how much she'd screw up. When her ice magic got out of hand, she froze everything in her surroundings. Breaking the minds of those around her was a lot scarier.

Styx's bequest might eventually help. The goddess had shown Devi how to control her own mind—she was completely ignorant of how Vale's power was supposed to work. It was best left alone for now.

Devi pulled another blackfire stone out of the supplies to heat for herself.

"May I?" Vale reached out for it.

She smiled as she handed it to him. He didn't share her feeling about the dangers of using magic he wasn't familiar with. Vale had taken to elemental magic like a duck to water. He was even comfortable with water and ice.

He placed the blackfire stone in his hands and closed his eyes, concentrating.

Devi felt a cold wave rise from Vale and put her hand on his arm to stop him. "Fire," she said. "You're accessing ice. It's the easiest element to get to because that's what's in my actual blood. Everything else is buried a little deeper. Fire feels like…" She thought it out for a second. "Rage. And love, and lust, too, but rage most of all. Remember something that makes you furious, it'll rush to the surface."

The energy around Vale changed suddenly, growing turbulent, unstable. The snow around their feet melted, and the grass underneath died.

He opened his eyes, stopping it as fast as it had come.

"Well, that was easy. Here."

He handed her the burning hot stone.

Devi didn't take it, focusing on him. "Too easy." When she called to fire, it took her a lot more effort, unless she was infuriated. "What were you thinking about?"

Whatever it was, it enraged him. Devi was annoyed at herself for having no clue. She wanted to know everything about her mate.

Their journey north was a cause of worry to him, because he wanted her to be safe, because he was concerned about the realm, and above all, his land, his people. Vale was also ambivalent about the prospect of ruling Corantius. Understandably.

She knew all that. They'd discussed it at length. None of these matters incensed him enough to be able to call to fire in mere instants.

Vale sighed. "My brother. Half-brother."

Devi grimaced. "I take it we're not talking about Aurelius."

His violet eyes settled on her. "He wants you. Marcus wants you. He's tried to blackmail you into giving in to him by using me. The prospect of dealing with him again…"

"I'd die before I let him touch me."

Vale snorted, finally looking away, eyes set in the distant north. "Yeah. I realize that. That's not exactly reassuring, little elf."

THIRTEEN
GAME OF WORDS

Kira glared across the small round table dressed with black candles and a green cloth. It was overflowing with all her favorite things, cooked precisely to her taste. Damn psychic.

"Come on. You're going to have to crack someday." The monster was amused.

She needed to reconsider her position. Her defiance was refreshing to him.

"My name is Marcus, not 'the monster', Lady Star."

"'The monster' suits just fine," she replied. "Especially when you keep digging into my head without an invitation."

He tilted his head. "Is that what's bothering you? I could stop."

Kira blinked. Was he for real? "What bothers me is that you're a sadistic, murderous psycho. And you've kidnapped me. Plus, locked me in my room."

Her door was open, and so was her window. She could even walk on her balcony and admire the view. Yet as surely as she hadn't been able to move when he'd paralyzed her in front of the gates of Carvenstone two weeks ago, she couldn't get out. He'd tricked her mind into it.

Things could be a lot worse. She could be dead. Or in a dungeon. Marcus brought her the nicest food and her closet was full of the prettiest clothes. He was trying to turn her into a pretty, compliant doll. But while he had access to her mind, he didn't know her at all. She'd never cared for dresses. She could last weeks without any food—though her energy suffered for it. There were only a few things that were essential to her.

One of them was her freedom.

The other was the woods. Nature.

They were in a white castle at the heart of a city glowing with shimmery lights. The gates were made of glass.

No, not glass. Crystal. The Court of Crystal was eerily beautiful. And everything she despised.

"Come on. One bite. Just one bite and I'll take you to the gardens."

She groaned. He'd just plucked her longing for nature out of her mind, too.

"I want nothing *from* you."

"I know. You just want to do things *to* me. Beheading, flaying, whipping. Somehow, all your dreams end in me roasted like a well-done piece of ham."

Marcus was smiling.

"Never mind sadistic. You're a total masochist."

"Hardly. I just find honesty refreshing. Go on, Kira. You need to eat, if you're to follow through on any of your brazen schemes to get out of here."

His contempt was like poison searing down her throat. She wasn't used to treatment like this. Kallan had teased her about her youth when she'd been unreasonably stubborn once or twice, but he'd never disrespected her or disregarded her strength.

"If you think I have no regard for your strength, you're sorely mistaken. I don't take note of weaklings. You're a challenge. Hence why you're here and not rotting in a cell."

"Five minutes," Kira said spontaneously. "Stay out of my head for five minutes, and I'll eat."

She would have done worse things for five minutes without his intrusive poking around her mind.

"Done. Starting now."

Kira grinned, immediately thinking about a thousand things that would have made him rise.

Devi. He had many questions about Devi, and she never answered them out loud. She also did her best to think of her sister as seldom as possible when he was around, just to deny him what he truly wanted from her.

She brought to the forefront of her mind everything Devi had ever told her of her life in Asra through their correspondences. She'd mentioned her friend Rook a time or two. The name Marcus used back then. "You would like him, Kira. He's so bold and unashamed, wings out in the open every day, in front of everyone. A little like you."

She hadn't been wrong. Kira might have liked Rook. Marcus, she despised.

She didn't get him. He had a nice life, friends who cared. He could do anything, go anywhere. Instead, he was harbinger of chaos, for no other reason than the fact he could.

"Are we to spend the next three and a half minutes in silence? If I can't distract myself with your fascinating little mind, I'd like to speak instead."

"Pardon me if I did anything to make you think I care what you'd like."

He laughed. "There she is again. In deeds or thoughts, always questing to wound my pride. You're good for me, Star. My ego could use checking on a regular basis."

"Your ego could use a good amount of deflation," she corrected.

Marks shrugged. "That too. Go on. While I can't get into your head, tell me why you think I'm wrong and evil for wanting what is mine by birthright."

He'd shared his sob story about being the first son of Orin.

"Because the laws of succession having anything to do with blood is bullshit in any case. The best person for the throne should rule. The end."

That seemed to amuse him. "Don't you think that's a little hypocritical, for the heir of Wyhmur?"

Kira rolled her eyes. "My father raised me to rule, in order to ensure I am the best option for Wyhmur when he passes me the throne."

"And do you believe you are?"

"Hell. No." She enunciated both words clearly. "I'd burn it down. Wage war on any realm that slights us. Which is why if he were to die tomorrow, I'd step aside."

Marks watched her a little too closely for her liking. "You know, I believe you would. Eat."

She could feel heat gather at her back of her eyes. No doubt they flashed. "You know, no female likes to be told what to do."

"A deal is a deal. Five minutes with no head-hopping. Eat."

Damn him. She wasn't one to go back on her word.

She cut a bit of boar, dipped it in green peppercorn sauce, and brought it to her mouth. Perfectly cooked, delicious, and still warm somehow. She moaned as it crossed her lips.

"I think I'm the best person for the realm. Not that weakling, Aurelius. Talk about middle brother syndrome. He's utterly average at everything he's ever done. And Valerius…well. Valerius Blackthorn, the dark prince, tortures, fucks, kills—"

"Yeah, yeah." Kira rolled her eyes. "You're into my sister, she's opening her legs to him, so you're pouting. I get it."

His jaw was set and his eyes, hollow.

Most of the time, Kira was facing Rook, Devi's friend, a male who was attempting to make his presence agreeable to her. An impossibility, but he still tried.

Right now, the monster was in front of her again. She steeled herself, expecting another jolt of pain.

"Valerius was spoiled. Permitted to give into his darkest impulses, nay, respected for them. He did well enough in his own land, I'll admit. He has his people's love, their adoration and respect. Do you believe a ruler ought to demand adoration?"

She remained silent.

"I will be feared. I will be their worst nightmare. I will be the reason why this Isle knows an unending peace. And my queen will give them hope."

"Devi will never fall for you. Ever. You deceived her. She doesn't deal well with betrayal."

Devi had been given away by their father, after losing her mother. She was loyal to Shea Blackthorn because her queen had welcomed her with open arms and never betrayed her trust.

Though Kira may not know her twin as well as she would like, still she knew one thing.

She'd never forgive the male who burned down her home.

Marcus got to his feet and started to walk away. Before leaving her room, he told her, "We'll see."

FOURTEEN
KING OF THE DALE

Elderdale, home to the seelie court in the southwest of the Isle, was a magnificent city built by the first of their kind, the fae who'd shaped their world.

There were towers so high they touched the clouds, marvelous fountains, small woods, tamed ash and willows planted at every corner so that the fae could stay connected to nature even amid the city, halls of crystals and painted townhouses with well-crafted carved roofs.

It had deserved its name, in the old days. The dale of the elders. Now it was also a fortress. Walls fifty inches thick, reinforced with spells, and soldiers patrolling the ramparts day and night. The moat dug around it was filled with a flammable substance, rather than water.

Their fire mages could light the moat, rendering their defenses impregnable.

The drawbridge was the only way in and out.

When the scions had come for them, Shea Blackthorn hadn't attempted to retain Asra—her home—because endeavoring to do so would have been pointless and cost too many lives. It had no such defenses. The only city that could hold for any length of time against such a powerful invader in the unseelie realm was Carvenstone.

When its master sat upon the throne, in any case. Currently, it was defenseless.

Shea had led whoever had a chance of making it out of Asra and called her armies. Now they were all standing in front of the closed gates of Elderdale. Thousands of civilians and soldiers. Everything left of the Court of Night. Most of the unseelie realm.

Shea expected the gates to remain closed until she revealed the card she'd kept up her sleeve, but the large iron doors were slowly pulling apart, in front of a man she had no issue recognizing.

Elder king Kraven Farel. He was handsome, with tanned skin, seasoned muscles and dark soft hair falling to his knees behind him.

He was also linked to the attack on Asra. Any imbecile could have surmised that much.

Kraven had voluntarily given up his throne in favor of his son. That wasn't unheard of, though it was out of character for a power-hungry scum like him.

What game was he playing?

"Your Grace. We have been expecting you."

"Indeed?" Shea prompted.

Kraven was all smiles. "It would be contemptible if the lord of the dale failed to notice an army marching to his gate."

He made it sound like they intended to attack, speaking loud and clear so that anyone watching from the ramparts could hear. Which they would, if it came to it. Shea needed the city, and she would take it.

"Lord of the dale," she repeated. "Isn't that title reserved for the king?"

The swine's charming smile faltered some.

"There's been no news from my son since he reached your land, my lady."

There was an accusation there. He played an angle, depicting her as the enemy.

Shea thought very little of Kraven, since he'd banished, then hunted down Loxy Rivers, and issued an assassination order simply because she wasn't inclined to marry him.

Even with all that, she hadn't believed him capable of having sent his son to die.

Until now.

It was clear that he'd expected Devin to be killed in the unseelie realm, whether by her or by the scions.

Shea wasn't easily surprised, and this, above all, shouldn't have come as a shock. Hadn't her very own father attempted to kill her? And for the same reason. Power. Immortals had no need for an heir. They weren't children as much as their replacement, after a certain age.

"Rejoice," Shea replied. "I do have news."

Devin's horse stepped forward. That Kraven hadn't recognized him was no wonder. He stood to Shea's left, dressed in the uniform of an unseelie soldier. They hadn't had any formal court attire to dress him in during their travel east. Besides, he'd needed his armor, his shield and swords.

Devin had changed in the last month. He used to be a softer boy. Shea had done her best to whip that out of him. Not literally, granting she'd been tempted once or twice. Devin took to intense training like a kitten in deep waters. There had been moaning. A lot of moaning.

"Devira Rivers at fifteen was less of a girl than you, a king!" she'd told him. Many times.

Still they'd persevered, and she liked to think that her mentoring might have had an impact on him.

It would be useful in the war to come.

Devin removed his helmet.

"Father," he said pleasantly. "It's good to be home. Open the gates."

Kraven's ire dripped from his pores as he found himself impotent. This was an order from his king.

Before Kraven could gesture or call for his men to lower the drawbridge, they did so. The word of Devin was enough.

He rode ahead unprompted, trotting past his father without sparing him a glance.

Shea wasn't one to gloat, but this memory would keep her warm in the many dark and cold nights to come.

Only then did she notice an oddity.

Jiya was riding right behind the king.

She smiled.

The girl had a bright future ahead of her. Shea could see as much, though the future had become uncertain since the fall of Asra. She could see no more than a few flashes, images that came and went, fleeting and unclear.

Jiya was in the snow. Her blood on the ground. Wounded and broken. Shea was resolved Jiya would not end this way. There was more to the girl's story. Shea saw a crown upon her head.

She'd have to protect her as long as she could, see that that future came to pass.

Because the alternative was darkness. Darkness engulfing the entire Isle.

"Your Grace?"

Shea looked to Loralei, the female who'd been with her since the beginning. Since before her beginning, back when she'd been no one. Just a girl in a cold castle, with enemies all around her and no hope.

There was no future for her favorite knight. Whatever vision crossed her mind, they never included the female by her side for long.

"I'm distracted. The thought of a nice feather bed was just too much for my poor old bones."

Loralei laughed. "I seem to remember a tale of our queen, content enough in a bunk built in a treehouse."

Shea managed a smile, but it didn't last. Like every other memory, this one was colored with too many deaths.

She advanced, entering the Court of Elders.

FIFTEEN
IN THE SNOW

Valerius looked at the crown in his hand, his frustration growing with every instant. The silver circlet remained still and quiet. No buzz, no energy had emanated from it since the moment he'd retrieved it. Some days, he wondered whether he'd taken the right device.

Devi had retrieved the sword and, from the very start, it had accepted her, despite the fact it was a divine instrument linked to his bloodline. That didn't surprise Vale. She was his mate, and over the course of the weeks preceding their heist in Staren, Vale and Devi had started to form the bond that made them one. She was a Blackthorn.

Vale could use the sword. He'd tried, and it responded to him. Nevertheless, he'd left it to Devi's care. She'd certainly deserved it; what was more, she'd claimed it.

His heirloom was this stubborn crown. Elden Star had warned him that the divine instruments had minds of their own and only worked when they felt like it, for those they considered worthy. It called to him. Yet when he attempted to connect with it, the ruby dulled, ignoring his pull.

Vale was glad of an interruption. A lone rider approached their hideout.

Their small company traveled by night and slept during the day. The cover of the night didn't help against scions or fae, but their enemies were known to live by day. Marching on a different schedule made sense, so long as they stayed away from settlements. Adequate concealment was growing harder and harder to find.

They'd found a hold far enough from civilization this morning, after marching for three hours past their scheduled halt.

"There's a larger town west, alongside the river. We can avoid it by heading east or west," Rula told them, dismounting her horse.

They generally conversed through notes except once every other day, the scout joined them during their break to sleep.

"Which side would you recommend?" Devi asked her, stepping forward and handing her a freshly spelled blackstone.

"Thank you." Rula wrapped her hands around its warmth and sighed in pleasure. "West. There's a mountain away from towns and villages some miles that way. I'm sorry to say, I think it's the last safe resting place you'll be able to use for a while. I reached the mountain. North, there are many towns, some cities, and no woods to speak of."

Vale's jaw tightened. He nodded. "Well, that means we're closer." The Court of Crystal was the northernmost city in the Isle, but it was surrounded by industrious towns filled with scions and fae alike. "We always knew it was going to get to that point. We'll have to blend in and risk sleeping in inns and taverns after we leave the mountain."

"We should wait," Telenar supplied. "I don't think the bulk of the forces have left to respond to the elven attacks thus far. We would have seen or at least heard them. Going in the surrounding areas of the capital while they're still teeming with soldiers is suicide."

Vale thought it out. "No, arriving right after the army leaves would only serve to make us more suspicious. The folks are bound to be watchful and apprehensive after they hear their kingdom is under attack. We should wait before we enter the Immortal City. It may be wiser to head over to the nearby towns now."

There was silence as all considered the way ahead.

"There's danger one way or another," Devi said. "As for me, I'll pick the option that allows us to sleep in a feather bed."

Even now, she managed to lighten the atmosphere. Vale wrapped his arms around her shoulder and kissed her forehead. "Feather bed it is. We'll see about sleep."

He was only half joking. He needed her. To hold her, feel her and make her scream his name. He needed her comfortable and happy. Letting her struggle in the snow went against his every instinct.

Struggle was all she'd ever done since they'd met.

She was strong. She could take it. The only thing enraging him was that she had to.

"I'll take the first watch if you'd like some time to yourself?" Gallal offered.

The healer-cook was decidedly growing on him.

"Oh no, I don't think so. I'll take the first watch. You guys sleep. I'm already exhausted and I know exactly what you would convince me to do if we had time to ourselves," Devi said, softening the blow by kissing him.

She was right of course. They all needed sleep to heal their physical aches and reset their energy.

As he lay on the cold snow, Vale stared at the crown in his hand for an hour, at least, willing it to respond to him.

In vain.

"I see something."

Vale was at Devi's side before her next breath, eyes forward as he watched shadows dance in the distance.

She was right.

"Two riders," she said.

"No, just one. Two horses. One rider." Vale kept his gaze on the approaching figured. Then, he smiled.

"By all gods!" Devi exclaimed when she recognized their horses.

"The gods have little to do with our fortune. As always, we can thank your kindness. That's our maid from the inn atop my horse, unless I'm much mistaken."

He hadn't gotten more than a glimpse of the high fae who'd served Devi at Vera's Roof.

Devi rushed back to their supplies, heated another blackstone and pulled out leftovers of their dry meat. By the time the horses had reached Vale, she'd returned.

"Jeryn! How in heaven and hell have you found us?"

The poor female was all but frozen, wearing a light coat entirely unsuitable for the weather. Her teeth were grinding, and she shivered like a leaf in the wind. Vale doubted she still had all her toes.

"I didn't. The horses just...kept going. Trust me, I tried to turn them back. A lot."

Vale didn't doubt it. He helped her down her horse and Devi handed her the blackstone.

"Here's some food. How did you end up following us?"

The better question was why. Another time, another war, Vale would have taken the answer from her mind, not thinking twice about invading it.

Now, he didn't.

"I just freed the horses. I think they're smarter than most. They understood I'd get in trouble for it, somehow. So, they let me tag along. And..." Hesitantly, the maid turned to him. "I didn't realize who you were when we met, so I didn't get to say it. My prince, I hope you're crowned. Many of us fae do." She almost managed a grin. "I'd curtsy, if I could feel my legs."

"I'll wake up our healer," Vale said, moving back to camp and feeling like he was running away.

He couldn't even begin to think how he could respond. She wanted him crowned? The very thought boggled his mind.

Valerius was prepared to take the throne if he had to. If he was chosen. But he'd imagined ruling over reluctant subjects, not unlike the court of night, who despised and disrespected him.

"Gallal." Vale kept and kept his voice low in an attempt to avoid waking the scientist cocooned next to the healer. "We have a patient for you."

Gallal yawned, before leaping into action.

Vale remained where he sat, his attention called away by the crown still in his hand.

Its ruby red stone shone in the night and it slowly hummed, as if singing.

Frowning, he placed it on its head.

The instrument was communicating, murmuring one word.

King.

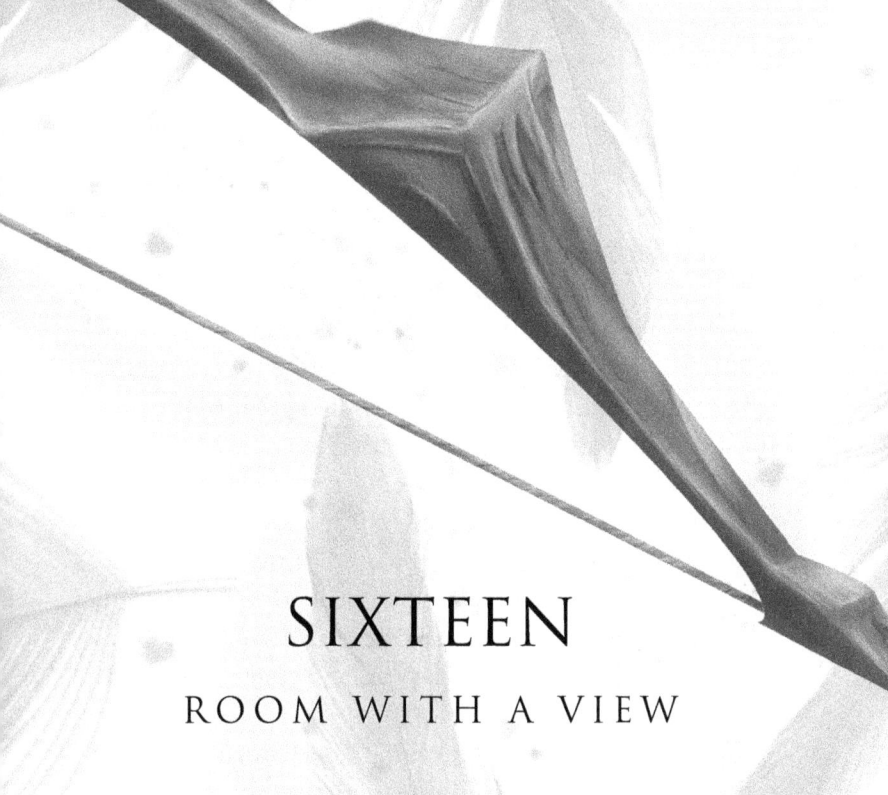

SIXTEEN
ROOM WITH A VIEW

Krea leaped out of the ship and rushed to the ground, kissing the wet sand under her feet.

In three weeks of sailing, she had grown accustomed to the turmoil of the seas. Still, there was nothing quite like standing on firm ground.

"Come on. Enough theatrics. You could have come ashore sooner," Kallan Blacks reminded her.

She grinned.

A week ago, their ships had headed south of Carvenstone land, in the mostly rural county of Farj. The children and non-fighters had been dropped off, along with a handful of soldiers. The rest of them were headed north to Corantius. Kallan had ordered that they'd join their prince, to fight for him. Finally.

So naturally, Krea hid below deck, only coming out when they were way too far for the commander to send her back.

He'd been angry at first.

She knew her impulse had been reckless, but what was she supposed to do in Farj? Look after the children again? She was terrible at it. It wasn't like she had family who wanted her around. She'd studied great battles and she knew that armies always needed messengers, scouts, cooks, people who ran errands.

After yelling at her for three minutes straight, their lord regent gave her a different kind of punishment.

She meant to be helpful. She needed to feel helpful. And strong. Stronger than she'd been down in the caves. The memory of the way she'd wept helplessly would haunt her till her dying day.

"Didn't you forget something?" Kallan glared at her.

Krea winced, returning to the ship. She came back with his sword. It was too heavy for her, but she had to carry it nonetheless, as his squire.

His *squire*. She expected to have been sent to the kitchens, or something equally dull. Instead, he made her polish his sword and write notes to the other ships, care for the ravens and eagles they used as messengers.

Krea pretended to be suitably inconvenienced and put out, so he thought she took her new appointment as a punishment. In truth, she couldn't possibly have been any more thrilled. Squires observed and aided their lords. Sometimes, they even became knights. She grinned each time she imagined herself wearing armor and kneeling to be anointed.

For now, her job was mostly cleaning and carrying things too heavy for her.

Like shiny swords she would love to wield someday.

"Where are we? The air is so cold here."

As a daughter of the north, she used to believe she was used to friskier weather but her feet were freezing in her boots.

"Twenty-five miles from Carvenstone. We landed away from the border as we anticipate it will be well guarded. And it's warmer by the sea than it is inland."

"Dragon's scales!" she cursed. "How are people living here?"

"They're more robust than unruly nine-year-olds."

Now Krea rolled her eyes. "What, so they don't have children here?"

Lord Blacks looked up to the sky, as he often did when she tried his patience, as if willing the heavens to give him the strength to put up with her.

"Go on ahead. We'll set up camp on the cliffs for tonight. Find the best spot for my tent."

This, like everything else he did, felt like a test. Or at least, Krea took it as such. The best spot? She looked ahead to the intimidating stretch of steep, tree-ridden cliff. The obvious answer was the very top, of course. It would have the best view and if their army was scattered around the rest of the forest, he'd be protected in case of an attack.

But this was Kallan Blacks. *The* Kallan Blacks, hero of the War of the Realm, companion and advisor to prince Valerius.

She lifted her gaze up the highest tree, and grinned, before starting a climb.

Yes. This would do just fine.

The tree was old, hard and sturdy. She lay back on one of the branches and sighed in pleasure.

"To me. Come to me." She whispered softly, her mouth and her heart calling to the frozen ground underneath her feet.

The leaves grew thicker overhead and new branches sprouted out of the older ones to form a floor under her feet.

"What have we here? A bird of some sort, I'd say."

She looked down to Kallan.

"The best spot, as ordered. I can see the entire forest from here, and the lands for miles ahead." When he made no reply, she added, "Or perhaps you're too old for climbing trees. I hear grownups get heavy, awkward bones and lose their agility with time."

"You have been sent to punish me, I swear." Even as he complained, he bent his knees and leaped so high he reached the first branch with his left hand. His feet joined it and he leaped again and again until he arrived right in front of her.

Kallan looked around, appearing confused. "Did you do this? It doesn't look totally natural."

Krea grinned. "When I was little, after my father passed away, I spent a fair bit of time by myself. You know, before the knights dragged me to Carvenstone. I've done a few treehouses."

It was one of her best creations. As the ash tree was so large, the room she'd built was as vast as Kallan's cabin in the blasted ship they'd just left.

"It's rather well insulated, too."

She shrugged. "Practice makes perfect."

Carvenstone may not be as cold as this place, but it was still the north.

"Thank you, Krea."

She felt rather awkward now. She hadn't expected any thanks. "Right. I'd better get the rest of your things."

"I think not. I'll not have you fall off the tree trying to get my suitcases. Go find yourself a perch. You're off for the rest of the day."

She certainly didn't need to be told twice.

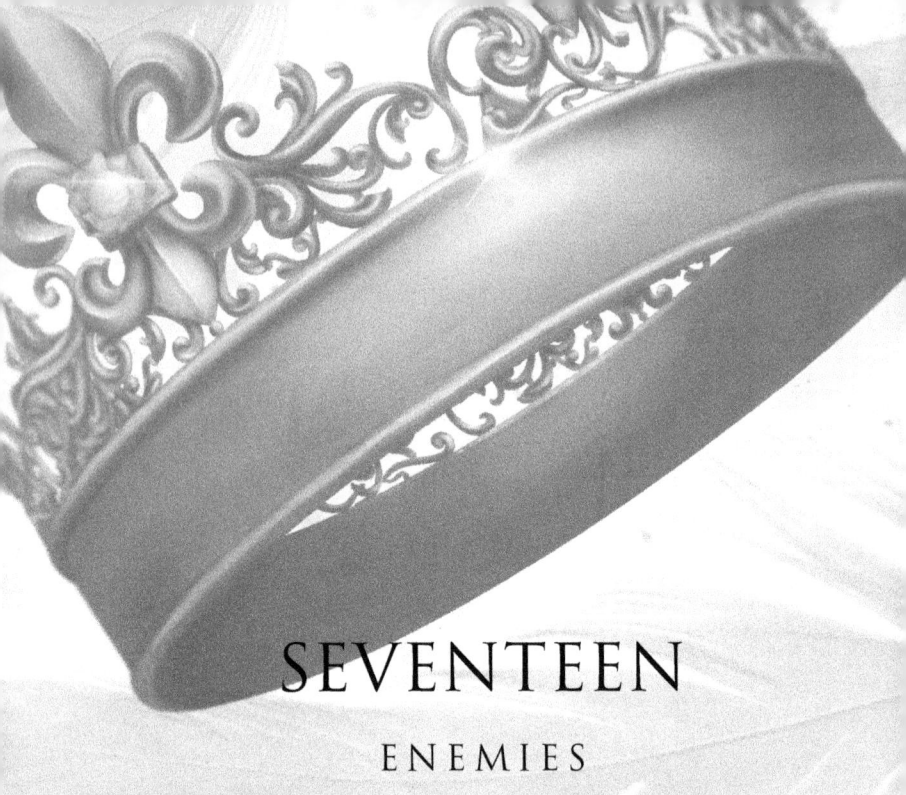

SEVENTEEN

ENEMIES

Rook was last to arrive in the emergency council session. He'd been bothering Kira, and though he'd received the summons promptly, he hadn't been inclined to stop his favorite activity right away.

The lords of Corantius awaited him in silence. Aurelius sat at one head of the table, and the only seat vacant was at its other end.

Rook kicked the back off in one hit, before sitting on what was now a stool. He'd not retract his wings now. They were his protection, his strength and pride.

In the middle of the large mahogany, to his left, sat Kelina Stormhale, the only person whose judgement mattered here.

She was of little skill and not half as clever as she pretended to be. But she was a seer, and that was all that mattered.

"Well?"

"An army arrived from the sea to the west. I did not see it. Water muddles the visions—and everything has been unclear since Orin's death anyway."

Rook leaned forward, eyes on her. "Then what use are you, exactly?" Kelina was angry. Incensing her was a pleasure he used to savor. Not of late. "Never mind. Can the locals deal with it?"

"I don't think so. Our spies report a hundred thousand strong. We'll need to move."

"No." Rook surprised himself. The answer was as firm as it was foolish. Of course, they should move against a hundred thousand enemies. "I'll stay here. Your last clear vision saw me—all of us—here, this summer, when our goal is finally accomplished. And yet..." He got up to his feet and all rose in response. Rook waved them down. "Sit. My chair is just uncomfortable." And he preferred to speak to them from a higher spot. "We have underestimated our enemy. We expected the lords of our city to stop them. For a month, they've raided our kingdom without failing once. The arrival of another force is the consequence of our inaction. So now, we must rid our land of enemies."

"If I may?" The duke of Stormhale was a formidable force. When he spoke, all listened. Even Rook. Most of the time. The man had taken him under his wing in his teens. Cared for him. For that, Rook showed him more patience than most.

"Yes, Father?" Rook prompted.

"It would be my honor to lead the forces heading east. Those heathens robbed me. Now they seek to rob our lands. Let me show them how we treat thieving low-lives in this kingdom."

"Perfect. Now for the west." Rook glanced to Aurelius. "What say you, brother?"

The blond-haired, blue-eyed boy sighed. "If you wish me to, I'll lead the forces heading west, of course. But I'd prefer to remain here. With my son."

Rook smiled. "Well, Kelina saw all of us here. You're off the hook this summer. We'll reassess if the war is prolonged past the season."

"Are we going to talk about the whore in your quarters?" Kelina asked.

Rook spun on his feet and growled before he'd even thought of it. His mind eventually caught up with his instincts. Then, he laughed. "Jealousy, dear? That does not become you."

"You're to be our king. You're to be our legend, our hero. You're to open these damn walls caging us in and let us see the rest of the world!" Her voice had risen to a shout. "There is talk in the castle. Soon, there will be talk in the street. If you're keeping a female who is not your queen, publicly, it undermines your position."

"You mean, unless that female happens to be you?" Rook questioned, before bowing his head toward Lord Stormhale. "Pardon me, Father."

"There's never any offense in saying the truth. Kelina, we have higher concerns than your feeling slighted on this council. If you can't concentrate on important matters, I suggest you return to your chambers."

The female was fuming. Rook fixed her with his gaze and entered her mind, reading her devious schemes. He rarely did so with her. Her mind was like poison.

"Kelina. I will only say this once and I expect you to understand it. I pray you understand it. Do not touch Kira. Do not think of harming her in any way. Should you do so, I will be obliged to treat you as an enemy. You know what I do to my enemies, sister."

He didn't think he'd ever threatened her before. He'd had no cause to until now. She averted her eyes, and he could feel she was tamed. For now.

"Again, who would ride west for me?"

All lords around the table volunteered.

Good. His attention had to stay focused on the one thing that mattered. For him. For his people.

Destroying those damn walls.

EIGHTEEN
NORTHERN FOLK

After marching north for a week on foot in the snow, traversing a good hundred miles each day, Devi's feet had been begging for mercy. She'd healed herself and the others with elemental charms at dawn after they were done, and Gallal had accomplished what he could with herbs and salves, with only moderate relief. She had never been so glad to see Alarik.

Beyond the relief that riding provided, she'd also missed the animal. They'd bonded on their journey; his presence was comforting.

Devi rode with Telenar behind her, and Vale walked alongside her. He let Midnight carry Gallal and Jeryn.

The poor girl was bundled in furs and holding on to a blackstone for dear life. She was of the north, but she hadn't been dressed for a journey like the one she'd embarked on to find them. It was lucky she'd survived.

They'd spent the night in the mountains as discussed, and now they were heading to the first town surrounding the immortal city. Rayon, a small town Jeryn had picked because she had family with whom she hoped to stay for a while.

It was little more than a hamlet; there were a hundred houses built around a town square with a deep well.

"I doubt we'll see any scions here."

Jeryn snorted. "Unless it's time to collect taxes, probably not. If you head down this alley, my family lives in the house with the blue door, I think."

Gallal headed in the direction Jeryn pointed to as Vale brought his hand to Alarik's reins and said, "We should patrol around the town. See if there's any store where we might buy adequate clothing."

Though they still had the Corantian habits they'd purchased on their way to Staren, the clothing marked them as foreigners from the east, which would incite questions. People dressed differently in each region of the realm.

Besides, Rula was more likely to be seen as she rode ahead, so Devi had given her the clothing. Gallal, Telenar, and Rula didn't have adequate disguises.

They rode around town, meeting curious and mistrustful eyes. All of the buildings appeared residential. There were no businesses at all.

"We're attracting too much attention," said Telenar.

"Unavoidable in such a small community. Here, it might be irrelevant, as long as they don't alert the authorities. Let's make a stop." Valerius put on his best smile and headed to the first door on their right. He knocked.

It took a whole minute for someone to open the door.

"Hello there. My companions and I are heading to Reguniev and we're almost out of supplies. May I enquire as to the best place to get what we need for the rest of our journey?"

The high fae male in front of him eyed them all, before echoing, "Reguniev, eh?"

He wasn't buying it.

Devi tensed on her saddle, half-expecting him to call for guards.

The villager crossed his arms in front of his chest and eyed Valerius first, then Devi. "You should hide your eyes. They all talk about them purple eyes. You have the kind of magic that can alter your appearance, right? And the lady has a reputation, too. They say she's stunning beyond belief, like a dark-haired goddess of death. Well, if Death came to me, I'd like her to look like you, that's for sure. Wear a cloak."

Devi dismounted Alarik. "Who talks about us?"

She exchanged a concerned glance with Vale.

The male snorted. "Who doesn't? That's a better question! That's all anyone wants to speak about at the pub. We hear news from the east, saying an army is claiming cities in the name of Valerius Blackthorn. And more whispers come from the west now. An armada from the sea, hey?" He grinned like this news warmed his heart. "Smells like change to me."

He didn't exactly sound upset about the fact that elves and fae were taking over his realm, just like Jeryn and many other fae. Regrettably, their loose tongues complicated matters.

"We aim to travel in secrecy," Vale told him.

If his brothers knew he was coming, they'd never make it past the doors of the immortal city.

The villager tsked, shaking his head. "We fair folk don't converse with the gods. We're too insignificant for their notice. However, whispering amongst ourselves may serve you well, Your Grace. For instance, birds whispered that a purple-eyed lord might be heading this way. So, we have food, and clothes and horses ready in the town square. Not great beasts like yours, but they'll suffice."

Vale twisted his expression into the bland mask he used whenever he didn't want to reveal what he felt, all while Devi could feel the turmoil inside him—inside her. They were one and his feelings were hers. He was terrified of taking on the weight of these people's expectations, scared to disappoint them, and perhaps even put them in danger by accepting their assistance.

If his feelings could reach and affect her, Devi reasoned hers might just calm his. So she told herself—and him—that he cared. Caring was enough. If he came into power, he'd do his best for them. If he failed, he'd do his best to see that no harm befell them.

He was enough.

The corner of Vale's lips twitched. "Thank you. This will not be forgotten," he said.

The villager nodded before closing his door, and they headed back to the town square, where two more horses loaded with supplies were indeed waiting.

Food, fresh bread that made Devi's stomach roar with anticipation, water, cloaks, and fur blankets.

This was not a rich village. They must have pooled all of their resources to provide that much for them.

"We should give them money."

"They aren't asking for money," Telenar interjected. "They're asking for a king in their corner. A greater request, in my opinion."

NINETEEN

LORD OF THE DALE

The great, noble fae of Elderdale were not fond of feeding their children at the breast. Or teaching their children. Or having much to do with them, until they were old enough to hold a debate on the taste of berry wine.

Like most nobles, Devin had been placed in the arms of a lower fae servant the moment his courtesan mother had expelled him from her body. The lower fae, Medera, had just had a son herself: Jibriel. They were fed together, and later, taught together.

Many lords forgot their breast-brothers when they were old enough to frequent their peers. Devin insisted Jibriel join him in the Academy.

Jibriel's father was never discussed, although Devin suspected that he must have been a high or at least common fae, because while he didn't have magic, Jibriel was stronger and faster than Devin at hand-to-hand combat. He was also clever.

When they graduated, Devin saw that his friend joined the Royal Guard. Now, they were too busy to meet often, but still they made time for each other whenever they could.

Devin had been sparring with Jibriel since they were children, and he'd never even come close to beating him without his magic. He hadn't realized how much Shea's tutelage had changed him until he got Jibriel on his ass.

The fae stared at him in disbelief, and laughed, getting back on his feet.

"Oh, it's on."

At Jibriel's first lunge, as fast and precise as it was powerful, Devin started to suspect that his friend had always gone easy on him. He managed to parry that attack, despite requiring all of his strength. Before he had time to regroup, Jibriel drew his arm back and leaped in the air, landing right next to Devin. He thrust the blade at him again, aiming for his breastplate-covered heart. Jibriel stopped when it hit against the protection. If they'd been fighting for real, he could have effortlessly pushed it past.

"You're dead, Your Highness."

"How strong are you, exactly?" Devin knew his breast-brother had never lost a fight, but this was ridiculous; his every movement seemed effortless.

Jibriel shrugged. "I do well enough."

"You should be guarding me." If Jibriel had been with him in the unseelie realm, things might have ended differently. "In fact, you shall."

Jibriel shook his head. "That's not how that works, you know it. The king is guarded by knights, people with the right name and the right ancestors. Not bastards. They might put up with me in the guard because we're friends. However, if you promoted me to a place I haven't earned, there would be a riot."

Devin snorted. "Who says the name is right? Who says you matter?"

Jibriel sighed. "The gentry."

"The *king*. As it happens, that's me. I left Elderdale with traitors who made underhanded deals with Corantius, and you know what happened. I only survived because of luck. Because they underestimated me. I need to be surrounded by people I trust if I'm to weather this storm." And he could count the people he trusted on one hand. "Say yes, Lord Jibriel."

His friend laughed. "That sounds weird. Lord of what, exactly?"

"You could have the Rivers lands. Their heir refused them."

"The Rivers lands are one of the largest estates in our realm. You'd make me more powerful than half your advisors."

"As I said, I need men loyal to me in places of power." Devin didn't make this request lightly. If he gave an irrelevant duchy to Jibriel, the lords would keep ignoring and belittling him. No matter his origins, the lord of Rivers would be of consequence in their realms.

"Why now?" Jibriel wondered out loud. "You could have done something like that anytime, even before you were king. No one would have questioned you giving away title and territories. You were the heir of the realm. So, why are you giving titles now?"

Devin thought it through. "I never would have guessed that you cared. That you wanted to be a noble."

"I don't want to," Jibriel replied. "Titles are nonsense to me. It won't change who I am, in or out. But a post in your guard? That means something. Still, you're not answering the question. Are you scared something might happen to you here?"

Devin's eyes darted to the door. "I wasn't meant to come back from Asra. Everyone who maneuvered to make me leave the realm has been plotting against me. I have many enemies and I don't know for sure who they are." That wasn't strictly true. "Except for my father. He's clearly against me."

It had never made sense why Kraven, at the peak of his health, had given him the throne. He'd meant to get rid of him. Which begged the question: why?

Jibriel whistled. "So, we're at war with the King Father. And possibly everyone else."

That covered it.

"What about the unseelie queen?" Jibriel asked.

Devin laughed. "Well, that's the one person we don't have to worry about. I was at her mercy for a month, and all she did was train my incompetent ass."

"Ah! Well, that explains why you almost made me break a sweat today."

Almost.

"You'd get along," Devin said. "And I'd pay to see you fight her."

If only to see Jibriel on his ass, for once.

"Yeah, right. Me, getting along with a queen."

"Why not? You're a fancy lord now."

His friend grimaced. "That's going to take some getting used to." After a beat, he asked, "So what are we going to do about them? The king, the advisors, everyone who's scheming right now."

Devin had wondered the same thing and come out without any answer since they'd entered the city. Now, he suddenly knew. Having Jibriel by his side had reminded him that with the right people next to him, he could feel stronger.

"I have an idea, actually. Could you call for a meeting with my advisors for me, for sundown? All of them, and Shea too. I need to get changed."

Despite his coronation, Devin had kept wearing his simpler clothing, and he'd removed the crown from his head as fast as he could after it had been placed on it.

Two hours later, he entered the council chamber in blue and silver damask, with a silk scarf around his shoulder, wearing his sword on his hip and the cumbersome, heavy silver crown on his head. Jibriel shadowed his steps.

His twelve advisors and the unseelie queen sat around a triangular table. Kraven had taken one angle of the triangle, and Shea, the other. The third remained vacant for him.

He remained still and wordless, standing next to his seat, until one of the lords had the decency to stand and bow.

"Your Grace," said Edevan Luwss.

He was the lord of war, protecting the borders of their lands north and west, everywhere except the coast.

Devin inclined his head toward him. Taking a cue, the other advisors stood. All save for Shea and Kraven.

"Good. Now that you're on your feet, you may get out. All of you."

They watched him with horror and hatred, barely veiled. Shea grinned, amused and, unless he was mistaken, proud. But not surprised.

"Sir…"

"I suppose you may remain, Luwss. Let it not be said that I do not reward common sense. The rest of you can find yourselves another king to counsel."

The deep, grave timbre of Farekin Persevel resounded in the entire room as he roared, "We have been serving the realm for longer than you have lived, boy!"

"Yes, and then you betrayed the realm. All of you, some of you, I care not. I will make the decisions brought to my attention alone, until I can vouch for advisors who will not betray me. Father, you may also go."

Now, he sat, pulling a stack of paper to him. They were the letters from the lords of each corners of the realm, detailing the issues they were facing.

The advisors remained on their feet, too shocked to move, but finally, the first cursed and walked away. Edevan took his seat.

Kraven was last to get up and walk away, then he stopped at the door, and turned back to his son.

"You will regret this."

"You will regret attempting to have me killed, Father. Next time you move against me, I suggest you don't miss. Otherwise, I'll have your head, as well as anyone still loyal to you."

Kraven's nostrils flared. Nevertheless, he finally walked away.

"Well, that's certainly a lot more comfortable," Shea stated. "Now, what's your decision about this war, seelie king?"

"I'll hear your counsel, first. You've left your city, your realm, to come here. I don't think you've ever told me why. It's time we talk. Queen to king."

"Yes, I believe it is." Shea's gaze lifted toward his new knight. "What do they call you?"

"Jibriel, Your Grace."

"Well, sit. If there's one person standing in the room, I prefer it to be me."

He didn't need to be told twice.

She glanced at Edevan before focusing on Devin again. "In a few days, perhaps a week—my visions do not come timestamped, unfortunately—the walls around the continent will fall."

Devin's eyes widened in horror and his expression was mirrored by the lord of war and Jibriel, all while Shea carried on as if she hadn't just told him that their world was ending.

"The orc lords know the secrets of Asra—its hidden passages, its weaknesses—as well as I. Asra will fall. The gates of Carvenstone, the other ancient land of my people, have already been breached by a force I could not have prevented. It would take a thousand sorcerers to rebuild the spells around the place. Elderdale will stand. If it is well protected," she added.

The certainty of her claim was the only comfort he could find.

"If the walls fall…how many orcs will we face?"

"There are billons scattered around the dead seas and the barren wastelands. Reaching us will take them some time. Time is our ally. The walls may be rebuilt. As long as another overking is crowned in time."

Devin exchanged a glance with two seelie in the room.

"What would you advise, Shea?"

"We'll recall the villages surrounding Elderdale, make everyone too far to reach us find shelter either in their lords' keeps, or in the Graywoods. The elves who remain there will harbor them. Then, we close the gates of Elderdale and prepare for a siege. But the real war is north. Our purpose here is to protect the people who cannot fight for themselves. I say, send soldiers you trust—the best you can spare—to take the portal of Daryn and join the forces in the north. The folks of Carvenstone have landed on the western coast of Corantius. The elves are attacking the east. However, they may not be enough. If the orcs swarm the immortal city before the overking rises, there will be no hope for any creature on the Isle."

"Even if our soldiers set out now, would they arrive on time?" Edevan asked.

"The portal will make them appear at the borders of Elvendale, cutting out half the journey. And if they ride our dyrmounts, then yes. They will."

Silence fell as Devin deliberated. "Very well. Lord Luwss, you have your orders. Send the city guard to aid the surrounding villages in their evacuation. See that messages are sent to ensure the rest of the realm gets to safety. Jibriel, you'll command the guard. Luwss, the knights are yours. Shea Blackthorn, will you protect this city, and this realm?"

The unseelie queen nodded. "That's why I'm here."

"Isn't it your duty?" Jibriel was confused for all of two seconds. Then he shook his head in disbelief. "You can't mean to go north."

"We have fifty dyrmounts. We can contribute fifty soldiers to the real fight. Do you think that would make a difference?"

"And how would your sacrificing yourself help anything?" Luwss raved.

"Because I can command the hundred thousand gryffins who live in our realm."

There was silence around the room, at first.

"Succession," Luwss stated. "You will make the matter of succession clear, in case your body rots under the snow in a month's time. I won't bow to your father again, understood?"

Then Jibriel turned to Shea. "Is he? Going to rot."

"Some things are yet unclear."

Devin's heart sank. But then, she added, "Others are not. Your king will see another summer."

TWENTY
HORN

Elden had questioned his promise the moment it had crossed his lips. Still, the words were out and could not be unsaid. He'd told his daughter and the fae prince that his army would support them, support their claim, if they managed the impossible.

He hadn't done it without cause. The sword and the crown rendered Valerius Blackthorn the single most powerful being on the Isle, whether he knew it or not.

The elven realm had been built to escape the wars of the realm, to ensure that his people stayed safe. Waging war on foreign soil wasn't their nature, or their purpose.

But for all that, he had to admit, it was rather fun.

He'd long despised the ways of Corantius, and taking their cities, turning them into what they should have been all along, havens of peace for fae and the remnants of humanity, was an incomparable pleasure.

Besides, Elden hadn't had the opportunity to stretch his muscles for some time. There were some scions who did almost pose a challenge.

Qirdess, the lord of Beraniel was a well-known warrior. He stayed behind his walls, letting his men die for him, while Loxy's forces held a siege for five days. Then, his people had snuck past the guards and opened the gates. Qirdess finally stepped out, along with a hundred knights.

"May I?" Loxy asked, watching him sway his axe as he rose to meet them in the field.

Elden wouldn't have civilian deaths on his head; he'd waited for him out of the city.

"You've had your fun for five days," Elden reminded her. "And you dispatched the lord of Denere, too."

She pouted—by far her most terrible weapon. Fortunately, he'd known her for long enough to grow indifferent to it.

"How about a wager?" Elden proposed, pulling a gold mark out of his cloak. "Heads for the lady?"

"I think not. If you propose heads, I'll take the tail."

"Do you believe me dishonorable? How shocking."

"I just know you usually get what you want, one way or another."

Elden made no answer.

Yes, he was used to things going his way. He planned details to ensure victory, always a step or two ahead of everyone else.

His most obvious move had been to send Kira away. The hotheaded girl was his pride and joy—he loved her as much as he loved her sister. They were his flesh, his mind, his power.

Unlike Devira, Kira was alone, weaker than she liked to believe, and too prone to jump head first into danger.

It had been a month since he'd received any news of her. His spies around the Isle, be they birds, beasts, or fae, had no word of her—not since the fall of Carvenstone.

If they won this rebellion, if they enthroned Valerius, a king who'd be fair to all on the Isle, but the cost for that victory was his daughter's blood, he would have lost the only fight that mattered.

"You're thinking of her, are you not?"

Elden lifted his eyes to Loxy. He often forgot she was their mother. Their coupling had been without much emotion, and they hadn't exactly co-parented either child.

"Which one?"

"Your favorite."

Elden laughed. "I don't have a favorite daughter."

"You so do. Clearly."

"Fine. Which one is my favorite?"

"Devira."

That showed how well the female knew him.

Elden launched the coin in the air and caught it in his palm. He extended his hand to let Loxy see the result.

"Heads." She groaned. "You knew I'd pick tails. You baited me into it."

"You're so very mistrusting, dear. Now excuse me. I have an idiot to dispatch to hell."

Elden dismounted his horse, lest the barbarian aim his axe at his loyal beast, and walked forward. "May I?" he asked, passing one of his foot soldiers, hand extended.

The female bobbed her head and handed him her lance.

He didn't need to use his sword for the likes of Qirdess the Coward.

Elden twirled the weapon in his hand to feel its weight while running forward, ahead of his armies. When he reached the front line, he aimed, drew his arm back, and threw the lance.

Qirdess was fast enough to attempt to alter his course, though it only resulted in changing his path by a fraction of an inch. The lance hit him on the side of his neck, instead of between the eyes, where Elden had aimed. The armor protected him some, delaying his suffering: the weapon had planted itself deep enough to guarantee his death, shallow enough to make it slow.

Elden grimaced. "That could have been cleaner."

"Mayhaps. But I'd wager it'll make a nice song, sir," one of his soldiers suggested.

"Marvelous idea. We'll try to compose it tonight after the people have elected their new ruler."

Whatever reply the soldier gave was drowned in the scream of a horn coming from the back of the forces.

Elden frowned, turning to face Loxy. That was one of their scouts; there was no mistaking the sound of their own horn.

Loxy didn't see him, gaze set in the distance, behind the army.

Elden drowned out the sounds around him and extended his mind to reach a greater distance.

Then he heard them. Thousands of hooves hitting the floor at a great speed. Shouts of orders muffled by the hundreds of miles that separated them.

Finally. The Corantians had responded to their attacks.

The real war was starting.

He returned to his horse and mounted it.

"I'll take the east," Loxy announced.

He nodded. As the mother of his children, she was given greater liberty than most of his commanders. The others awaited their orders.

"Veran, west flank. Revere, I want your archers with boards on the surrounding hills to cut their retreat. Ylli, I need to know their numbers. Sirel, you stay hidden until we know whether we're outmatched."

All acquiesced and moved to surround the Corantian forces.

Now, Elden was thinking about his second daughter.

Playing at war against ridiculously unmanned cities was one thing, but an open conflict against thousands of scions, quite another.

He prayed Devira came through, and fast. Otherwise, win or lose, there would be too many losses on both sides.

TWENTY-ONE
LEGACY

"Are you sure about this?"

Devin smiled at Jibriel. "Why? Do you want to go back to the city and tell and tell Shea Blackthorn I've changed my mind?"

The fae shivered, then replied, "I will, if you order it. You're our king."

Devin smiled. "Perhaps. Yet she'll defend the city. Her people are here, too."

Devin embraced his breast-brother, before stepping outside the gates.

Among the fighters mounted on the fifty dyrmounts, one face stood out. Devin smiled, approaching Jiya. "Are you coming north?"

"Someone has to make sure your pretty head stays on your shoulders." She grinned. "Besides, my best friend is in the north with Shea's son. I'll help however I can."

She was the loyal sort. "Glad to hear it."

Jiya looked around, to the five thousand soldiers on foot. "So, we have awesome horses, but we'll have to trot alongside soldiers on foot again. That blows."

Devin laughed. "Not precisely. This time, it's your turn to try keeping up."

He whistled a clear command and spelled his voice with airshadow to reach far and wide. Before long, the first wave of winged beasts appeared from the nearby woods and plains. Then more came, and those who lived down in the south, the beasts hiding north and west. All landed before the gates of Elderdale and bowed their heads low.

Devin stepped in front of the closest creature and spoke out to his men. "All right, those of you who haven't ridden a gryffin before, it's quite simple. Sit astride them like you would a horse, and while you may hold on to their neck, it's not necessary. They will not let you fall, and if they do, they'll catch you again. Talk to them; they understand as much as any of you. The more they like you, the greater your chance of survival. And above all, there's one rule. *Do not pull their feathers.*"

"Really?" Jiya yelled as Devin climbed his beast. "I get your old boring horse and you guys get *gryffins?*"

"Are you ever content with your lot, female?"

"I would be if I had my own gryffin."

Devin laughed and whispered, "Rise."

He would have given the unseelie soldier a gryffin if he could, but Jiya wore the green cape of Shea's officers, indicating that she was in charge of some of their soldiers. It wouldn't do to separate them from their captain.

His beast punched the ground with its sharp talons and took flight, heading to the portals in the Graywoods.

They could have reached it in mere hours, except they had to stop frequently to let the dyrmounts catch up.

Devin had felt some guilt at the thought of roping in wild creatures for war; it felt like abusing his power over the gryffins. Despite that, they seemed happy. Every time they stopped, the beasts played with one another, sparring in displays of strength and brutality that made him glad they were on his side.

He realized that the gryffins were probably more enthusiastic about going to war than any of the fae forming his company. Fighting was their nature, their predilection.

Devin wondered how the relationship between the Farels and the beasts had started at the beginning. It was a pact sealed in blood, that much was clear; otherwise, the beasts wouldn't obey him now. Whatever deal his ancestors had made, they'd ensured it was linked to their bloodline.

"Do you know why your king answers me, I wonder?" he asked, looking in the eyes of his mount.

The beast was silent of course. Gryffins had never been able to speak. Still, looking in its dark eyes, Devin was sure that the beast knew. Perhaps it even remembered it.

The gryffin puffed out its chest and opened its mouth. A high-pitched screech resounded, and suddenly, as surely as if the beast had spelled out the words, Devin knew.

"A blood debt."

He frowned. It didn't compute. "Saving one of you wouldn't have warranted the fealty of all of your kind, I don't think."

The beast lowered its head to Devin's chest. He instinctively lifted his hand to its side, and the moment he touched it, he saw the image of another time.

Small, hungry, thirsty, wounded gryffins were locked in cages, eating whatever rats or worms wandered into their prison until a little boy with dark hair and eyes was locked up among them. Their prisoners had expected the beasts to eat him, and they would have, had he been grown, but they didn't feed on children, no matter their race.

The boy took sharp bones from the floor and used them to unlock the doors as soon as the guards were distracted.

Devin's gryffin stepped back.

"Ah. One of my ancestors saved you. All of you. From..."

There had been something peculiar about the guards. They didn't look quite like fae. Bulkier, taller than common fae, with rounded ears. Their skin had seemed pale, almost bluish.

The gryffin screeched again and Devin knew.

"Orcs."

No wonder they were so enthusiastic about going to fight against more orcs in the north.

"Do you have a name?"

The gryffin's talons scratched the ground impatiently, as though Devin should have known, or at least guessed.

"Queen. You're the queen."

The beast shook its head proudly.

"Well, it's an honor. And glad that we can communicate, Queen."

The dyrmounts and their knights were approaching again.

"Up for another ride?"

Queen screeched. "All right then. Let's go."

TWENTY-TWO
CITY OF STENCH

In Verdessa, a larger village, an old couple had prepared them rooms so they could rest during the day. Right before they reached Kevanon, a river town large enough to have a regular posting of scion guards at its gates, a merchant awaited them with a wagon full of hay under which Vale and Devi hid so they could enter without being seen. And when Rula rode back to them after scouting Romel, the last stop before the immortal city, she told them the guards were gone when she'd reached the gates.

"Some fae slipped them sleeping draughts during their lunch break. We have an hour or two."

Everyone was taking risks, and no one seemed to have mentioned their arrival, though, no doubt, Rook would have handsomely rewarded information about Vale's and Devi's whereabouts.

Finally, a week after reaching the first village surrounding the Crystal Court, they were inside the immortal city.

They'd entered via merchant gates, along with a long line of artisans who'd thoroughly, purposely ignored them.

Devi didn't think she'd ever seen a city so rotten. In the distance, the inner city was white and opalescent, but once they entered downtown, the streets were marred, stinking of waste and sewer.

"The fae live here," Telenar told them. "The scions, in the clean, gated territory a mile forward, right at the feet of the Court of Crystal."

No wonder that they'd be so willing to aid a prince they didn't even know. Anything was better than being condemned to a life of suffering, living on top of each other in fetid streets because of what they were born.

Devi had thought about the unseelie realm, her home, about her own survival, and about the prospect of having billions of orcs invading their land, at first. Now, it was more. Corantius was everything that was wrong with the differentiation of the castes, only a thousandfold, and flipped on its head, because in the rest of the Isle, the high fae were the apex of the food chain.

Devi remembered Rook telling her this, many times.

"You generally just hang out in your room until the last possible second. Not that I blame you. It's like the size of my entire place. Plus the neighbor's. And you have people wiping your butt too."

She'd dismissed it, thought that he was unfair to envy her, because she did her best for her people; she was a good lord, compared to the rest of the court. Now she understood what he'd meant to make her comprehend. That her privilege was wrong at the core.

Devi was starting to understand Rook, and she hated it. She wished she could have painted him with a villain's brush and been done with it. But if any of the fae condemned to live in such conditions had had the power to put a stop to it, would they have done anything different?

Devi remembered her father's tale of a Prince of Worms, desperate and starving, alone in the woods. If his orc mother had shown him kindness before she passed away, there was no surprise in his obsession for that part of his family. Rook's tale was a tragedy. Nevertheless, if they let him win, the entire Isle would share his fate… his doom.

Her eyes remained ahead, on the shimmering castle beyond the gates of the inner city.

She felt sorry for her former friend. All the same, she'd drag him to the throne and then let him rot in a dungeon for the rest of his days.

"Naelynn?"

She and Vale had fallen back into their borrowed names with ease. She turned to him.

"It's getting late. We should rest. Let's find an inn, shall we?"

In other words, they should get off the street before they became too noticeable. This wasn't a village or a small town. They'd passed a soldier on every street corner.

"Any recommendations?" she asked Telenar.

He rode one of the village horses by behind her. "I left a thousand years ago," he reminded her. "I haven't stayed up to date with the city gazette. But I'd say anywhere in this part of town should do nicely."

In order for them to be inconspicuous, in any case.

Devi nodded and scanned the storefronts, in search of an inn. This street seemed to be the province of fish and meat vendors, however. If there had been lodging here, she might have ignored it. She doubted she could sleep with the smell all around.

They reached an intersection and took a larger avenue, better presented and marginally cleaner. The streets of tanners, shoemakers, and dressmakers kept going until it reached a square with pubs.

Devi bit her lip. "Ruven?" she called to Vale, still sticking to their pseudonyms.

He shook his head. "It might be a little too busy for us."

They went down that street and reached a serpentine alley with a few inns. That was more like it.

"No."

Devi lifted a brow, turning to Vale questioningly.

"These aren't the pleasant sort."

"We've traveled in the snow for a month. Pleasant is relative."

"He means to say they're whorehouses, brothels, that sort of thing," Rula translated.

Oh.

"Would they rent us rooms?"

Telenar snorted. "Certainly. Although their rate may be by the hour, and they'd have certain assumptions about you ladies."

Devi rolled her eyes. "I don't care about assumptions."

She tugged Alarik's reins to turn toward the alley, when Vale made Midnight step forward and bar the way. "I said no. These…establishments will be owned by scions," he added in a whisper.

Ah, that certainly changed things.

They'd spent too much time here already, and some eyes were darting toward them.

"All right. You pick a place, then."

Valerius rode forward, until they reached an option he approved of—a small bed and breakfast along the outer city wall.

He paid for four rooms for a week in cash, keeping his demeanor friendly and open, making a show of staying downstairs for a drink as though he had nothing to hide.

The city was different from the villages and towns they'd crossed. The gazes on them were not merely curious; they felt greedy. Desperate. Devi guessed half of these people would sell them out for a hot meal.

When they finally headed up to their rooms, she said, "I'll take the first turn of guard. We're going to need you at the top of your form. We have to keep our appearances hidden."

Vale smirked. "No, you sleep first. I'm just fine."

He felt fine. He looked it, too. She wondered why; back in Rhionhave, changing their features in the minds of those they came across had drained him.

He answered her unasked questioned, pulling his crown from his cloak and handing it to her.

"Is it working now?"

He shrugged. "I'm not sure? A little, at least. It's certainly replenishing my energy. I doubt that's all it's supposed to do, though."

Devi smiled, giving it back to him. "Well, every little bit helps. And if you're sure, I'll sleep."

She didn't even get undressed, instead heading right to the bed, and she was asleep before her head hit the pillow.

She didn't think she'd been out of it for more than a couple of minutes before Vale whispered in her ear softly, waking her up. The light outside had waned, giving way to a soft reddish dusk, so she must have crashed for hours. Or days, who knew?

Vale's alarm poured through her veins as surely as if it was her own. "What is it?"

He shushed her by bringing one finger to her lips before pointing to the window. She followed him, staying close to the wall and looking out to the streets.

Soldiers in armor. Too many of them, all entering this place.

The others had been right, they'd brought too much attention to themselves earlier in the street. Dammit, it was all her fault

She had so many questions, but could speak none aloud. Then she remembered she didn't have to. Not with a psychic who was bonded to her mind.

"What about the others?" she asked, directly reaching for his mind.

"I've warned them. We have to separate. They'll get out of here easier than us."

The scions would be after Vale, and her, his known associate. There was no knowing whether his mind tricks would work on this lot. Vale was powerful, but some were naturally well protected against mind invasion.

Abandoning their friends went against all of her instincts. Devi's hand went to the hilt of the Enlightened sword she'd never removed. *Let's fight,* she wanted to challenge.

And then an annoying, overly smug voice echoed in her mind. Words that shouldn't have made such an impact on her.

If you value the lives of the few over the many every time you have a hard choice to make, you are doomed.

She hadn't heeded them when she'd seen an alternative. But now, so close to their goal?

She nodded, opening the window, and leapt on the banister, then on the roof. It was lucky that night had fallen; scions could still see as clearly as they, but nature was still on their side.

Devi called to her air power and clouds gathered overhead, mist shrouding the streets.

She jumped down, and Vale joined her, equally silent and agile.

With a last glance toward the inn, seeking the window next to theirs, she turned back and followed Vale's steps north.

Toward the castle.

It was time.

In the distance, bells started ringing, loud and incessant. Even if she couldn't feel the unease of the crowd below, she would have been able to tell that those sounds weren't usual.

They were bells of war.

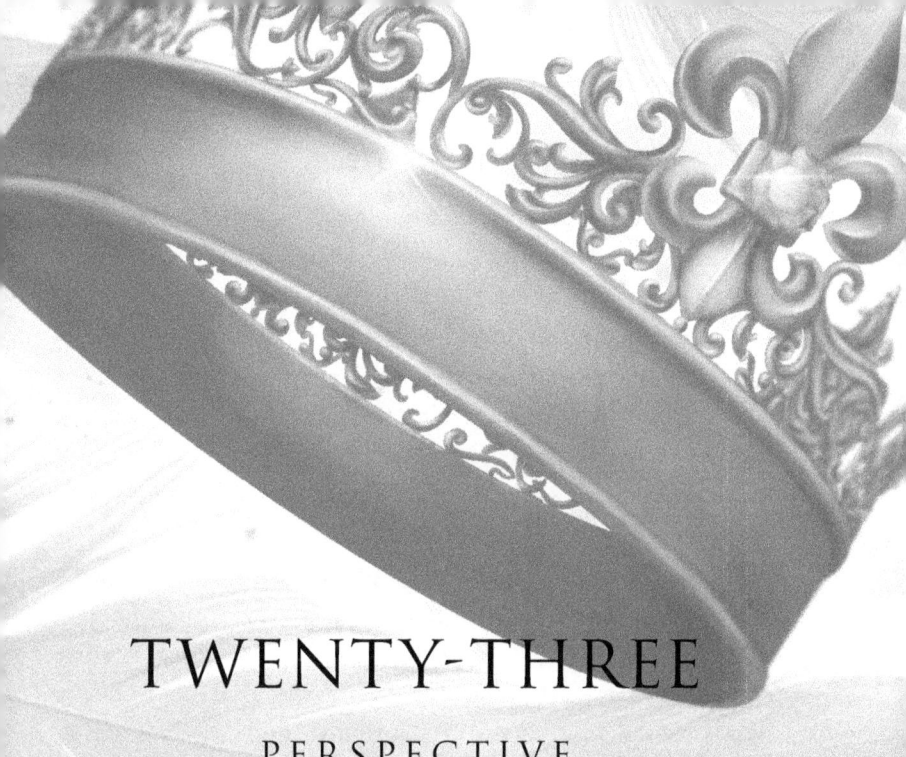

TWENTY-THREE
PERSPECTIVE

Atop the highest tower, Rook observed the city below, eyes narrowing on the crowd beyond their gates.

It had been faint at first, but know he could feel it, feel him. His second brother. He was close.

Good.

Rook needed to conclude the matter, one way or another.

Rook closed his eyes, trying to decide on a course of action. Inevitable as his brother's presence was, it had come sooner than he'd expected it, considerably changing his timeline. His goal hadn't changed. And if life had taught him anything, it was that there were many paths leading to the same summit.

Now that Valerius had made it here, alive, Rook had to face the possibility that he might take the throne. Sitting on a dusty old chair wasn't what he'd aimed to accomplish, all these years. Let the boy take the throne if it chose him. Becoming overking wasn't the only way to gain the power Rook needed.

An idea had been skirting the edge of his mind since he'd heard of his brother's adventures in Staren. Valerius had blown the security by destroying the generator operating the walls surrounding the Stormhale keep.

Rook's gaze now lit on the highest tower in the immortal city, directly overlooking the overking's keep. The cumbersome steel building was an eyesore, yet it was necessary—it generated the power that kept their walls closed around the city, and around the Isle itself.

Rook jumped down the roof, his wings extending so he could soar until he landed. He winced, and then laughed. Kira and her damnable fire had certainly done some damage. Most wounds healed fast. His wings were so sensitive he still felt the burn. He should have, could have, might have, killed her for it.

He hadn't. A strategic mistake that had considerably weakened him, he realized now. It was too late to do anything about that.

Rook was all for taking the world as it was and molding it to his purposes. Regretting the past was a waste of time and energy.

He marched forth, until he'd reached the bottom of the power structure. A dozen guards had been posted around its entrance. They wore a different, unfamiliar silvery armor. Fyriron, he realized. The moment he approached, they pointed their spears at his chest.

Rook smiled. "I don't believe you're up to speed with the change of hierarchy in this kingdom."

The closest guard replied, "We do not answer to any entity in this world, child."

Rook stilled. He felt it in their voice and energy; these were true ancients, like the handful of gods scattered around their world. But they didn't feel like Enlightened.

"Who do you answer to, then?"

"The crown."

Rook canted his head. "And if I win the crown and my first order is to dismember you for disrespecting me now, what will you do?"

"*The* crown," the guard emphasized. "The crown ruling over all gods, the crown of light and shadow. We answer to Nalini Krane and Kai Lor Hora. Their order is that none shall pass. And none shall."

Rook stilled. He recognized the names from tales of Elden Star, who mentioned the tales of rulers of the Enlightened world when he'd had a little too much wine on a cold night. Nothing he'd seen in his thousands of years had indicated that those entities still had a presence anywhere on the Isle, on Ertia.

His eyes narrowed. He wasn't going to win this fight by butting in. He had to think his way around it.

His gaze went skyward again, and Rook smiled.

No, not around it. Above it.

"Suit yourself." Rook waved a goodbye, turning his heels and returning to the palace.

He could get in through the air, if the guards were distracted. Maybe. Though he doubted he'd have more than once chance.

He had to get in, and do what needed to be done, before these creatures realized he'd slipped by.

Rook headed to the cavernous throne hall inside the palace. He did his best to avoid it in general; just being in the presence of the large throne on its imposing dais was enough to drain some of his strength.

He pushed the door open. The blue chamber was not empty. Since the night he'd killed Orin, it had been guarded by two. Pallas and Iapetus, often. Thea and Hyperion. A few weeks ago, Styx had also arrived and taken a turn.

The gods wanted to be there at all times, so they could witness the rise of their new leader when one of them was finally enthroned.

He was glad to find Iapetus present. That titan didn't seem to wholly detest him. Yet.

Styx was another story. She'd never said a word to him, and she didn't even bother to glare, but when her dead eyes were on him, Rook had the impression she was picturing the thousands of ways she could extract his soul from his dying corpse.

He tilted his head to invite Iapetus to step out in the corridor. The Enlightened got up from his seat at the foot of the dais and followed him.

"I have a hypothetical question for you."

"Hypothetical." Iapetus snorted. "I find that likely."

"And answering it would grant you a favor of your choosing," Rook added.

The god watched him and smiled. "I'm listening."

He wasn't about to pass up a favor from a male who could become his king.

He, like all other Enlightened, had grown used to doing what they wanted, scattered through the Isle and the rest of the world. Instead of following convention, whoever was enthroned would have the power to order them to stay at court, force them to fight for them, or worse.

They'd pay a high price for their freedom.

"If one wanted to disable the wards around the Isle, would it be possible from the tower?"

The god narrowed his eyes. "Why one would want to undo the wards that have protected this territory for thousands of years is a better question."

He could have given him a reason; instead, Rook shrugged. "One answer. One favor."

The god narrowed his eyes. Moments passed before he stated, "It's impossible. The tower only generates power. The controls are linked to the throne."

"If it generates power, wouldn't destroying it undo the wards?"

Iapetus's eyes flashed. "One answer, one favor," he repeated.

"Certainly. Except I'm under the impression you've given me a misleading answer. Is it impossible, Iapetus?"

The god started to walk away.

"You may not know me well, but I trust you understand that I will blast it into oblivion on a maybe."

"You'd destroy this kingdom's technological advancement in one single strike. Including the throne you so desire. You'd plunge us into a dark age. And we will be free to do as we please," Iapetus said, a threatening edge to his last words.

"I do not care for your electric toys. Let them burn."

For a moment, Rook wondered if the Enlightened would hit him, before remembering he couldn't. As long as Rook was one of the contenders for the throne, none of the gods could harm him. Their laws dictated it.

"The top floor. The generators for the outer shields have to reach farther than any others, so they're on the top floor. If you destroy the highest level of the tower and affect nothing else, the wall will fail, and the rest should still function."

Rook grinned, and tapped his shoulder. "There. It wasn't so hard, now, was it?"

Iapetus's teeth flashed. "One favor," he reminded him.

Now that he was done, Rook could have headed right back to the tower. And not so long ago, he might have. Instead, he walked up the flights of stairs leading to his apartments, and knocked twice on an ornate gold door, before pushing it open.

He knew better than to expect an invitation to come in.

"Dinner?" he asked Kira.

She stood next to her open window, facing away from him.

Then she turned to glare.

"How long do you intend to keep me locked up in here?"

"Who knows? One day, one month, one year, one century. Did you enjoy your walk in the garden?"

She grabbed the first object on her left—a foot-long statue—and chucked it at him. "I'm not some damn dog you can walk for an hour a day! I won't yap, heel, and be happy because I've had a bit of fresh air."

Rook laughed. Her spirit, her strength, all were fire, to the bone.

"Come, sit. I have things to tell you that may comfort you. Only with food."

She wasn't eating enough. And while it definitely had something to do with the fact that he was keeping her captive, he still hated it.

Rook rang a bell and ordered some more of her favorite dishes when a servant came.

"I hate you," she reminded him.

"I'm aware. But if you eat well, I'll tell you a thing or two about Valerius Blackthorn's whereabouts. And your sister's."

Kira's eyes widened. She ate everything on her plate, so Rook told her they were in town.

"Here." Kira's voice was a whisper, just a breath full of feelings.

Rook couldn't keep track of all of them, though he tried. Joy, happiness, relief, fear, confusion, anger.

Some made sense. Others didn't.

"I've lost you. Are you pissed or happy?"

"Stop reading my mind!" she yelled.

Rook shrugged. "Well, tell me what you're thinking and I won't have to."

A lie. He read her mind because he couldn't help it. He had to physically shield himself from her thoughts, otherwise *they* reached out to him without his even trying.

"I'm thinking that you're going to get what's coming to you. I'm thinking that Devi's going to find you and kill you."

She was telling the truth, he felt it.

Rook grinned.

Because she wasn't happy about it.

"Well, I do have a trick or two in my sleeves. Relax. I have no intention of harming your sister."

"No, you're under the impression she'll marry you, for some reason."

Now, he laughed. "No such designs, but she's a good friend of mine. I'll keep her out of what's coming next, if I can."

"Devira won't stay out of your power trip. She'll stop you."

"She'll try," Rook admitted. "You and I both know I can stop people from doing anything. With my mind. Easily."

Kira rolled her eyes.

"But…in case things don't go as planned," he said, "know that you'll be free to walk out the moment I'm killed. The spell will break if I'm not maintaining it."

Kira's gaze stayed on her glass of wine. She took it and held it up in a toast. "Here's to your funeral, then."

Again, Rook smiled.

TWENTY-FOUR
TWO PATHS

"The bells mean the city is under attack, don't they?"

Vale nodded. "I felt the wards erect around it while you were passed out. Your father must be close."

Her heart beat in her chest. Devi had been trained as a protector of the unseelie realm and as such, she would have liked to believe that she was at least a little prepared for things like these; attacks, fleeing guards, sneaking into places. Instead, while it was going on, she could hardly breathe properly.

She let Vale's calm and focus soothe her nerves.

"How do we get to the palace?" Devi asked.

It had been one thing to discuss their plan but now that they were in the city, she wasn't sure how they were supposed to manage. In Staren, it had been easy enough, with an unsuspecting lord who welcomed just about anyone at his doors. And no one had been specifically looking for them back then.

"I only visited the city once—there's one thing I remember. I was received through the main gate, right ahead. Huge, elegant high fences of iron and gold. During my short stay, however, when I wandered, I found another entrance. One no one was supposed to see from the outside. See, even in the Court of Crystal, nobles eat, sleep, and piss. They need servants."

"Fae, no doubt," Devi guessed.

He nodded, pointing at a large building on the left. "That's our ticket in. The service entrance. It goes underground and leads to the kitchens, so that they remain out of sight."

Devi bit her lip. "Won't Rook expect that?"

She'd given up trying to use any other name in order to distance herself from him. He'd been her friend, and she'd have to accept it. Embrace it, if she was to succeed in her one mission.

When—she wouldn't say "if"—they made it to the court, she was supposed to find him and lead him to the throne room.

Somehow.

"Perhaps. Still, if I know one thing after our time here, it's that we have allies in the fae of this realm. I'd say we have a better chance with them than we do aboveground, among the scions."

Devi opened her eyes and closed them again. She knew what she had to say, but the words wouldn't come out.

"It's a great idea, little elf," Vale said softly.

Damn psychic.

"Really? You made a huge fuss when Kallan offered to do just that."

He laughed. "He was volunteering to pretend being me, against enemies who clearly wanted me dead. You want to go through the main entrance so your friend keeps his attention on you while I sneak in underground. That's not remotely the same thing."

She hated it. She abhorred the thought of being away from him while they'd both be in danger.

Valerius tugged her hand, pulling her close until she was right against him, and took her mouth, slow and purposefully, his every touch making her understand what her mind already knew. He hated it too. He would do anything so that she was safe, happy, without worry. For the realm, and so that they might both bask in thousands of years of peace after this, he'd do just about anything.

"All right. If anything goes wrong, you reach out to me. Promise?" She didn't think she could bear it if she didn't know he was safe at all time.

She didn't state the obvious. That they'd never tried to communicate through a large distance. They'd always been relatively close. Even if he did end up calling her if he needed her help, there was a chance she wouldn't hear him. And vice versa.

"As long as you promise the exact same thing."

Vale handed her the charm Telenar had put together using Vale's blood before kissing her forehead one last time, leaping down to the street below.

He pulled his cloak's hood over his head and disappeared through the crowd.

Devi waited until he turned at the end of the street before making her way down herself, device firmly in hand. She walked north, through the increasingly clean and elegant streets. Higher up in the fae town, the homes were grander, larger, and the pavement, white and shining. By the time she reached the gates, every single house was as beautiful and dignified as the home where she'd grown up in Farj.

Devi looked at the device in her palm, mistrustful and unconvinced. It hadn't so much as twitched as she walked through the city. No sign of a single vibration, and it certainly wasn't lighting up.

She was going to have to look for Rook the old-fashioned way in the gargantuan palace before her. It wasn't so much a keep as an inner city, a hundred times the size of Wolvenfort.

Telenar said it should react when she was close to Vale's blood; it remained stubbornly still and dull. She sighed and stepped toward the main gates.

Watching the twelve guards behind the large barrier, something told her they weren't going to be as simple to fool as the knights of Staren.

"I wonder what you'll do. Fight them, jump the gates, just walk through the doors and tell them you're looking for me? I see all these possibilities floating above your pretty head."

Devi froze, and turned. Right behind her, Rook stood, his presence absolutely masked, just like Styx's had been. It revealed just how much power the male wielded.

"And I would have let you choose. It might have been entertaining. Regrettably, I'm in a hurry, and I don't want you harmed, Devi. Follow me and let us have a chat."

The crowd waiting in front of the gates parted to let him through, and spotting him, the guards immediately lowered the barrier. Devi remained where she stood, hand inching toward the hilt at her belt.

The only thing stopping her from drawing it was the knowledge that if Rook had read her intentions, her plans, he must have seen this too.

Seen what she hadn't said out loud to anyone. Not her father, the elven commanders, Telenar, Gallal, or even Vale.

The fact that if she couldn't force him to follow her to the throne room, she intended to kill him. That had been his initial plan for Valerius; if he was dead, the throne would only consider the remaining heirs as potential overking. But if he was alive and didn't attend, this conflict would never end, tearing the Isle down as they fought over who was supposed to rule over the ruins.

"Come on, Devi. We don't have time to waste."

He sounded bored, not even bothering to turn back and face her, which was a testament to his belief that he was in no danger from her.

Because he was stronger than her. Or because he thought that she wouldn't have the strength to kill her friend.

Devi decided she didn't need to know whether he was right on either account. For now.

She followed as he led her past the guards and left toward a flower garden.

"Are we to walk in silence? We're old friends, after all, you and I."

Devi snorted. "Right. Friends. Then you attacked my city, hunted your brother like it was a game, shot my horse, kidnapped me, and threatened to hurt my—" She stopped herself.

Pissed as she was for all the reasons she'd just listed and more, angering him might not be the wisest course of action right now.

"Mate? That's what you were about to say, right? Congratulations, by the way. When will you hold a ceremony?"

He'd either grown considerably better at hiding his rage, or he wasn't angry.

Which made no sense.

"I'll admit, I might have been hasty in my decisions, on most of those fronts. Asra had to fall. Asra was never a fae court to begin with. It had to be emptied so that my people can have it back. I'd rather send a few hundred scions to scare the little fae out of it than let thousands of orcs claim it, killing anyone within."

This again. "I don't get you. Why this obsession with orcs, Rook? You said it yourself: they kill indiscriminately."

He shrugged. "So do I. So do you. The only difference is that they don't feel bad about what they are. I am obsessed with them because they're my folk, my clan, my blood. Unlike everyone on this Isle."

"Orin had your blood. Vale has your blood."

He sent her a look full of derision and amusement. "Orin raped my mother. As for Valerius, yes. He has my blood. And he would never have cared."

"I guess you'll never know, as you started to hunt him down before he had any idea you existed."

Rook sighed. "We're not here to rehash past decisions, mistakes or otherwise."

Devi shook her head, downright confused now. "Wait, was that an apology of sorts? If so, try again."

Rook's grinned uncovered his teeth. "I don't apologize for what I am. When you have nothing, you learn to do whatever is necessary to gain what you desire. Something you wouldn't have a clue about."

Devi knew it was stupid, and she took a swing at him anyway. He blocked her fist with nonchalance and amusement. "Feisty as always. Yes. I remember how much you dislike your elders reminding you of your inexperience. That wasn't my intent, Devi. I never saw you as a naïve little child. You're quite mature. Life forged you that way. However, you are and have always been privileged, and unwilling to look at the other side. Yes, you help your people, aid them when they need a new roof. But you never have nor will you spend a day working a field or trying to see what it's like to live on a copper a week."

"None of your bullshit excuses your behavior, Rook."

"As I said, I'm not making excuses. Just telling you who I am."

He stopped now. They were close to a solitary building in the gardens, away from the castle.

"What's that, your dungeons?"

He rolled his eyes. "Hardly. This tower powers the walls around the city, the Isle, as well as most of the technology around Corantius, I understand. I'm going to blow up the top."

She stepped forward, opening her mouth to protest, when she found herself incapable of saying a word or moving a finger.

"Don't bother. I don't have time to explain myself, or hear you enumerate every little protest I've already fetched from your pretty skull. The walls come down tonight. To give me time to do that, I'm going to have to ask you to distract the guards."

Her eyes widened in shock as her limbs started to move toward the building against her will. He was really doing it: forcing her to aid him in his madness.

"They're very strong. Do whatever you need to do to stay alive, Rivers."

On that note, he unfurled his wings and took off into the air. Leaving her to grasp her sword and catch the attention of twelve scions.

No, not scions.

These things felt bigger, stronger.

Dammit.

If she got out of this alive, she really was going to kill Rook.

TWENTY-FIVE
TALES IN THE TOWER

Rook laughed at the volley of mental insults that followed him as he reached a window on the last floor of the tower. He definitely was going to pay for this trick later, but how could he resist?

All afternoon, he'd attempted to find ways to keep the Enlightened guards distracted long enough to allow him to do what he had to do, and then boom, she'd appeared. One of the handful of people in the Isle who could survive them.

He blasted the window into pieces and snuck through the opening. Inside, the dark room was filled with large, heated boxes stacked one atop each other, bright and beeping in a rhythm that was going to give him a headache soon.

He knew little about technology. His upbringing hadn't exactly been full of expensive toys for him to experiment with, and he'd never developed the taste later. He was going to have to improvise.

For a moment, he wished Kira were right here, next to him. He could certainly use her fire magic. Then he remembered that if she were present, she would have been trying to stop him, just like her twin.

Rook winced. She was also going to kick his derriere for what he'd done to Devi.

One problem at the time.

Iapetus was right; he didn't actually want to destroy all tech if he could help it, which meant that he had to try to only affect this floor. Simply unplugging the devices from their sockets wouldn't do the trick—presumably, they could simply replug it to fix it later.

He followed the dozens of entangled cords to their source. There was a round energy sphere against a wall—the generator. Frowning, Rook looked around, trying to understand how it worked, what else it might power.

"What the hell do you think you're doing?"

Rook smiled as he turned his head toward the window, impressed.

"You managed to take out all the guards?" he asked Devi.

"No, idiot. I told them what you were up to."

"And they listened?" Now, that was surprising.

"After I froze their feet. They didn't have much choice. I give you two minutes before they get out of the trap, then they'll be here to kick your ass. Rook, please. You have to see reason. Your quest to open the wall is madness. Shea told me there's billions of orcs—billions. Even if they didn't mean to destroy us, their numbers alone would put an end to our world as we know it."

"Would that be such a tragedy?"

She stomped her foot in frustration, only serving to amuse him further. "You have got to stop with the self pity! You have everything at your fingertips. More power than almost everyone here, a title as noble as titles can get, as much money as you want. Come with me to the throne room. You might be overking. And if you aren't, if Vale is chosen, he'll leave you in peace."

At that, Rook laughed. "You're incredibly naive."

"He will. Because I will make him. I'll beg and plead until he gives you a chance, if you show me you deserve one."

And she meant it. Even if he hadn't been listening to her mind, he would have been able to tell. Devi was such an open book.

"The Isle is dying. Every year, our resources go down. The elemental mages have to beg the earth for every crop. The wars that have plagued this continent for thousands of years have destroyed it to the core. You're young. You've never seen the flowers bloom at midnight or tasted fresh apples picked a few thousand years back. Now, everything is tainted. Old. The lords of Corantius are behind me because they've seen it, and they know that our solution lies beyond our wall. We need trade from the other lands. We need the orcs as much as they need us. They can bring fresh soil, grain. Before we end up a dead continent, like two of the ones in this world already."

"What makes you think that anything is better beyond our borders?"

"What makes you think that closing our doors to change is such a terrible thing? Someone needs to act. I am opening the doors because I want to see my family. I'm not pretending that it's a selfless act—it's just about me. But there are actual reasons why this needs to happen. Ostracizing ourselves is madness."

"Blowing our walls down is madness," she countered. "Not until we have some answers about what's beyond them."

"We have them! Didn't your dear queen tell you about Álfheimr?"

Devi paused. She knew that name, he could tell. "The third continent with fae, right?" she asked when she'd caught up.

"And elves. And men. And orcs. And scions. All living in harmony. They're led by a line of scions powerful enough to keep everyone in line, just like us. They brought their walls down centuries ago. And for hundreds of years, they sent messages of friendship to the leaders of this world, including Shea. Who ignored them."

"Maybe because those powerful scions, the ones strong enough to keep everyone in line, might have meant to conquer us," she shot back.

Rook shook his head. "Paranoia aside, you're missing the point. Their walls are down. They're just fine."

Both of them turned left, hearing footsteps rushing up the stairs.

"We're out of time," Rook said.

He reached out his hand, touching the edge of the round power source, and pushed a blast of energy through it, like he'd done when he destroyed the window. When nothing happened, he made it stronger, and stronger again.

"Rook, please stop this, all right? If what you say is true, we can talk. Find a way to reasonably fix our problems here."

The door opened, and the Enlightened walked in, lances pointed toward him.

No time.

He increased the amount of power, extending both hands, and finally, the sphere cracked.

Instantly, the twelve guards fell to the ground, like puppets without strings.

They hadn't been Enlightened at all. Just…devices, now powered down.

At first, nothing happened, then he felt it. An excess of power brewing beneath his feet. The ground began to shake.

Devi was at his side, pulling his arm. "Come on. Let's get out of here."

For the first time today, he thoroughly agreed with her.

They both started to run to the window, and jumped.

Too late.

The tower was imploding, large rocks the size of four horses blasting in every direction with the power of cannons.

Rook followed one specific one, his mind anticipating its trajectory. It was heading toward the castle. Worse yet…to his apartments in the west wing.

As the blast pushed him backward, Rook concentrated one hundred percent of his strength on one single thing: shouting.

Mentally yelling as loud as he could, begging Kira to hear him. He saw her rush to the balcony, and gasp in fear as she saw the huge stone heading right to her.

It hit him then. The spells. She *couldn't* get out.

Rook didn't think he'd ever performed magic with as much speed, distress, and fear, unsealing all of his hexes and blocks. He barely noticed the pain when his body crash-landed on the ground, too desperate to care that his ribs, arms, and legs hurt like hell.

There, done.

Get out now!

She jumped right out, not questioning his order for the very first time since they met.

Rook might have laughed, if what was left of the tower hadn't exploded in a second detonation made of fire so powerful it engulfed all of the gardens and half of the castle.

And him.

High in the air, Devi watched in horror. Half a mile had been blasted into oblivion, now blackened ruins. Through the thick dust, she couldn't see a thing. She needn't have stayed to know Rook couldn't survive that. With all her elemental powers, she wouldn't have made it alone. If he'd flown out, maybe. He was faster than she when flying. But he hadn't even bothered to try.

Devi looked up to the creature holding her by the shoulders, his sharp talons digging into her flesh. She wasn't going to complain.

The phoenix certainly had timing. She wondered if he'd just seen her from a distance or if he'd stayed close ever since she'd let him out of his cage in Staren.

He carried her through the air a lot faster than she was capable of, leading her out of danger.

"I need to go back now," she told him. "Please."

Her voice sounded broken to her own ears. So was her heart.

The death of the monster she'd met in Low Crest Bridge would have been one thing, but today, she'd had her Rook back. Too stubborn, too opinionated, nonetheless it had been Rook. A protector attempting to do what he considered his duty.

Just like she had to do hers.

The phoenix dropped her off on top of an intact roof, and she snuck in through an open window, twitching her hood around her head again, as she tried to find her way to the throne room.

TWENTY-SIX

BLOOD

Something felt wrong. Too easy. The guards and fae he passed were watchful, all seeming to notice him and yet, he wasn't stopped once. Not in the long underground corridors, the kitchen, and not on his way up from the servants' quarters to the vast, bright, Spartan halls.

He didn't know his way through this castle—one visit hadn't made the humongous stronghold familiar. Thankfully, with the aid of Telenar's device, he found his way to two large blue doors.

The stonelike tracker in his hand, warm and bright as a light, was telling.

Vale stilled in front of the door, hesitant. He'd never spoken to his brother. Not really. Aurelius had been at a few dinners during his one visit to the immortal city, where he'd thoroughly ignored him, and Vale wasn't one to beg for attention. Now, he had to speak to him, convince him to listen to reason.

Or kill him. Preferably not kill him.

He knocked.

Every door was warded against mental intrusion here, with spells and seals, so he was surprised when the door was opened by a beautiful brunette holding a child in her arms.

"Yes?"

Vale's eyes remained on the child. He had crystal-blue eyes and the woman's dark hair, but his frown and nose were familiar. Not unlike his own.

"Excuse me, I am…"

"Going to step away from my child now. Unless you wish to find out who among us *should* have been called the dark prince. Brother."

Vale turned on his heel to find Aurelius behind him, his eyes cold, holding a sword in each hand.

"Aurelius." Vale lifted his hands in gesture of peace and took a cautious step to the left, away from the female and child. "You look well."

"What are you doing here, Valerius?"

"You mean, what am I doing alive?"

Aurelius didn't lower his guard, frowning. "Do I detect an accusation?"

With his free hand, his brother beckoned the female close. She remained at the door, ignoring him.

"Well, Corantian soldiers have done their best to remedy that, so I inferred you might have something to do with it. You're one of the few who could command them."

"I have never in my life cared whether you lived or died. Until now. Step away from my son or I will save those soldiers the trouble."

"Oh, for the sake of everything holy in the universe!" The female swore, stepping between the two brothers. She glared at Aurelius. "He's my son too, if you recall. And his uncle can greet him if he wants to." She turned back to Valerius and attempted a bright smile, no doubt in defiance to Aurelius more than as a kindness to him. Regardless, it produced a clear change in his brother's stance, from aggressive to protective, and now that she was close, Vale used it.

He bowed low in greeting, before leaning forward, and smiling down at the child. "I see more of you than my brother in his smile. A blessing, truly."

The female laughed, offering her hand. "Lyn Reyland," she introduced herself. "And your nephew is called Syd. Sydiven." She rolled her eyes. "I wasn't given much say in the matter. Come. Would you like some wine?"

"Lyn, Valerius could be here to hurt you, *and* our child."

"Sure. He looks like a baby-killer." She rolled her eyes. "If you want to enter my quarters, Aurelius, you'll sheathe your sword."

Devi's ice was warmer than the atmosphere between his brother and his nephew's mother. Vale stepped into the apartment, was invited to sit, and presented tea.

"Would you like to hold Syd, Valerius?"

"I don't think—"

"Sit down, Aurelius."

"I'm not quite used to children," Vale admitted. "But I'll try. I believe I should hold the head. Anything else?"

"That's about it. There."

The child smiled and wriggled when she transferred him to his arms. Vale couldn't help smiling back. He hadn't lied; in his long life, he might have carried a child in his arms perhaps a handful of times at most, and often reluctantly. They were fragile, bothersome, thoughtless things, not of use yet. Despite that, this one felt different. Not just because he looked a little like him. The boy also *felt* like him, too. Like kin, a part of his clan. It made him want to say, *no one's ever going to hurt you, little one.*

"He's perfect, Lyn. Aurelius."

His brother's glare only grew in hostility now that he held his child. Vale wondered how many times Aurelius had held Syd. His relationship with the woman who'd given him the boy was obviously strained, at the very least.

All of her overtures of friendship to him were just slights aimed at his brother. Knowing that, he got up and went to hand the child to its father while Lyn prepared tea.

"I'm not here to hurt him, or you. I'm here because the continent is at war and will remain at war until the throne here is occupied."

"I am not interested in the throne. I would remove myself from the line of succession entirely."

"If you could, but that's not your decision. Unfortunately. It's my understanding that the throne is to choose a successor only when all of us are standing before it."

"And you'll have me—and my child—go so you may claim it. Very well. Pray, tell, how do you propose we convince our elder brother to follow suit?"

He seemed almost amused at the thought of anyone convincing Rook to do anything.

"Ah, well. Thankfully, that's not my job."

Lyn served them tea—Valerius first, before placing Aurelius's next to him, on a small round table.

She'd only just taken her own seat when the ground started to shake—then there was an explosion, so harsh and powerful Vale was on his feet, building shields before he had time to think of it.

Aurelius, with Syd in his arms, didn't try to use magic that could harm the child.

Valerius enveloped all three of his relatives under his wards before the violent blast hit them.

TWENTY-SEVEN
SANDS

Shea was the only one to remain undisturbed when the wards fell. Elderdale was only a few miles off the shore, and the echo of the destruction made the entire city vibrate. She was prepared for it. She was also prepared for Jibriel rushing through the room, informing them, "Ships! Ships coming from beyond the wall through the sea."

"Yes, indeed. Have the defenses been prepared to the southeast as ordered?"

"Yes. But they won't hold. Not for long."

Shea smiled. "Long enough. I need you—every single one of you—to fight tonight with the sole goal of surviving till morning. This ends when the light shines again."

She grabbed the sword at her side, the sword Orin had given her almost a thousand years ago, and got to her feet.

This night had been a long time coming.

The orcs took hours to reach the shores as Shea awaited them ahead of the army, seelie and unseelie alike.

The first to come to shore were different from what she'd imagined. Less bestial. Occasionally, a few orcs made it through the wards, and they were always grotesque, pungent, malformed creatures. This time, the one before her was handsome, though his skin was light blue and his eyes filled with nothing but white. Shea would have been hard-pressed to remember any man as well formed. He wore tight leather over his thick thighs and a white silk shirt that did little to hide his musculature. Except his teeth were filed to sharp fangs and he grinned as he watched her, as though he savored the thought of eating her.

The orc led hundreds similar to him. Shea waited until they reached the beach, their feet firmly planted on the ground. They screamed, rushing forward, weapons at the ready. The moment they were all debarked, she lifted her hand and the ground beneath their feet collapsed, swallowing them like quicksand.

Shea leaped into action, and all her soldiers followed without her having to say a word.

The first wave was easy. The second, less so, as two more ships had landed. By the time ten arrived, she ordered her soldiers to fall back to Elderdale. They'd delayed the inevitable for long enough.

Her entire life, she'd lived for this encounter. She'd suffered and fought for her people, her country, her race. Over a thousand years of unceasing struggle.

There had been some comfort, even some happiness. Every time she saw Orin. Every time Valerius allowed her to embrace him. Every time Kallan joked and smiled. Every time Devi showed how much strength and grace she had.

But her true reward was today. The day when she'd stop fighting.

The day she joined her mate in death.

TWENTY-EIGHT
HALL OF KINGS

Styx sat on the dais on which the throne stood and by her side, there was another god who felt just as terrifyingly powerful.

"I am the first one to get here?" Devi asked her.

The large bald man wiggled a brow. "Why, was there a party we haven't been told about?"

She hesitated. "We were going to…Valerius was trying to get Aurelius—and I, Rook. We wanted to start the throne, if we could."

Why did it sound like she was asking permission? Probably because if they were against that idea, she knew there was nothing she could do.

The male shrugged, and Styx perked up. "This certainly is good news. It is past time this world returns to order."

Just then, Valerius came in, walking in front of Aurelius, his wife and child following moments later.

Vale rushed to her, cupping her face in his palms.

"What happened? I felt you suffer and then, it just stopped. I feared the worst, before I felt you again."

"Turns out, letting that phoenix out was a pretty good idea. The tower blew up. One moment, I was feeling the impact of the blast before I could put my shields up, and the next, the bird got to me. The moment it touched me, everything stopped hurting."

He pulled her into a hug and kissed the top of her head.

"Rook?" he asked.

Devi's throat tightened. She would not have made it, given the strength of the blast, if it hadn't been for the bird. And Rook had been a lot closer.

"I think he's gone."

Vale had no reason to regret his death. Instead, he felt her sadness, and hugged her closer. "I'm sorry you lost a friend."

"Well. Not quite."

Devi gasped, turning as she recognized his voice. Rook was standing at the door, cocky as usual, his wings out, singed but in one piece.

"How the hell…"

Then, she knew.

A few steps sounded on the ground, though she recognized the presence before the female appeared. Kira came to stand right behind Rook.

Devi rushed to her sister. It had been over a decade since their last meeting, but it might as well have been yesterday. She held her close, caressing her back.

"You saved him?" Devi questioned.

Kira shrugged. "He saved me first. Anyway, shall we get this thing over with?"

Vale stared at his brother, his hatred apparent. "Why are you suddenly fine with going through the selection?"

Smug as always, Rook shrugged. "I accomplished what I set out to do. I don't care who sits on the throne now. Let's get this over with, unless you object?"

"We need Telenar. I have no idea how to operate the throne."

"No matter." Rook was casual and stolid as always. "They do." He tilted his chin toward the gods.

The man laughed. "We are bound to not interfere in your affairs for now."

"'For now,'" Rook echoed. "Do you truly want us to remember you as the ones who would not press the damn button when you were asked to?"

"This threat again, Marcus?" The titan laughed.

Devi stepped between the two males reeking of testosterone and rolled her eyes. She glared at Rook, before turning back to the stranger. "Please? Telenar will arrive eventually." Unless he was dead. "And let's face it, the likelihood of these three staying in the same room without starting a fight is pretty low."

The Enlightened assessed her in one intense stare. "I'm no throne tech, but there should be a lever on either side."

She thanked him and headed up the dusty stairs on the left side of the throne. It was clear that no one had walked them since Orin passed away a couple of months back.

The shimmery, transparent surface of the throne was smooth and devoid of anything that could pass for a lever at all. She knelt and traced her fingers against it, trying to feel for nooks.

Nothing.

"I don't see anything."

"Here, I'll do it. It'll only work for one of us."

Devi rolled her eyes as she stepped away to let Styx operate the device. Of course. No one in Corantius seemed to be fond of inclusion.

Telenar finally made it, rushing in hastily, his eyes wide open. "There's an army at the doors."

"Yes, we're aware." Rook replied dryly. "Our brother is invading with your elven liege."

"No, not Elden. They're coming from the north."

There was nothing north of the immortal city. Just the sea.

Devi blinked. "You mean, from outside of the Isle? How many are we talking about?"

"Hundreds of ships in the distance. Some already landed."

She glared at Rook, who smiled, smug and self-satisfied.

"Well, that's a matter for the next overking to deal with," Valerius stated. "Let us start."

Taking the steps on the other side, Telenar joined Styx and started to type on the smooth surface.

"It has been some time since I operated one of these, Styx. Old friend."

"Yeah, same. See, my brother stabbed me in the back, and my husband didn't see fit to go looking for me for a few thousand years, so I haven't been here for a while either. Still. If I recall, we just need to reset the protocol?"

"Yes, both sides at once. No one can touch the throne once it's started, understood? It'll kill you on contact. The device is set up to defend itself."

Devi grimaced at Styx's warning and shuffled away from the throne.

"Press in three, two, one..."

Suddenly the room was dark, every large widow covered by an opaque black screen. The one source of light was the throne, now bright blood red.

"*Kneel.*"

The voice came out of nowhere. Devi couldn't tell whether it had been intoned out loud or if she was just hearing it in her head. All she knew was that she had to obey.

She was already sitting next to Styx, but she got to her knees, head down. From the corner of her eye, she saw everyone in the room do the same, even Rook.

There was something in that voice. It wasn't metallic, or impersonal, like she would have imagined the voice of a thing, an object, to be.

"*You're here to claim the throne from which you can rule this Enlightened outpost. What will you do when you take it?*"

Devi attempted no reply, knowing the question wasn't meant for her. She fervently hoped Valerius could tone down the sarcasm and have enough confidence in himself to articulate everything he'd done in his own land. To explain the deeds of both of his brothers and his quest to foster peace in the Isle.

He could be a great leader, given half a chance. He would be. She believed that, to the bottom of her heart.

"*Rise.*"

All got to their feet.

"*Forward, children. Let us see which of you may be worthy.*"

Vale and Rook each took one step. Aurelius surreptitiously glanced at the woman behind him, before facing the throne again. "My child is a few months old. I would forfeit any right to the throne, on my behalf as well as his."

"*It is not for you to decide. Forward.*"

Aurelius cradled his boy, taking him from the dark-haired female's arms, and did as he was bid, joining his brothers.

They were all so very handsome, despite having few features in common. Perhaps the shape of their mouth and their eyes. Otherwise, they'd taken after their respective mothers. Rook, dark of hair, Aurelius, blond, and Vale with his dirty ash hair. One pale, one tanned, the other almost white.

The presence of the child bothered Devi, somehow. That something so innocent had to come in the middle of this bid for power pissed her off.

Now there was silence, and stillness. The red light dimmed.

"Are we out of power? Did something go wrong?" Devi asked.

When the tower has been blown out, the energy remained functioning in the castle, but maybe there wasn't enough electricity left for the throne to do what it was supposed to.

"Everything's fine." Telenar frowned, eyes on the side of the throne. "It's just…paused. Waiting for something."

"Maybe Father had another bastard running around somewhere. He's obviously been rather busy."

"The throne would not have started if all candidates weren't in this room, boy," the giant god said.

"Is there anything on the screen?" Devi asked, peeking over Styx's shoulders.

She didn't expect to see anything; moments ago, she couldn't even discern whatever the gods were typing on. Now that she was scrutinizing the device, she noted it had changed.

There were letters along the smooth surface. Glyphs that seemed to move like waves.

She leaned forward and reached out.

"*Careful.*" Styx stopped her hand before it had reached it. "No one may touch the throne. Not now. No one but the overking."

Ah, yes, she'd said something about that just moments ago. Even as the ominous warning came back to her mind, Devi felt a pull she couldn't resist, as though the device was calling her, whispering her name.

Devira. Devira. Devira…

The letters were foreign to her eyes, though she would have sworn that they, too, formed her name. There were only six, repeated over and over again.

"Don't you see it? Will you read what it says?"

Styx glanced at the throne. "It says nothing, child. There's no writing."

There was.

Devi opened her mouth to explain herself, when, in the next moment, the throne physically pulled her to it, and her palm fell flat on its cold surface.

She gasped.

And then she stopped moving, thinking, breathing. She remained frozen in time, frozen in place, as far as anyone in the throne room could see.

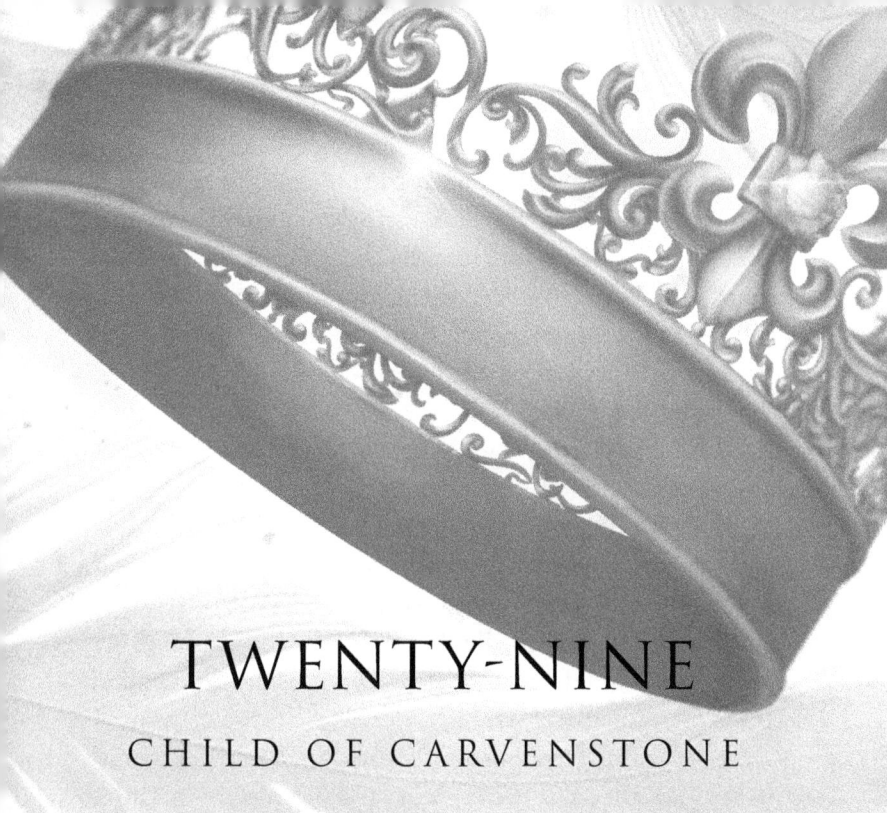

TWENTY-NINE
CHILD OF CARVENSTONE

The sky darkened on the horizon, but Kal's vision was clear in the night, and he could see the number of approaching ships increasing in the distance.

"Give the order," he stated. "Everyone back on land. We can't keep this coast clear anymore."

They'd done their best to keep them at sea, but now they'd be a hundred against one. He wasn't sacrificing more Carvenstone blood here.

Kal's ship was the last to reach dry soil again. As soon as he alit on the beach, a short, annoying little girl ran up to him, asking, "What are we doing now?"

He'd told Krea to stay away, hide in her woods, again and again. He didn't bother to waste his breath a third time.

"We're letting them reach the shores. We've already lost ten ships and there's no stopping them without condemning ourselves. Here, on the ground, we can take them. Your kind can take them," Kal amended. "Mages. You're at your strongest on firm ground."

The little girl beamed.

"What can I do?"

"Hide. Stay away. Don't die. I won't have a little girl's blood on my hands."

"Okay. I'll get your swords sharpened."

She was going to drive him mad. Or, she would if they weren't all dead by morning.

"Fine. Try not to die. And if you do, please don't haunt me." He left his two swords with her and headed to his captains for a strategy meeting. Such as it was.

They didn't have much of a choice. The mages would form a line ahead of the archers, and behind them, those who couldn't wield elements or a bow would wait for their turn on death row.

Kal knew he'd only bought his people time. But the folks of Carvenstone were earth-dwellers, and making them die at sea had seemed cruel beyond belief.

They were all in position, Kal at the forefront, when Krea returned with his swords. She was carrying a dozen others in her little arms, practically falling beneath their weight.

She handed them to their rightful owners as they passed.

When she reached him, Kal got to his knees to be on her level and looked directly into her brown eyes as he said, "Krea. Daughter of earth, child of Carvenstone. If there's any future for us, for our people, it resides in you. In your goodness, your strength, and your powers.

Please, I beg of you, listen to me this time. I need you to leave. I need you to *live*."

She threw the three swords left in her arms on the ground and yelled back, "Why? Why would I go and hide while everyone else is fighting?"

Dammit. "Because you're *nine*. You're a child."

"No one cared about my being a child when I was abandoned. I had to fend for myself. I had to learn how to take care of myself. And I have magic, so I'm more useful than *you* here."

Kal blinked. He'd heard that insult before from magic users; coming from her, it just made him laugh.

"All right. Let's try again. I want you to go away and hide because you remind me of me. Because no one truly cared if I lived or died either. I always came second to the real heirs, the true children of the gentry." To Valerius. "I see it in your eyes. For that reason, I care, Krea. I care about you being alive come morning more than anyone else here. If I'm worried about you, I can't command everyone else or protect myself as I should. Understood?"

She blinked in confusion, then blushed and bent to the ground to gather the swords.

He watched her walk away, handing them to their owners, before walking up the hill, and finally disappearing in the woods she'd claimed.

He breathed and concentrated on the matter at hand as the first enemy ship, made of steel and painted gray, blue, and white, landed on the beach.

The sound of screams, the roars of triumph and despair burned his ears almost as much as that of the crashing blades. The air was heady with the stench of death and blood.

Elden tightened his infernal device in his grasp. This might be how he fell. This might be where his legacy, his people ended. The orcs were no match for his skills, or that of his brethren, but they outnumbered them at least a hundred to one now. Soon, it would be a thousand. And another thousand.

This wasn't just a reversion to the old days; it was worse.

"Should we fall back?" Loxy asked him.

Once, he might have acquiesced. During the first war, there had been a limited number of orcs on the Isle, and they'd stuck to their cities, leaving the olden woods alone. This time, their numbers were greater and there would be no stopping them without the help of everyone else. The Corantians, the Carvenstone folks.

"If we do not stand here today, we'll have to face them on our own tomorrow."

She nodded. "Then let's do this. So long, Elden."

It sounded like a goodbye.

"It's not the end. It can't be."

He infused his words with as much faith as he could, when even to his ears, they sounded empty.

"The walls are open. As long as they are, they'll keep pouring in."

He closed his eyes, willing this reality away. A high-pitched cry broke his moment of peace. Elden looked up in its direction, expecting a greater danger, as from the southeast, hundreds of great beasts approached, carrying fae on their backs.

"Well, I'll be damned." Loxy laughed. "When the seelie court comes to help, we know it's the end of the world."

That wasn't quite right though.

The seelie court only acted when there was a profit in it for them, for their people. Their presence meant that there was hope.

THIRTY
HAIL TO THE HEIR

She'd never seen a world like this.

Smooth, tall, towering buildings higher than any mountains. Floating vehicles in the skies. Lights. So much light, although it might have been midnight.

Devi moved away from the window and turned around, confused and frightened. Where was she?

Dammit. She'd touched the throne. Was she dead? Was this the afterlife?

No, that couldn't be. She could still feel the pain in her legs and arms.

Although her body felt…wrong. Far away. As though this was nothing except a dream.

"You aren't dreaming. Not precisely."

She'd been alone moments ago, but now there was an incredibly tall male at her side, and a beautiful female with scars along her arm and neck. She had markings that seemed to emphasize rather than hide them.

"Your consciousness has traveled to us. The throne can serve as a communication device when needed." The female spoke to her like they were acquaintances catching up, whereas Devi remained speechless, not understanding a thing.

"Oh, we are. Acquaintances. This isn't the first time I've reached out to you."

She felt like she was embroiled in some sort of a test; the male scrutinized her, his gaze demanding and cold.

"Don't let Kai intimidate you. His bark is often worse than his bite. I've reached out to you in dreams, in the past."

"The warnings," Devi realized. "You were warning me about Rook, and everything else."

The female ruefully shook her head. "Yes. That darling boy. I never give up on my descendants, as a rule, but I must admit, that one is a little bit of a work in progress. Never mind that. You're here, and in time to fix this."

"This isn't how it works, Nalini," the male, Kai, said. "She's a child of clay, built as a weapon by mortals. She needs to be tested."

The female rolled her eyes. "Fine. Do your worst. I remind you, husband, that only one of us happens to be a seer."

The moment Nalini disappeared from the strange vision, Devi felt incredibly out of balance. As if her worst instincts, her darkest impulses, were all she could think of.

"Why are you here, Devira?"

"I don't know. I touched the throne and…"

"Why are you here?" he repeated, his voice darkening.

Her mind felt like it was set ablaze, a burning sensation starting inside her very soul.

A punishment. A warning.

If she lied or obfuscated the answer, he'd torture her.

She repeated, forcefully, "I *don't* know. I should be home, with Vale. I should be trying to figure out the mess we're in. The wards protecting us are down and they need to be fixed."

"What will you do? Once the wards are fixed and the war is over. Once there's peace."

She blinked. Devi didn't think she'd truly asked herself that. "Get married. Visit Carvenstone. Travel everywhere, without being chased. Help Valerius with his duties." That wasn't all. "I'll try to learn to be better, too. My friend Rook might have been wrong about a great many things, but he was right about me. I am privileged, and as such my duty should be to take care of those who have less. Not just the handful of peasants under my responsibility. Everyone. I'll…help."

The words were pouring out of her mouth, bleeding out of her like she couldn't help it, and she knew. He'd demanded the answer. He was a mind-manipulator like Vale.

A thousand times worse than Vale.

"If I tell you that you dying right here, right now, is the only way to recreate those wards? That you need to sacrifice yourself to save your world. What will you do?"

A single tear fell down her cheek. She would have answered faster if her throat hadn't felt so tight and dry. It took her three long calming breaths before she said, "I would wish I'd said goodbye first."

The male rolled his eyes. "Pull yourself together, child. That was a rhetorical question. Another one for you. If I said the only way to save everyone in your little Isle was for me to sacrifice your mate. What will you do then?"

Her fists curled at her side. She glared. "Kick your ass and let the world burn."

There was a laugh all around her before Nalini appeared again, looking up at Kai. "Told you so," she taunted. "She's it."

What was she?

Devi was about to ask when Kai interrupted her.

"The castle planted in your little city is the ship inside which our children arrived to your world. The tower that was destroyed was one of four antennas. The walls can be rebuilt if you restart the power. The damage sustained won't have affected the core of the mechanism. Let me teach you."

He proffered his hand, and after a second, realizing she had no choice, Devi took it.

She yelled as a jolt of energy flew through her. Not unlike when Styx had shared her experience, her control, but this was faster, stronger—a series of information that had been entirely foreign to her moments ago. Science and algorithms. Technicalities. Weapons forging? So many skills, accrued over the space of thousands and thousands of years, flew from his palm to hers.

When he took a step back, she sighed in relief.

"We're out of time. You're ready, child," Nailini said kindly. "You'll make a marvelous queen."

Wait.

What?

Before she had time to say a word, she blinked, and was back in the throne room.

The blinds on the window had disappeared, letting in the soft light of a waning moon.

And she was seated on the throne.
Worse yet...
She belonged there.

THIRTY-ONE
UNDER THE KEEP

Vale didn't think he breathed the entire time Devi remained frozen like a statue, cold and white, her eyes wide open and dead. If it hadn't been for her heart, its beat echoing in his chest, and their bond telling him that she was fine, he would have despaired.

He stayed seated on the side of the crystal throne, his hand over hers, caressing it, willing her to come back to him with his every thought.

"She's fine. She's syncing with the throne. It always takes a few moments," Styx assured him.

"How can this be?" Aurelius questioned. "She's not of our bloodline, is she? I know Father dearest appreciated females, but I don't feel a kinship with her."

Valerius ignored them all, concentrating on Devi.

"She's Valerius's mate," Telenar stated. "Their bond makes her part of him, down to the flesh. As far as the throne is concerned, that makes her a candidate. Obviously."

Vale wasn't surprised that the throne had chosen her over him, over anyone else in the room. Young as she was, she was good, fair, smart, and above all, she was selfless. No misplaced ego would make her ignore someone else's advice, nor was she likely to erupt in a temper tantrum that shook the Isle from one coast to the other. If he'd ever considered that she was a contender for the throne, Vale would have known she'd be chosen.

Finally, she inhaled deeply, and her eyelids fluttered.

They zeroed directly on his, and Devi smiled, as her skin recovered its color, her eyes their focus. Her hands lay on the armrests of either side of her seat, and her fingers started to tap on the smooth surface with alarming speed and precision. Before he'd opened his mouth to ask what she was doing, the tops of the armrests parted, opening up to reveal a device that lifted to her wrists. Two cuffs closed around her forearms, the silver devices identical to the ones his father had worn.

"These are remote commands for the throne," Devi explained. "So is your crown, by the way. It should work better now."

Valerius blinked in confusion, before taking out the device in the breast pocket of his cloak.

He handed it to her.

"Keep it." Devi winked. "Just because I sit on this stupidly gaudy chair doesn't mean you can't hold power."

Though he hadn't questioned it before, now Vale knew exactly why the throne had chosen her.

He would have named her his. Finally marrying her, after all this time. He would have seen that she had all the luxuries and distractions that she wanted. He would have also asked for her advice and heeded it when he could.

But Vale was self-aware enough to know that he would not have shared the throne. The crown. The actual power.

She didn't even think on it.

She got to her feet and immediately, as one, everyone in the room went to their knees, heads bowed deferentially.

"No time for this. I've seen a glimpse of our future and it isn't pretty. Rook."

His elder half-brother lifted his head. Vale could tell he was awaiting his punishment, though he did it with equanimity.

"I need you to look at what's going on beyond our walls. Fly to the coast. And see what side you want to take."

He frowned. "You're letting me go?"

Devi rolled her eyes. "I have no time for this. We need to fix your mess, and I don't want you in the way."

Though he hesitated for half a second, Rook turned his heels, leaving the chamber before she could change her mind and lock him up in a dungeon, no doubt.

"Telenar, with me, please." Now, she turned to the ancient gods. "Do any of you have any idea how to operate your spaceship? The original one you used to get here thousands of years ago."

The Colossian bald titan bobbed his head. "Aye. I used to pilot it."

"Good. Follow. The rest of you, we have an invasion. Deal with it."

The gods brought their fists to their heart and clicked their heels before rushing out of doors.

Devi led them through the palace's corridors and down endless flights of stairs.

"Where are we going?" Vale asked, catching up with her.

She was jumping two or three steps at once, as she had the very first time they'd run into each other. She was still Devi. With the command of the entire Isle.

"Underground, to the very last floor. This castle isn't a castle at all. It's their spaceship. It's been modified to blend in and provide living accommodations, but everything we need to rebuild the walls is still there. The tower Rook blew was an antenna. There are another three, under and above ground. As the ship was piloted by a team of four to six, I might need help."

"Accurate enough," the Enlightened said. "This begs the question of how a child of this world, born not even a century ago would know this, however."

"You can thank your grandfather, Hyperion," Devi replied.

The titan gasped. "Kai Lor Hora?"

"Sure thing. The throne synced me with him and Nalini. This way."

She touched a part of the wall and pressed on a few commands; a panel slid aside, and a dark, dusty room full of spiderwebs lit up.

Devi grimaced, lifting her hand and pushing through enough air and ice to clean some of it and build a front walkway.

"Wait, are you saying that you were actually in contact with our lords in Vratis? They've not talked to us for an era."

"Wrong. They talk to the overking. Or overqueen, I guess. And as long as we do well enough on our own, they have no reason to interfere with our affairs. Right now, we aren't doing well. If we don't fix this, they're sending a ship to bring us back and throwing the key to Ertia in a black hole. Or something."

Shit.

"All right. Let's go save the world, I guess."

The chamber was a smooth, triangular-shaped room littered with half a dozen seats that had seen better days. Now they were bare and disgusting enough for Vale to thoroughly ignore them. Standing sounded like a great idea.

Each chair was in front of a console table.

"I should be able to start this somehow..." Devi frowned, concentrating on her wrists.

"There's a manual lever, if I recall," Hyperion said, heading to one of the walls. He tapped on it until he found a spot that sounded hollow, and pushed it until a small part of the wall collapsed.

He pulled the lever within, and the tables came to life, revealing five blue screens. The fifth, at the forefront of the room, before a more imposing chair, was red.

"Okay, everyone, take a seat. Those of you who can read alien languages, now's the time to show off."

The moment she actually tried to decipher what could potentially be written on the bright screens, she found that she could understand the unfamiliar signs as clearly as her own alphabet. Hell, she wouldn't have been surprised if she could fly the damn vessel. Had it been in one piece.

Just like they had in the throne room, her hands flew over the consoles.

"Unless I'm mistaken, this should start the ship. We've amassed enough solar energy over the last thousands of years…I just need you guys to fire the auxiliary engines, as the main one was damaged in the blast."

"Do the words you've just said somehow make sense to you?" Valerius questioned.

Inexplicably, they did. "Sort of? You should see a command popping up on your screen right about…now."

The command room roared as it came to life, each panel lighting up in cold blue lights, the floor under their feet cool and white. Though they couldn't see it from there, the screen in front of Devi indicated that the entire ship was online.

She got up to show Vale how to operate his station. "There, see?" She clicked on the model of the ship and turned it around, face down, so that they could see the castle rather than a horizontal vessel. "This was the antenna Rook blew up." She pointed to the rear end fixture that had been the tower. "There are others like these."

Vale's fingers traced the identical towers. "Here."

"The ground level is right about here." She traced a line toward the rear of the ship. Like an iceberg, their vessel was much larger under the surface. "So, they're underground, which means less reach. One may be enough, but just to be safe, I want to start two. That means both sides of the ship need to be functional while we set them up. You're on the left command, so your station is connected to this side. If anything pops up—a light, a sound demanding your attention—while we're working, let us know. You'll be prompted to tune up the power in a moment." She pointed to a lever at his right. "Pull it up when we say it's time."

The ship was old and cumbersome. With the updated knowledge of the latest technology that Kai had provided, she found it awkward and frustrating. The fact that part of it was missing certainly didn't help. Still, they managed, with time and patience, as a team.

Finally, the walls were back up again.

Devi laid back on the strangely comfortable skeleton of a captain's chair, and breathed.

Their problems weren't solved by a long shot. There were still orcs on the continent. Hundreds, maybe thousands. Ships surrounding them, waiting for the next weakness, no doubt. And then, there was everything Rook had told her just hours ago. The fact that the Isle was dying, held together only by magic. Then there was another potential threat at the edge of her mind. Álfheimr, who'd offered overtures of "friendship", according to Rook. An empire strong enough to let their outer wall collapse, and still keep the orcs in their place.

They could be an ally. Although everything in Devi's mind, including the newly acquired knowledge of a million-year-old warlord, said that they weren't.

Regardless, this specific catastrophe had been averted.

She'd only closed her eyes and taken a calming breath for a short instant when her heart screamed in sharp pain, as surely as if it had been pierced.

A thousand miles away to the south, in the kingdom of the fae elders, Shea stood alone at the city gates, four ugly, thick arrows planted inside her limbs, a fifth in her chest, so very close to her heart.

"Open the gates!" Jibriel yelled.

It was his third attempt to give that specific order, and Shea yelled back, "No."

There was no saving her. Each of these arrows had been poisoned; the last was her undoing.

There was only one thing left for her to do. The one thing that had moved her since she'd been little more than a girl.

Protect her people.

With a battle cry, she plunged Orin's sword deep in the earth, burying it to the hilt, and pushed whatever was left of her power through, letting her self, her mind and soul, dissolve into the soil.

There was nothing at first. Then a thundering earthquake rumbled, surrounding the city, from the beach to the borders of the Graywoods.

The millions of orcs surrounding the gates of Elderdale, attempting to climb its wall and force its door, turned to follow the sound and fell silent, motionless. As one, they all ran west, attempting to reach safety, desperate. But it was too late.

The ground collapsed, crumbling like sand, and the ocean rushed to claim its new territory.

All drowned, joining the strongest queen the Isle had known.

And Elderdale stood alone in the New Sea.

Rook stood on the battlefield, stepping over a broken corpse with light blue skin. His gaze took in the endless sea of corpses. Elves and fae and orcs, all dead because of his gullibility, his mommy issues.

He's grown up with tales of his people. Lies for a scared, hungry little boy. And he'd been stupid enough to believe them. He was sentient, intelligent, worthy of affection, safety. His mother had been just as civilized. Imagining that his people had been grossly wronged, betrayed and robbed of their heritage, their lands, he'd been consumed by a desire to right the wrong. As if it could fix his own life, fill his own emptiness.

And now, it had come to this. The orcs were monsters. Not even a hundred thousand had come through in the time the walls had remained open, and they'd ravaged, hunted, and killed everyone in their path until they encountered an army ready to stop them.

These deaths were on his shoulders. And there could be no atoning for them.

Rook looked back over his shoulder, to the crystal court high on the hills of the immortal city. He'd come to see it as his birthright, another thing that he'd been robbed off. As the firstborn son of the lord once ruling there, he should have been given a soft bed in the most comfortable room since the moment he'd opened his eyes. And his rage had been based on the fact that he hadn't.

He had a soft bed now. He knew he could return to it. The overqueen wouldn't turn him away. It might take her consort time to warm up to him, but he could go back. He wanted to. Not for riches or titles, not even to attempt to redeem himself. He wanted to go back because she was there. The one person in the world who'd seen through him, who'd looked straight at the monster and found something worth caring for.

Kira Star Rivers.

Another thing he'd never deserve.

Rook outstretched his wounded wings and took off into the night.

At first, he roamed the sky without a clear direction, as his wings took him southwest.

There was one place in darkness and shadow, under a harsh bed of rock, enclosed by many spells he could restore.

It looked like he couldn't stop coveting his brother's dues, after all, Rook thought, as he stepped inside the empty halls of Carvenstone.

EPILOGUE

The immortal city woke to a red dawn, and though no one called for a rally, all meandered uptown to the inner city that morning. Full of questions, apprehension, confusion.

Yesterday, the bells signaled war, invasion. Now the gates were open. Yesterday, they'd all felt the shift in the energy around them, the deep knowledge that something had changed. And some had seen the golden walls disappear far offshore.

The orcs that had landed on their northern beaches had been pushed back by the armies—all-inclusive armies, elves and fae and scions. As one folk of the Isle.

And now the walls were back. And now the Court of Crystal shone with a blue light, beckoning them. And when they reached the gates of the inner city, they found them open.

The crowd was thick by the time the gates of the royal keep opened, in front of a dozen fae, scions, elves, and gods. The king's son Aurelius and his fae mate, with their child. The bastard prince of the unseelie realm. Others that weren't recognized on sight.

Ahead of them, a woman in battered, burned leather gear, with a fyriron cloak around her shoulders, and two silver armbands around her wrists.

Then they didn't have questions anymore. They knelt to the overqueen.

Elden had never called himself sentimental and it wasn't going to start now. He hated waste. Waste of time, waste of resources, waste of lives were all equally evil notions.

He shouldn't be wasting his time here on the battlefield littered with corpses. Anyone alive had already returned to their camp, or made their way to the immortal city. He should be there, gloating over his daughter's triumph.

Overqueen.

Even he hadn't seen it coming. He wondered whether Shea had. Annoyed when he realized this might all have been her plan all along, he started to turn, when he heard it.

A heartbeat. Faint but distinctive in the silent mile-wide grave.

Elden followed his hearing, trying to trace the muted beat. He heard it right at his feet, coming from an orc corpse. Elden pushed it with the tip of his boot.

Underneath, there was a short, redheaded fae female with dark golden skin and beautiful markings on her arms. He glanced at her wound. Her stomach had been pierced by the blade of a lance still lodged inside.

Not pretty. She should already have been dead. Elden should pull his sword and end her suffering. Letting her bleed out like this was cruel, and Elden was never cruel. Brutal, cold, yes. Cruelty was the toy of boys, not the weapon of kings.

He remained on his feet, towering over her, listening to her heartbeat. It should be slowing down. Fading.

It didn't.

"What's your name, little fighter?" he asked.

He didn't expect her to reply. Her eyes were hazy, almost hollow. He didn't think she saw him at all.

"Ji—" she tried. Then she coughed up blood. "Jiya."

Elden remained where he stood a little longer, telling himself she'd be dead in an hour at most. She wasn't worth his time, or energy. She certainly wasn't worth soiling his clothes over. He liked his silken shirt.

Still he got to his knees and carried her all the same.

"If you die after ruining my clothes, I will curse your name till the end of days."

The End

To stay in Ertia, look out for the tales of Álfheimr: *Wicked Court*, *Into The Fae Woods* and *Noblesse Oblige* in 2020.

Lightning Source UK Ltd.
Milton Keynes UK
UKHW011941180522
403172UK00004B/434